THE
IRON LADY
GILBERT MORRIS

BETHANY HOUSE PUBLISHERS
MINNEAPOLIS, MINNESOTA 55438

Published by Bethany House Publishers
A Ministry of Bethany Fellowship, Inc.
11300 Hampshire Avenue South
Minneapolis, Minnesota 55438

Printed in the United States of America.

Library of Congress Cataloging-in-Publication Data

Morris, Gilbert.
    The iron lady / Gilbert Morris.
       p. cm. — (The House of Winslow ; book 19)
    ISBN 1–55661–687–2
    I. Title. II. Series: Morris, Gilbert. House of Winslow ; bk. 19
PS3563.08742I76   1996
813'.54—dc20   96 10058
                                               CIP

To Kermit and Frances Bryant

Kermit, you always said that if I'd listen to you more—I'd know more. I think you're probably right! I've always admired you, and I am proud to call you my friend!

Frances, I wish every young woman in America could take lessons from you on how to be a godly wife. You are a real darling—and in my eyes you've been what a woman of God should be.

BOOKS BY GILBERT MORRIS

THE HOUSE OF WINSLOW SERIES

★ ★ ★ ★

1. *The Honorable Imposter*
2. *The Captive Bride*
3. *The Indentured Heart*
4. *The Gentle Rebel*
5. *The Saintly Buccaneer*
6. *The Holy Warrior*
7. *The Reluctant Bridegroom*
8. *The Last Confederate*
9. *The Dixie Widow*
10. *The Wounded Yankee*
11. *The Union Belle*
12. *The Final Adversary*
13. *The Crossed Sabres*
14. *The Valiant Gunman*
15. *The Gallant Outlaw*
16. *The Jeweled Spur*
17. *The Yukon Queen*
18. *The Rough Rider*
19. *The Iron Lady*

THE LIBERTY BELL

1. *Sound the Trumpet*
2. *Song in a Strange Land*

CHENEY DUVALL, M.D.
(with Lynn Morris)

1. *The Stars for a Light*
2. *Shadow of the Mountains*
3. *A City Not Forsaken*
4. *Toward the Sunrising*

TIME NAVIGATORS
(For Young Teens)

1. *Dangerous Voyage*
2. *Vanishing Clues*

GILBERT MORRIS spent ten years as a pastor before becoming Professor of English at Ouachita Baptist University in Arkansas and earning a Ph.D. at the University of Arkansas. During the summers of 1984 and 1985 he did postgraduate work at the University of London. A prolific writer, he has had over 25 scholarly articles and 200 poems published in various periodicals, and over the past years has had more than 70 novels published. His family includes three grown children, and he and his wife live in Orange Beach, Alabama.

CONTENTS

PART THREE
Esther (1903)

PART FOUR
Ruth (1903)

THE HOUSE OF WINSLOW

★ ★ ★ ★

THE HOUSE OF WINSLOW

★ ★ ★ ★

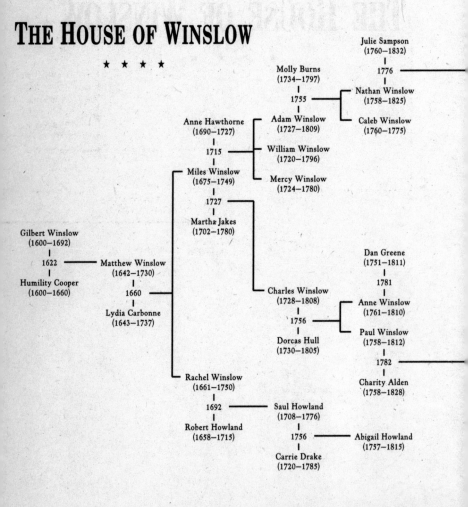

Julie Sampson
(1760–1832)

1776

Molly Burns
(1734–1797)

1755

Nathan Winslow
(1758–1825)

Adam Winslow
(1727–1809)

Caleb Winslow
(1760–1775)

Anne Hawthorne
(1690–1727)

1715

William Winslow
(1720–1796)

Miles Winslow
(1675–1749)

Mercy Winslow
(1724–1780)

1727

Martha Jakes
(1702–1780)

Gilbert Winslow
(1600–1692)

1622 — Matthew Winslow
(1642–1730)

Humility Cooper
(1600–1660)

1660

Lydia Carbonne
(1643–1737)

Dan Greene
(1751–1811)

1781

Charles Winslow
(1728–1808)

Anne Winslow
(1761–1810)

1756

Paul Winslow
(1758–1812)

Dorcas Hull
(1730–1805)

1782

Charity Alden
(1758–1828)

Rachel Winslow
(1661–1750)

1692 — Saul Howland
(1708–1776)

Robert Howland
(1658–1715)

1756 — Abigail Howland
(1757–1815)

Carrie Drake
(1720–1785)

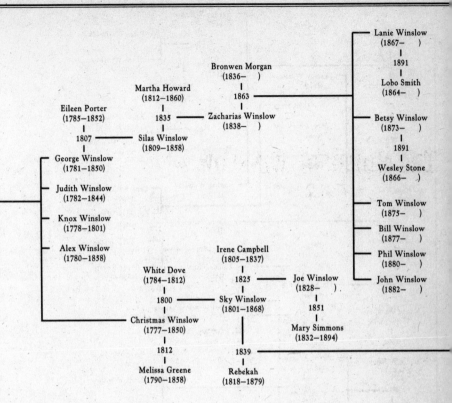

Lanie Winslow
(1867–)

1891

Lobo Smith
(1864–)

Betsy Winslow
(1873–)

1891

Wesley Stone
(1866–)

Tom Winslow
(1875–)

Bill Winslow
(1877–)

Phil Winslow
(1880–)

John Winslow
(1882–)

Bronwen Morgan
(1836–)

1863

Zacharias Winslow
(1838–)

Martha Howard
(1812–1860)

1835

Silas Winslow
(1809–1858)

Eileen Porter
(1785–1852)

1807

George Winslow
(1781–1850)

Judith Winslow
(1782–1844)

Knox Winslow
(1778–1801)

Alex Winslow
(1780–1858)

Irene Campbell
(1805–1837)

1825

Sky Winslow
(1801–1868)

White Dove
(1784–1812)

1800

Christmas Winslow
(1777–1850)

1812

Melissa Greene
(1790–1858)

Joe Winslow
(1828–)

1851

Mary Simmons
(1832–1894)

1839

Rebekah
(1818–1879)

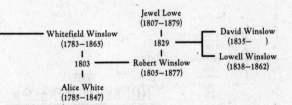

Jewel Lowe
(1807–1879)

1829

Robert Winslow
(1805–1877)

David Winslow
(1835–)

Lowell Winslow
(1838–1862)

Whitefield Winslow
(1783–1865)

1803

Alice White
(1785–1847)

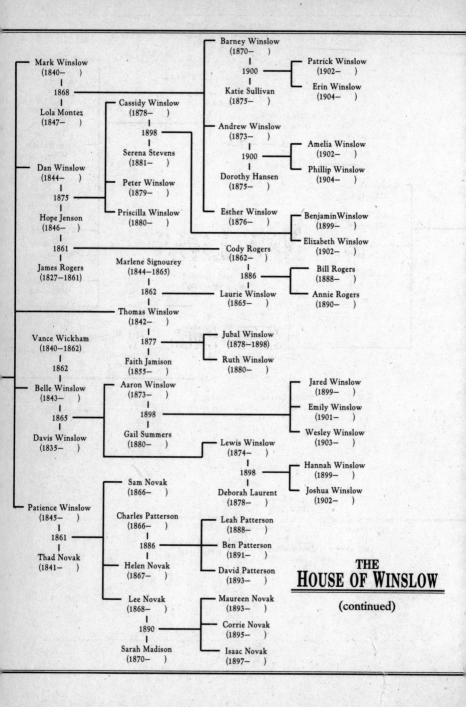

THE
HOUSE OF WINSLOW

(continued)

PART ONE

NEW LIVES

★ ★ ★ ★

1900–1902

CHAPTER ONE

SENTENCE OF DEATH

★   ★   ★   ★

A pale November sun beat down on the African veld as the column of mounted men wound slowly through a valley, then emerged at the top of a ridge. There was a serpentine quality to the line of horsemen as the troop descended, moving through the broken ground. All of the men wore floppy hats that shaded their faces. Some were fresh-faced boys, still in their teens, their eyes gleaming with excitement at the thought of the action that was to come. More of them were men in their sixties with full, bushy beards, their faces lined by a thousand suns under the African skies. Bandoleers were draped across the shoulders of most of the commandos, and they carried modern rapid-fire Mauser rifles capable of killing at immense distances.

Jan Kruger rode at the tail of the column. His throat and nostrils felt thick with the dust raised by the horses' hooves, and he was weary from the long ride that had brought the column almost thirty miles in the last eight hours. Kruger was a tall man, just over six feet, with tawny hair that crept out from under his brown floppy hat, and a pair of steady hazel eyes set in his squarish face. There was a lean strength to his body, and his sunburned hands that gripped the bridle looked immensely strong. He rode the black horse easily, as did all of the men, for they were all expert horsemen. Far ahead, down the column, a splotch of color caught his eye, and he saw the *vierkleur*—the national flag of the Transvaal. For a moment, Kruger sat and enjoyed the slight breeze that stirred the air. When he saw the banner suddenly flutter, Kruger felt a trace of emotion, half pride and half apprehension. In the battle that was to come he would take no part in the fighting, but afterward he would be in great need, for many of the men, he knew, would be wounded. As the surgeon of the commandos, he had gained considerable experience patching together the mutilated and fragmented bodies of the South African soldiery.

"Well, are you going to join in the fighting, Doctor?"

Toby Eloff, a short, muscular young man of twenty-two, had pulled his gray stallion alongside Kruger's horse. He had a pair of clear blue eyes, bright as ingots, that gleamed in his round face, which was sunburned to a brick red. Eloff was a farmer in the Transvaal when there was no war. Now, he was a member of Louis Botha's trained commando unit. Excitement stirred in the young man as he lifted himself in the saddle and stared ahead. "Looks like we're going to ride all day. I don't see why General Botha don't give us a shot at the English."

"I think you'll get your chance soon enough, Toby," Jan said, smiling at the young man. The two had become fast friends in the fighting that had erupted—now known as the Boer War. Kruger himself had been serving in a hospital at Ladysmith. He had been caught up in the struggle that had erupted between England and her South African possessions. Looking down at his dusty uniform, a wry smile tugged at his broad lips as he thought how different this was from the clean white smock he had worn in the hospital. He slapped the dust from his coat ineffectively and shook his head. "I hardly think the general brought us out here just on a little ride—especially me."

Eloff's grin flashed quickly. "No, we've got to have a regular sawbones when we get shot up, don't we, now?" The thought of getting shot did not seem to trouble the young soldier, for he rode along with Kruger speaking humorously of the last leave the two had taken. Then he broke off, saying, "Look—there's the general giving orders. Looks like we're going to set up camp."

Sighing wearily, Jan Kruger lifted himself in the stirrups, arching his back. "None too soon for me!" He glanced down at his horse and shook his head. "I wasn't made to ride like you farmers."

"Why, Doctor, you're a natural-born commando! Why don't you take a gun and help us knock a few of the English off in this battle that's coming up?"

This was a question that had been put to Jan Kruger by more than one of his comrades. When he had joined General Botha's commandos, he had done so with the understanding that he would serve as a noncombatant. Kruger was well enough aware of the international law to understand that civilians were either noncombatants or they were considered spies. If he were found with a rifle in his hand, and it could be proven that he was not a soldier, the firing squad would be his fate. But this decision not to fight was a choice that came from his own philosophy as well. Jan Kruger had decided long ago—even when he was in his teens—to be a healer and not a destroyer. When the war had exploded in South Africa, his loyalty to his homeland, the Transvaal, was enormous. He felt that the English were totally in the wrong, and so he had chosen to pledge his loyalty and his medical skills in service to his people. Deep inside he felt a sense of hopelessness, for everyone knew that England had the most powerful army on the face of the earth. Their regiments were spread out over vast areas of the world from India to Africa, exercising a highly disciplined power and might that few dared to challenge. The Boers were a hard-fighting lot—expert marksmen, tremendous horsemen, and they knew every foot of the wild African terrain they were defending. Nevertheless, their numbers were few, and when one of them fell there was no replacement to step into his place.

Lieutenant Groeber pulled the men into a long line, spread out and looking down on a slight plain. The most obvious feature that Kruger saw was the railroad track. The twin rails gleamed in the sunlight, and he said to Toby, "I do believe you're going to be taking some action against a train."

"Yes, that's what the word is." Toby had been speaking to several of the other soldiers and now said, "There'll be an armored train coming down there. The British will be shipping troops." His eyes swept the scene, and he nudged Kruger with his elbow. "Look over there. They've got guns set up and the artillery is in place." A gleeful note crept into his voice as he said, "Why, that train will get blown clean off the tracks!"

Shortly after, the men were ordered down onto the plain, where they began rolling rocks onto the track. Kruger took no part in this, but he watched as the men labored hard. A tall, broad-shouldered man rode up—General Louis Botha, the man in charge. He sat straight in his saddle atop his large stallion and watched silently. A man of medium size, he wore a bandoleer across his chest, as did the common soldiers. In his right hand he held a Mauser rifle carelessly, as if it were part of his body. Louis Botha was a fighting man. He had eyes that never stopped searching the ground in front of him, and a dark, short-cropped beard under a strong nose. There was a fearlessness about him that inspired his soldiers, and though he was a hard man, most of them idolized him. When he was satisfied with the pile of rocks, he uttered, "Enough! Back to your places!" then wheeled his stallion around and rode at full speed across the field.

Toby came scrambling back to his place, and his voice was high with excitement. "We'll get 'em! You'll see, Doctor."

"I suppose I will," Kruger said calmly, "but I hear it will be at dawn. Let's cook up a bit of supper, all right?"

★ ★ ★ ★

Just before dawn the next day, Jan Kruger nudged Toby Eloff in the side with his dusty boot.

"Eh, whot's you doin' that for?" Toby moaned from his rumpled bedroll.

"General Botha is wanting us up early, remember?" Jan said.

Off in the distance, a low rumble was heard as Jan doused the small fire with his remaining coffee. A final wisp of smoke curled up from the ashes as Jan packed away his tin cup in his saddlebag and rolled his blanket. "Come now, Toby, we don't have much time before the train gets here."

Moments later, the train appeared on the horizon. It was a troop train with a hundred fifty men, flanked by three armored trucks on each side of the armored engine. It was steaming north toward Chiveley, and as it approached, both Toby Eloff and Jan Kruger held their breath. As the train neared the bend in the track,

Botha's gunners loosed off a couple of shells. At the sound of gunfire, the engineer put on more steam to gather speed. The train swept around the corner and crashed directly into the pile of rocks blocking the track. The engine remained half on the rails, but all three of the cars were derailed.

Botha's men poured shells and bullets into the stranded train. The upturned trucks gave little cover, so some of the British soldiers scattered across the field, trying to escape. Botha ordered units to be sent out to capture them. The action was soon over, for there was little hope for the stranded Englishmen.

"Come on, let's go see what they look like!" Toby exclaimed. He began scrambling down the hill, with Kruger hurrying along beside him. When they got there, the commandos had already disarmed the men, and the process of transporting the captured English soldiers to the prison camp at Pretoria began.

All of General Botha's soldiers were curious about the English, and Jan Kruger no less. He moved among them, studying their faces, and finally stopped beside a man wearing a field jacket, knee-high boots, a pair of light khaki trousers, and a sun hat on his head. He had blue eyes and a pale round face. "How do you do?" Kruger said. "Bad luck for you fellows."

"Yes." The single word returned by the young man was clipped, and the blue eyes were fixed on Kruger. "You're not a soldier?"

"No, I'm the surgeon with this unit." Kruger examined the man and said, "You're not a soldier, either, I take it?" The others were all wearing helmets and uniforms.

"No, I'm a newspaper reporter."

"Ah—and your name?"

"Churchill—Winston Churchill."

"Are you a famous reporter, Mr. Churchill?" Kruger asked, smiling slightly.

"Not yet, but I shall be when my reports get back."

"That may not be for some time. I understand you're going to the prison camp in Pretoria."

"So it seems." Churchill seemed to find the doctor interesting, and for some time the two men spoke freely.

Kruger discovered that Churchill was the son of an influential family in England and had a taste for adventure. Finally he asked,

"How do you see this war ending, Mr. Churchill?"

The round eyes opened, and Churchill shrugged his shoulders. "Back home they think it won't be much of a fight." He looked around at the efficiency of the commandos and added, "I'm inclined to think it may be a bit more difficult than that."

An officer came along and, seeing Churchill in civilian dress, said, "Come along." Churchill turned as he left. He smiled and said, "Good luck to you, Doctor."

"And to you, too, Mr. Churchill. I hope you do become a famous reporter."

★ ★ ★ ★

English military leadership in South Africa proved to be rather dismal during the early stages of the Boer War. One Highlander said that his regiment had been "led into a butcher shop and left there!"

One poetic private in the Black Watch wrote of his regiment's experience:

Tell you the tale of the battle, where there's not much to tell;
Nine hundred men went to the slaughter, and nigh four hundred fell;
Wire and Mauser rifle, thirst and a burning sun,
Knocked down by hundreds ere the day was done.

When the details of the wretched battles reached England, the empire's reputation was shattered. The flower of the British infantry in defeat—and at the hands of an inferior force of Dutch farmers!

But the empire was not about to allow such a military defeat to tarnish her name. Lord Roberts, known as Little Bob, was commissioned to take command of the troops in South Africa. When Roberts reached Cape Town in January of 1900, act two of the war began. His keen military mind quickly saw that their failure had resulted from inept leadership among the troops and lack of mobility. Quickly he rid the army of incompetent generals and collected every horse he could find to form units of mounted infantry. Victory followed quickly, and on May 17, the city of Mafeking, under the command of Robert Baden Powell, was relieved from their siege.

★ ★ ★ ★

The war ended abruptly for Jan Kruger. His commando unit had been rushed to fill a breach in the line and stop the English from advancing any farther. Kruger had set up a crude field hospital, and almost as soon as the guns began firing, the wounded were brought back. Supplies had become scarce, and he operated as best he could, praying that the chloroform would hold out.

Hour after hour, he worked feverishly as the wounded were placed under the branches of a spreading tree, the only shelter from the unrelenting heat of the sun.

So engrossed was Kruger with his work that he was unaware that the troops were moving back from the front. He did hear the cry, "Move back! We're moving out!" But he was intensely engaged in removing a bullet from the back of one of the officers and could not look up.

The operation proved to be quite risky, taxing his skills under such primitive field conditions. He had just straightened up with a sigh of relief when he saw mounted riders wearing English uniforms come sweeping around to surround the hospital tent.

The officer in charge, a tall, arrogant captain with frosty gray eyes, shouted, "Take them all! Cut them down if they offer any sign of resistance!"

Kruger had no intention of offering a fight, for he was totally exhausted from the surgery. He wiped his hands slowly on a stained cloth, and a heavy sadness settled over him as he realized he was bound for a dirty and crowded prison camp. The somber thought disturbed him greater than the fear of being wounded, but there was no help for it.

He approached the officer and said, "I'd like to arrange for transportation for my wounded." His voice was calm, and he stood erectly before the officer.

"You'll do as you're told! Take this man away."

"But the wounded—"

The officer had a riding crop in his hand, and he slashed at Kruger. The leather struck him across the neck, and a fiery pain shot through him. "Is this the way English soldiers treat their captured?" Kruger inquired quietly.

The officer's face flamed. "Get him out of here!" he shouted.

"He's not a soldier. Probably a spy for the blasted Boers!"

For the next twenty-four hours, Jan Kruger was roughly treated. Somehow the word *spy* had been picked up by his guard, a beefy-faced corporal, who forced him to walk to the English camp. By the time Kruger arrived, his legs were trembling, and his tongue was swollen from lack of water.

The corporal said to the short officer, who came to stand before him, "Captain Mayling says this one's a spy, sir."

"A spy, you say? Well, we know how to take care of those!" The officer was a pale man with dark eyes that seemed to glitter. "See that he's locked up safely. We'll have his trial in the morning."

"But I'm not a spy! I'm a doctor," Jan protested.

"You're all rotten spies if you're not wearing a uniform!" the major shot back quickly. "Lock him up, Corporal."

Kruger was led away roughly by the corporal and confined in a shed. The guard shoved a tin of tepid water at him, but nothing to eat. He sat there in the semidarkness all day long, unable to believe what was happening. "I'll be able to explain everything when I get before a proper court," he muttered to himself.

But he never saw a proper court. The "court" was composed of three officers, including the short, dark-eyed major and the tall captain who had captured him. They outranked the lieutenant, a young man in his early twenties, who seemed somewhat sympathetic. "But, sir," he said to the major, "if he is a doctor. . . ?"

"Nothing to that. They're all 'doctors' here. They take care of their own wounded," the major snorted. "What do you have to say for yourself?"

Kruger spoke urgently, offering to prove his identity, but he had no papers.

"Of course, he doesn't have papers!" the tall captain sneered. "They're all a bunch of rabble, and this one's a dirty spy. Nothing to do but shoot him."

"You're right!" the major agreed shortly. He gave the lieutenant, who appeared about to protest, a harsh look, and the lieutenant swallowed and nodded feebly.

"You've been found guilty by court martial," the major snapped. "You'll be shot at dawn." The officer glared at Kruger, then turned and walked away.

The captain remained for one moment. He looked at Kruger,

triumph in his eyes. "You won't be shooting any more English soldiers," he smirked, then left, followed by the lieutenant, who seemed distressed by it all.

Kruger was thrust back into the darkness of the rough shed. He was a man of considerable courage, but the idea of being falsely accused as a spy and shot revolted him. It brought a sickness to his throat, and he sat down and placed his head on his arms folded across his knees. Outside, he could hear the noises of a prison camp, the shouts of the soldiers as they ordered their prisoners around. Hours seemed to pass, and finally night cast its shadows on the camp.

The guard, a bulky private, brought him a plate of food. "Here you are. I tried to get you something better than the standard grub they serve around here," said the guard. He stared at Kruger curiously, knowing the fate that awaited him only hours away. "Anything else I can get you, Dutch?" he inquired in a voice that was not unkind.

"No, nothing," Kruger said flatly.

"Well, good luck."

The guard stepped outside, and Kruger heard the scraping of the latch being fastened. He tried to eat, but he had no appetite. The water was tepid, but he drank some of it, then sat back. He had no watch, and so he had no idea of the passage of time.

As he sat in the quiet of the night, a disturbing thought came to him again and again. Now that death was imminent, he realized that he had never made his peace with God. He thought back to his mother, who had died when he was young, and remembered how he used to sit on her lap as she sang hymns about Jesus and urged him to never stray from God. *I have strayed far, though*, he realized as he waited in the stygian blackness. Though a great deal of his life had been given to the preparation to become a doctor, that part of his life his mother had often spoken of had been greatly neglected. Now as the final hours and minutes crept by, he thought about it.

As a doctor, Kruger had seen many men die. Death was not something rare in his experience. He had often been at the bedside of many patients and soldiers during their final minutes. And in every instance as he watched death approach, he thought, *Where did those souls go?*

The sobering thought gave him no rest, for all night long he sat awake, shocked and stunned by what was happening to him. Sometime just before dawn, he finally began to try to pray, and yet he found himself unable. "Oh, God!" he would say and then stop, unable to speak another word.

Finally tiny lines of gray light appeared through the slats of the window, and he knew that sunrise had come—and with it, his death. He tried again to pray but could not. Groping around, he found the water and drank some of it, then sat back. Closing his eyes, he leaned his head back against the rough wood and sat there waiting for the inevitable. He was not praying, but somehow a single sentence framed itself in his mind. Jan Kruger was not a mystic; indeed, he had a great deal of doubts about prayer. He was a scientist, and as a doctor he had learned to trust his senses—but this was not a thing of reason.

The words that came to him were unimpressive, but very strange to him. They were simply, *I will spare you—but you must show my love to the poor by service.* Again and again the sentence came, each time stronger. Finally, with a shock Kruger straightened up and whispered, "Is that you, God. . . ?" But again there was no answer, just the sentence, *I will spare you—but you must show my love to the poor by service.*

There was little hope, and almost no faith lay in Jan Kruger's heart, but as he sat there in the darkness, the lights growing brighter through the cracks, he whispered, "I will do it, God!"

There was no stirring of emotion—but somehow Kruger *knew* that something had happened inside him. He knew that God—the God he did not yet know—had made him a promise. He knew also that he had made a commitment, and somehow that both frightened him and gave him a feeling of exaltation. "There *is* a God out there!" he whispered. "I just have to find Him."

One hour later the door rattled. Kruger got to his feet at once and faced the officer who came in. He was surprised to see that it was the youthful lieutenant.

"I have good news for you, Kruger," the lieutenant smiled. "Your sentence has been commuted. You're being sent to a prison camp."

"How did that happen?" Kruger demanded. "The major and the captain; they don't seem to be men to change their minds—

especially about condemning a spy to death."

The youthful lieutenant pulled his hat off and scratched his patch of tow-colored hair. "I can't rightly explain it," he admitted, puzzlement in his eyes. "They never did anything like this before, but just thank God they did."

"I do thank God," Kruger said earnestly. "I thank Him very much indeed."

★   ★   ★   ★

Kruger was taken that same day to a station where he was transferred with other prisoners to a prison camp far inland. As the train rattled over the uneven tracks, again and again in his thoughts he heard the words, *I'll spare you—but you must show my love to the poor by service.*

Jan Kruger reached the prison camp, which was located in Helpmakaar. When he stepped off the train, Jan knew he was not the same man. Something real he could not fully explain had happened to him in the darkness of the prison shed just before dawn. He found life at this new prison camp endurable and did his best to use his medical expertise to help the men there. All the time, however, the expectation that something more lay ahead of him grew with each passing day.

The *something* proved to be a result of the turn that the war took. Lord Kitchener, unable to pin the Boers down in battle, instituted a scorched-earth policy. Blockhouses were hastily built along the railway lines. Every man, woman, and child was swept into these poorly built concentration camps. It was in one of these crowded camps where Jan Kruger found the way he could obey the word he had heard from God. General Kitchener sent thousands of women and children into confinement, but he left the details to inept administrators, who failed miserably. With the squalid living conditions, the camps proved to be deathtraps. Women and children died every day as plague swept through the camps. It was here amidst such suffering and dying that Jan Kruger was able to show the love of God to thousands of prisoners. He became a famous man among the prisoners, and though twenty thousand prisoners had died through the course of the war, the authorities denied that anything was amiss within the camps. Throughout this time Jan Kruger labored faithfully for the God who had spared his life. From sunup to sundown he tirelessly spent every moment bringing help and hope to those who only saw despair all about them.

By the time the war wound down, Jan had come to know this God who had spoken to him in the darkness, and now his faith was strong. Deep inside he knew that no matter what happened, or wherever he would go, he would find a way to show God's love by serving the poor.

CHAPTER TWO

"MY LIFE IS A FARCE!"

★ ★ ★ ★

New York City, 1902

"Will you *please* be still for just one second, Dickens!"

The dapper black-and-white cat stared at Esther Winslow with utter disinterest. Leaping out of the silk-lined wicker basket with lazy grace, he stretched, then yawned. He deliberately began to lick the white fur on his chest, ignoring the young woman who stood behind the camera a few feet away.

"You are a worthless feline!" Esther wanted to throw the camera at the cat but knew that she would not. Putting the camera down on a rosewood table, she came over and picked up Dickens, then plumped him firmly back into the basket. "Now, won't you please stay there just for one minute?"

Whirling, she rushed back, picked up the camera, and raised it to eye level. Dickens stared at her, then before she could move, he leaped out, raced along the floor, and with one jump launched himself upward onto the windowsill. Esther, in exasperation, moved toward him, and then suddenly the clear white light streaming down through the window caught the animal in such a way that she paused. Throwing up the camera, she held her breath, froze her hands, and snapped the picture.

"There, you ornery thing!" she said in disgust, then set the camera down. "You don't deserve to have your picture made!" Then she went over and picked him up. Placing her cheek against the smooth fur, she whispered, "If I didn't love you so much, I'd shoot you!"

Leaning back against the windowsill, Esther stroked the silky fur and let the sunlight warm the back of her neck. She was a tall young woman of twenty-six. Her black hair, for the moment, hung down almost to her waist, as glossy and dark as hair could possibly be. Her eyes were dark brown, very large and wide spaced, and her lashes were thick and luxurious. She had smooth skin, somewhat of an olive texture, and her lips were full and red without the aid of cosmetics. She was wearing a red-and-black wool plaid skirt and a finely laundered shirtwaist of French percale. The outfit graced her figure smoothly and was buttoned loosely at the neck. Her only jewelry was a brilliant green emerald enclosed in a delicate setting that glittered on her right hand.

With a sudden impetuous gesture, Esther put Dickens down and picked up the camera. She moved across the room, which was unheated, and shivered from the cold. It had been her playroom when she was growing up, or *their* playroom. A smile softened the contours of her lips as she thought of how she and Andrew and Barney had spent many happy hours using this large room for the games that children played to pass the time away.

Moved by a sudden impulse, she crossed to stand by the tall bookcase on the wall and saw the books that they had read together. She let her eyes run over the covers—*Captain Kid's Goal*, a Horatio Alger novel, caught her eye. She pulled it from the shelf and opened its familiar worn pages. It gave off a dry musty odor, and her lips curved upward in a smile as she remembered how the three of them used to sit there for hours reading about how the young men found their way to fame and fortune.

Fond memories filled her thoughts as she found other books that she had enjoyed—such as *Gulliver's Travels*, *Robinson Crusoe*, and *King Solomon's Mines*, a book which she had always loved for its romance. She suddenly remembered a particular book and, after a few minutes of browsing, found it. It was simply entitled *She*. Esther opened it and, turning through the pages, found her favorite passage. Her eyes sparkled and she laughed aloud, saying, "That's what you used to call me, Andrew, 'She Who Must Be

Obeyed,' and Barney used to punch me when I insisted on having my own way."

Sitting down in a plush chair, she began to read the book, and more memories came floating back. She thought of Barney, who was a missionary in Africa, and Andrew, who was now traveling around the country telling people about missions after returning from working in Africa with his brother for a couple of years. The thought of her two brothers brought a fond look into her dark eyes, and for a time she sat there thinking of the pleasant times of the past. Finally Dickens came and brushed against her legs. He made a noise that sounded like "wow!" Looking down she said, " 'Wow,' yourself, Dickens. Are you getting hungry?"

"Yow!"

Laughing at the dapper appearance of the huge tom, she put the books back on the shelves and left the attic room. Taking the camera downstairs with her, she thought of her fifteenth birthday when her father had given it to her for a gift. She looked at it as she entered the kitchen and thought of how many pictures she had made with it.

Esther poured a cup of rich cream over some broken bread scraps and placed Dickins' bowl on the floor in front of him. She ran her hand over his head as he nestled down in front of his feast. "It's a good thing I don't feed you a treat like this every day. You're plump enough as it is."

Sitting down at the large table, she studied her camera. It was a small black box, cut from metal sheets that had been enfolded and soldered together. It had a photographic plate two and a half by four inches that had to be loaded in the dark through a narrow slot, which was then closed with a slide. It could only be used effectively in strong sunlight, since its single convex lens was very slow. She held it and ran her hands along the worn surfaces, noting the small hole in a tube holding the lens, which served as a diaphragm to improve the definition of the image. She had received, on that birthday, a box of six plates, a package of printing paper, trays, a tripod, and a few tubes of chemicals. *How many pictures have I made with this camera? Surely in the hundreds—maybe a thousand—but I haven't made any lately.*

Esther had dug out the camera from time to time in her life, and now sitting there in the silence of the kitchen, she suddenly realized that it had often served as some sort of therapy for her. She thought uncomfortably, *Every time I got in trouble, I'd grab this camera and go out and take pictures. It was like . . . like I thought taking pictures would make everything go away, or maybe when I took pictures I couldn't think of my problems. . . .*

"What are you doing, Esther?"

Lola Winslow entered, wearing a black sateen dress that was very becoming on her. She had the same lustrous dark hair as her daughter and the same dark eyes. Her name had been Montez before she had married Mark Winslow. She was half-Irish and half-Spanish, a spirited combination. Now, at the age of fifty-five, she was still a stunningly beautiful and graceful woman. Sitting down beside Esther, she asked, "Are you back to that old camera again?"

"Oh, I just thought I'd take a few pictures of Dickens. I haven't made any since he was a kitten."

"I don't think there's any room left on the walls to hang any more of your pictures," Lola said, smiling. Looking down at the camera she said, "Why don't you buy a better camera? If you had one of the newer ones, you could get clearer pictures."

"Oh, I don't know—I guess I'm partial to this one. Taking pictures is just something I like to do. This one's all right." Still her mother's questions caught at her, and her eyebrows rose. "You know, Mother . . . I think you might be right. You think I could get the money out of Daddy for a new one?"

"I think you could have his right eye if you asked him for it. He spoils you rotten—you've always known that."

"But, Mama, I *deserve* it!"

Lola laughed at her daughter's assurance. "I know you think so," she said. "Now, you'll get your camera, I'm sure. Have you decided about the ball tonight?"

"Oh, I don't know. I don't really look forward to it. They're all the same."

"Everyone will be there, and you have that new dress. I think Simon will be dazzled when he sees you in it."

"I suppose." Something in the lackadaisical response of her daughter caught Lola's attention. She cocked her head to one side and studied the young woman for a moment. "Is something wrong, Esther?" she asked quietly.

Quickly Esther looked up and saw a calculating light in her mother's eyes. "Oh no," she said. "I guess I'm just having old-maid blues."

"Nonsense! You're not an old maid."

"I'm twenty-six—and I think every girl I went to school with is married by now. Some of them have already started families."

"That's foolishness!" Lola said promptly. "You could've been married a dozen times. You've had enough young men chasing you."

"Not all of them were chasing *me*; some of them were chasing Daddy's money or our position," she said matter-of-factly.

Lola was somewhat disturbed by Esther's words and said, "Our social position isn't all that exemplary. Have you forgotten I was a saloon-hall girl once, and your father was a gunman of sorts?"

"Oh, Mother, that was a thousand years ago!"

"Perhaps, but society has a way of never forgetting, it seems. Your father may be vice president of the largest railroad in America, but Mrs. Guggenheim won't ever forget."

"Who cares what Mrs. Guggenheim thinks?"

"Quite a few people," Lola remarked. "Some young women I know would give anything to receive an invitation to one of her parties, like the one tonight."

"Well, I wish *they* could go instead of me. I'm not really in the mood."

Lola suddenly reached out and smoothed a lock of Esther's dark hair back from her forehead. "We'll have to fix your hair. I'll help you, dear," she said. Then she asked curiously, "Are you and Simon having difficulties?"

Esther hesitated for one moment, then shrugged. "No, not really. He keeps pressuring me to set the date for our wedding."

"Well, after all, Esther, he has been very patient. Aren't you sure of yourself about marrying him?"

"I wouldn't have agreed to marry him if I wasn't sure, would I?" Esther's voice was somewhat sharp, and she realized it. "I'm sorry, Mother," she said. "I don't know what's wrong with me lately." Forcing a smile, she said, "I'll have a good time at the ball tonight. I wish you and Daddy were coming."

"He hates those things with a passion," Lola shrugged. "I don't care for them myself, but I'll wait up for you. When you come home you can tell me all about it."

"All right, Mother, I will."

★ ★ ★ ★

"I think Daddy will have to start a branch line on the Union Pacific to pay for this dress."

Lola looked up from where she was carefully plaiting Esther's hair into a circle around her well-shaped head. "Stand up and let me see it," she said, giving a final touch.

Esther stood to her feet and looked in the mirror at her ball gown. It was primarily an airy yellow with part of the skirt given over to green insets. The skirt was train and flounce, decorated with lace and velvet. The low décolletage was off the shoulders and ornamented with deep lace. The sleeves were short and puffed with velvet and ribbon bows. "I look like a huge canary!" Esther laughed at herself.

"A very attractive canary. Here, let me finish your hair."

"Oh, it's all right, Mother." Twirling in front of the large mirror, Esther smiled and said, "I look good enough for Mrs. Guggenheim!"

Right then the two women heard the doorbell ring, and Esther said, "I suppose that's Simon. For once I'll be ready on time."

Gathering her matching reticule and coat, she left the room, followed by her mother. When they reached the bottom of the stairs, she looked across the foyer to see Simon Barfield, who had entered and stopped midstep as he caught her eye.

"What! You're ready? I can't believe it!" he exclaimed.

Simon Barfield was a tall, strong-bodied man. He was wearing a square-cut evening suit with the skirts narrow at the bottom. His single-breasted waistcoat had a deep V-shaped front, while the trousers were narrow with a braid running down each side from the waist. Simon looked strong and confident, and at the age of thirty-two, he was considered one of the handsomest and most eligible bachelors in New York City.

"You look beautiful, Simon," Esther said quickly, knowing those would be his exact words about her.

Caught off guard by Esther's remark, Simon flushed and

glanced at Lola. "Has she always been so outspoken and out-of-step with the world?"

"Always," Lola smiled, "but you do look very handsome, Simon."

"Thank you, ma'am. Now, if I may get a word in, you look very lovely, Esther." There was a driving force in Simon Barfield that kept him always at full speed, and he said energetically, "Are we ready?"

"I suppose so." Esther leaned over and kissed her mother and whispered, "I'll tell you all about it when I get home."

"Good night, dear. You two have a good time."

Snow was lightly falling as they crossed the sidewalk and Simon murmured, "Careful, the street is treacherous." He helped her into the phaeton and spoke to his driver, saying, "To the Guggenheims', George."

"Yes, sir!"

The carriage was closed and Esther found something underneath her feet. "What's this?" she asked.

"Something to keep your feet warm," Simon nodded. "It's a comfort in this sort of weather." He explained how the foot warmer worked, and then leaned over and put his arm around her. "I always want you to be comfortable."

The weight of his arm lay heavy on Esther's shoulder. He smelled of shaving lotion, and she was aware of the intense masculinity of this man who had pursued her for over two years. As they moved along the street, there was an eerie silence, for the snow had padded and cushioned the entire city, and she said, "This is lovely, isn't it? I wish it would stay like this all the time."

"Well, I don't. Tomorrow it will all turn to dirty slush—nothing but cold and discomfort."

"Oh, Simon, don't be so *practical!* Look," she said, gesturing at the streets. "It looks like a fairyland out there."

The snow was falling in swirling fragments of white flakes that glittered as they caught the soft golden beams from the glowing lamplights along the street. There was, indeed, a fairyland quality to the scene as the houses appeared somewhat ghostly now with their sharp corners rounded and smoothed by a soft downy mantle of snow. Chimneys emitted smoke, which was a foil to the whiteness of the snow. As the wheels of the carriage rolled along,

Esther watched the wintry scene pass by and was pleased. "I wish we didn't have to go to the party. Why don't we go down to the waterfront? I'd like to see what it looks like all covered with snow."

Simon Barfield turned his head to stare at her, as if she had said something almost obscene. "Why, we can't do that! What would our hostess think?"

Esther had a perverse desire to shock this strong man out of his rather rigid ways. "We could ask her to go with us, Simon. Why, I bet she's never been down to the Bowery in a snowstorm. She might find it interesting."

Barfield saw her coy smile and realized that she was teasing him, as she usually did. There was something in her that he found very appealing; otherwise, he would not have pursued her so carefully. He could have married a dozen different women. Mothers were constantly throwing their daughters at him, and he was well aware that it was not just his personal charm, but the fact that he was very wealthy. Perhaps that was one thing that had drawn him to Esther Winslow. During some of the social events when they first met, he had tested her out. And even shortly after their first times together as a dating couple, Simon could tell that she cared nothing for money—not his, not her family's. From their talks while strolling through the park, or dining at an expensive restaurant, Simon quickly realized that Esther had no fanciful whims—or even the slightest interest—in becoming another rich socialite. Her calm self-assurance and poise were so different from the other women he had dated. So many of them seemed to spend all their time and money scheming to become the wife of a wealthy and handsome businessman who could guarantee them a social position. Esther's obvious indifference to the whole thing had been intriguing to him, and he found himself drawn to the freshness of her beauty and the rather startling independence of her mind.

He tightened his grip on her and said, "If there's time, we'll go down to the wharf after the ball, if that's what you want."

He leaned closer and studied her carefully. There was color and warmth in her that seemed to reflect a vibrant spirit that glowed like live coals. She possessed a self-sufficiency, he had noticed, and was usually on her guard. Still, she was beautiful and robust, with a woman's soft depth and fire that drew him. Now, as he looked at her, her eyes held his. Even in the darkness, he could see the beauty of her face when they passed a lamplight along the way.

"You're a beautiful woman, Esther," he whispered huskily. She had the power to stir him, and now he leaned forward and put both arms around her. As he drew her close, she resisted for one moment, but he ignored that. His lips came down on hers hungrily, and he savored the softness, yet firmness of them.

Esther was taken aback, for Simon was not a man to steal kisses in the carriage. He had kissed her a few times, but tonight there was something in him that she had not sensed before. His arms were strong and held her pinioned, and there was a dominance in his affection that she had seen in his dealings with others and found disturbing. He was an attractive man, and she enjoyed being kissed, but somehow this was different—almost possessive. She managed to turn her head aside and whispered, "Please, Simon—"

Simon released her and then said sharply, "What's wrong with you, Esther? We're going to be married. I trust you won't find my kisses objectionable after the wedding."

"Of course not." Esther's voice was sharp. She did not understand herself. She had told herself she had refused many other men because she had not found the strength in them that she desired. Now, Simon Barfield had strength enough—of that she was certain. The trouble was—she was not completely sure that she was in love with him.

"When will we get married? Set the date, Esther. I've been patient and waited a long time."

Impulsively she put her hand on his and held it. "I know," she said. "I'm so indecisive that you ought to throw me out of the carriage."

"I'd never do that." His hand closed on hers, and he smiled. "Let's enjoy ourselves at the ball; we'll talk about it later."

"All right, Simon," she said, trying to suppress the doubts that rose within.

The ball took place at the Waldorf-Astoria Hotel, and Esther, who had attended these gala events before, was mildly amused at how the newly rich jostled each other for position. She noted that Mrs. Randolph Guggenheim, the hostess, had hired night-ingales singing from transplanted rose trees. The liqueurs that were served had been bottled before the French Revolution occurred. For a time Esther enjoyed the spectacle of dresses and gowns and gems worth hundreds of thousands of dollars, but after a few hours she grew tired and was glad when she found Simon and he took her home.

As he stood at the entrance of the Winslow home, he urged again, "I want to get married soon, and it's time for you to think about it, Esther."

Esther quickly agreed, "Yes, of course, I will." She let him kiss her again, then turned and moved inside the house. It was late, but she saw a light burning in the study as she moved down the hall. Peering in, she saw her mother sitting up reading a book.

Looking up, Lola removed her glasses and said, "Well, you're home fairly early for this sort of thing. Did you have a good time?"

"Oh, it was interesting, I suppose," Esther sighed.

Lola sat there for a while as Esther recounted some of the amusing things of the evening. Finally she asked, "Did Simon press you about getting married?"

Esther shifted uncomfortably, then rose to her feet. "Yes, he did, but I put him off again." She paced the floor of the carpeted study restlessly, seeking for some way to explain to her mother her reluctance to get married. Finally she changed the subject. "I'm going into town tomorrow. I've decided to buy a new camera. I think I've outgrown my old one."

Lola sat there quietly for a long time after Esther kissed her and left the study. She was troubled about this daughter of hers. Esther had a lot of good traits like her two brothers, but she had not found her place as they had. "There's something going on in her that I don't understand," she murmured quietly. Going upstairs, she found Mark sleeping soundly. She considered waking him up to talk about Esther but then decided not to. Slipping off her robe, she slid into the bed beside him and moved over to the warmth of his body. Even in his sleep, he turned to her, put his arm around her, and held her close. She felt secure and safe in his embrace. She kissed his cheek and smiled in the darkness, then finally drifted off to sleep.

★　★　★　★

"Miss, this is the finest folding camera that we have in stock," said the short, foreign-looking man in a dark suit, with a cravat neatly folded at his throat. He had laid out a variety of cameras on the glass cabinet, and for the past thirty minutes had been trying hard to sell one to Esther. He had known, at once, that she had money, for her dress and coat were very stylish and expensive— and besides this, she had that unmistakable air of a wealthy young woman.

"Look here," he urged. "It's fitted with the Victor shutter, you see? This is an iris diaphragm with a pneumatic release, but it can also be released by this lever. It has a new center swing back, and it's adaptable either to being hand-held or being placed on a tripod."

Esther examined the camera closely. Somehow, since the ball, she had been nervous about Simon's insistence on marriage and had decided to spend some time making photographs. "What's this?" she asked.

"This has a reversible viewfinder, and it has a spring-actuated ground-glass screen," the clerk explained. He went on for some time and drew a sigh of relief when Esther finally nodded.

"I'll take it, and I want quite a bit of film to go with it." Esther waited for the clerk to get all her purchases and wrap them. Then she reached into her reticule and paid for them in cash. Taking the packages in her arms, she turned to leave.

"I hope your pictures turn out well, miss," the clerk said. He looked out the window, where snow was falling lightly, and shook his head. "But you'll have to wait for a sunny day. No one wants a picture of bad weather, I suppose," he said, a jocular note in his voice.

"Why not? We have as many bad days as we have good days," Esther challenged.

"Yes, but who wants a picture to remind you of them?" the clerk shrugged. He watched as she left the store, then spent a few moments thinking how nice it would be to have money to buy any camera or anything you wanted. "Some people have all the fortune," he muttered. Then a customer entered and he pasted on his artificial smile and moved forward to say, "May I help you, sir?"

Outside, Esther turned her face up to the gray skies. The snow had been falling hard and had packed the streets with its downy white blanket, but it seemed to be tapering off. The sky, however, remained dark and foreboding, hinting of more snow to come.

Esther moved along and noted that the passersby had their heads drawn in as far as possible, like turtles, against the piercing cold. She was wearing a new, long, double-breasted overcoat fastened with large buttons. It was a brilliant yellow, which drew many open stares, and she was glad for the warmth that the inner lining furnished. She wore a rather frivolous boat-shaped hat made of fur. It shielded her hair, but her ears and nose were nipped by the frosty wind that whipped around the corners of the buildings.

Finally she hailed a hansom cab.

"Yes, miss?"

"Take me to Fifth Avenue, Madison Square Park."

"Yes, miss. Right away. Careful now, watch your step."

The streets were not as crowded as usual, for the cold weather had kept most people in, except those who had to be out. The hansom cab passed by wagons loaded with kegs of beer, pulled by large draft horses straining against their heavy loads. Ordinarily their hooves clattered loudly on the streets, but now they seemed to float over the soft fluffy surface of the snow. By the time the driver had reached Madison Square Park, the skies had cleared so that there was more light.

Esther dismounted from the hansom, fumbled in her reticule, and came up with the cash to pay the driver. He thanked her, touched his hat, then drove off. The park was almost empty, except for a small group of children that were yelling and having a snowball fight. Esther watched them for a time, smiling as she remembered the snowball battles she had had with her brothers. Her father and mother had joined them, too, and it had become a tradition to have a melee when the first snowfall came. For one brief moment, a bittersweet nostalgia rose in her. *I wish Andrew and Barney were here, and Mama and Daddy. We could have another great time.*

Then suddenly she became aware of the passage of time. It seemed like such a short time ago that she was only ten years old. And now—that little girl, where was she? For a while longer, she allowed herself to ponder those warm thoughts of her childhood, then she shook them off.

She strolled over to a park bench, dusted off the soft layer of snow, and took the camera out of the package. Once she had everything ready, she began to take pictures. She had a keen eye for composition, and for a time stood beside the street, photographing the cabs and wagons and horses that made their way down the lane. Somehow the black figures of the horses against the whiteness of the snow caught her attention. She got a shot of a very heavy woman convoying three small children along the snowy walkway like a hen would her wayward chicks. The woman glared at her when Esther snapped the picture, but she merely smiled back.

Finally she moved around and took pictures of some of the buildings. The Flatiron building caught her eye. It was the architectural triumph of the century. The immense structure was shaped like a flatiron, and it dominated Fifth Avenue. It rose to a great height over the other buildings around it. Somehow the building itself had been an affront to those who loved the old styles with turrets and porticos. The sheer simplicity of it offended art experts. To them it was "modern" in the very worst sense of the word.

Now Esther came to stand at the very point of the building, the sharpest edge. She spent some time composing the picture, but she finally found the right angle that pleased her. The skies were lightened, for a time, with a pale iridescence outlining the buildings on Fifth Avenue. Fifth Avenue itself disappeared to the vanishing point with the older buildings lining the snow-clad streets. To the left of the picture, a small group of bare trees lifted their black arms, reaching to the skies, almost in prayer. Underneath the trees, a few men and women dressed in black were making their way along the sidewalks. *Why, they look like awkward penguins!* Esther thought and giggled at the idea.

In the foreground, one of the newfangled horseless carriages rolled along. Beside it skimmed an old-fashioned sleigh with a young man and a young woman being pulled by a dapper horse with his harness decorated gaily. *The old and the new—and I like the old best!* she thought, snapping a quick shot.

Finally, after capturing this shot, she turned and gathered her gear. The taking of the pictures pleased her, and she could not wait to get home and do the developing. This part of photography pleased her almost as much as the taking of the pictures. Waving her hand, she hailed a cab, which pulled up in front of her. She got inside and then gave the cab driver her address. She had been tense for days, but now as the cab seemed to glide over the snow, like a clipper ship through the seas, a sense of relaxation and release came over her. Leaning back, Esther closed her eyes, and a smile softened her lips. As the cab moved along the street, she hugged herself for warmth.

★   ★   ★   ★

"So what have you been doing, Esther?"

Mark Winslow had appeared in the door of Esther's bedroom and stood smiling at her. At the age of sixty-two, he still had the rough good looks that had been his when Lola Montez had first seen him, in a jail in Mexico. He had penetrating blue eyes, and his dark hair was now sprinkled at the temples with gray. His face was lean, and he still had the muscular form of a much younger man. Walking across the room, he gave evidence of the strength that had driven him from a penniless cowboy to become vice president of the Union Pacific Railroad—the biggest railroad in the United States. He still looked able to handle himself in any situation, and though his past had been hard, there was a gentleness in him that manifested itself as he sat down on the sofa beside Esther. He was wearing a pair of fawn-colored trousers, a brown open-collared shirt, and short low-heeled boots, which he preferred to the patent leather shoes that most businessmen wore.

"Sit down and let me show you what I've done," Esther said eagerly. She adored her father and had always been somewhat sad that there were no young men like him to pick from. "I've been taking pictures with a new camera I bought. Look, let me show you!"

As Esther began opening the pages of the album, where she had fastened her new photographs, Mark sat there quietly commenting from time to time. He was, at the same time, aware of the fact that Esther looked very much like Lola the first time he had seen her. He had a fondness for this girl, his only daughter. The two had been closer than most fathers and daughters, and now he felt a slight tinge of apprehension at the thought of how Lola had warned him that Esther was unhappy.

"Look! Here's the best one. What do you think?"

Mark took the album and studied the picture of the Flatiron building. With surprise faintly in his voice, he exclaimed, "Why, this is wonderful! I've stood there a hundred times, I guess, and looked at that building." He examined it carefully and said, "Now, there's something about this picture that's different. Maybe it's the snow—or that sky. By George, you can almost *feel* the cold! When did you take this?"

"Just three days ago," she said. "The storm had just stopped for a little while, and I went out to the park and took pictures. Do you really like it, Daddy?"

"Yes, I do." He studied the picture carefully and said, "You know, any fool can go out and point a camera and push a button— but your pictures always have a way of portraying something— well, *different*. Have you ever thought of putting them in a book, a published book, I mean? You've got pictures going all the way back to your childhood."

Esther laughed and her lips pursed delightfully. "I know the title: *The Story of a Useless Rich Young Girl in Pictures*. Who would buy such a thing?"

"You're not useless!" Mark protested.

She reached up, patted his cheek, and smiled. "Not to you, but I am to everybody else."

Mark looked back at the picture and studied it for a moment, then turned his light blue eyes on her. "I'm concerned, Esther. When did you start feeling this way? I don't like hearing my daughter talking like this."

Esther had not intended to throw her woes on her father, but she always had been able to tell him her problems. Tracing the pattern in her dress with one forefinger for a time silently, she looked up at him, her eyes filled with unhappiness. "I don't know, Daddy. I suppose I'm crazy. Thousands of girls would like to be in my position. I've got a good family, all the money in the world—and I go around moping like a sick calf!"

"What is it, Esther? Can you tell me what is causing you to feel this way?"

"I don't *know* how I feel. That's the trouble. It's like being almost sick, but not quite. When somebody asks you, 'Where do you hurt?' you don't know—it just hurts more or less all over. That's the way I've felt for the past few months. My life is a farce!" she exclaimed suddenly.

There was such grief in her voice that Mark knew this was more serious than he had thought. He put his arm around her and said firmly, "You're not useless. You just haven't found your way yet. Let's talk about this thing. . . ."

For the next hour they talked, until finally Mark said, "You need a goal, and I thought it might be marriage. Your mother's made a pretty good career out of that."

"But she dealt blackjack in a saloon before she married you. At least she's done *something*."

Mark grinned recklessly, his teeth white against his tanned skin. "That's not much of a goal. I'd hate to see you set up dealing blackjack in a saloon. Not that a woman can't survive it—your mother did."

"All the Winslows have done things. I've studied the family history, and all our family, men and women alike, have done some impressive things with their lives. I'm just a slug."

"You're not a slug," Mark said, shaking her gently. She was wearing a new scent, and he leaned forward and remarked, "You smell good. I'll bet I paid a bunch of money for that."

"You did, but you've got lots of money." She looked up at him and tried to smile. "Look at you, Daddy. You were just a cowboy—now you're vice president of a railroad. What have *I* ever done? Just eat and sleep and take up space, and don't contribute to anybody. And look at your brothers—they've all done so well."

"That reminds me . . ." he said. "I haven't told you about Tom. He's retiring from the army."

"Why, I'm surprised about that. I thought he'd stay in uniform forever!"

"Well, for a long time he's wanted to go to Wyoming. He's going into ranching with Dan. Plenty of land out there. He'll do well at it."

Esther was almost as fascinated with her uncles as she was with her father. They were all tall, strong men, much alike, and now she asked about their families. "I try to write once in a while, but I haven't lately."

"Dan's family is fine. It's hard to believe that Cass is married now. He and Serena have a son. Peter's not married, and Priscilla—well, she's about to drive them all crazy."

"How old is Priscilla now?"

"Twenty-two. Should have been married a long time ago, but she hasn't found anybody yet."

Esther raised her eyebrows. "Maybe we ought to get together and have a club of old maids. We could get Ruth to join, too."

Ruth was the daughter of Tom Winslow. A thought came to her and she said, "She's twenty-two also."

"Ruth's not going to be any trouble to her folks," Mark said, and a fond look came into his eyes. "She's a fine girl—but Priscilla, that's another story."

The two sat there talking for a long time, and finally Mark looked down at the photographs again. "I wish you would do something with your gift for taking pictures."

"I wouldn't call it a gift."

"Why not? A picture like that ought to be preserved. A hundred years from now that building will be gone. Only a picture of it will be left, and this ought to be the one people remember it by."

After her conversation with her father, Esther went back often to her collection of pictures over the next few days. His words seemed to cling to her, especially his remark that taking good pictures was a gift she should use. An idea struck her, and so she hurried off to find her father. Finding him sitting in his favorite leather chair in the library, she came up and said, "Daddy, if I decided to become a professional photographer, what would you say?"

Mark looked up at this beautiful daughter of his and smiled. "I'd say that when the Winslows do something, they do it with all they've got. Now, are you ready to give that kind of dedication to this thing?"

Her father's words seemed to strike a deep part of Esther's spirit. All her life she had dabbled in the arts. She had been fair at music, had not done so well with painting; but now she knew that there was something in her that enabled her to take memorable photographs. Looking down at him, she nodded and said soberly, "I think I am, Daddy." Straightening her shoulders, she gave him a fierce look and whispered, "I'm ready to do something besides just being an ornament...!"

CHAPTER THREE

RUTH AND PRISCILLA

★　★　★　★

Ruth Winslow pulled the roan mare up sharply, and when the horse bucked slightly, she said with some irritation, but firmness, "Be still, Lady! Stop acting up!" The animal turned a wide eye toward her, shook her head rebelliously, then bent and began to nibble at the short grass that grew along the ridge.

Ruth sat easily in the saddle, sweeping the scenery that lay before her. She was a tall girl, well formed, with red hair that she allowed to hang down her back, tied by a single green ribbon. Her eyes were light blue, large, and well spaced, and her cheeks were tanned by the Wyoming sunshine. There was an efficiency in her movements, and though her hands were square for a woman, they were well shaped. She was wearing a light brown riding out-fit, consisting of a divided skirt, a pale blue blouse, a fawn-colored vest, and a small, low-crowned black hat that shaded her face from the sun.

She took pleasure in looking out over the ranch that lay be-low—her uncle Dan's place—and she sat quietly, letting the horse graze as she took it in. The ranch sat on the south bank of a small creek that passed diagonally from the white-hooded peaks of Cash Mountain to the west. Cottonwoods bunched about the house, for her aunt Hope loved trees and growing things. Ruth took in the lodgepole corrals, the pole-and-shake barn, and the smoke curling leisurely upward out of the stone chimney. The brilliant morning sun streamed through the apertures of the trees. Far down where the creek made a serpentine path across the land, the sparkle of frost made the ground look as if a giant had scattered a handful of diamonds across the valley.

Lifting her eyes, she looked through a line of trees to see a distant mountain pull and hoist itself some thousands of feet until it met the sheer, glittering glacial peaks far away. A solitary white cloud floated across the serene blue sky overhead. As she spoke to the mare and continued her way down the gentle slope, she soon was surrounded by tall, yellowing cottonwood trees. The leaves fell gently down around her, and there was a sharp threat of winter in the air. As the horse came down the last of the slope and the land flattened out, Ruth gave a light touch with her heels, saying, "Come on, Lady, pick up your feet!" The mare responded at once and broke into a swift gallop. Ruth, who had ridden all of her life, sat easily in the saddle, swaying to the movements of the smooth muscles of Lady. She swept up to the corral, where three men were sitting on the top rail watching while a fourth was snubbing a steel gray stallion to a post.

"Hello, Ruth."

Ruth dismounted and glanced to see her cousin Priscilla Winslow, the daughter of Dan and Hope, step out from the barn. Priscilla was wearing men's jeans and a white shirt, and a pair of rather worn low boots. Even these garments seemed to take on style, and Ruth thought, *She could put rags on from a scarecrow and look like she's going to a fashion show.* Smiling, she said, "Hello, Priscilla."

"You got here just in time to see me ride that horse."

Ruth looked over to the steel gray horse as a tall, lanky cowboy clapped a blanket, then a saddle onto its back. The horse bucked and pitched, and the cowboy had to follow him around until he finally got the mount calm enough to pull the cinches tight. "He looks like a lot of horse to me," Ruth said, giving a critical eye at the animal. Her father was Colonel Tom Winslow—or had been until recently—Commander in the United States Cavalry. Ruth had been around horses all of her life, and now, studying the animal's wild whitish eyes, she shook her head. "He's no gentleman, Priscilla." She looked around at the cowboys grinning on the fence. "You better let some of these desperate characters get *their* necks broken instead of you!"

The tall cowboy working with the horse looked at her and nodded. He stepped away from the horse, which was bucking and fighting already, then ambled over to where the two girls were talking beside the corral gate. "I reckon that's right, Miss Ruth," he said. "Why don't you try to talk some sense into Priscilla?"

Ruth looked at the cowboy, remembering that his name was Jason Ballard. He was at least six feet three with a tough, lanky body, a crop of fiery red hair and a set of light gray eyes. When she first came with her family to settle in Wyoming, Ruth had seen that Ballard was hopelessly stricken by her cousin Priscilla.

There was an air of concern about him as he added, "This hoss might do fine in a rodeo, but he's no good for a working animal. Why, look at him! This crazy animal is planning some outrage right now."

Priscilla glanced carelessly at the horse. She was a beautiful girl with honey-colored hair, blue-green eyes, and a flawless complexion. Her lips were wide and mobile, and there was a smoothness and complete femininity to her form, even in the shapeless old clothes she was wearing. She was afraid of virtually nothing and had a daring recklessness in her. Now she said, "Don't be such a grandma, Jase. You've ridden Buster. I can ride anything you can."

Laughter went up from the cowboys perched on the fence. One of them, a short heavyset man with untidy black hair poking out from under his worn Stetson, called out, "You tell him, Miss Priscilla! He thinks he's somebody because he won first money at the rodeo in Cheyenne, but you'll show 'im!"

Jason Ballard shot an irritated glance at the cowboy—who stared back innocently. "You shut up, Shorty," he said, "or I'll put *you* up on Buster." Then he turned to Priscilla and said slowly, "I'm not kidding about this, Priscilla. This is a bad hoss. I think we ought to get rid of him before he hurts somebody."

Priscilla took this as a dare. She had ridden bad horses before and had taken her share of falls, but there was a measure of daring in her. Her blue-green eyes flashed and her mouth drew into a stubborn line. "You worry too much, Jase. Now, I'll show you how to ride a horse."

Ruth moved over to where the cowboys sat, and as her cousin walked toward the horse, she said, "Is that horse really as bad as Jase says?"

"Sure is, Miss Ruth," Shorty said, "but you know Miss Priscilla. When she gets her head set on somethin', ain't neither perdition nor high water's going to change her mind!"

The tall, lanky puncher sitting next to Shorty, whose name was Bill Dixon, nodded sourly. "Jase ought not to let her get on that horse."

"When did Jase ever make up her mind? Only her pa can do that, and he ain't here," Shorty announced. "Well, one thing about it, Buster ain't bad to stomp a rider after he tosses 'em off. If she don't break her neck, she'll be all right."

"You're a real comfort," Dixon muttered and then lifted his head. "There she goes!"

Ruth looked out into the middle of the corral with apprehension as Priscilla put one foot in the stirrup, then in one light graceful pull mounted the saddle. Jase Ballard was holding the animal's bridle. He leaped backward, and at once the horse began to plunge around the arena. The dust rose and Priscilla sat securely, swaying to the violent jolts. The cowboys on the fence were yelling, and Ballard moved around, keeping out of range of the bucking horse, anxiety drawing his face into tight lines.

For a time it seemed that Priscilla would manage the ride, but suddenly Buster rose high in the air, sunfished and swapped ends, then came down on one hoof. The sudden jolt tore Priscilla from the saddle. She catapulted over the bronc's head, turned a somersault, and landed on her back. For a moment, she lay absolutely motionless on the ground.

Jason Ballard was by her side instantly. He raised her up and said something that Ruth could not understand. Ruth watched as Priscilla struggled to her feet, helped by Ballard, and then brushed the dust out of her clothes.

Watching the horse, which continued to buck with the stirrups flailing against his sides, Priscilla said stubbornly, "Catch him, Jase. I'll ride that horse."

"No, I don't reckon," Jase said in a stern voice.

Priscilla looked up at the tall man. "You heard what I said!"

Jason Ballard was wearing a Stetson that had seen good service. He pushed it back now with one forefinger, and as he did several reddish curls caught the sun with a glint. He had a lean face, strong and noble, and now there was no give in him as he said, "Nope, you're not riding Buster again. It's too dangerous."

Ruth glanced at Priscilla and saw that her cousin's face was flushed with anger and embarrassment.

"Then I'll catch him and ride him myself!" Priscilla said stubbornly. She turned to go after the horse, but Ballard reached out quickly and caught her arm.

"You're not riding Buster, and that's final!" he said, his voice flat.

Aside from the snorts of the horse, which had stopped bucking now and was running around in a meaningless circle, there was quiet about the arena. Ruth and the cowboys on the fence were still, caught by the drama of it. Priscilla had always been a willful girl. Ruth saw that Priscilla's shoulders were set back and her lips were drawn into a line. Her hat had fallen back, held by the lanyard, and her honey-colored hair made a dot of color in the drab corral.

When she spoke, her voice was edged with anger and impatience. "You're the foreman, Jason, but this isn't your ranch!"

"No, it's your father's ranch, and he'd run my tail right off this place if I let you ride that horse again. I shouldn't have let you do it in the first place."

"Let go of me!"

"I'll let go, but you're not riding the horse. Come on!" Ballard swung the girl around easily. She began to fight, and when he turned around to speak reasonably, her free arm swept in a swift movement. Her hand caught him on the cheek, and the slapping sound was sharp on the stillness of the air.

Ruth was appalled. She knew Jason Ballard to be a fine foreman. She also knew that he was right in this matter. Quickly she moved through the corral gate and came over to say quietly, "Priscilla, don't carry on like this. Jason's right. That horse *is* dangerous, and your dad wouldn't like it if you tried riding him again."

Priscilla's eyes were wide and bright with anger, but Ruth's quiet words seemed to calm her. She looked at Jason and said briefly, "All right, have it your own way." When Jason's hand fell away, she turned and walked away, her head held high.

Ruth gave Jason a brief sympathetic smile to let him know that she agreed with his decision, then she turned and followed Priscilla out of the corral.

When they disappeared into the shadow of the house, Shorty said, "Well, I guess that's what you draw foreman's pay for—getting punched by the boss's daughter."

Ballard gave him a wicked glance, started to say something, and then grinned sourly. "I guess you're right, Shorty. Well, this animal goes to market. We don't need anybody's neck broke by a hoss, not this time of year." He moved across to the horse, stared at him for a moment, then grabbed the horn and swung into the saddle. The anger that was in him came out then, for as the horse rose and fell, he wrenched at the bridle, swinging at the horse's head. He rode until the horse finally squealed with pain and stood trembling in the cloud of dust that he had raised. Ballard suddenly reached out and slapped the animal on the shoulder. "Didn't mean to take it out on you, Buster, but I just couldn't help it."

When they were inside the house, Ruth was greeted by her aunt Hope, who had the same blue-green eyes and honey-colored hair as her daughter, Priscilla. "Why, Ruth," she said with a pleased expression on her face, "I'm so glad you've come in. Your parents are coming over later for supper, aren't they?"

"They said so, Aunt Hope."

Priscilla said only, "I'm going upstairs and change clothes." She left the room abruptly, leaving an air of dissatisfaction behind her.

"What's the matter with her?" Hope Winslow asked.

"Oh, she got thrown from a horse, and I think it hurt her feelings."

There was something in Ruth's reply that caught at Hope and she said, "Sit down and tell me about it. I'm worried about Priscilla."

Hope Winslow had a way of getting people to talk, and soon she had the whole story. "I'm worried about Priscilla," she repeated. "Dan and I have been so fortunate with our children. Of course you know how well my son, Cody, and your sister, Laurie, are doing. I can't believe how much Bill and Annie have grown. Cass and Serena are doing so well out in Seattle. He's in the lumber business now, and those grandchildren of ours are doing fine."

"What're their names, Aunt Hope?"

"Their son is named Benjamin, but of course, everyone calls him Ben. He's three now. Let me show you the picture they sent." She rose and went over to the piano, which looked slightly out of place in a ranch house, picked a photograph framed in gilt, and brought it back to Ruth. "Isn't Ben something? He looks just like Dan to me, shrunk up. And that is the baby with him, Elizabeth."

"A fine boy! Very handsome. And baby Elizabeth is beautiful. Now, if you ever get Peter married off, you could have more grandchildren."

Peter Winslow was twenty-three, but had shown no sign of settling down and getting married. Though he was a fine hand on the ranch, he had decided he wanted to become a mining engineer. He was away at school and doing very well.

"I wish Priscilla were as steady as Cody and Cass," Hope said. She then glanced at her niece and smiled. "Or as you. I'd hoped you would be a good influence on her—and you are."

Since her father had retired from the army and had brought Ruth and his wife, Faith, to start a belated career as a rancher, Ruth had known that Priscilla's parents had welcomed her as a stabilizing influence on their daughter. Ruth had done her best, but Priscilla had a willful streak in her that nothing seemed to tame.

"She'll be all right. She's just growing up," Ruth said, trying to reassure her aunt.

But Hope shook her head with an unusual air of doubt in her fine eyes. "She's twenty-two years old, and she hates this ranch and is dying to get away." She twisted her hands together in a hopeless gesture and looked out the window at the mountains rising far away. Then she looked back to Ruth and shook her head. "She's going to leave soon, Ruth, and I'm afraid of what will happen if she does."

Ruth moved over and put her arm around her aunt. "We'll just have to believe that God will do a great work in Priscilla's life," she said gently.

Hope responded at once by reaching up and placing her hand over Ruth's. She had been impressed with the deep spiritual quality of this young woman's life and had longed to see some of it in her own daughter. "Yes," she whispered, "we'll ask God to do a work in her. . . ."

* * * *

The main street of Warpaint was lit up brightly as darkness began to cast long shadows on the town. Drawn by the promise of some color and activity to break the monotony of their lives, the ranchers and farmers and their families had come from miles around to take part in the dance that was being held in the community building. Ruth had spent the night with Priscilla, and the two of them had come into Warpaint together, accompanied by Dan and Hope Winslow. Dan pulled the wagon up, then stepped to the ground lightly. He had loose, easy movements of a man accustomed to the saddle. At the age of fifty-eight he looked at least ten years younger. Reaching up, he helped his wife, Hope, down, and when she got to the ground, he unexpectedly put his arm around her and squeezed her. "I better keep a close watch on you. Why, a woman as good-looking as you is a menace."

Hope laughed up at him. "Let me go, you fool!" she said. "People will think you're crazy. I think so myself."

Priscilla stepped to the ground and nudged Ruth with her elbow. Her eyes danced with fun as she said, "They embarrass me every time we get out in public."

Dan looked at his daughter and winked. "She's something to look at, isn't she? When a man marries, he knows he's gonna have to wait on a woman." Then glancing down at Hope he nodded, as if making a judgment, "Sure am glad I got one that was worth waiting for!"

"Come on, the dance has already started," Priscilla said.

As she hurried inside, Ruth looked around and saw that the floor was already filled with dancers. At one end of the room a band of musicians, including two fiddlers, one banjo player, a harmonica player, and a small man seated at a tinny piano, were beating out a melody as twirling couples moved around the floor.

"Reckon this is my dance, Miss Priscilla."

Priscilla turned to see that Jason Ballard, wearing a blue suit and a white shirt with a string tie, had come at once to claim the first dance. She hesitated, for she had been upset with him and had snubbed him since he had refused to let her ride Buster. But she loved to dance, and the music was a powerful influence on her, so she said, "I forgive you, I guess." She put her arms up, and he swept her off to the floor.

At once Ruth was besieged with offers to dance, and she took the hand of a young man who stepped up. She did not know his name, but these dances were all informal. Before the dance was over she knew that he was Clyde Jones, and that he was looking for a steady girlfriend. Jones, however, was quickly shoved aside, and Ruth danced with a series of partners.

Finally she took a rest and went over to where her parents had come to stand by the refreshment center. As she glanced at them, she was thinking how handsome a couple they made. Thomas Winslow was sixty, tall and erect as ever. His hair was silver now, and his face was tanned with years of hard work spent out under the western sun. He was a big man with the slim hips of a rider. He turned to his wife, Faith, a careful affection in his manner. Faith, at the age of forty-seven, had gray eyes, and her raven hair was still rich as it had been when she was a girl. Her eyes caught Ruth's and she said, "There you are! We've been watching you dance."

"This must be my dance," Tom Winslow said. He led Ruth to the middle of the floor, and soon the two were waltzing around. "I like these slow tunes," he said. "This fast, jiggly music never got me anywhere." He was a good dancer and had taught her well. "We're the best-looking couple on the floor," he announced. "Just look around."

"You're not broke out with humility, are you, Dad?" Ruth smiled.

"We have to face up to the truth of things," he said. "We can't help it if we're better looking than the rest of these folks." He spoke solemnly, his eyes twinkling with fun. They danced around the room and he remarked suddenly, "Times like these I think about Jubal." Jubal had been Tom and Faith's only son. He had been killed in an avalanche in the Yukon four years earlier, and the loss was still keen in all of them.

"You think about him a great deal, and so do I, and Laurie, and Mother, too."

Tom said nothing for a while, then murmured, "It makes

heaven richer when one of your loved ones goes there. Makes me homesick, a little bit, for heaven."

"Me too, Dad."

Quickly he shook off his mood and glanced across the room. "Priscilla's a beautiful young woman. I think there'll be some fights over her tonight. Is Jase still mooning over her?"

"I think so. She doesn't seem to care much for him, though." She repeated the incident about the horse and added, "Priscilla just doesn't want to be told what to do."

"Dan and Hope are worried about her—and so am I. She could go wrong if she doesn't do something pretty quick."

Ruth agreed silently but said nothing more about her cousin. She enjoyed the dance, and when they were on their way home, Priscilla sighed, "I wish we could have a dance every night."

"That would get pretty boring," Ruth said as the wagon rolled along. "A dance is fun only because it comes seldom. That's the way it is with pleasures, I think. If we had strawberries all the time, we wouldn't think anything about them. It's because we get them rarely that they're so good."

"Oh, don't start talking philosophy, Ruth," Priscilla said sharply. She slumped down in the seat. The two girls were speaking quietly, for Dan and Hope were in the front seat discussing some matters about the ranch. "I think I'll just *die* if I have to live in this place another year!" Priscilla whispered. "Don't you hate it here?"

"No, I rather like it," Ruth said with surprise. "If you had to live in some of the isolated army posts that we've lived in, you'd think this was heaven. Some of them are pretty grim, Priscilla."

"I suppose so—but I get so *bored* with everything."

Later, when the two girls were undressing for bed, Ruth noticed again the pictures on Priscilla's wall. They were all portraits of famous actors and actresses. Most of them were signed. She had discovered that Priscilla had written to them, asking for pictures, and many of them had responded. When they were in bed and the lamp had been turned down, Priscilla began talking about the stage. She knew a great deal about it, for she had read everything she could about plays and the world of drama. There was silence for a while, and she said, "I'd give anything just to go to New York and see some dramas."

"Have you ever seen a play?" asked Ruth.

"Oh, just amateurs, but once Daddy took Mother and me to Cheyenne. It was wonderful, Ruth! Lillian Russell was on tour there. She was in a play called *Heartbreak House*. Oh, I can just see it now! I think I remember every word of it."

Ruth lay quietly listening as Priscilla went on and on about the play and Lillian Russell, and all about how fascinating the world of drama was. Yet something about the whole thing just didn't seem right to Ruth, but she dared not say so. Finally she drifted off to sleep, and her last thought was of the rather sad look in the eyes of Jason Ballard as he had stood on the outskirts of the crowd watching Priscilla dance by.

★　★　★　★

"Dad, I've been thinking a great deal about what to do with my life."

Tom Winslow looked up with surprise. He had been going over the books of the ranch. Sensing the seriousness in Ruth's voice, he now shoved the papers away and turned his chair around. "Sit down, Ruth," he said. When she was seated, he clasped his hands together in a familiar gesture and looked at her knowingly. "I take it you don't want to stay here and live on a ranch for the rest of your life."

"Oh, I like the ranch. I love horses and the out-of-doors, but you're right. I need to do something, and I think I know what it is now. I've already talked to Mother about it."

Tom grinned at her. "You always did talk to her first. I guess that's the way it is with girls and their mothers. I remember when you were just a little thing. When you wanted something you would go to her and get her approval, then come to me and say, 'Mama says I can do such and such.' "

"Well, I've done it this time." Ruth was sitting quietly in a horsehide chair. She was dressed modestly, as usual, in a plain green dress, and her red hair was tied back with a single ribbon. She had a serious air about her and hesitated for one moment, then said, "We've talked before about this, Dad. I can't get it out of my mind that God wants me to serve Him in a special way."

"You've talked about being a missionary. Is that still in your heart?"

"Yes, it is, Dad. I don't know where or how—but it keeps coming back again and again. As I went through the Scriptures, I read about men and women, too, who carried the gospel during those first days of the church."

"I guess you have a biography of every missionary who ever lived. You always loved the stories of those men and women who went to the mission field." Tom considered this young daughter of his, and the thought was in his mind, *She's all that Faith and I have left, now that Jubal is gone and Laurie is married and living on her own ranch*. It had been his hope that Ruth would marry and settle down close so that he could see his grandchildren grow up, but he knew that somehow this was not to be. "Are you worried about me and your mother?"

"Yes, I'd hate to leave you," she said, "and I wouldn't for anything else." She went on to speak for some time about how her thoughts and her heart had been turned toward the mission field, and finally she said, "Will you help me, Dad? I don't know what to do next."

"Of course, I will," Tom said. "It would be like tearing an eye out to lose you, but if God is calling you, then that's all there is to it." He sat there for some time and the two talked, and finally he straightened up and said, "I know what! Write a letter."

"A letter? To whom?"

"Why, to Andrew. He was a missionary." He spoke of the son of Mark and Lola Winslow. Andrew and his brother, Barney, had gone to Africa as missionaries. Andrew had returned, but Barney was still on the field. "Andrew's come home now to tell people about the need for more missionaries. I got a letter from Mark just last week, and Andrew's going around the country speaking at the churches about the mission field in Africa. Why don't you write him and ask him what he thinks about your problem?"

"I will. I'll write him right away and mail the letter tomorrow." She rose and came over, put her arms around her father, and kissed him on the cheek. "Probably nothing would come of it. Can you imagine me traipsing around Africa or somewhere?"

"I can see you doing whatever God puts you to," Tom said fondly. He took her hand and held it, noting that it was strong.

Looking up at her, he seemed to see her mother as she had been at that age. "You're very like your mother," he said, "and I can't think of anything nicer to say about any young woman."

★　★　★　★

"Mom—Dad, look! I got the answer from Andrew."

Tom and Faith had been eating supper when Ruth had come in waving a letter, her eyes flashing. She had ridden in from town, and her excitement made her more alive than ever. "I'll read it all to you, but he says he thinks I ought to get some medical training."

"Medical training?" Tom asked. "Well, that might be hard to get out here in Wyoming."

"Yes, it would, but he says there's a Dr. Burns at Baxter Hospital in New York City. There's a training program there for young women, and he says that your nephews have both married young women who went through the program there."

"Yes," Tom nodded. "That would be Aaron and Lewis. They're sons of Davis and my sister Belle."

All three of them had heard of the part that Dan's nephews had played in the Spanish-American War. Lewis had been awarded the medal of honor, and his brother, Aaron, had served as well.

"Who was it they married? I've forgotten those girls' names," Faith asked.

"Aaron married a young woman named Gail Summers," Tom explained. "They've already got a son named Jared and a daughter named Emily, and Lewis married a girl named Deborah Laurent. They got married at the same time as Aaron and Gail. They've got a daughter now, named Hannah, and a newborn son named Joshua."

"Anyway," Ruth went on, "Andrew says that if I want to come to New York, I could apply for the nursing program at Baxter hospital." She read the letter then at length.

When she was through, Tom said carefully, "Are you sure this is what you want to do, daughter?"

Ruth lowered the letter, looked at her parents, and suddenly felt overwhelmed with the thought of leaving them. It would wrench her heart apart to be gone from them, but she knew she had to follow God's leading. She would miss them dreadfully, and yet there was a certainty in her voice as she said, "Yes, Dad, I have to go. God is calling me."

Faith leaned forward then and said, "If God is calling you, He will make a way."

★　★　★　★

"You're going to New York?" Priscilla stared at Ruth almost in shock. Then she sat there and listened as Ruth tried to explain that she was going to serve in a hospital to prepare to be a missionary.

As soon as she was finished, Priscilla said abruptly, "I'm going with you, Ruth!"

"Why, Priscilla, you've never even *thought* of such a thing. You certainly aren't going to be a missionary."

"No, but I'm going to New York. I'm going into the nursing program with you. It's something I can do."

Ruth was taken aback by Priscilla's instant decision. She, herself, made very few decisions on the spur of the moment, but Priscilla was impulsive to a fault. She at once besieged her parents, telling them that it was a career for her, and when they argued that she would be away from home, she said, "But Ruth is going. I'll be with her, and Uncle Mark and his family are there. They'll be glad to look out for us."

Ruth was not completely happy with the situation, for she felt responsible for Priscilla. She said as much to Priscilla's parents, privately.

"I wish that Priscilla hadn't decided to go with me. I'll feel responsible for her."

Dan Winslow reached over and patted her on the shoulder. He glanced at his wife and said, "Hope and I have prayed about this. It may not be a bad thing."

"Yes," Hope nodded quickly. "Priscilla was going to leave one way or another. This way she'll be close to you and to Mark and his family. We're praying that God will touch her while she's there."

From that moment on, it was settled. The mail moved slowly, but after a few weeks, all the arrangements were made. Finally the day came when the two cousins were ready to leave, and they stood at the station saying tearful goodbyes to their parents. As the train pulled out, they found a place at the window and were waving at them. Suddenly Ruth said, "Look, Priscilla, isn't that Jason over there?"

Priscilla turned and saw Jason standing silently, without moving, beside the station. She waved at him, and he lifted a hand in reply, then turned and walked away.

"He's going to miss you. He's in love with you, you know," Ruth said.

"He'll get over it. He'll find a girl who wants to do nothing but keep house and raise children." When she saw that her words struck Ruth as being hard, she immediately said, "Oh, I don't mean to be harsh, but I'd make Jason miserable! Come on, let's look at the maps of New York that we got. I want to see the whole city as soon as we get there. . . !"

CHAPTER FOUR

NEW YORK—NEW YORK!

★ ★ ★ ★

"Oh, look! There they are—see . . . see, getting off at that car."

Esther tugged at her father's coat sleeve and began hauling him along the crowded railroad station toward the passenger cars. The wood-burning engines that pulled up in New York train terminal had fogged the air, making it a gloomy-looking spectacle, but Esther ignored this. She had brought her new camera along and had taken several good shots of the mammoth locomotives as they slowly chugged into the busy station. Anxious to greet her cousins, she called out and waved as they approached, "Ruth!—Priscilla! Over here!"

The two young women who dismounted from the train were travel weary from their long journey from Wyoming. Their dresses were rumpled, and their hair was not as natty as it had been when they had first gotten aboard. Despite their fatigue, both of them brightened when they saw the tall man and the young woman smiling at them as they approached.

Mark Winslow reached out both his hands, and the two young women took one apiece. "Well, now this *is* exciting!" Mark exclaimed. He pulled them close suddenly and gave them a warm hug, saying, "I will avail myself of an avuncular privilege by hugging two of the best-looking nieces in the country. Welcome to New York!"

"Oh, Uncle Mark, it's so exciting!" Priscilla's eyes were like stars, and she turned to greet Esther, who, at once, gave her an enthusiastic hug. "I'm just so excited to be here I can't even talk."

"And what about you, Ruth?" Esther asked, turning to greet the taller of the two young Winslow women.

"I don't think anybody can be as excited as Priscilla," Ruth smiled. There was a calmness in her manner that contrasted with the almost frantic excitement of Priscilla, and she turned now to look up into her uncle's face. "It was so kind of you to make all the arrangements and to get us tickets on the railroad."

"Why, what's the use of being a big shot with the Union Pacific if I can't push my weight around a little bit from time to time?" Mark was studying the two young women—Ruth, who was wearing a rumpled, dark-colored dress, and Priscilla, whose two-piece outfit was a bright blue-green that matched her eyes exactly. Mark saw, at once, the difference in the two and studied Priscilla the longest. He had received a long letter from his brother Dan who had pleaded with him to keep an eye out for the girls, especially Priscilla. He thought wryly, *Well, if a sixty-two-year-old man can keep up with a twenty-two-year-old girl—especially one who looks like this— it'll be the first time.* Aloud he said, "Come along, Esther. You take the girls to the automobile while I go and collect the baggage."

The two young women followed Esther after she collected her camera and tripod from the station agent, who had been standing guard over them. Leading her cousins outside, Esther walked down the long street crowded with a mixture of automobiles and carriages. Finally, she came to a black automobile with a curved front dash and bicycle wheels. "Here," she said, "you get inside. I want to get your pictures while Daddy's getting the luggage." She arranged them in the front seat of the car and then set up her camera in a very professional manner. She had already made three pictures when Mark appeared with a porter carrying luggage on a two-wheel dolly.

"Here, let's see if we can fit all this stuff inside," he said as the porter began to unload the luggage. It took some maneuvering and ingenuity to get all the luggage and four people into the automobile.

"What sort of automobile is this?" Ruth inquired curiously. This was a new experience, for she had never ridden in one before.

Indeed, the two girls had rarely seen one. She ran her fingers over the black painted surface of the dashboard.

"It's an Oldsmobile," Mark Winslow replied proudly. He tipped the porter, then got into the automobile and said, "Believe it or not, this fancy contraption cost six hundred and fifty hard-earned dollars!—and I'm still not sure I wouldn't rather have a good team and a buggy."

Priscilla sat in the front seat with her uncle, and the other two young women got into the back. After a series of complicated manipulations, the internal combustion engine exploded with a roar that caused a team passing by to rear and scream with terror. Mark glanced at them and shook his head. "Sorry, boys," he muttered. "You don't hate it any worse than I do." He advanced the ignition, and the car jerked into motion and chugged out from the line parked along the side of the street, and soon they were breezing along through the streets of New York.

The wind tore at the hats of the two new arrivals. They noted that Esther was wearing a huge white linen coat. Her hat was tied down with a luminous scarf, under which was a dust-proof veil. Mark Winslow was also dressed for the outing, wearing a bright orange-colored overcoat with black plaids. He had a cloth cap with a small peak and a bill and wore goggles as he steered the automobile along the streets.

Priscilla could scarcely keep her seat as Winslow made his way through the crowded avenues. She was enraptured with the thrill of being in such a big city, while Ruth, on the other hand, sat quietly smiling at her cousin's excitement. As they passed a magnificent structure with towers rising out of a large square-shaped building she cried out, "What's that, Uncle Mark?"

"That's Madison Square Garden."

"Do they have plays there?"

"No, mostly circuses and bicycle races." He turned to smile at her. "They're having a national horse show right now. Maybe you would like to see that."

"No, I've seen enough horses to last me awhile," Priscilla said. "Could we go to the theater sometime, do you suppose?"

"I don't see why not. You'll have to talk to Esther about that."

They finally reached their destination, the Winslow home, which was a tall two-story red-brick house with white columns in front, gables on three sides, and a sweeping driveway under a canopy of towering chestnut trees. As they stepped out of the car, Lola Winslow, Mark's wife, came outside to greet them. "Well, come in, girls," she said after hugging them. "I've been cooking all day. I know you must be hungry after that long train ride."

"I'm not hungry, but my backside is about dead!" Priscilla exclaimed, rubbing that part of her anatomy with a pained expression.

Lola laughed aloud. "I don't think you need to mention that in public, but I know what you mean. Those trains are murderous on a person's body." Lola, at once, took the girls to their rooms, saying, "You can have separate rooms. Andrew should be dropping by tomorrow night."

"I'm so anxious to meet him," Ruth said quickly. "He was kind to answer my letter so quickly. I'm interested to hear about his time in Africa. Will his wife be with him? I would love to meet her as well."

Andrew had married Dorothy Hansen before returning to the United States. Dorothy was the daughter of Myron Hansen, who was serving as a missionary in Liberia. Mark and Lola had not been pleased with the sudden marriage, as Dorothy seemed more concerned with her station in life than in serving the Lord. Despite their concerns, Andrew seemed oblivious to this and lavished his attention on his beautiful wife.

Lola answered stiffly, "Dorothy is staying with some relatives in town. She hasn't fully recovered from having our granddaughter, Amelia." A look of concern passed across her face; then a smile lifted the corners of her lips upward, and she shook her head. "Andrew's out recruiting right now. I think he wants Mark and me to go and help Barney preach to the savages in the villages of Africa."

Ruth's face glowed. "It's so exciting to think of carrying the good news of Jesus to foreign countries. I don't know a thing about it, but it all sounds so exciting to me."

The girls spent the rest of the afternoon settling into their rooms. By the time the girls unpacked and each took a long, relaxing bath, it was time to get ready for supper. The entire meal that night was excellent. Lola did most of the cooking herself, although the girls had volunteered earlier to help. When they sat down, Mark looked over the table and smiled. The table had a fresh white linen with a vase of flowers in the middle. Lola had used the china with the delicate floral pattern she reserved for special occasions when she entertained important guests. "I think I'd like my nieces to stay for a long time if I get meals like this." He looked over the platters of roast beef, fried chicken, and fish and shook his head. "Let's get busy and dig in. I wish Andrew were here." He asked the blessing quickly, and then said, "Andrew was telling us last night that he ate monkey over in Africa."

"Monkey! I can't believe it!" Priscilla gasped, almost dropping her fork. "I wonder what it tastes like."

Mark laughed. "I asked him about that and he said it tasted a little bit like goat—which doesn't help a lot."

As the meal progressed and they caught up on family news, Mark noted the difference between the two girls. Priscilla was volatile, excited, her honey-colored hair and blue-green eyes shimmering under the gas light. She was a beautiful girl, but he thought, *She's not as stable as her mother. I wish she were.* His eyes then turned to Ruth, and he admired the quiet beauty of the girl. Her auburn hair was neatly pinned back, and she sat quietly, her light blue eyes observing those around her, saying little, but listening a great deal.

Esther said, "Tomorrow I'll take you girls shopping."

"I don't think we have money for that," Ruth said quickly.

"What has a man got good-looking nieces for if he can't buy them a new outfit? You take them around, Esther, and the sky's the limit!"

Esther laughed aloud. "We'd better take him up on it, girls. This is one of those rare weak moments here, and I'd hate not to take advantage of it."

★　★　★　★

The next day the three young women got into a carriage, and the driver drove them into the city. As they came through a line of carriages between Eighteenth and Nineteenth Streets, Ruth noted that the coaches were a rich maroon, a deep olive green, and some even a bright canary yellow. She was more interested in the horses and saw that most of them were a matched team.

They were all colors: black, brown, gray, and white.

They finally got out of the carriage, and Esther led them along Broadway, which was crowded with shoppers. Priscilla stopped in front of the windows of the glittering stores as they walked along, noting that each store was crowded with women dressed in the finest of clothing. "I've never seen so many new fashions," she said excitedly.

"No more hoop skirts," Esther said fervently. "I'm glad of that."

"That's right," Priscilla said, although she had never worn them. She pointed to a dress in a window and said, "That's a pretty one, isn't it?"

"You like it?" Esther asked. "Come along." She led them inside, and they examined the dress that was displayed on a dressmaker's form. It was a walking suit of green and blue plaid poplin, with a short-fitted jacket and a ruffled under blouse of light blue percale. Lifting the skirt, Esther found only one petticoat and one underskirt and said, "This ought to look very nice on you, Priscilla."

"Oh, do you really think so?" Priscilla beamed.

When the saleslady came and led Priscilla away to the fitting room, Esther found it more difficult to find something for Ruth.

"I really don't need fancy clothes, Esther," Ruth said quietly. "I'll be working at the hospital long hours, from what Andrew says, and I won't be going out much."

"Well, you need one nice dress to celebrate in," Esther insisted. After a few minutes of looking at a number of outfits, they found her a simple-cut dress. "This is a cashmere tea gown," Esther explained. "Look, it has a new Stewart bodice, close fitting down to the waist. Come on, try it on."

Ruth allowed herself to be persuaded, and when she had donned the garment, she stood still and stared into the full-length mirror. The color perfectly matched her blue eyes. The wide collar had velvet rosettes, and the sleeves ended at the wrist in a frill. There was a vest of oriental silk threaded with gold, and the bell-shaped skirt was one such as she had never seen. "Oh, this is lovely, Esther," she said, "but it costs so much."

"Let Daddy worry about that," Esther said firmly.

As soon as the dresses were wrapped and Esther paid for them, the three cousins left the shop and moved along Broadway.

They lingered at the window of an excellent milliner's shop, where hats of all colors with trims from netting to jet to feather vied for their attention. Next to it was a ribbon shop, and then a shop that sold shoes. At Nineteenth Street was the elegant marble Arnold Constable and Company, where they bought a pair of light blue satin gloves for Priscilla, and a pair of beige ones for Ruth.

Finally they reached Lord and Taylor's, a five-story building that had a "vertical railroad." They entered the elevator and a young boy, attired in a man's miniature suit, took them to the fourth floor. When they stepped out they saw hundreds of women sewing madly.

"Well, I have a dress to pick up for myself. They're specially made," Esther said, then turned to speak with a seamstress.

For the rest of the afternoon Esther took them to more shops, but instead of going home Esther said finally, "I have a surprise for you girls. We're going to have dinner out." Then she turned to Priscilla and smiled. "We're going to see Mrs. Fisk. She's starring in a performance of *Macbeth*. Mr. Gillette is playing the part of Macbeth."

Ruth had heard of people lighting up from the inside, and that was exactly what happened to Priscilla. The girl's lovely face suddenly became illuminated, and her eyes were so wide that they seemed enormous.

"Really, Esther?" Priscilla gasped. "I've heard about her and read everything about her. She's a wonderful actress, isn't she?"

"So everyone says. I'm not one much for the theater, but if you don't like that we can go see a vaudeville act."

"Oh no. Let's go see *Macbeth*," Priscilla insisted.

They had a rather elegant dinner at an expensive restaurant, then made their way down Broadway to the Palace Theater. A picture of Mrs. Fisk was on the outside, and the line of patrons trailed a long way down the block.

"Maybe we won't get in," Priscilla said anxiously.

"Don't worry about that. I've already made reservations. Come along. I used Daddy's name," she explained. "It's helpful to have a father who's important and well known. I use it as often as I can."

Esther stepped up to one of the attendants and handed him

her father's card. Noting the name and the reservation, he smiled and ushered them ahead of the line and into the theater, where they made their way almost to the front and took their seats. Priscilla could not keep still, and finally Ruth said, "For heaven's sake, Priscilla. You're as jumpy as a cat. Settle down, will you!"

"But it's so exciting, Ruth! I don't see how you can be so calm— oh, look, the curtain's opening. It's going to start!"

Neither of the girls had ever seen *Macbeth*, and they were spell-bound by the dark and rather violent play. From time to time Ruth would turn to see how Priscilla was taking the thing in and saw that the girl was transfixed. She was completely out of herself and caught up with the action that was taking place on the stage. *She likes this too much, I'm afraid*, Ruth thought. *I wish we hadn't come— but she would have come eventually by herself.*

After the play Esther said, "Let's go back and meet the actors."

Priscilla stared at her as if she had invited them to go to the moon. "Why . . . can we do that, Esther?"

"Of course we can. It happens all the time. Come along." Esther had the self-confidence of a born New Yorker. She had been to a number of well-known plays before, and afterward her father had taken her backstage to meet famous actors.

They found Mrs. Fisk surrounded by several admirers and waited patiently. Finally Esther stepped forward and said, "Mrs. Fisk, my name is Esther Winslow. I'm a photographer. I wonder if I could ask you to let me come some night and photograph you after the performance?"

Mrs. Fisk was a beautiful woman, tall and dignified. She smiled rather wearily and said, "Perhaps you could come to my apartment. It might be better than here."

"Oh no. I think here would be best," Esther said confidently. "This is where your life is. The action's all here. I don't want a pretty photograph. I want one of an actress who is giving herself to her art."

Mrs. Fisk was impressed by the young woman. "You have a rather definite idea of what you want. I'd be most interested to see what you could do. Bring your camera tomorrow night."

"Thank you, Mrs. Fisk. These are my cousins, Ruth and Priscilla—both Winslows. Priscilla has never seen a play before, but I think she's struck by all of it."

"Oh yes, Mrs. Fisk, you were so wonderful," Priscilla breathed. She took the hand which the great actress held out and said, "I'd give anything in the world if I could be an actress!"

Mrs. Fisk studied the beautiful young girl and thought suddenly of herself as she had been at that age. "It isn't always as enticing as people think," she said quietly. "There's a lot of hard work, and a great many disappointments along the way—the same as with any profession."

"Oh, I'm sure that's true, but just to be able to do what you do! Why, I think it's the greatest thing in the world."

"I need to hire you for an agent," Mrs. Fisk smiled. She studied the young girl's glowing beauty and was touched by her eagerness. "I trust that you'll always feel that way about the theater."

"Oh, I will! I promise I will," Priscilla said.

They finally left the theater, and on the way home Priscilla talked incessantly. "Can I come back tomorrow night to see the play again, Esther?"

"Why, of course you can. Would you like to come too, Ruth?"

"No, I understand that Reverend James McGowan is preaching. He's such a wonderful preacher, at least his sermons are wonderful, and he's doing so much fine work in evangelism. If you don't mind, I'd rather go there."

"I'm sure Mother will be going," Esther said. "You'd rather hear a preacher than go to the theater?"

"I think so."

Priscilla seemed stung by Ruth's calm manner, and she said, "Well, not me. I'd like to go to the theater every night of my life."

"When do you have to be at Baxter Hospital?" Esther inquired.

"In three days," Priscilla said rather mournfully. "Can we go to the theater every night?"

"If that'll make you happy. Maybe I can do a series of pictures and get one of the papers to buy them."

★ ★ ★ ★

Baxter Hospital was a square three-story red-brick building that appeared to explode, like a mushroom, among the shabby tenements of the Five Points District. The streets outside were filled with ill-clad immigrants, whose faces were drawn and weary from the incessant struggle against starvation, illness, and poverty. The builders had spent no money on ornament or decoration to grace the front of the building. It was a simple glum-looking building in the middle of ramshackle tenements that crowded around it.

David Burns paused briefly as he entered the building. Looking up, he wished that some touch of color or beauty had been given to the structure. However, bringing beauty to the tenement district was not what the founder of Baxter had in mind. It had been built for the express purpose of treating the enormous number of poor people that flooded from Europe and now inhabited the district as if it were a rabbit warren. *The slums were grim enough without making the hospital so ugly,* he thought suddenly and shook his head as he entered. As soon as he was inside he was met by the head nurse, Mrs. Agnes Smith. Mrs. Smith was a homely woman with an almost mannish look, but despite the strict manner in which she ran the nurses' program, she had a genuine, caring heart. "Hello, Nurse Smith," Dr. Burns said, taking off his coat, "things have been all right, I take it?"

Nurse Smith's lips pursed and she shook her head. "We're crowded and overflowing as usual—and three of the nurses have reported in sick."

"I suppose we'll just have to make do," Dr. Burns said. He examined the nurse's face carefully and said, "You're tired, Agnes. You're working too hard."

"So are you, Doctor." Nurse Smith studied the young man with a maternal air. He was not an impressively handsome-looking man at all. He stood no more than five feet nine, but there was a straightness in his posture. He had a Highlander's look about him with light blue eyes, brown hair, and a carefully trimmed mustache. His face was thin, but there was a cheerful gleam in his steady eyes that women found attractive enough. Nurse Smith had been indignant when he had been assigned to the hospital, insisting he was too young, but she had sensed at once that he was a young man far more dedicated to his profession than many of his older colleagues.

"We have two young women waiting to meet you."

"New recruits?" Dr. Burns said with surprise.

"Yes, Doctor, and we need them."

"What did you think of them?"

"Oh, they have little sense, either of them, I suppose. Young people don't these days, but if you'll give me a free hand, I think I can do something with them."

David Burns smiled suddenly, and the change made his face almost attractive. "That's what you said aboot *me*, Agnes, when I first came here."

Agnes blushed slightly. "Well, I've done a good job, I think." She turned and walked down the corridor with the doctor toward his office. Glancing at him she said quietly, "I got a letter today from Gail Summers—I mean Gail Winslow." The mention of the name brought the doctor's head around, and Nurse Smith saw something in his eyes that she recognized at once.

He said, "Oh, how is she?"

"Fine enough. The letter's mostly about that girl that she and her husband have. Emily is her name."

"Yes, I know. I hear from them very often."

When the doctor said no more, Nurse Smith thought at once, *He hasn't gotten over Gail yet. I don't know as he ever will. Some of the Scotchmen are pretty steady in their feelings. He might wind up a crusty old bachelor, which I'd hate to see.*

When they reached the door of his office, Dr. Burns opened it and allowed Nurse Smith to go in before him. When he entered, he saw the two young women, who stood at once.

"This is Miss Priscilla Winslow," Nurse Smith said, indicating the fair-haired girl with exceptional blue-green eyes. "And this is Miss Ruth Winslow," she said, waving a hand at the taller girl with the red hair. "This is Dr. David Burns, young ladies."

"It's a pleasure to meet you," Burns said. There was a Scotch burr in his speech and he smiled briefly. "Winslow? Would you be related to Aaron and Lewis Winslow by any chance?"

"Yes, sir," Priscilla said quickly. "We're cousins. Our fathers and their mother are brothers and sister."

"And where do you come from? You don't talk like New York girls or Virginia girls."

"No, we're both from Wyoming. This is our first time in the city." It was Ruth who answered this time, and she added quickly, "We're anxious to do our best in the hospital with the program, Dr. Burns, but I must confess I know very little about nursing."

"Aye, weel now, Nurse Smith here will be a great help to you. She's a bit stern"—his smile lighted his features again, and he looked fondly at Agnes Smith—"but she is with me, too, so mind that you please her. Let me show you around the hospital."

Burns took them on a quick tour, and Ruth studied him carefully. This was the man she would be working under for the next year, and she was pleased with what she saw. Nurse Smith had given the two girls an account of Dr. Burns' activities, including his service in the Spanish-American War with Aaron and Lewis. She told them how he had taken Gail and Deborah, both nurses at the time, along to Cuba, and the three of them had served the wounded troops well there. "You're lucky to be learning under such a man as Dr. Burns," Nurse Smith had said stringently. "He's fair and he lets himself be put upon. See to it that you don't add any to his burdens."

Ruth noticed that almost every patient that they passed in the hall sought to get the doctor's attention, and he had a good word and a smile for each of them. He led them down through several wards, and Ruth was appalled at the thinness of the faces that she saw. She said as much quietly to Dr. Burns once. "They all seem so thin and undernourished. I suppose that's the way it is with the poor of the city."

"It's worse than ye think, Miss Winslow," Burns said rather glumly. His jaw seemed to set firmly and he added, "These businessmen force the people to live in tenements, sometimes seven or eight in a small apartment, or even more. They're the ones that need to answer for it."

"The little girl back there," Ruth ventured, "is she going to be all right?"

"I pray God she will. It's almost out of the doctors' hands now—but the Lord himself is the healer."

Ruth stared at him quickly. He turned to see the expression on her face and said, "What's the matter, Miss Winslow? Did you not expect a doctor to say such a thing?"

"Not really, but I'm glad to hear it," Ruth said. Her hair was pulled back, and her blue eyes studied him carefully with a pleased expression. "I don't know if Nurse Smith told you, but I'm here to learn nursing so I can go as a missionary. My cousin Barney Winslow is a missionary now in Africa."

"Indeed! Why, I know about him," Burns said. "I sometimes attend services at the mission where he was converted."

"Do you really!" Ruth exclaimed. "Oh, I'd love to go there."

"Why, indeed you shall if you would allow me. We're going for a service there tonight. Perhaps you and your cousin would join me for a brief supper, and then we'll go to the mission."

"Oh, I would love to do that!" Ruth exclaimed, though she noted Priscilla did not look interested.

★　　★　　★　　★

Late that afternoon after a rather difficult time of indoctrination to their duties, Burns met them at the door and said, "Now, for something a wee bit more enjoyable than nursing or doctoring." He stepped outside and hailed a carriage, which took them down the street.

"I never saw so many saloons," Priscilla said timidly as she stared at the saloons that seemed to line the streets.

"There's too many of them, but *one* would be too many, in my mind." As they rode along, Burns spoke to them about the vicious conditions that existed along Water Street, and then finally they came to a simple frame building, whitewashed, with a sign out that read simply, *Water Street Mission*.

Burns stepped out of the carriage, paid the driver, and helped the young ladies out. As they walked inside, they found themselves in a large rectangular room with rough benches. At the front stood a single table with a pitcher of water on it. The benches were half-filled with men and women, all roughly dressed. Some of them were going to sleep on the benches and Burns whispered, "Some of them come in just to get out of the cold. I don't mind, for they need the rest. Come along, we'll sit down front."

They made their way to the front of the building, and Burns introduced them to a tall, muscular man named Ralph Vincent. "Reverend Vincent has taken over the mission, and a fine job he's doing, I might add," Dr. Burns said.

Vincent greeted both the young ladies with a smile and said, "Perhaps you would like to give your testimonies. There'll be an opportunity for that."

"Oh no," Priscilla whispered, "I couldn't say a word!"

Ruth hesitated, and seeing the hesitation on her face, Vincent said, "You, miss. Perhaps you might say a word for Jesus."

"I . . . I might try," she said, "but it won't be much."

"Any word for Jesus is a good word," Vincent smiled.

The service that followed was very simple, consisting of half an hour of songs sung rather roughly to the accompaniment of a tinny piano that was at the front to one side. Then the testimonies were given, and most of them were from ex-drunks and prostitutes. Finally, Vincent said, "We have a visitor—a Miss Winslow. Would you stand, Miss Winslow, and tell us what the good Lord Jesus has done for you?"

Ruth's heart was beating fast. She was not an accomplished public speaker, and she had never been in a place like this mission in her life. Nevertheless, she heard Dr. Burns whisper, "Now, say your piece, Miss Winslow." And it encouraged her.

"I am glad to be with you tonight," Ruth said rather timidly, and then cleared her throat. She lifted her voice and began, "Almost all of you have led harder lives than I. God has blessed me with so many things, but I realized when I was just a young girl, no more than twelve years old, that I needed a savior. I was in a church, not much larger than this one, and the preacher preached on John 3:16. He talked about how Jesus died to save the world, and when the invitation was given I went to the front. It was a simple thing—I just yielded my heart to Him. He came in that morning and has been there ever since." She hesitated, and quiet had fallen over the room. The sight of the well-dressed, healthy young woman was such a contrast to the derelicts who occupied most of the seats and was quite dramatic. After a quick look at Reverend Vincent, who was smiling, Ruth went on, "I think God is calling me to go as a missionary to Africa, and I . . . I would ask you to pray for me that I will be faithful to His commands. Thank you."

A rough chorus of "Amens," "God bless you, sister," and "God will be with you, dear girl" came from the congregation. Vincent smiled at her again and said, "God will have His way with you, Miss Winslow. I feel it in my heart."

After the service was over and they were on their way back to the hospital, Burns turned to Ruth, saying warmly, "I was blessed by your words, Miss Winslow. It's exciting to see a young woman giving her heart to Christ and her life to Him in service."

"I'm a little bit afraid, Dr. Burns."

He smiled at her in the darkness of the cab. "If God has called you, He'll be with you." He hesitated, then said, "Perhaps you'd like to come again sometime."

Ruth agreed at once, but Burns was aware that Priscilla had not said a word. He turned to her and studied her beautiful face, but she turned away from him, saying nothing. Burns felt that there was a resistance in this young woman. From watching them during the service, he knew that the two young women in this cab were far different.

The next day Agnes asked Burns, "Did the young ladies enjoy the service at the mission?"

"Well, Miss Ruth Winslow did," Burns said, and his face fell as he added, "Miss Priscilla Winslow—she was not at all impressed."

"They're very different, aren't they, Doctor?"

"Yes, they are. Keep your eye on them, will you, Nurse Smith? I know you'll have to keep strict with these girls, but Miss Priscilla Winslow might need a little extra grace."

"I'll do that. The other one, Ruth, she's a fine girl. I already can see that."

"Aye, indeed she is! She gave a fine testimony."

"She's pretty too, isn't she?"

"Weel, I didn't notice so much about that."

"Didn't you?"

Burns flushed, for Nurse Smith knew him very well. "She is vurry attractive—both of them are."

Nurse Smith turned away to hide her smile. Several times in the days that followed she noted that Dr. Burns seemed to be drawn to the quieter of the two young women. Once she said, "She'll make someone a fine wife, won't she, Doctor?"

"Aye, I suppose she weel."

The doctor's words were short and clipped. As he turned and went to check on some patients, Nurse Smith shook her head and said, "Ah, poor boy. He's lost one love and he's afraid to risk himself. He can't take another loss like when he lost Gail Summers, but he'll have to risk, because love is taking a risk." She laughed at herself, whispering aloud, "I'm getting to be quite a philosopher." Then she turned and said sharply, "All right, you young women! You're going to have to make these beds better. Mind you now!"

CHAPTER FIVE

GOD HAS DIFFERENT CALLINGS

★   ★   ★   ★

Ruth threw herself into the training at Baxter Hospital with every ounce of her strength. She was always up early in the morning and often worked late at night. All the medical training was exciting to her, for at the back of her mind was the thought, *Maybe I'll learn something today that I can use when I get to the mission field*.

Her dedicated efforts did not go unnoticed by the staff. The director, Dr. Henry Cameron, remarked one day to his assistant, "Well, Dr. Burns, we are getting a few quality people in the nursing program. I noticed that the young lady with the red hair always seems to be around. What's her name again?"

"Her name is Ruth Winslow, Dr. Cameron." Burns smiled, pleased that the director had noticed the young woman's efforts. "She is an exemplary, fine young woman, indeed!"

"She has a sister here, I understand."

"No, sir, that's her cousin, Priscilla."

"And how is she doing?"

A slight hesitation broke the conversation for a moment, and finally Burns had to admit ruefully, "Well, sir, she's not as committed as Miss Ruth Winslow—but I have hope that she will improve."

"What's the matter with her?" Cameron demanded. "She's fine looking, but that may be a handicap. Back during the Civil War,

Dorothea Dix wouldn't hire a nurse unless she was downright homely. Good looks can be a distraction, although it doesn't seem to bother Miss Ruth Winslow."

"Well, sir, the girl is stage struck, I think. She spends every moment of her spare time at the theater, but she does her work, and I'm hopeful that she'll grow out of this foolishness about the stage."

★ ★ ★ ★

Later on, when Burns was on his way to Ellis Island, accompanied by Ruth, he repeated the conversation to her. He ended by shrugging his trim shoulders in a gesture of despair. "I'm not sure that we'll ever make a nurse out of Priscilla. She's just got her head set on the stage."

"Don't give up on her, Dr. Burns, please! She's a fine girl underneath, just not quite as mature as she should be."

Burns turned and smiled faintly. "I get the impression that her parents sent her here with you to accomplish that. Well, they couldn't have chosen a finer teacher. Dr. Cameron commented very favorably on you today, Ruth."

Ruth's cheeks were suddenly touched with red, and she looked out the window of the carriage. "That was very nice of him," she said quietly. She spoke no more, until they arrived at Ellis Island. She had never been there before, and was pleased when Burns had invited her to accompany him. As she dismounted from the carriage and the two of them moved inside the building, she saw that the reception center was enormous. It was two hundred feet long and one hundred feet wide with a fifty-foot-high ceiling.

"This is the main registration and examination hall on the island," Burns said.

"Do all the immigrants have to come through here?"

"Well, more or less. A few of the higher-class people have ways of getting around waiting in lines. Rich people are the same, I suppose, whether they're from America or Europe. Come along now, and you can watch as I do my examinations."

Ruth accompanied Dr. Burns, noting that the ground floor was used for baggage handling facilities, railroad ticket offices, food sale counters, and money changers. After observing for a few minutes, she realized that the immigration service employees wore dark uniforms that frightened many of the immigrants. "Why are they so afraid of the attendants?" she asked the doctor.

"Well, they think they're army officers. To Europeans any army officer is potentially dangerous."

They arrived at a station where a long line of poorly dressed immigrants stretched out beyond Ruth's view. "How many people come through here?" she asked, looking at the nurses and other employees bustling about.

"Probably about four thousand today." Burns slipped his coat off and added, "The flood tide from Europe is at its peak. Every day ships arrive from Hamburg, Liverpool, and Naples. They never seem to stop."

Ruth was surprised that the medical exam was very brief. Burns examined them very quickly, and she noticed that he marked some of their coats with chalk. When she asked him what that meant, he said, "Well, if they are obviously diseased, I pass them along so that another doctor can examine them more carefully."

"What will happen if they don't pass?"

Burns' thin face took on a melancholy look. "Why, they'll be shipped back to where they came from, of course."

Ruth looked at the men and women, some of them holding very small infants, and saw the fear in their faces. "It seems rather cruel to travel so far and then be sent back."

"Aye, it does at that, Ruth, but it's got to be like that. Look at it this way, though, eighty percent of them pass the examinations."

At that moment a family approached. The man was short and squat with a sunburned, lined face. He was approximately fifty years old. His wife wore a handkerchief over her head, and her clothes were patched. She cradled one child in her arms who appeared no more than six months old, and held the hand of a second. Two more, both boys, in shabby clothing, huddled behind her, their eyes filled with fear.

"Do you speak English?" asked Dr. Burns.

"Ya!"

"Open your mouth." Burns checked the man's teeth, then said,

"I see you limp. Is something wrong with your leg?"

"*Nein!* My leg is fine." A fine sweat broke out on the man's brow, and he pleaded, "Please, Doctor, I am strong. I work hard, ya, very hard."

"Well, your leg will have to be looked at."

"Nothing wrong with my leg."

"I'm sorry, it'll have to be looked at."

The woman, who evidently spoke no English, began to cry, and the man turned and spoke to her sharply. "Please," he said, turning around, "don't send me back."

Burns hesitated for a moment and then shrugged. Reaching out, he dusted the chalk mark from off the man's shoulder and said in a kindly fashion, "Move along."

"Thank you, Doctor."

After the family had been given a quick check and had passed through the check station, Ruth moved close enough to whisper, "That was very kind of you, Dr. Burns."

Burns turned around and found himself looking into her clear eyes. He noticed that her skin was the smoothest of any he had ever seen and that there was a glowing health about her. She was wearing a simple white uniform, but the attractiveness of her figure was not concealed. Startled at his reaction, for he had been with her for some weeks now, Burns said briskly, "Well, I may not be doing them a favor, but I couldn't say no." He saw that her eyes were filled with admiration and turned away in some confusion. "Next!" he said and turned to look at a tall man wearing the shabby uniform that all immigrants seemed to be issued at some point.

Burns worked hard all day, examining a never-ending line of immigrants. Ruth did nothing but watch for the most part, admiring the doctor's gentle manner with everyone he examined. More than once she would go to a woman with fatigue showing in every line of her body and take a baby and hold it. She seemed to have a certain charm, for not once did the babies resent her taking them. Several of the women spoke to her, mostly Italian. She could not understand a word, but she smiled at them warmly and assured them that America would be good for them.

One woman, who did speak some English, talked with her considerably. Ruth was appalled at the conditions that the poor woman had endured on the ship, and she said finally, "But now you are in America. Things will be better."

Shyly the young woman looked at her and said, "If all peoples be as kind as you, ma'am—everything will be wonderful."

Finally the day ended, and Burns took Ruth back to the hospital. "It was a hard day," he said, helping her out of the carriage.

"Not for me, although you worked awfully hard," Ruth smiled.

He paused for a moment and turned to her. "You're really interested in all of this. Some nurses would be offended by the poverty. They don't all smell too good after weeks on a crowded ship."

"They're God's children," Ruth said softly. "What kind of a missionary would I be if I was offended by a little dirt?"

A smile then came to Dr. Burns. "That's vurry good, Ruth," he said quietly. "I'm glad you've come to Baxter."

★   ★   ★   ★

Ruth delighted in her training at Baxter, but Priscilla found the program and the work almost unbearable. All of her life she had enjoyed the freedom of the outdoors, and now to be confined within the rather dark, smelly interior of the hospital with sick patients was torturous for her. The only thing that kept her from giving up was the fact that she spent every evening at the theater. Every penny of the money that her parents sent her she spent on tickets. Since she was a child, Priscilla had been fascinated by plays and dramas. And by coming to New York City, she had come to the theatrical center of the world. New York, of course, was full of amusement resorts—music halls, dance halls, concert saloons, and nickel house movies. These were not classified as "respectable," but the big city offered high fare. Priscilla soon knew every theater in town and had seen such romantic comedies and melodramas as the *Rose of the Rancho, Julie BonBon,* and *Barbara's Millions.* She had tasted of the witty plays of George Bernard Shaw, and her favorite was a rather light play called *Florodora.* It had played over five hundred performances and proved so popular that local railroads were running *Florodora Expresses* throughout the city. The story took its title from a perfume made by an

American on a mysterious Philippine Island. The plot dealt with engaging proper young ladies to proper young gentlemen. The show's hit was Leslie Stewart's "Tell Me Pretty Maiden," sung in the second act by six women dressed in full-length skirts with flounces, ruffled shirtwaists, and ostrich-plumed hats. The song was addressed to six men wearing silk hats and gray morning coats, bearing walking sticks, who responded on bended knee.

Priscilla liked it so much she saw the show three times, and on her last trip persuaded Ruth to accompany her. When the hit song was being sung—"Tell Me Pretty Maiden"—Priscilla leaned over and whispered, "I could do that, Ruth."

"Why in the world would you *want* to!" Ruth exclaimed. It seemed to her the height of frivolity, and she was not at all impressed with the play.

After that Priscilla ceased her attempts to get Ruth to accompany her, but she continued to go every night. She saw *Winchester*, a war play about the Filipino War that was coming to an end, and she was enraptured over Lillian Russell's performance in a musical version of *As You Like It*. She even managed to buy tickets to Oscar Hammerstein's *Victoria*. At the famous Paradise Roof Garden, she saw the famous escape artist, Houdini, perform his magic, and on another night she watched as a young Charlie Chaplin put the crowd in stitches with his clowning.

It was, for Priscilla, a dual existence. All day she drudged away at the mundane, dirty, hard work at Baxter Hospital—and every evening, as soon as she could eat and dress, she fled to the Great White Way of New York to Broadway, where theaters lined the streets. There was an insatiable hunger in her for this life. Yet when morning came, at times she despaired and even wept when she had to rise up and do her ten hours of work at the hospital.

Ruth, naturally, was distressed with her cousin's consuming infatuation with the theater, and in her letters home she tried to put the best face on things, but there was little of a positive nature that she could say about Priscilla's work. Ruth grew rather close to Esther and shared some of her concerns with her.

On her day off, Ruth decided to spend the afternoon visiting with Esther. As they were sitting in the parlor, drinking tea, Esther listened as Ruth expressed her concern about Priscilla's lifestyle. When Ruth had finished, Esther said, "I hate to hear that. From everything I understand about the theater, it may be colorful and exciting—but for most of the actors and actresses, it's not a good life."

"Even before we came to New York, it's all she ever talked about. Her room at home is covered with autographed pictures of actresses and actors, and all she ever reads is plays and stories about them." Wearily she tucked a strand of hair back in place. "I'm worried about her, Esther. She's got to find a better life than going to the theater every night."

"What about you, Ruth?"

"Me? Why, I'm fine." Ruth's face glowed, and she spoke for some time about how happy she was at Baxter Hospital. She ended by saying, "I've been going with Dr. Burns out to Ellis Island. I can't do much, but I help with the women and babies as much as I can." Her face clouded, and she shook her head. "It's so pitiful, Esther. I wish you could see it."

Esther suddenly straightened up. "You know, I think I'll go with you—if Dr. Burns would permit it."

"You would?" Ruth was rather surprised at Esther's sudden interest. Going to Ellis Island was not a normal thing for wealthy young women to do. "Why would you want to do that, Esther?"

"I'm looking for some sort of subject for my pictures," she said slowly. "I've taken quite a few around the city, but so far nothing has really fallen into place. Ellis Island is really a most unusual setting, isn't it, Ruth? I doubt if there's anything like it in the country."

"It's dramatic, all right, but it's sad to see all those people coming with such hope . . ." She hesitated, then added, "Then you know they'll end up in a tenement, ten to a room, and half starving to death."

Esther considered that for a moment, then said, "Ask Dr. Burns if I could accompany you with my camera next time."

"I'm sure he wouldn't mind."

When Ruth returned to the hospital, she found Dr. Burns in his office. She walked in, and when he looked up from his paper work, he said, "Hello, Ruth. I hope you enjoyed your day off. You certainly deserve it for all the hard work you do."

"Why . . . thank you, Dr. Burns, I did. I spent a nice afternoon with Esther. She is wondering if you would mind if she accompanied us the next time we go to Ellis Island. She's interested in taking some pictures."

"Why, I think that would be fine. Tell her we'd be pleased to have her company."

★　★　★　★

On the following Thursday, Esther loaded her camera, tripod, and equipment, then accompanied the doctor and Ruth to Ellis Island. She was stunned at the enormity of the main hall, where lines and lines of immigrants were waiting to pass through the examinations. "Why, there must be thousands of people!" she whispered.

"Aye, and they're all pretty weel penniless, and fugitives from the worst kind of poverty," Dr. Burns said.

"Will they mind if I take their pictures?"

"Some of them might—they are frightened of any attention, but I'll talk to some of them for you."

It was a tiring afternoon for Esther Winslow. She had never spoken with the very poor, nor come in close contact with them. It was one thing to ride down the street and see the shabby tenements with clothes strung outside the windows—ragged, tattered, worn clothes—but it was another thing to stand face-to-face with a woman whose possessions consisted only of what was stuffed into a black cotton sack. Esther was coached by Ruth, who had learned how to gain the confidence of people. Some of them had never seen a camera before, but Ruth was fortunate to find one group whose leader could speak very good English.

"They're from Russia," Ruth said as she brought the group up, "and they'd be happy to have you take their pictures."

Esther, at once, went to work posing them, taking their pictures individually. The last picture she made she felt would be the best. The whole group was standing, all nine of them, including a baby in the woman's arms, three men wearing shabby coats with vests, one of them boasting a ratty bow tie. The woman wore a skirt that reached to the floor. She had a handkerchief tied over her head, as most of the women did. One little girl, no more than three, had eyes like saucers and black curly hair. She sat on one of the suitcases and stared at the camera, fear and curiosity mingled in her eyes. It was the eyes, Esther saw, that would make the photograph. Men and women stared into the camera, the men all with bushy mustaches, wearing soft-brimmed hats that had seen much use. Now they were in America, and they were all facing a life that they had dreamed of for years. Along with the hope that each treasured in their thoughts, Esther did not miss the fear that lurked in every face.

When they were on their way home, Dr. Burns said, "Did you get some good pictures?"

"I think the best I ever took," Esther said.

"What weel you do with them?" Burns asked. "Who would buy pictures like that?"

"I'm not sure," Esther said slowly, "but I keep up with the newspapers pretty well and the magazines, too. There's never been a story done like this. If I could get enough good pictures, I might sell the *Times* on the idea of doing a series on Ellis Island."

Burns stared at her. "For what purpose?"

"I don't know," Esther said slowly. "When I came I just wanted to take pictures, but now that I've seen these people, how pathetic they are, that doesn't seem quite right. I'd like to do some good for them, if I could."

★ ★ ★ ★

The next day Andrew arrived at the home of his parents, and they all met him with a great deal of joy. Andrew Winslow had thick auburn hair and bright blue eyes. His six-foot frame was lean and smoothly muscled, allowing his movements to be sure and graceful. After supper that night, he and Esther sat up after everyone else had gone to bed and talked endlessly.

Finally Esther said, almost woefully, "You and Barney are doing such a wonderful work—Barney as a missionary in Africa, and you as a traveling speaker for missions. But I don't do anything, Andy."

Andrew sensed the hint of despair in his sister's voice. "Why, sis," he said, "you shouldn't talk like that."

"But it's true. I'm just like an ornament, and what good is an ornament?"

"It makes the world nice to look at," he said. "What would a

Christmas tree be without an ornament?"

Esther got up and began to pace about the room. It was a cold night, and the fire crackled in the fireplace. The light reflected on her black hair, and when she turned her large eyes on him, he saw a plea in them that he had never seen before. Esther had always been a rather selfish girl, taken up with her own affairs. Andrew had always had a soft spot for his younger sister, and now he felt a sudden urge to do something for her.

"Why, Esther, God has something for everybody to do. Some can sing, and if they can"—he shrugged his broad shoulders—"they can sing for the glory of God. Some can preach, and some can teach. Look at Ruth. She's found her niche already. Dr. Burns tells me she's going to be the best nurse he's ever had. I'm going to try to talk her into going to Africa—and the doctor, too, if he would."

"That's just it. They've found their place, both of them, and they're doing good work." Esther shrugged her shoulders with discontent. "I'm not doing anything, Andy. I'm just, as you say, an ornament. Like a ball one hangs on a Christmas tree."

Andy said, "Come over and sit beside me, sis." When she came, he put his arm around her, and the two sat there quietly, listening to the fire crackle. Andy was praying in his spirit, and finally he asked, "What would you really like to do? Is there something?"

"Well, I've been caught up with photography lately, but that's just a hobby."

"I don't know that that's true. Paul was a tentmaker. He made tents for the glory of God. Why couldn't you make pictures for the glory of God?"

His words caught Esther by surprise. "Why . . ." she paused, her eyes opening wide, "I never thought of such a thing. How could I do that?"

"I don't know, but I know that God gives talents, and as I've often said, be the best steward of what God has given you. What about this Ellis Island thing? Is there any way your pictures could alert the public to the terrible plight of the poor people you've been telling me about? And, you remember, I spent a lot of time in the mission on Water Street. I know a little bit about the drunks and the prostitutes. Nobody cares for them, except a few people that run the missions there. What if the whole city could suddenly see the awfulness of it? Now *that* would be doing a work for God! Perhaps it would get the churches stirred up to help," Andrew said. He became excited and talked at length about the possibilities.

As for Esther, she was struck deep in her spirit with all that Andrew said. She had always respected him and the work that he did, and now to have him approving what had been, to her, only a hobby thrilled her deeply.

The two talked on until very late, and when they stood up to go to bed, Andrew said, "God has different callings, Esther. It seems to me that He has put this gift in you. Now, the Bible says whether you eat or drink, do *all* to the glory of God." He smiled at her and kissed her on the cheek. "Let me add to that, when you take pictures, take pictures to the glory of God!"

CHAPTER SIX

THE IRON LADY

★ ★ ★ ★

The world had survived the year 1901 as it had survived thousands previously. Some of the captains and the kings had departed, the most spectacular being Queen Victoria of the British Empire. She had died at the age of eighty-two on the Isle of Wight. Beside her, as she passed from one world to the next, was the Prince of Wales, who came to the throne as Edward the VII.

Another death that rocked the world had taken place on September the sixth. President William McKinley fell to an assassin's bullet, and eight days later died, feebly mouthing the words of his favorite hymn, "Nearer My God to Thee." President Theodore Roosevelt, a forty-two-year-old former governor of New York, took the oath of office at once and put his hand to the helm of America.

In France, Henri de Toulouse-Lautrec, painter and lithographer, who chronicled the Parisian night life, died at the age of thirty-six. The Spanish-American War wound down with the capture of the Filipino rebel leader, Emilio Aguinaldo. William Howard Taft went at once to rule as governor of the Philippines, while General Arthur MacArthur ruled as the military head.

Many died in South Africa. The Boer War dragged on, its end not in sight. The British could not seem to defeat the guerrillas who struck like lightning, then disappeared into the vast wastelands where the British troops could not follow. Lord Kitchener herded all residents into concentration camps. Thousands of family members had been confined, and large numbers of women and children had died from starvation and the diseases that resulted from the squalid conditions in the camps. Kitchener had warned that he would use even more serious measures to defeat the Boers.

Jan Kruger had been one of those who had nearly died of starvation in one of Kitchener's concentration camps. He had given himself wholeheartedly to the job of treating as many of the diseased Dutch families as he could. In the end he had been able to make his escape and had stowed away on board a ship that was docked at Durban. He had been ill with fever, but by the time he had been discovered, the ship was well out to sea and, of course, could not turn back. The vessel had been bound for Italy, and when they finally reached port, Kruger had been roughly dumped ashore and left to his own devices, which were very few!

November had come to the world, and now overhead a pale, almost lifeless sun sent down rays that seemed to carry no heat whatsoever. Jan Kruger was thirty pounds under his usual weight. His face was drawn with fatigue, his eyes glazed with fever, and his cheeks flushed. As he staggered along the narrow street, the local inhabitants turned to stare at him curiously. They were accustomed to poor sailors coming ashore from foreign countries, but this tall man with the tawny hair and the feverish eyes looked somewhat dangerous. He wore the remnants of the uniform that he had managed to hang on to in South Africa. The brown canvas jacket, with multiple pockets, and the low-crowned hat with the brim pinned up on the right side gave him an alien and menacing look.

As he passed by a bakery, the delicious odor of freshly baked bread wafted out into the street to him. He stopped, leaned up against the building, and thought hopelessly of the impossibility of his situation. He had not a single coin in his pocket and had been poorly fed on the ship during the voyage. Now he was so weak he could barely stand.

No sense tempting myself, Kruger thought and moved away from the bakery. For two hours he roamed the streets of the city, growing more feeble.

He had just passed into one of the poorest sections of town, and through fever-dimmed eyes, he could barely make out the features of those peasants who passed by him. Too proud to beg for something to eat, he decided to go back to the harbor. Why, he did not know. As he stumbled along, suddenly the world seemed to tilt under his feet. He stopped, planted his feet wide apart, and closed his eyes. A wave of dizziness came to him, and he desperately tried to hold his balance—but the hard pavement seemed to rise up and smite him a heavy blow. He knew he was lying on the street, and his fingers clutched at the stones as he tried to pull himself upright. The sun overhead was dim enough, but it grew dimmer, and finally he was swallowed up in a heavy, thick, cold blackness such as he had never known. . . .

★ ★ ★ ★

He was aware that voices spoke out of the darkness, but they were faint and seemed far away. Sometimes hands pulled at him. Some of them were rough and others more gentle, but always he would slip back into the warmth of the darkness. The light that broke into his dark world seemed to bring pain and discomfort. It was much easier to simply fade away into the oblivion and comfort that the darkness brought with it.

But finally there came a time when the voices grew louder, and he realized that he could not understand the words. He felt hands touching his face, and with an effort he slowly opened his eyes. The light from some source blinded him, and he shut his eyes quickly and turned his head to one side. He coughed, and pain like that of a hot poker thrust through his chest.

"Look, he's awake!"

With an effort Kruger opened his eyes again, keeping them turned away from the light that he now saw streaming through a small window. Twisting his head he saw that he was lying flat on his back in a bed. A woman was sitting beside him, but the light was behind her, so that he could not see the outline of her face. He tried to speak but began to cough, and she put out her hand and held it on his chest and said, "Here, you drink-a this."

Her strong hands were under his shoulders then, and he turned to see a man standing on the other side of the bed. He felt the man's rough hands under his arms, pulling him upright, then the young woman held a cup to his lips. He discovered he was ravenous for water and gulped it down. Some of the liquid ran down his chin, and he whispered, "More!"

"You can-a have plenty."

Kruger drank three cups of the water, then the young woman said, "Later, you have more. What your name?"

"Kruger—Jan Kruger."

"What kind of a name you have-a there?" The man spoke this time. He was a short man, stocky, with black hair and black eyes, and a droopy mustache of the same color. His eyes were curious, and when he leaned forward, Kruger could smell sweat and the pungent odor of garlic.

"Dutch. I'm from South Africa."

The young woman said, "You hungry?"

Suddenly Kruger realized he was very hungry. "I . . . I think I am." He looked around and said, "Where is this place?"

"This-a my house. My name—Tony Scarlotta. This-a my daughter, Maria."

"How did I get here?"

Maria moved away from the light. She was, he saw, no more than sixteen or seventeen. She had olive skin and enormous eyes, and wore a handkerchief over her head. "My papa—he bring you in on his back. He found you in the street. You been sick a long time."

"Maria, fix-a him some soup—onion soup. That's-a good for sick folks with fever."

"I think the fever, it's gone," the girl said, but she turned and left the small bedroom. As soon as she left, what seemed like a whole herd of children came trooping in.

"These are my other children," Tony said. "This is Emila, she's-a six, this is Michael, eight, this is my two older boys, Mario and Dino, thirteen and fifteen. My wife, she's-a be back soon."

Kruger's head was pounding, but his thoughts began coming more clearly. He surveyed the dark faces surrounding the bed and said, "You've got a good father—to take in a sick man."

"They don't understand English good like-a me and Maria. How come you here, you gotta friends in Rome?"

"No, Mr. Scarlotta, I don't know a soul."

"Well, you pretty sick fella. I learn English good, working on

English ships," he said proudly. "How you like-a my English?"

"Very good, much better than my Italian."

The children seemed fascinated by the tall man, and when Maria came back in carrying a steaming bowl of onion soup, she cried, "Shoo, get away. You gonna smother him!"

Kruger accepted the bowl and the spoon she put in his hand and began eating ravenously. "This is good," he murmured, taking time between swallows, "the best I've ever had."

As he was finishing, a heavyset woman with the same dark coloring as the others came in. "Ah, Lucia," Tony said, "he's awake."

Lucia Scarlotta shoved children aside, almost callously. She said something in Italian and put her hand on his brow, then she nodded with approval. She spoke to her husband, who interpreted. "She no speak English good like-a me. She-a say your fever all gone. You be much more better soon."

"I feel better already. I think maybe I could get up now."

"No," Maria said quickly, "you're too sick. You stay here, rest." She turned to the children and spoke to them in Italian, and they all scattered, leaving the room. "I fix-a you something solid tomorrow."

"Thank you, Miss Scarlotta."

The girl stared at him and murmured, "My name is Maria."

"You can call me Jan." Kruger smiled at her. Then the weakness came back like a wave, and he tried to say something else, but his eyes would not stay open. This time, however, he did not drift back to a restless black darkness, but a peaceful, natural sleep. Just before he lost consciousness, he had time to pray one prayer. "Thank you, God, for bringing me to good people."

★ ★ ★ ★

The new year came, almost unnoticed by Jan Kruger. He was not aware of it as he walked the streets of Rome all day looking for work. Every place he went, he was turned down, for even native-born peasants were having a struggle finding work to stay alive. As he passed down the street that led to the Scarlottas' small apartment building, he thought, *Thank God I'm getting my strength back*! He had regained most of the weight he had lost, but he was depressed, for he was a man of strong independence. Never had he been totally dependent on anyone since he left home at the age of fifteen. Now, every bite he took at Tony Scarlotta's house was a bite that this kind man's children would not get. "Got to find something to do," he said briefly. He had one possession that had come with him from Africa—his father's watch. It was a fine Swiss watch, gold, and worth a considerable amount of money, he supposed. He had never considered selling it because it was the only possession he had from his father. Now, however, he found himself touching it as it nestled in his pocket. He knew that sooner or later it would have to go if he couldn't find work.

When he reached the building that housed the Scarlottas' apartment, he stepped inside and smelled the familiar aroma of soup and cabbage, and, as always, garlic. He entered without knocking, for there was little privacy in the Scarlotta apartment. It consisted of one fairly large room which served as a kitchen, dining room, and living room, plus two small bedrooms, one of which was used by Tony and Lucia, the other by Maria, Emila, and Michael. Mario and Dino slept on pads in the main room, and it was here that Jan was allotted a space for sleeping. Maria turned from the stove where she was cooking spaghetti and smiled at him. "You been gone all-a day. Any luck?"

"No, not at all," Jan said dejectedly. He was swarmed by Emila and Michael, who came at once, pulling at him and pestering him to play games with them. Mario and Dino were not far behind, for they loved to learn to speak English, and he had served as their teacher.

"Let him alone, he's tired," Maria said sharply. She spoke to the younger children in Italian, and then said, "Supper will-a be ready soon, Jan. Go wash up."

"Haven't done anything to get dirty," Jan said. However, he moved over to a table that held an enamel pan and pitcher and washed his face and hands. Drying them off on a clean white cloth, he walked over and said, "I wish I could help you cook, Maria."

"That's-a no job for a man!" She turned to him and shook her head as she stirred the pot of spaghetti. Her hair was as black as hair could get, and there was a pleasing fullness to her youthful figure. Jan had noted that many young men dropped by, for the girl's beauty attracted them from far away across the city.

"I think any work would be good. I wish I could get a job washing dishes, anything—but there's nothing."

"You'll find something. What did you do in Africa?"

Strangely enough no one had bothered to ask this question in all the time that Jan had been under their roof. He had mentioned being in the army, and they assumed he had been a soldier. Now he looked at her and smiled. "Believe it or not, I was a doctor."

Maria turned and stared at him. "You are a real doctor?"

"Well, as real as I could be." Jan smiled. "I think I saved more than I killed." He saw a puzzled look on her face and quickly added, "That was a joke that we doctors make about each other."

"Why, you must go to the hospital. You can get a job there. There's always a need of doctors in Rome."

"No, I'm afraid not," Jan said, shaking his head.

"Why not?" she demanded.

"Because you have to qualify, which means in this country, or any country, I'd have to go back to school for several years."

"What foolishness! If you're a doctor, you're a doctor." The girl gestured dramatically with the wooden spoon that she had used for stirring the pot of spaghetti. "All you need to do is get a black bag and start curing people!"

Her youthful innocence somehow pleased Kruger, and he shook his head with a smile. "That would be a good way to wind up in prison," he said. "Every country has a law against practicing medicine without a license. I don't know exactly what it is here in Italy, but you can be sure there is one. No, I need a job digging ditches or cutting timber or some work I could do with my hands."

Maria was caught up with the idea of Jan being a doctor. "Maybe you could be an assistant to a doctor," she said. She continued to speak of the possibilities with excitement. When her parents came in, she began speaking to them rapidly in Italian, explaining that their guest was a genuine doctor. This, of course, triggered Lucia and Tony, who became quite excited.

Tony beamed and said, "Now, you no tell us? That's-a no good to keep-a secrets from Tony!"

"Well, it wasn't a secret, Tony," Jan shrugged. "It doesn't help any, either. As a matter of fact, I wish I were a stone mason or a carpenter instead of a doctor. Then maybe I could get work here."

Tony's brow furrowed and he frowned. "It's-a bad time," he said. "Change of government always bring-a bad times."

Maria interrupted by saying, "Sit down, we eat now."

The meal was simple enough, consisting of spaghetti and fresh-made bread. It was the staple fare, along with a few extras which Maria sometimes wheedled out of the store owners. As they gathered around the table and ate, Tony talked about the hard times, and suddenly he looked up and said, "I need to talk to you."

"You mean now?" Jan asked.

"Yes," Tony hesitated, then said, "what do you know about America?"

"Not much—never been there. Big place, though. Plenty of room to spread out. Why do you ask, Tony?"

Tony Scarlotta bowed his head and stirred the spaghetti on his plate with his fork. Deep thought came hard for him, and everyone was quiet as he seemed to struggle to bring forth what was on his mind. Finally he looked up and said, "I'm-a think it be good to go to this place America."

Jan Kruger stared at his host with surprise. "But this is your home, Tony!"

"It's-a good place for some, Italy, but many are with no work and hungry now. My job, it won't last. I'll be outta work soon. I think of America a long time now. My cousin, he go two years ago. Got good job, fine job in Chicago. He say plenty of work in Chicago."

"But it would be leaving all that you know. Like me . . ." He paused, then said, "I'll never go back to South Africa. Things would never be the same now that the English have taken it over."

"You no can stay here," Tony said, extending his hands in an eloquent gesture. "No work, nothing to do. The same for me. I worry about my family," he said simply. "I wanna my boys and my girls to have more than I had. There nothing here for none of us."

"Have you really thought about this, Tony?"

"Yes, me and Maria. We talk about it a long-a time." He shook his head. "It cost much-a money. We no have enough right now, but we save every penny. Then we go."

"It'll take a long time," Maria said sadly. "But when we go," she brightened up, "you will go, too, Jan."

Jan Kruger said nothing. He smiled but shook his head. "I don't have a penny," he said.

"We save enough so we all go," Maria nodded. "It take a while, but we'll do it, you gonna see!"

From that moment on, all of the talk in the Scarlotta household was about going to America, and soon Kruger discovered that this family was not alone. The whole neighborhood was talking about America. Men in the shop talked of it over their accounts. Even the market women made up their quarrels so that they might discuss it from stall to stall. People, who had relatives in America, went around reading the letters they received to the less fortunate folk. Even the children made games, playing at immigrating, pretending to be on the ship, pretending to get off in America. Of course, the old folks shook their heads and prophesied no good for those who braved the terrors of the sea, but everyone talked about it, although scarcely anyone knew the true facts about the faraway land.

For a month Jan strove as hard as he had ever striven for anything to get work, but he did not speak the language. He had no skills, save that of a physician, and since he was not licensed here, no one would acknowledge that. He even went to a hospital trying to find a job as an orderly but was looked at with suspicion by those in charge.

He was present one evening when Tony brought out the box that held all of the funds that the Scarlottas had scraped together. Even the children had brought their small coins in, and Tony counted it up. When Maria heard the total, she shook her head. "Not enough! Got to have more lira!"

"How much more?" Jan asked.

Maria named the sum and shook her head dolefully. "Take a long time—a long time."

Jan looked at Tony and his family and saw the hope mixed with the stark realization that it would take a long time of saving before they could make their plans. As they finished their meal in silence, he made a decision.

The next day Jan went to the business district of Rome. He entered a fine jewelry store and was at once approached by a man who had come, no doubt, to order him to leave. However, he made a striking figure with his field hat pinned up to one side, and though his jacket was worn, Maria had patched it nicely and kept it clean so that he made a prepossessing appearance. "I have a watch that I want to sell. A very valuable watch. Do you speak English?"

"Certainly," the clerk said, as if insulted. "Let me see the watch."

Silently Kruger handed the watch over. The clerk examined it carefully and shrugged. "Not worth a great deal, but I will give you a hundred lira for it."

Instantly Kruger reached out and took the watch. "I didn't come to make it a gift. I know the value of this watch. It has twenty-one jewels, it's made of solid gold, and it was created by one of the finest craftsmen in Switzerland. I'll take it to your competitor down the street."

"Wait!" The clerk held up his hand. "I'll let you talk to the manager. He will have to make the deal."

Thirty minutes later Jan Kruger left the jewelry store with a wad of bills tucked in his shirt pocket. There was a sadness in him, for the watch had been the last physical evidence of his family. Now there was nothing left to look at to remember them. *I had to do it*, he thought as he made his way back toward the poor section of town. *There's no other way.*

When he got back to the apartment, he said nothing until suppertime. After they had eaten, he pulled the wad of lira out of his pocket and handed it to Tony. "Is this enough to get us all to America—along with what you have, Tony?" he asked.

Tony Scarlotta stared at the bills. Slowly and deliberately, he unfolded them and began to count. When he had totaled them all, he placed the wad of bills on the table and looked up.

Maria exclaimed, "That's-a plenty. We can go to America!" Without thinking, she threw her arms around Jan. Her lissome figure pressing against him gave him a shock, but then all of the others rushed him, so that he was swarmed by hysterical Scarlottas. Lucia stood back and wiped her face as tears streamed down her face.

Finally he got them calmed down enough to say, "When can we leave, Tony?"

Two tears ran down Tony Scarlotta's ruddy cheeks as he said, "We leave as soon as we get a place on the boat. Tomorrow we sell everything that we can't carry, and then—here we come America!"

★ ★ ★ ★

Leaving their homeland had been hard, and the voyage itself was a nightmare. The ship that carried them out of the Mediterranean and across the Atlantic was named the *Victor Emmanuel*. They were all huddled together in steerage, almost like cattle. The Scarlottas arranged themselves in the narrow bunks, but they could not eat the ship's food for the first two days because all of them were seasick. Fortunately, Kruger was spared and was not affected by the swells that rocked the boat, and here he proved his worth, for he managed to secure some hot tea and kept them from succumbing to the sickness.

But soon the Scarlottas became utterly dejected. The dark, filthy compartments in the steerage contained wooden bunks in two tiers. Constantly, people had vomiting fits, and the confusion of cries became unbearable.

"I wish we'd never left Italy," Maria moaned one day. She was sitting on the lower bunk holding Emila and Michael, one on each side. Her face was pale, and she was drenched with sweat. "I never think it be this bad!"

"Try to stick it out, Maria. It's pretty rank, but we'll make it." Kruger looked around at the crowds, jammed like rabbits in a warren into the ill-smelling bunks. The odors of scattered orange peelings, tobacco, garlic, and disinfectants all blended together to form a horrible stench throughout the steerage. The food, miserable as it was, was dished up out of large kettles into dinner pails provided by the steamship company.

"I'll see if I can get some washing done," Jan said.

"You no do that, that's woman's work."

Kruger reached out and squeezed her hand, which was draped on Emila's shoulder. "It's anybody's work as long as it gets done. You rest here. I'll bring some tea and maybe something light, maybe some soup later."

He made his way down to the washroom, which was about

seven by nine feet. It contained ten faucets of cold salt water—five along either of its two walls—and had as many basins. Most of them were already in use, serving as a dishpan for greasy tins and as a laundry tub for handkerchiefs. There were also a few basins for shampoos, but none of them were ever clean. It was all there was, however, so Kruger threw himself into the work of washing the soiled clothing of the entire family. He found the dirty job gave him a sense of satisfaction. These poor people had done so much for him, and now this was a small way to return their many kindnesses. Besides, he kept remembering the word that had come to him in the darkness of the night he was waiting to be executed, *I will spare you—but you must show my love to the poor by service.* "Well," he said aloud as he scrubbed the clothes, "they can't get much poorer than Tony and Lucia and their kids."

He began to whistle, and after he had washed all the clothes, he wrung them out as well as he could. He was almost fully recovered now, and his hands were strong. An elderly woman was struggling to wring her clothes out, and he said, "Here, ma'am, let me help you with that." He wrung the woman's clothes until they were as free of moisture as possible, then said, "Let me carry this back for you."

The old woman seemed very fragile. The veins on the back of her hands were large and blue, and she moved slowly, as if each step sent darts of pain through her tired limbs. Kruger wondered how she would fare in the new land which required youth and strength, but hopefully she had relatives there. He saw her settled in her bunk with her clothes hung out as well as could be, then he returned to the makeshift washroom to take the Scarlottas' laundry back to their bunks.

Leaving the clothes there, he went to the galley and cajoled the cook into filling his bucket with soup, then he used some of his precious cash to buy some fresh-baked bread.

When he got back, he found them all looking apathetic and pale. "You've got to eat," he said.

"I throw up," Maria complained.

"Then I'll feed you some more until you keep it down. Come on, especially the tea, and the milk for the children."

Fortunately there were no storms at sea, which helped the seasickness pass away after a few days. The Scarlottas gradually all improved, and they managed to make the best of the hardships. More than once Maria said to Jan, "It's a good thing for you to be here, Jan. We have real trouble without you."

"You're the one who picked me up out of the streets," he reminded her. "I think I might've died if you hadn't taken me in, so I guess I owe you my life."

The next day Jan and Maria were standing on the rail of the *Victor Emmanuel* watching the gray waters churning along the side. The sky was blue overhead, but the wind was sharp as it whipped through their thin clothing. "You know," he said, "since you saved my life, I'm sort of your prisoner. I'll have to owe you that debt as long as I live. What can I do for you, Maria, when we get to America?"

"I don't know what you mean."

"I think we'll need to stick together, the Scarlottas and this poor Dutchman. I think God meant it that way."

Maria did not answer for a time. When she turned to him, however, there was a pleased smile on her youthful face. "That's-a good," she whispered. "I like that very much."

They stood on the rail as long as possible, for the air was fresh and clean, but finally they were forced to go below to take care of the children.

★ ★ ★ ★

The *Victor Emmanuel* approached the Ambrose channel, and the rail was crowded with the steerage passengers who had come up at the word that America was in sight.

"There it is!" someone finally cried out.

"It's so big!" Mario said, staring toward the land.

"It's the biggest thing I've ever seen," Dino echoed.

They were all standing on the ship's fantail, staring at the huge Statue of Liberty that seemed to rise up out of the water and welcome the ships that sailed by. The *Victor Emmanuel* had dropped anchor in the narrows, placed in the quarantine pending clearance, and medical teams had come aboard. The doctors gave perfunctory medical examinations to the first- and second-class passengers, making sure the ship was not infested with lice and there was no epidemic aboard. The steerage passengers had nothing to do but wait and gawk at the impressive Statue of Liberty. Their examinations would come when they disembarked at Ellis Island.

As Jan Kruger stood at the rail, penned in by Maria on one side and Tony Scarlotta on the other, he stared up at the magnificent piece of sculpture—the figure of a woman holding a torch high in the air. Looking around he saw tears running down Maria's cheeks, then turning he saw the same on the countenance of Tony.

Tony wiped his eyes with a red bandana, blew his nose with a honking sound, then he turned, and his lips trembled under his heavy mustache as he said, "It's a dream come-a true, Jan!"

Maria heard his words. She was pressed against Jan's side, and she asked in a faint whisper, "Do you think we will be happy here?"

Jan Kruger looked up at the statue and said, "That Iron Lady there, she stands for something." He tried to put his thoughts into words, and said finally, "As far as I can understand it, she's inviting the poor and the mistreated to come to this country of freedom and opportunity. Now we're here, and we will see what this place called America is like!"

Maria stared up at the structure for a long moment—then she whispered, "I'm glad she's a woman, Jan—I think maybe she can understand a woman's heart. . . !"

PART TWO

PRISCILLA

★ ★ ★ ★

1902

CHAPTER SEVEN

ELLIS ISLAND

★ ★ ★ ★

"It's-a so beeg!"

Maria Scarlotta moved closer to Jan Kruger, unconsciously reaching up to take his arm. Jan looked down at her, noting that her face was tense, her eyes clouded with fear. "It'll be all right, Maria," he said quietly. "The worst of it is over."

"How long we-a stay on this ship?"

"Not long, I guess. Look, they're starting to unload some of the passengers now."

The two were standing on the deck of the *Victor Emmanuel* watching the crowds that thronged the deck. Hundreds upon hundreds of people from all over Europe were packed together waiting anxiously to disembark: jowled, close-cropped Germans, the full-bearded Russians, scraggly whiskered Jews, and Slovak peasants with smooth faces. There were smooth-cheeked and swarthy Armenians, the quick-witted Greeks, and stoic Danes with wrinkled eyelids.

"Well, we're a colorful bunch, I'll say that for us," Jan grinned. He looked over the matrix of vivid costumes—speckled green-and-yellow aprons, flowered kerchiefs, embroidered homespun, the silver-braided sheepskin vests of the men, gaudy scarves, yellow boots, fur caps, caftans, and dull gabardines. "Let's be sure we got all of our things together, Maria," he said.

They moved along the deck, which was swarming with activity, amid the guttural voices highlighted by high-pitched voices, astonished cries, gasps of wonder, and exclamations of gladness that rose from the milling, shoving crowd that thronged the deck of the *Victor Emmanuel*. They found the rest of the Scarlottas clustered together forward, and they were, Jan saw, all frightened. Cheerfully he moved over, slapped Tony on the back, and put his arm around Lucia. "Well, we're here," he said loudly. "We've finally come to America, and we're going to have a great life here."

The voyage had worn all of them down so that there was a paleness underneath the natural ruddy color of the cheeks of both Tony and Lucia. Tony shot a frightened glance at Jan, muttering, "Sometimes, I'm-a wish we had not come."

"Why, don't be foolish! We're going to make a new life for ourselves here, Tony." Suddenly Jan reached over and picked up Emila and Michael, one in each arm, and held them tightly. "Look out there. That's America—our new home. You're going to love it here!"

Mario and Dino were clutching their scant possessions, and like the others, they looked at Jan with a hope dawning in their liquid brown eyes. They had picked up much English on the ship. All of the family had practiced every day with Jan, and now Maria said warmly, "It's-a good you with us, Jan."

"We're all together," Jan replied cheerfully. Looking down toward the gangplank, his eyes lighted up. "Come along—let's get all the things together."

Like the other immigrants, they had brought all the necessary possessions they could carry. As they moved down the deck, they were pressed against those who carried their belongings tied up in huge bundles in sheets. Some of them had bulky wicker baskets, and a few even carried their prize featherbeds. Jan also noticed that some had almost nothing at all besides small cloth sacks or worn luggage tied together with frayed string.

As they passed off the ship, Jan was interested to see the great variety of behaviors on the part of the new arrivals. The most volatile races, such as the Italians, sometimes danced for joy, whirling each other around and pirouetting in ecstasy. Swedes, he noted, sometimes just looked at each other, breathing through open mouths like panting dogs. The emotional ones, such as Jews, wept, while Poles roared and gripped each other at arm's length. A few, who were English, kept aloof, gravitating toward embraces, but never quite achieving it.

Bells clanged now, and the gulls wheeling over the crowd of the *Victor Emmanuel* rose with screeching cries from the green water. The white wake that stretched from Ellis Island grew longer and raveled wanly into melon green. On one side lay the low, drab Jersey coastline, while on the other the flat, water-towered Brooklyn was evident. Rising on her high pedestal from the scaling brilliance of a sunlit water to the west stood the Statue of Liberty. Amongst the luminous sky, the rays of her halo were spikes of darkness roweling the air. The torch she bore was lifted high, and the immigrants all stared up with hope dawning in their eyes.

The struggle ended when all of the passengers were disembarked on Ellis Island. Soon Jan and the others were marched into the vaguely Romanesque reception center with its four towers. The building lay low in the water, for the island had originally been a sandbar. A number of ferries and barges were tied up by the side in the ferry basin. It was a hot April day promising to get hotter, and beyond the island the New Jersey dock shimmered in the distance.

A silence now fell over the newcomers, for they all understood that this was going to be one of the most important days of their lives. They moved four abreast under the canopy that stretched from the entrance of the reception center all the way out to the ferry landing. The shade gave some relief from the April sun. Nearby a pushcart vendor was crying out, "Bananas—ham sandwich—twenty-five cents!"

"What is 'banana'?" Maria whispered, looking up to Jan.

"It's a fruit. Here, let's try some." Jan hailed the vendor over and bought a dozen bananas. He had little money left, but he felt that it would be a break from the tension. "Do you take lira?" he asked the vendor.

"Sure!" the vendor replied, grinning broadly. "I'll take anything."

Jan paid for the fruit, then turned to see that Emila had bitten off the end of her banana and was making a sour face.

"No like!" she cried.

"Wait a minute, you're eating the peeling," Jan grinned. "Here, let me show you." He peeled the banana back and said, "Now, try that part."

Emila tentatively took a bite, then a smile broke out across her tanned face, her white teeth gleaming. "That's-a good!" she exclaimed.

"You shouldna spend your money!" Lucia scolded Jan. She was a woman who worried a great deal as, indeed, did most of the women who had left everything familiar to come to this strange new place. They were all accustomed to poverty, but in a new world with no friends, no family, the specter of poverty was one that never completely left their thoughts. It showed in the tension of their shoulders, in the dartings of their eyes, and in the tightness of their lips.

"Don't worry, God's going to take care of us, Lucia," Jan said. "He brought me all the way here from South Africa and put me with the best people in the world." He reached out and ran his hand over Dino's curly black hair and took his smile. "We're going to be all right. Now, what do you think of bananas?"

Tony had taken a bite of the fruit and was chewing it thoughtfully. He smiled and said, "That's good. They grow these in New York?"

"No. I think they're grown in South America. Then they ship them all the way by boat in big bunches."

"Do they grow on a vine, Uncle Jan?" Michael piped up, his mouth stuffed full of banana.

"No, they grow on a tree."

Maria took her time and enjoyed her banana, savoring the new taste. "It's good," she said, "our first meal in America. Thank you, Jan."

The line moved on, slowly and imperceptibly, like a glacier. Finally, however, they entered the reception center where long lines crept up the central stairs to the great hall. The immense room was the main registration and examination hall on the island. Everywhere they looked, there was confusion. The floor was cluttered with baggage, with a throng of tired, anxious human beings all standing very close together. Moving among the lines of people and trying to direct them were the stern-looking immigration service employees, who wore dark uniforms.

Tony's eyes narrowed. "That's-a the police?"

"No, they're not police," Jan said.

"Must-a be soldiers, then," Lucia added, her eyes cautious as she stared apprehensively at the officials.

Right then a tall, raw-boned Swede standing in the front of the Scarlottas turned and said nervously, "I'm worried about what they do to your eyes here."

Jan asked, "What do you mean—do to your eyes?"

"They tell me they stick a button hook into your eyeball."

"That's foolish," Jan spoke up at once. "They won't do a thing like that."

"My brother, he came to America. That's what he said. They stick a button hook into your eyeball."

Jan shook his head. "I imagine they use it to turn the eyelid back for an eye examination."

"What's the difference?" the Swede demanded. "They don't stick anything in my eyeball! I'll go back home first. . . !"

Maria had taken all this in. She now seized Jan's arm almost in a panic and asked, "That's not so, is it, Jan?"

"Of course not! All kinds of stories get told when people get frightened. He just misunderstood what his brother said. Don't worry." He reached over and gave her shoulder a squeeze. "It's going to be fine," he said encouragingly.

After what seemed like hours, they reached the top of the stairs and entered the huge room which was packed with people. It was divided into a maze by a series of steel bars, and Jan quickly understood that this was designed to guide the immigrants through the intricacies of the various inspection stations.

They passed two doctors at the very top of the stairs, and as they watched, they saw the doctors reject an elderly woman, marking her coat with chalk. The woman was Lithuanian and spoke no English at all. Her husband begged and pleaded in broken English, but the doctors were adamant. "I'm sorry, but you can't be admitted."

It was a heartrending scene to watch the man leading his sobbing wife away. Tony Scarlotta gave Jan a worried look and said, "Poor woman, poor man. Why they send them back, Jan?"

"She's crippled and old," Jan said tonelessly. "I suppose they have to have some medical standards." As they waited their turn, he watched carefully and saw that it was not uncommon for the elderly and the infirm to be turned back. Later he found out that if one of the inspectors saw a crooked back or a vacant facial expression, he could reject the immigrant out of hand for anything, calling it tuberculosis or simplemindedness.

When they finally reached the two doctors, one of them asked, "Do you speak English?"

"Yes," Jan said.

"Open your mouth," the doctor ordered. He glanced incuriously into Jan's mouth and held up his hand. "How many fingers?"

"Four."

"Move on." The Scarlottas all went through the same charade, and finally, looking ahead, Jan saw a small group clustered around what appeared to be an examination station. "I think this will be all," he said. "If we get by this one, we're all Americans." He studied the group ahead and was surprised to see an attractive young woman with black hair, dressed in a rather shiny black dress, standing beside a large camera mounted on a tripod.

"This is a funny place to take pictures," he murmured. But at this point he was committed to anything he had to do to get through this last station with the Scarlottas.

★ ★ ★ ★

Esther had already made two trips to Ellis Island with Dr. Burns and Ruth, but the pictures she had made had not been to her satisfaction. There had been no unifying principal in them, which was something she always looked for in any series. She had joined the pair once again today when they came to Ellis Island. As Burns quickly made his examinations, Esther made several pictures. Ruth had come to stand by her and said, "Don't you see anything that would make a good photograph, Esther?"

"Well, they're all interesting," she said as she positioned her tripod for another shot. "Exotic, I suppose you might say." She still was quite shocked at the depth of poverty she witnessed as the lines of immigrants passed by her. She began to feel deep stirrings of compassion as she stared into the eyes of so many who had courageously made the choice to risk everything to start over in a new land. Many of them were undernourished, some of them diseased, all of them obviously in the last stages of poverty. "What I'm looking for, Ruth," she said, "is something to tie pictures together."

"I don't understand what you mean," Ruth said.

Esther tried to explain the sort of picture she was after, keeping her eyes at the same time on the long line that wormed its way by slowly. "You see, if you go out to a horse race, obviously there are horses there. And there are people that go to watch them. You can take a hundred pictures, but none of them might have anything to do with the others. Each one might be interesting in itself, but pictures should tell a story." She struggled to put her concept into words, for it was a theory that she had arrived at some time ago. "For instance, it might make a series of pictures of people who just lost their bets on the race. They might be rich people, poor people, working people—they might be anything, but they have that one thing in common—the anguish of losing. And then you could take pictures of the losing jockeys—and the losing owners of the horses. You see what I mean?"

Ruth nodded at once. "Of course. That makes sense, and you haven't found anything like that here at the island."

"Not yet, but I will," Esther said with determination. She was a stubborn young woman, this Esther Winslow, and underneath the fashionable, smooth exterior, and good looks there was the heart of a pioneer. She had thrown herself into this new profession of hers with all of her strength. Ever since that talk with Andrew late that night, Esther had taken his words of encouragement seriously. With a new purpose and enthusiasm, she spent her days taking pictures and her nights developing them in the small, hot darkroom that always held the pungent order of chemicals. Fortunately, money had been no problem, so she had been wasteful, almost, of film, and had thrown away literally hundreds of pictures that did not please her.

Suddenly a group of people moved forward, and something about them caught Esther's eye. They were obviously a family— a husband and wife, both short and swarthy—and as soon as she heard one of them speak, she knew they were Italian. The children were stair-stepped from a child of no more than six up to a rather striking young woman of, at least, seventeen. But they all shared a family resemblance—except for a tall man who was with them.

One of the smaller children held to his hand, and they all looked at him nervously as one looks to a natural leader.

He's not Italian, that's certain, Esther thought as she studied the man carefully. He was at least six feet tall, with tawny hair that fell out from under a strangely shaped hat. It was a worn hat, khaki colored, with the left side of the broad brim pinned to the crown with a silver pin. She recognized it from the pictures she had seen of the Boer War that was taking place in South Africa. Once that clicked in her mind, she looked more closely. He turned to meet her gaze, and she noted that he had direct hazel eyes set in a squarish face. His clothes were clean, but patched, and she saw that his hands were tanned and looked very strong. There was a Nordic look about him, so that he could pass for a Norseman if he had worn a steel-pointed helmet and carried a sword.

Dr. Burns walked over to the tall man and said, "You speak English?"

"Yes, I do, Doctor."

Burns reached out and thumped his chest, then put his hands on the larger man's wrists and took a pulse for a moment. "Well, you're healthy enough," he said. He looked with some question at the others and said, "Are you with this family?"

"Yes, I am, Doctor. Obviously I'm not one of them in blood."

An amused light touched the hazel eyes, and Esther saw the lips turn up.

Something about his speech was different. The man's English was good, but there was a British inflection that caught at Burns. "Where are you from?"

One moment's hesitation occurred, and then Kruger shrugged and said, "Originally from South Africa—but I've been living in Italy with these good people."

"I see." Burns did not see, but the lines had come to a halt. Quickly he took out a button hook and said, "I'll have to check your eyes."

"Go ahead, Doctor."

Kruger stood still while Burns took the button hook, skillfully turned the eyelid back and looked quickly, then checked the other eye. Kruger turned toward the others and said, "See, it didn't hurt a bit. The doctor here knows his business."

"Thanks for the recommendation," Burns said. "Now, let's see the rest of you." Quickly he checked Tony's and Lucia's eyes and then Maria's. He had found it better to let the children watch as he did this, and, indeed, he had become so skillful that there was very little discomfort involved. When he had examined them all, he smiled at Tony. "You're all just fine, Mr. Scarlotta. All in good shape except this young fella. What's wrong with your leg, son?"

"He broke it," Dino burst out.

"No," Kruger said quickly. "He just dislocated the patella."

Instantly Burns turned to look at the tall South African. "The patella? His kneecap?"

"Yes, it floated a little but it's all right now."

"How did you know a kneecap was called a patella?"

Kruger hesitated. He had already decided that there was no point in revealing the fact that he had been a doctor. Technically he was an escaped prisoner of war, and doctors would be easier to find than laborers. He held Burns' eye for a moment and said, "I'm not sure how I knew that."

Burns examined him carefully and thought, *He knows more than he's telling. Not one person in a million knows the name of a kneecap in medical terms.* However, he said, "I'm vurry glad it's healed."

Esther had been watching all this and suddenly knew she had to film this particular family—especially the tall man from South Africa. "Please," she said, coming up, "would you mind if I took some pictures?"

Kruger turned to her quickly. The last thing he wanted was pictures circulating! He asked almost rudely, "Pictures? What for?"

"I'm trying to make a record of the lives of those who come to this country," Esther said. She made a pleasing sight as she stood there, and now she turned on all the charm she had. "I'd be glad to pay you."

Instantly Kruger grinned. "In that case, go right ahead." He had weighed the dangers and found them minimal, and every penny they could get would help.

Instantly Esther began taking pictures, instructing Burns to continue with the examination. She got several very fine shots of the doctor examining the eyes of Emila, who was a beautiful child. The various shots would make excellent ones for the series she was trying to compose about Ellis Island.

As she worked, she noticed that the tall, fair-haired man served as an anchor for the rest of the family. "What's your name?" she asked as she managed to include him in several shots.

"Jan Kruger."

"I see you're wearing a uniform. Were you in the Boer War?"

Again the slight hesitation that Esther noticed at once.

"Yes, after a fashion. I spent most of the time in a prison camp."

"I see," Esther said as she continued to take pictures.

Finally, Burns said, "We'll have to let the line move on, Esther."

She smiled and said, "Of course." Moving back, she found her reticule and plunged her hand into its depth. Coming up with a roll of bills she removed several of them. Then looking at the poverty of the family, she added at least that many more. "You've been a great help," she said. She held the money in her hand, not knowing who to give it to.

"Give it to Mr. Scarlotta," Jan said. When Tony took the money he said, "There, you've already done your first day's work, Tony."

Tony Scarlotta stared at the bills. He bobbed his head and said, "Thank-a you, miss! Thank-a you very much!"

Esther had a desire to talk more to the family, but there was no time. On impulse she put her hand out to Tony, who took it with surprise and said, "I hope you find a good life here. You have a fine family, Mr. Scarlotta." Then she turned to Jan and extended her hand. When he took it, she was aware of the warmth and life and strength in his hand. "And . . . and you, Mr. Kruger," she said rather breathlessly, "I hope you have a good life too."

"It'll be better than what I've had lately," he said soberly. "Thanks for helping the Scarlottas out. It was very kind of you."

Then they moved on, and after the family had disappeared, Burns looked at Esther. "Well, I think there's a little mystery about that fellow. I wonder what he's up to?"

Esther could still feel the warm pressure of Kruger's handshake, and she shook her head slowly. "I don't know, but it'll be interesting to find out, won't it?"

★   ★   ★   ★

America, at least the part of it that the Scarlottas found themselves in, seemed like a very confusing place to them. None of them knew a soul, and it was Jan Kruger who, by talking to several of the guards, led the way when they left Ellis Island. After a short ferry ride to shore, Jan and Tony managed to hire a wagon to carry them and their belongings. He had heard that the Lower East Side of Manhattan had the cheapest places for rent, and soon they found themselves on Mulberry Street. They stood there looking around, for the street was lined with vendors on both sides. Food, clothing, shoes, and all kinds of household goods were sold from stalls. Some of them were under awnings that extended from the buildings, but many vendors had erected small portable stands along the sides of the streets. There was barely room for carriages and wagons to make their way down the packed street. On each side of the street, tall buildings, which had an unhealthy look to all of them, arose like sentinels watching the waves of immigrants that flooded into the already-crowded city. On the front of each building, everything that could hold a garment seemed to be used for drying clothes. Colorful petticoats and white shirts and long underwear fluttered in the slight breeze, some hanging from poles and looking like flags with arms.

"It's noisy, isn't it?" Jan said. "It reminds me of the story of the Tower of Babel. When everybody spoke nobody could understand anyone else."

"Lots of Italians," Tony said in a pleased voice, and he looked around at the tall buildings. "We no gotta much money. Let's-a find a place."

Finding a place to live did not prove easy. Tony had spoken the truth—there was not much money and the question of work lurked in both men's minds, and the women and children as well. Finally, after walking many blocks, they found themselves exhausted in a sunless court off a tenement building on Mulberry Street. They had looked at several places, but all were too expensive.

Now, Jan said almost harshly, "We're going to have to take what we can get, Tony. This is pretty bad, but surely we can find *something* here. You stay here, and I'll go look."

Jan made his way through wash-hung courts, trash-laden alleys, and even near-open privies. He passed through an odorous open-air marketplace where wagons and temporary stands offered every kind of article, fresh and otherwise. It was a slum, which he hated the moment he saw it, but he finally stopped a man and inquired and was told that apartments were for rent in the building he was standing in front of. He moved to the door, and a short, heavy man with a three-day growth of beard grumpily informed him that he had vacant places.

When Jan returned to the Scarlottas, he shook his head. "I've found a place. It's cheap enough, but it's pretty bad. We'll just have to make do until we can find jobs."

"We find something better," Maria said. She was exhausted and frightened by the hubbub and the strange surroundings, as were all of the Scarlottas, especially the children.

When Jan led them up to the third floor, to what was basically a three-room apartment, he said, "It's filthy, but soap and water can fix that." He did not mention that the only water in the place was down the hall at a single tap. All water for drinking, cooking, and washing had to be hauled in buckets. "We'll make do here," he said.

Maria looked around. It was a gloomy, dirty place with pitiful excuses for furniture. The few chairs only had three legs, and the few mattresses were so filthy that no one would dare to sleep on them. But when she saw the pained expression on her mother's face, she went over and said with a smile that she had to force, "It's all right, Mama. We'll do fine. At least we got a roof over our head, and we weren't sent back like some who were sick."

Lucia looked at Maria and tried to smile. "You-a right. We will work hard and make it." Then she turned and started to pile their belongings in the corner while Tony and Jan went to get some water so they could begin cleaning the apartment.

They spent the rest of the day cleaning and finding food and fuel for the ancient stove that served for heating and cooking. When that was done, Jan went out to find some clean bedding that would do for the family. When he got back, he smelled the familiar aroma of Lucia's cooking before he even opened the door to the little apartment.

While everyone had worked hard cleaning and unpacking, Lucia had cooked their first meal in America on the stove, which had heated up the entire apartment. By midnight all the children were settled down, and the elder Scarlottas fell into bed exhausted also.

Jan had stepped outside onto the fire escape to get a breath of air. He had been standing there some time enjoying the slight breeze when he heard a sound and turned quickly. "Come out here where it's cool, Maria," he said. When she stepped beside him, he asked, "Are you tired? I know you must be."

"Yes, very tired."

After the fierce commotion and activities of the day, the streets below now seemed quiet and almost placid. The darkness was broken by the yellow gleam of gas lights, and overhead the skies were spangled with stars. A huge full moon looked down benignly on the sleeping city.

"Real peaceful," Jan murmured.

"Yes, I like it better like this."

The two sat down, and both enjoyed the relatively cool breeze that brushed against their faces. They spoke about the problems that lay ahead, but each of them seemed occupied with thoughts that did not surface into the conversation.

They were sitting very close together on the rather small fire escape, and finally Maria turned to Jan and said, "I'm worried."

Jan turned to her, and her face was bathed by the silver moonlight, and her eyes looked enormous. The light gathered in them so they almost seemed to be filled with diamonds, and he said quickly, "What's the matter?"

"It's a strange place, and I don't know how we make it here."

Jan put his arm around her shoulder and squeezed her, hoping to give her encouragement. To his surprise she turned to him and lifted her face. Jan Kruger was aware that Maria Scarlotta was an attractive young woman, but she had been no more than that. Now, suddenly, he felt her pressed tightly against him. Without thinking he put his free hand on her hair and stroked it. "You have beautiful hair," he said. "You're a lovely girl, Maria."

Jan's compliments pleased her. She had grown close to him while nursing him back to health when her father had brought him home that day. During their voyage on the *Victor Emmanuel*, she had become more aware of the handsomeness of this tall, blond man. Her beauty had drawn boys and men to her since she was a young girl, and she had been slightly puzzled that Jan Kruger had never shown the slightest interest in her as a woman. Now, however, as she felt his lean strength, she was suddenly aware of him as a man and wanted to make him aware of her as a woman. She pressed against him, lifted her face, and shyly put her free hand on his neck. "You're very good to us, Jan." She pulled his head down and kissed him then.

A shock ran along Jan's nerves, and her soft lips moved slightly under his. Old hungers raced through him, and he realized that Maria was, indeed, a fully mature and attractive young woman. He held her, savoring the moment, then suddenly he pulled away. "We'll have to get up early in the morning," he said hastily. He released her, got to his feet, and then said, "Good night, Maria."

After Jan had left, Maria sat there, and a strange smile touched her lips. *He is a man*, she thought. *He liked kissing me. I wonder if he's ever been married. He must've had sweethearts, he's so handsome!* She sat for a long time on the balcony. Finally she got up and went back inside the apartment. But for a long time she lay awake thinking of the pressure of his lips on hers.

CHAPTER EIGHT

PRISCILLA MEETS A MAN

★ ★ ★ ★

For Priscilla Winslow life had become even more sharply divided between two worlds. During the day she put in long hours working at Baxter Hospital, which she now was starting to despise. She had discovered at the beginning of her training that she did not have the temperament for dealing with sick people. It was not that Priscilla was unkind, but she felt inadequate and quite unfit to carry out her duties in this respect. Truthfully, sick people frightened her a little, and she said once to Ruth, whose talent lay in this area, "Ruth, I don't see how you can be so patient with these people! I know they're sick, and I feel sorry for them, but you just seem to do it so easily."

Ruth had commented quietly that it was only the love that God gave her for the sick that enabled her to carry out the rather difficult tasks that were a part of caring for them. Her words were not of particular help to Priscilla, who had not been to a church a single time since her arrival in New York. The only service of any religious influence was the one she had attended with Dr. Burns and Ruth at the Water Street Mission, after which she never went back. Week after week had gone by, and Ruth begged her to go with her to attend services, but Priscilla always made some excuse.

So the days for Priscilla became increasingly more boring, difficult, and a part of life to be endured. She washed patients, changed bandages, carried the food from the kitchen, then back again. She changed the patients' clothing, made beds—and through all of this she simply endured. Her lack of dedication became more and more evident in the quality of her work, drawing the concern of the staff. Her only means to survive the drudgery of her days was her anticipation of the night.

After her duties ended at five o'clock, she followed a strict ritual. She ate with the rest of the staff, then at once took a quick bath and changed clothes. She left the hospital as soon as possible, and as she hurried out into the night, it always seemed as though a weight lifted off her shoulders. Her step became lighter, and her eyes would brighten as she headed for Broadway. She had little money and saved practically every penny for the admissions to see the plays along the Great White Way. She would stay out as late as possible, and when there was no other choice, she would return to her room, undress, and fall into bed dreading the daylight, when she would once again have to face another grueling day at the hospital she was despising more and more.

For weeks this went on, until one day in the first week of May, Priscilla got sick of the same dresses she had been wearing. She marched defiantly out the front doors of the hospital and headed for the shops on Broadway. She was determined not to return to her room until she had picked out a new outfit. She may not have been good in her dealings with sick people, but Priscilla Winslow was an expert in the area of clothes. Since she had the whole day off, she entered shop after shop, looking at and trying on various gowns and hats. The sales clerks grew impatient with her, but she would not allow them to rush her selection.

Finally, after spending most of the day choosing the right outfit that pleased her, she bought a gown after hammering the price down considerably. Looking at it in the mirror, she decided to wear it out of the shop. It was a dress that emphasized the extreme femininity of her form. The gown was a mixture of rust and gold with a touch of fuchsia pink. It was an unusual design with a pointed waist, a pleated bodice, and floral trimmings. As she studied herself in the mirror, Priscilla saw that it made her look both alluring and fragile. She was one of those women who could defy the current trend in clothing and make her own style seem the right one and all others ordinary and unimaginative. As an accessory she chose a wide-brimmed straw hat that perched slightly to one side and down over her forehead, tied with stiff taffeta ribbons. It gave her a rakish look, and she turned sideways and smiled to herself in the full-length mirror. She was pleased with her appearance. She also selected a pair of fine black leather boots that buttoned on the side, and a small reticule made of some exquisite fur that she did not recognize.

When she had paid for all the items, Priscilla had the clerk wrap her old clothes in a package and she left the store. It was only five o'clock, and the theaters would not open for two hours, but this was no problem for Priscilla. She enjoyed walking along the broad sidewalks and observing the pedestrians that made their promenade along this section of New York. Her quick eyes took in the fashions of the women she passed, and she filed in her memory those items which she would like to try. She studied the men almost as carefully, for she had become a student of male fashion, as well. After a few minutes, she went into a small restaurant, took a table, and ordered a sandwich and a glass of milk. She ate hungrily, and more than one man passed by her table, trying to catch her eye. She ignored them, for the most part, but she had become used to such things since she had arrived in New York City. She was accustomed to male admiration, for all her life her rich beauty had drawn the eyes of men. She was astute enough, however, to know that most of the men that would have accosted her in New York were sensualists and would have but one thought in mind. She was, in many respects, not a serious young lady; but she had seen enough of life—even in the West— to know that women had to protect themselves.

When she had finished her meal, she rose and left the restaurant. As she moved down the street, she knew that she did not have enough money to attend one of the first-rate theaters. This grieved and annoyed her, for she had her heart set on seeing William Gillette at the Palace starring in *Sherlock Holmes*. Tonight, however, it was beyond her means—as were all of the other ornate and expensive theaters. After a while she sighed and turned off Broadway to a side street, where several small theaters offered less expensive fare.

As she studied the playcards outside the theaters, she saw

nothing that really appealed to her. Finally she came to an extremely small theater, almost crushed between two large buildings, with the name Golden Nights Theater over the entrance. She moved closer and studied the advertisement, which proclaimed that the offering was a musical called *Lilly Goes to Paris*. A young woman named Nellie Byron was the star, and her name was larger, by far, than the names below. Priscilla had never heard of her. She was reading the names of the other actors and actresses when a voice said, "Thinking of seeing a good show?"

Priscilla turned to face a man who had come up to stand beside her. He was not tall, no more than five eight, but very good-looking, in a flashy way. He had dark hair and brown eyes, and a set of perfectly formed teeth that he exposed in a wide smile. He was wearing straight-cut brown-checked trousers, a waistcoat with a collar buttoned with brass buttons, a scarlet knotted tie at his throat, and a coat cut short in the fashion of the day. He wore a beaver top hat, and his hair was long and rather curly. There was a cheerful expression on his smooth face, and when Priscilla started to turn away, he said, "I can recommend it, you know."

Priscilla was rather amused at the young dandy. "You've seen it?"

"Seventy-two times."

His words caught at Priscilla, and she stared at him with amazement. "You saw the play seventy-two times?"

"Well, more than that, really, if you count rehearsals." He took off his hat then and smiled at her.

He was an amiable man, probably twenty-seven or twenty-eight, Priscilla judged.

"I'm Eddie Rich." He reached out his finger and placed it on the name just below that of the star. "That's me."

"Really?" Priscilla said, her eyes opening wide.

She made an attractive picture as she stood before the actor, and he did not miss the honey-colored hair and the blue-green eyes that seemed to swallow him up. "Well, there are some who would say that you haven't met much of one now." He laughed cheerfully at his own words and said, "Do you attend the theater much?"

"Every night."

"Every night!" Rich's eyes opened wide and he exclaimed,

"You must be a lover of the drama!"

"Yes, I am. I just love it—everything about it. What's the play like?"

Rich shrugged his shoulders. "Well, to be truthful, it's not a very good play."

Priscilla was surprised at his honest appraisal and studied him more carefully. "What's wrong with it?"

"For the most part, Nellie Byron is what's wrong with it." His face turned sour for one moment, then he shook his head. "I've been around spoiled actresses before, but Nellie takes the cake. She thinks the world revolves around her and expects everyone to fall over and bow when she passes by."

Priscilla turned to look at the photograph on the advertisement. "She's very beautiful, though."

"Oh yes. She's that." Eddie shrugged his trim shoulders carelessly, then added, "But there's more to being an actress than beauty. Nellie couldn't act if someone pointed a gun at her head. All she has going for her is that she's a pretty good singer, and she's good-looking."

"Well, that seems like a lot to me."

"I suppose it is." Rich shifted his feet and said, "Look, you don't want to spend your money seeing this, but I have a little influence. He took out a card and a pencil from an inner pocket, wrote on it briefly, then handed it to her. "Just show this at the door. They'll give you a good seat down front."

"Oh no, I couldn't take it."

Eddie Rich laughed. "You're not from New York, are you?"

"No, I'm from Wyoming."

"The Wild West, eh? Well, I must say the Wild West is sending a good quality of young women to the big city." He studied her and grew more serious. "I suppose your mother told you to beware of strangers?"

"My mother never said much, but I am careful of men I meet on the street."

"I think that's very wise," Rich nodded. "However, there's no obligation. Go see the show. You'll probably never see me again."

"All right—I will." Priscilla smiled suddenly. "Thank you very much, Mr. Rich."

"Oh, call me Eddie. We're not very formal in the theater." He put his hat back on and bowed. "I hope you enjoy the show."

Priscilla felt somewhat awkward. She knew better than to take gifts from strange men, but somehow this seemed quite innocent. She looked at the card, which read, "Give this lady a good seat, Max," and was signed "Eddie Rich." Suddenly she decided. Lifting her head, she moved into the doors, and when a young man glanced at her and reached out his hand for a ticket, she handed him the card. He took it, studied it briefly, then smiled, "You're a friend of Eddie's? Well, come along this way, miss. I'll give you a good seat." He led her down into the theater itself, which was smaller than most that she had attended. It did have a high ceiling, and the seats were fairly comfortable. She took the seat, which was in the third row center, and waited with some excitement until the show began.

The curtain opened, and music filled the theater, and for the next hour and a half Priscilla avidly watched the play. It dealt with a young farm girl who set out for a visit to her uncle and aunt in Missouri, and through a series of misadventures, she found herself in Paris being courted by a prince. It was a totally unbelievable plot, but then no one expected musical comedies to be realistic. The star, Nellie Byron, was a tall, statuesque blonde, with a large mouth and a pleasant voice. When she was singing, she was very good, but the instant she was forced to act, all illusions of theatrical talent vanished. She was wooden, awkward, and spoke all of her lines in a high-pitched, totally unnatural voice. *She ought to sing everything instead of speaking*, Priscilla thought as the play continued to the next act.

And, of course, she was very interested in Eddie Rich. He played the part of an American in Paris who competed with the prince for the hand of Lilly. He had a pleasant tenor voice, and, if anything, underplayed his role. He was rather good, Priscilla noted, and somehow that pleased her. He had three solo numbers—one of them a sentimental ballad titled, "You're Only a Bird in a Gilded Cage," which he performed well, and his acting was far better than anyone else's in the play.

When the final song was sung and the curtain closed, the actors and actresses came out for the obligatory bow. The house was half-full, and the applause was lackadaisical. Priscilla, herself, applauded more loudly, standing with the others. She suddenly saw

Eddie Rich looking down at her from the raised stage. He smiled and nodded, and she returned the smile and the nod.

As she moved down the aisle to leave the theater, she stepped into the lobby and was about to walk out when she heard a voice.

"Just a minute!"

Turning, she looked back through the doors and saw Eddie Rich leave the stage and come up the aisle through the theater. He was still wearing his costume, a tuxedo.

When he came over to her, he asked at once, "How did you like the play?"

"Oh, I thought it was wonderful. Miss Byron is a good singer." She hesitated, then said, "But you were the best, Mr. Rich. I really enjoyed your singing, and your acting, too."

Rich flushed slightly. "Why . . . thank you. That's nice of you to say so." He hesitated one moment then said, "Look, do you have to be home right away? We usually have supper at a cafe down the street. Some of the cast, you understand. We'd be glad if you would join us."

If Rich had asked her to join him alone, Priscilla would have instantly refused. However, since there would be others there, she said, "Why, I suppose that would be acceptable."

"Good! Let me go get out of this rig. If you'll just wait right here it won't take long. Oh, what's your name?"

"Priscilla Winslow."

"A pretty name! Now, you wait right here. . . ."

After Rich left, Priscilla waited in the lobby. The crowd had scattered, and she was alone, except for the employees of the theater. She felt a sudden reluctance about accepting Rich's invitation. She knew that her parents would disapprove—but to be around real actors and actresses! It was a temptation greater than she could resist.

After a short while Rich came out with a small group and said, "May I introduce you to the cast, Miss Winslow?" He introduced her first to Nellie Byron, then to the other members he said, "This is Miss Priscilla Winslow, a fair immigrant from the wide open spaces of Wyoming."

Nellie Byron studied the young woman for an instant, her eyes taking in the fashionable costume, the clear eyes, and the fresh beauty and nodded. "Glad to meet you," she said briefly, then turned and walked away. The other actors and actresses were more pleasant.

Eddie soon took her arm and said, "The restaurant is just around the corner. I hope you're hungry."

The restaurant was not fancy, but the actors ate as if they were starved. Priscilla enjoyed her meal, for the sandwich which she had eaten earlier had not been enough. She said little during the meal but listened to the actors avidly. They talked of the world that they knew of, plays opening, and those which were being closed. They gossiped casually about the great names, the gods and goddesses of Priscilla's life. Once when Rich mentioned the name of Lillie Langtry, she whispered, "Do you *know* Lillie Langtry?"

"Oh yes, of course. I've been in plays with her twice."

"What's she like?"

"You'd like her, I think. She's in England now, you know—but I hope she'll come home soon."

"Tell me all about her."

Rich smiled, then for the next ten minutes told anecdote after anecdote about Lillie Langtry. As he spoke he was thinking, *What a beauty—and green as grass! You don't see this kind in New York very often!*

After the meal was over and the actors rose, Eddie said quickly, "I'd like to see you again. Now that we've met, it would be a shame to lose each other. Do your parents live here?"

"No, they live in Wyoming. I'm in nurse's training at Baxter Hospital."

"Really!" he exclaimed. "How interesting. I had no idea you were such a serious young lady."

"Well—I'm not really, but it was the only chance I had to get away from cows and ranching. I hated that most of my life."

"I always thought it would be rather fun."

"I suppose it might be for a few days, but when you go weeks without seeing anything but a cow, it can get pretty boring. But *you* have such an exciting life!"

"Acting isn't always exciting. Sometimes it's hard, too," he shrugged. "Look," he said, "why don't you come to the theater again tomorrow? If you can endure the play again, that is."

"Oh yes, I could—but I'm not certain I should."

Eddie hesitated for one moment. "I know this isn't the proper way to do things, but I'd like to see you again. Just for a meal. We can have dinner, and you can tell me about your cows out in Wyoming. I can tell you some more about Lillie Langtry." He knew this was a powerful temptation, and he saw her eyes light up. Quickly he said, "I've been around quite a few stars you might like to hear about. I do wish you'd come."

"All right, I will," Priscilla said impulsively. Then as if she had frightened herself, she said, "I really shouldn't, and I'll have to leave right after."

"That's quite all right. I'll be glad to see you tomorrow. Shall I pick you up?"

"No, I'll meet you here."

Eddie Rich was a man who had known many women. He knew when to be aggressive and when not to. This young woman, he saw, would be frightened off by his more flamboyant tactics. Being an actor, he knew how to play any role he chose, and now he smiled and said, "It will be something to look forward to, Miss Winslow." As he turned and walked away, he thought, *What a doll!—but she can't be rushed. She's like a young deer, one loud noise and she'll bound off. But she'll be worth the trouble. . . !*

★　★　★　★

"Ruth, I think you ought to try to talk to Priscilla."

Looking up from the bandages she was rolling, Ruth stared at Dr. Burns. "You mean about staying out so late?"

"Yes." Burns had stopped on his rounds and now leaned against the wall. His brown hair was caught in the sunlight that filtered through the window to his left. He looked very much the Highlander as he lolled there. There was an intensity and driving force in Burns that kept him at a high pitch, usually. Now he seemed to relax and looked younger than his years. "I'm afraid she's going to get into trouble, staying out till these late hours."

"She goes to the theater every night."

"I saw a man bring her home in a carriage two or three nights ago. Do you know him?"

"I met him," Ruth said cautiously. "His name is Eddie Rich. He's an actor." She put the bandage down, stood, and came over to stand beside Dr. Burns. The sunlight now caught her hair and brought out the rich red color that Burns had never noticed.

He said, "You have beautiful red hair. I never really noticed that before."

"Some of our people are redheaded," she said. Ruth was quiet for a moment, thinking, *This is the most intimate remark that Dr. David Burns has ever made to me, this comment about my hair.* They had worked together for weeks now, and he had kept himself aloof.

She had learned from Agnes Smith that he had been disappointed in love, and Nurse Smith had said once, "He's gun shy, that's what he is! He'll have to get over that before he opens his heart to another again."

Now as she studied Burns, Ruth thought how very much she had learned to admire him. He was totally dedicated to his work, and his Christian commitment was deep and broad. He had taken her several times to the mission, which she had enjoyed tremendously. They had also attended church together more than once, and she had become a member of his church.

"I'm worried about Priscilla too," she said finally. "This man Rich is in a play on Broadway. He seems like a gentleman, but she doesn't really know anything about him."

"Actors can be a bad lot. Some of them are not known for their high standards of morality. I wuid not like to see her come to harm."

"She's very impulsive and so in love with anything to do with the theater. I wish she wouldn't go out every night. I've tried to talk to her, but she won't listen."

"You know the book of Proverbs says about a hundred times, a fool will nay listen to counsel. That's the way with this, I suppose. We're proud creatures, and we all want our own way."

Ruth smiled, her light blue eyes bright and clear in the early morning light that came from the window. She looked fresh, and there was a gentleness, yet a strength, in her that struck everyone she met. "What about you, Doctor?"

"Me? Why, I suppose I'm like everybody else." Burns was surprised at her question. "Do you mean you find me foolish, not willing to take advice?"

"Oh no," Ruth laughed, "I didn't mean that. I mean most of

us, at some time or other, do things like that—refuse to take good advice. I know I have."

"I can't imagine it!"

"You've never seen me when I throw one of my fits."

"A fit! You? Why, Nurse Winslow, you're incapable of such a thing." Burns smiled suddenly. "I'd like to see one someday. What usually brings them on?"

"When I don't get my own way, I suppose."

"Well, I'll not believe it until I see it." He suddenly seemed to feel embarrassed at the moment of intimacy. He straightened up, pulled his jacket together, and said rather brusquely, "Well, I best get to my patients. Try to talk to Priscilla. She's headed for trouble."

His abrupt departure caught at Ruth. She knew that he was a man who was not given to expressing his emotions, and his broken-off love for Gail, she suspected, had made it even worse. *What a shame*, she thought. *I can tell he's got a loving heart, but he's got it cooped up and won't let it out.* Then she thought of what he had said about Priscilla, and her brow creased with worry. "I'll have to talk to her," she murmured. "She can't go on like this."

★　★　★　★

"I've got to go home, I tell you, Eddie," Priscilla protested. "Nurses in training can't be out late. It's a rule!"

"Rules were made to be broken." Eddie reached over, put his arm around Priscilla, and drew her close. They were proceeding down the street inside a carriage, and the lights flickered as they passed by the lamp poles. They had gone out to eat after Eddie's performance now for five nights in a row. This night they had stayed longer than usual. Afterward he had gotten a cab and had directed the driver to take them around Central Park. Priscilla had protested, but inwardly she had enjoyed seeing the play again and the attention Eddie was giving her. It had been a good evening for her. Earlier, at the restaurant, Eddie had been sparkling with hope. He told her he was about to be offered a part in a better play—perhaps the starring role—and he was overflowing with good will.

Now as he pulled her to him in the carriage, he kissed her—

and for the first time she returned his affection. In the last few days, she had more fun with Eddie than she had ever had in her life, and now as his arms pulled her close and his lips touched hers, she thought, *I shouldn't be doing this!* Still she was a young woman who loved life, and Eddie was terribly attractive. He grew more insistent, and at that she pulled away and laughed, "Now, that's enough!"

"You shouldn't tempt a man the way you do," Eddie complained.

"I'm not tempting you!" Priscilla argued.

"Yes, you are! You're such a beautiful girl. A man can't help being drawn to you. You're the most beautiful woman I know— and that's the truth!"

"Why, you can't mean that, Eddie. Look at all the beautiful actresses you know."

"There's a freshness in you, Priscilla. Everybody notices it. Most actresses get hard sooner or later. Look at Nellie," he shrugged. "She's like a piece of granite. Why, you're ten times prettier than she is, and you can sing better too." Rich had been surprised to find that Priscilla had a beautiful singing voice. She had no formal training, but she only had to hear a tune one time before she could sing it through. She had amused him once as they had gone for a ride around the park during her afternoon off when she sang all the songs from the show. "Now," he said, "most actresses would like to have your voice and your looks."

"Don't be foolish, Eddie." Priscilla knew he was an actor, and secretly she was always suspicious that he was playing a role with her. "You say that to all the girls."

"No, I don't. It wouldn't be true."

"Oh, you're always true and innocent in your relationships with women?"

The sharpness of her words caught at Eddie Rich. He flushed slightly and drew back, then laughed shortly. "Well, I've known women," he said. "They play a game with me, and I play back, I suppose. But now with you—" He reached over and took her hand, lifted it, and kissed it gently. "You're *different*, Priscilla." He found himself, to his surprise, actually meaning what he was saying. "You're innocent—and that's refreshing in my world. Not much innocence in the theater, but you have the real thing."

"You wouldn't want to take it from me, then?"

Eddie's face flushed an even richer color. "You're very attractive," he said. "I can't help being drawn to you, but I admire you and respect you, too."

Most young women were easy for him. Girls loved actors, were fascinated by them—and with his good looks and skilled charm, they sooner or later fell to his persuasions. Priscilla had, however, been different, and he said, "I wouldn't want to do anything to harm you. I have a great affection for you, Priscilla."

There was an earnestness about the man, and suddenly Priscilla found herself confused. What had begun as an entertainment for her suddenly seemed to be getting serious. It disturbed her, and she was rather quiet for the rest of the evening. Finally when they pulled up in front of the hospital, she let him kiss her again, then got out and said, "I'll see you tomorrow night." It had become standard procedure that she would attend the play, then afterward go out with him.

"Good night, sweetheart," he said. "Sleep well."

Priscilla mounted the steps and entered the hospital. She was greeted at once by Agnes Smith, who evidently was waiting for her. Agnes was wearing a robe over her gown and said, "You know the rule, Priscilla."

"I . . . I'm sorry, Nurse Smith. I forgot to watch the time."

Agnes Smith stared at her impatiently. "There are watches and clocks all over New York. You know the time well enough. I'm telling you this for your own good, Priscilla. The doctors and the administration had a meeting about you. They're dissatisfied with your work."

Priscilla's heart sank, and the first thought was, *If they turn me loose, I'll have to go back home.* Quickly she said, "Oh, I'll be very careful about coming in late."

"It's not just about coming in late. Your work is unsatisfactory. You don't care anything about your profession. Your work is slovenly, and you're no help to the patients."

Priscilla knew that the woman was speaking the truth. She made no defense but finally said quietly, "I am sorry, Nurse Smith. I . . . I'll try to do better."

Agnes Smith studied her carefully. "Well, see that you do!" she said, relenting. "Now get to bed. I'll expect to see better things out of you tomorrow and from now on."

Priscilla quickly went to her room and was surprised to find Ruth up and waiting for her. She was still smarting from Agnes Smith's words and said, "I suppose you have a sermon for me, too?"

"No sermon. I just couldn't sleep." Ruth was in bed, reading by the light of a gas light fixed in the wall over her head. She put her Bible down and said, "Did you have a good evening?"

Priscilla looked at her directly, suspecting sarcasm, but she knew Ruth was incapable of such things. "Oh, Ruth," she said, going over and plumping herself down on her bed, "I'm so unhappy."

Ruth got up from bed and came over to sit beside Priscilla. "I know you are, dear," she said. "I wish I could help."

"Nobody can help. I'm just not cut out to be a nurse—but I can't stand the thought of going back to Wyoming."

The two women sat there, and for a time Ruth did her best to comfort the girl. Finally she said, "It will look better tomorrow. Good night."

She went back to her bed and closed her eyes. She did not fall asleep as Priscilla prepared herself for the evening's rest. Finally, when the light did go out, she began to pray silently. She sensed that Priscilla was in great danger, and she somehow felt helpless in the face of it. "Oh, God," she whispered, "don't let anything happen to Priscilla. She's so young and vulnerable. Watch over her. . . !"

Priscilla was not praying—she was thinking of how terrible it would be if she had to go back home. After a taste of the bright lights and the excitement of the theater, she could not imagine anything else. "I'll just have to do better. I've *got* to keep my job," she said. "They just can't send me home!"

CHAPTER NINE

THE SMELL OF POVERTY

★ ★ ★ ★

New York City was the scene of a spectacular murder trial that had drawn newspapermen from all over the country. The judge had strictly prohibited any photographs from being made inside his courtroom. Therefore, reporters and photographers alike were caught in the throngs that filled the halls and spilled out into the streets.

"Excuse me—let me get through, please!"

Some of the crowd on the second floor of the courthouse where the courtroom was located turned and frowned with irritation. One man, whose back was suddenly probed by a sharp-pointed instrument, turned and began to curse, "Who do you think you're poking—!" He halted abruptly when he looked into a pair of lovely brown eyes, and his eyes opened wide as he took in the trim figure of the young woman who held a box camera in one hand and a tripod in the other. It was the pointed end of the tripod that had probed him, and despite his irritation he grinned and took off his hat. "Sorry about that, miss," he said. "Pardon my language."

Esther smiled up at him, saying, "I didn't mean to poke you so hard, but I do need to get through."

The man, whose name was Mack Edwards, was a reporter for the *New York Journal*. He was a big man with red hair, light blue eyes, and an Irish lilt to his speech. "You wouldn't be intendin' to take a picture of the courtroom would you, miss?"

"That's exactly what I intend to do."

Mack was pleased by her spunk. "Well, now," he muttered and winked across at some of his cohorts, "I think we ought to give the little lady a chance. What do you say, boys?"

A hum of assent went up, and one of the reporters, a short, tubby man with a balding head and a full cavalry mustache, spoke up, "Who does that judge think he is anyhow, barring the press? Make way here, men."

Esther found herself escorted through the crowd by the two rather burly men. She followed in their wake, and soon they arrived at the door of the courtroom.

A policeman was standing there, and Mack winked down at Esther. "Wait here. Let me get the law out of the way." He moved over and said, "Hey, Charlie, come over here. I want to speak to you a minute."

"Can't do it," the policeman said, "got to watch the door."

The rotund reporter said, "Oh, I'll keep the door for you, Charlie."

The policeman stared at the reporter and grinned. "That would be like putting the fox to guard the chicken house, wouldn't it, Roland?" Nevertheless, he moved away to where Mack held up some tickets in his hand and winked.

"Couple of tickets for the baseball game, Charlie—but I want to talk to you first."

Roland, the short reporter, waited until the two had disappeared into the crowd, then said, "Now, what next? What's your name, anyway?"

"Esther Winslow." She smiled at the heavyset man and said, "I'm going to take a picture that'll get me a position with the *Journal*."

"Do you tell me that?" The reporter winked. "Well, now! If we open this door, the law will be on us, and some of us might end up in jail. I don't suppose that camera will take a picture through solid oak."

"No," Esther said. Then she glanced up and said, "If you'll hold me up, I can snap it through the transom."

Roland laughed aloud and said, "Jerry, Taylor—come here, will youse? Let's give the pretty lady a hand." Four reporters crowded around, and the rest began to call encouragement.

"Are you ready now?" Roland asked.

Esther had removed her camera and made ready to take the picture, knowing she would not have long. She looked up at the transom. It was a high transom, for the doorway was massive. "Lift me up," she said.

Roland winked and said, "You boys be careful, now. Don't insult the lady."

Esther suddenly felt hands grasping her ankles and knees. She was pushed high into the air, and a whistle went up, and catcalls sounded from the onlookers. She ignored the rude and ribald remarks concerning the men holding her by the legs and concentrated on taking the picture. She rose up to the height of the transom and looked in, where she had a perfect view of the judge, the jury box, and the backs of the heads of the spectators that packed the room. Instantly she whipped the camera up, focused, and snapped a picture. "Hold on just a minute," she whispered. Quickly, conscious of the hands holding tightly to her legs, but ignoring them, she took three more shots.

Then Roland said, "Watch it, boys, here comes Charlie! Let her down!"

Esther found herself lowered to the floor, and she laughed at the faces of the men, saying, "Thank you, gentlemen." She gave the camera to Roland, saying, "Hide it!" Roland quickly turned around and disappeared into the crowd.

When the policeman named Charlie appeared with Mack beside him, he said, "What have you been doing, young lady?"

"Why . . . officer. I just want to make a complaint."

"A complaint!" Charlie exclaimed. "About what?"

"I think I'll report you for permitting so much dust on top of that transom." She winked at him broadly, then laughed aloud. Laughter went up from the crowd, and Esther disappeared. She was joined by Mack and Roland, who returned her camera and tripod.

"Did you get some good shots?" Mack inquired.

"I think so. I'm going to develop them right now. Then I'm going straight to your publisher and ask for a job."

"If the shots are good, you'll get it," Mack replied. "Won't she, Roland?"

"Sure, but there ain't any lady photographers working for newspapers."

Esther turned and smiled at both men. "There will be!" she said, and then with a laugh she turned and made her way out of the building.

When she was outside, she hailed a cab and went to a photographer named Gustave Smith who had helped her do some of her film processing. She rushed in and told Smith what she had just done. He laughed when he heard the whole story. Taking the glass negatives, he gave them a quick rinse, then bathed them in wood alcohol so they would dry quicker. A few minutes later they were ready to produce the prints. Fast production of prints was no easy matter, for in addition to other technical problems, the developing paper was thin and tended to curl at the edges.

A few minutes later, Esther took one look at the finished prints and threw her arms around the photographer. "They're *beautiful*, Gus!" she beamed. She danced around the room waving the prints in the air. "Wait till William Randolph Hearst sees these! He'll have to give me a job, then I'll be able to get into some places where they've kept me out."

Esther rushed out of the studio, and as she made her way toward the office of the *Journal*, she thought, *I've got it this time. They shouldered me aside long enough. When Hearst sees these, he'll have to give me a card.* She wanted a card identifying her as a representative of the *Journal*. This would give her entrance to the scenes of crime or to advance past the lines of firemen at the terrible fires that sometimes swept the buildings of New York. In fact, it would make her a professional indeed!

She had some difficulty getting in to see the editor, for William Randolph Hearst was a celebrity of stature. He had entered New York City's newspaper publishing wars by acquiring the *New York Journal*. Lavishly using immense mine and ranch wealth of his father's, he had made a riotous success of the *San Francisco Examiner*. Now he intended to oust Joseph Pulitzer's *New York World* and dominate the newspaper business. He had come to fame when he had taken a large staff to Cuba and publicized the Spanish-American War. There were many that claimed—Hearst among them!—that he was primarily responsible for starting the war by his yellow journalism. But, no doubt about it, Esther had chosen the right man, for he believed in lots of photographs, which he used for his feature stories.

Finally, after charming the secretary, Esther was admitted to see Hearst. He rose at once from behind his large walnut desk. He was a tall man with short-clipped hair and pale blue eyes set in a long face. "What can I do for you?" he asked brusquely.

"You can give me a job, Mr. Hearst."

"Why should I?" He had many applicants for employment at the *Journal* and had grown hard toward them. Seeing a bold young woman standing in the middle of his office and asking for a job amused the newspaper tycoon.

"Because of these." Esther handed the prints over and stood waiting.

Hearst looked at them, and his eyes flew open. He lifted them and said, "Are these from the Keller trial?"

"Yes, taken less than two hours ago. You can get them in the afternoon edition, I think."

Hearst yelled, "Willie, come in here."

The clerk popped in and Hearst said, "Here, I want these pictures in the afternoon edition. They're of the Keller trial."

"Yes, sir!"

After the clerk had disappeared, Hearst grew more genial. "Well, now," he said, smiling faintly, "sit down. I think we can do some business. . . ."

★　★　★　★

Simon Barfield cast his eyes around the crowd with exasperation. "Really, Esther," he muttered, "we could've watched the parade from a more advantageous position than this!"

Esther had, against her better judgment, allowed Simon Barfield to accompany her on an assignment. She was to get shots of the huge parade that would take place down Broadway, and he had insisted on going with her. Now she gave him a rather harried look. "Simon, I've got to get the pictures. Why don't you go back, and I'll meet you later."

But Simon shook his head grimly. "No, if you're going to make a spectacle out of yourself, I suppose there is nothing I can do about it."

His attitude suddenly angered Esther. They were standing next to a hardware store, and the crowd was enormous, making it impossible to get near the street. The spectators lined the streets ten deep, at least, and she could think of no way to get to the front of the crowd with her camera and equipment. Now, Simon had made the matter more difficult, and she was frustrated. Then she touched the card in her pocket that identified her as an employee of the *Journal* and tried to relax. Hearst had been so impressed with her pictures of the Keller trial, he had hired her on the spot. He had marched out into the main office and, ignoring the disbelieving stares from his staff, ordered her card to be typed up right then. In the weeks that had followed, her career with the *Journal* had been successful. Standing there now, her mind worked to figure out a way of getting a shot of the parade from an unusual angle.

"Look!" she said. "That's what we can do. . . !"

"What's that?" Simon demanded. He was startled to see Esther turn and dash inside the hardware store.

"Watch my camera, Simon!" she called back over her shoulder.

Before Simon could protest, Esther had disappeared. He stood there glowering at the people who crowded around attempting to see the parade, and then when he looked up he saw two men carrying a twenty-foot stepladder outside with Esther directing them.

"Set it up right here—right next to the building," she said. The two men winked at each other and set up the high stepladder.

Esther, at once, came and took the camera from Simon and approached the ladder.

"You're not going to climb up that stepladder?"

"I can't think of any other way to get a shot over the crowd," Esther said. "Here, anchor this end of the ladder, will you?—and if you gentlemen would take the other end, I would be most grateful."

"Right you are, miss," one of the clerks said. The three men then anchored themselves, Simon looking harassed and wishing he were anywhere in the world but at the foot of that stepladder! He watched, apprehensively, as Esther climbed to the very top, leaned over, and held the speed graphic eight-by-ten camera while bracing her arms against the top of the stepladder. Over her shoulder hung a leather case which held glass plates. The case weighed thirty pounds and pulled her backward, but she gritted her teeth and held on. As the parade passed by, she took picture after picture, expertly removing the glass plates and replacing them. Finally, when her arms felt as though they were going to give out, she pulled the camera back and carefully lowered herself down the ladder.

"Thank you so much, gentlemen," she smiled.

The owner bowed slightly and grinned. "Any time, miss."

Esther saw that Simon was fidgeting and said, "If you'll bring the tripod, I can carry the camera and the slides."

The two made their way around to a side street where they climbed into his carriage and headed back to the offices of the newspaper. When Simon helped her down and would have gone inside, she said quickly, "No, Simon. This will just be boring for you. I have to develop these plates, and then I have to work with the writer who'll do the story."

Simon Barfield stared at her in exasperation. "For goodness' sakes, Esther! What does all this prove?"

Esther had heard this before. She was frustrated by his brusque attitude and now stood still, looking into his face. "It's something I have to do, Simon. I don't think you're ever going to accept it."

"If you want to take pictures, there are better ways of doing it than running around to fires and scenes of violent crimes. I'll buy you a studio. People can come in for portraits and you'll be able to meet important people—maybe even Teddy Roosevelt—I know him slightly."

Esther was at a loss to explain what she wanted to do. She wanted to take pictures that would change things. She wanted her efforts to bring forth more than a pleasing photograph—even of the President of the United States. She had tried to explain this to Simon before, expressing her desire to have a work that meant something, but he seemed incapable of understanding it. Now she said wearily, "We'll talk about it later, Simon, but I *must* hurry right now."

She smiled her thanks and turned and moved inside the office of the *Journal*, her mind already working on some projects that she was planning, plus those Hearst had assigned to her. After she had developed the films and the plates and delivered them to the copy editor who would do the actual writing, she went to Baxter Hospital where she found Dr. Burns making rounds.

"Come to take more pictures of the hospital?" Burns inquired.

"No, I just thought I'd like to go back to Ellis Island with you."

"Well, that won't be until next week," Burns said. "What have you been doing?"

"I'll tell you after you're through with your rounds." Esther went to his office and waited patiently until the doctor was finished, and when he came back she said, "I've been taking pictures of a parade, but that's not what I wanted to talk about."

"What is it, Miss Winslow?"

"Please call me Esther. I think we know each other well enough for that." Esther's eyes began to glow, and she said, "The pictures I made at Ellis Island—the editor is pleased with them, but he wants more depth. Can you think of any way that we can show the plight of the immigrants through pictures? I want to do a series that would move people to do something to alleviate their suffering and poverty."

Burns shrugged. "Well," he said, "it's as I've said before, why don't you do a project on one family?"

"I've been considering that," Esther said, "and I keep thinking about the Scarlottas. You remember the family that I took the pictures of the first time I went with you and Ruth?"

"Yes, of course. There was a big tall fellow from South Africa with them. I remember him now."

"I've been thinking I could go see if they'd agree to let me take some pictures of their lives just as they are."

"Weel now, that's a touchy situation. People don't want their lives revealed, and you're offering to put them on the front page of a big newspaper. It might be a wee bit difficult."

But Esther had made up her mind. "Have you seen them since that day?"

"As a matter of fact, I saw Tony last week. I was on an errand down near the docks, and I ran into him. He has a job down there. Says they're doing all right. They're living in an apartment now on Mulberry Street."

"I thought of taking some of the pictures I made. Maybe they'd be glad to have those."

"That's a good idea. Why don't you do that."

The two talked about it for some time, and then Esther stopped to talk with Ruth and explain her project. "I'm going to the Scarlottas today."

Ruth said, "I think that's a fine idea. Would you like for me to go with you?"

"No, I can't wait. I'm going now, but thank you, Ruth."

Esther left the hospital, hailed a cab, and got in after loading her equipment in the opposite seat. As she sat back, her thoughts went to the tall, hazel-eyed man from South Africa who had caught her attention, and she wondered if he were still with the Scarlottas.

*　*　*　*

The boss entered the warehouse and hollered, "Quitting time—!" Then he began to shut the doors.

Jan Kruger wearily put down the heavy crate that he was carrying on top of another, then stared at his sore hands. They were blistered, and one of the fingernails was blue and about ready to fall off from an incident a few days earlier when he had crushed it. He turned and joined the other men as they filed out of the crowded warehouse packed with barrels and heavy crates. He had been working now for twelve hours, and since it was payday, he followed the others to the small office to collect his meager pay. *Not much for a week's work*, he thought as he took the money and pushed it into his pocket. As he left, the backs of his legs were aching. His shoulders were knotted from the strain of moving heavy boxes of crates for twelve hours with one brief half-hour break for a quick cold sandwich.

He moved slowly through the streets down Canal Street, where he turned off on Eleventh Avenue and finally came to the tenement where the Scarlottas had finally found a semipermanent residence. He reached the first large block of buildings, and as he turned down a narrow alleyway, he noticed the clotheslines running out of every window. They were the constant reminders of countless housewives struggling against dirt. The pungent odors of a dozen national traditions of cooking hung heavy on the air, and the inadequate provision for sewage, and the difficulty of air-ing out mattresses cast a miasma over the neighborhood which he never got accustomed to.

Turning into one of the narrow doorways, he wearily climbed to the third floor and made his way down a dark hallway until he came to the apartment. It was much better than the first apartment the family had endured when they had arrived, but the rent was high—twelve dollars a month. This, along with the necessities of life, took all that the Scarlottas could scrape together—along with the money that Jan himself brought in from his job at the warehouse.

Inside the largest of the rooms was a table where Maria and her brothers and sister sat, making paper roses. They received twenty cents a gross for these, sometimes earning as much as two or three dollars a week. It was not much, for in the tenements of New York City in 1902, the edge of starvation was an ever-present threat to many immigrants who were struggling to survive.

Maria got up at once and flexed her fingers. "Hello, Jan," she said. "Supper will be ready soon. If you want to, why don't you go wash up?"

"All right." Jan moved over to the table that contained a pitcher of water and a chipped blue enamel basin. He poured some of the tepid water, washed his face and hands as well as he could, and thought longingly of how he would love to have a complete bath. This was a luxury that few people in the tenement district could afford, and he resolutely forced it out of his mind.

Sitting down, he began to help with the roses, talking with the boys as he twisted the paper. Their English had improved tremendously, for young people picked up the language easily.

Lucia came in with a small sack in her hand, followed by Tony, who was dirty and sweaty from his day's work at the docks. Lucia said, "We fix-a supper, Maria." She also was doing much better with her English, and when Jan complimented her on it she flushed and smiled at him.

Thirty minutes later the meal was ready, and they had just sat down when a knock came at the door.

Tony glanced up in surprise but went to the door. They had very few visitors, and they all looked to see who it could be.

Opening the door, Tony blinked with surprise. "Yes, miss? What is it?"

"Don't you remember me, Mr. Scarlotta?" Esther stood looking at the squat, powerful figure of Tony Scarlotta and smiled at him. "I took the pictures of you and your family the day you arrived at Ellis Island."

Tony nodded. "Yes, I remember." He hesitated, then said, "Won't you come-a inside?"

"Thank you."

Esther had left her camera in the carriage. She felt it would have seemed presumptuous to have brought it. In the hall, she saw the pump, which she supposed all the tenants on this floor shared. She stepped inside, and her eyes swept the barren room that bore all the signs of poverty, worse than she had ever known. Now, at once, she saw the tall form of the Dutchman, who rose as she entered. "Mr. Kruger," she said, "I remember your name, you see."

"I'm surprised," Jan said. He took in the trim figure of the young woman. He had thought of her often since they had arrived, and saw that she was even prettier than he had remembered.

Esther was conscious that the children were all looking at her intently, especially the rather pretty daughter who had risen to stand by the stove. "I apologize for interrupting your meal, but I've been meaning to come by for some time. Please go ahead—I can come back later."

"No," Tony said. "Come in—I forgot-a your name."

"Esther Winslow."

"Miss Winslow, will you have something to eat?"

"Oh no. I couldn't eat a thing."

There was an embarrassed silence, and Esther said quickly, "I thought you might like to have these pictures. I made copies of those I made of you at Ellis Island." She was carrying a flat carrying case around her shoulder. Quickly she removed it, opened it, and took out the photographs. She handed them to Tony.

He took one look and said, "Mama, come-a look! Kids come-a see what Miss Winslow has done!"

Soon the room was a babble as they all crowded around, ignoring the food. They were delighted with the pictures.

Kruger stood back slightly, not knowing what to make of the woman's visit. She was well dressed, wearing a gray skirt with a black coat and a pert hat cocked over her forehead, giving her a raffish look. He moved closer at the urging of Dino.

"Look, Jan, it's you!" said Dino.

Jan looked over the boy's shoulder and saw the picture of himself staring into the camera rather defiantly. He lifted his eyes and studied Esther's face for a moment, then said, "You're a fine photographer."

Esther flushed, saying, "Thank you very much, Mr. Kruger."

Finally Tony said, "Now, you have cup-a coffee, at least, Miss Winslow?"

"Very well, just one, then I'll go. I don't want to interrupt your meal."

Lucia brought a cup of coffee and apologized, "No sugar."

"I never use it," Esther said, which was not exactly true. She sipped the black, bitter liquid and smiled graciously. "This is very nice," she said. "Now, tell me. What have you all been doing with yourselves since you got to America?"

For some time Tony told her of the events—how they had moved twice, how it was hard to make a living, but they were all healthy and well.

When Tony was finished, Esther glanced at Jan Kruger. "And how have things been with you, Mr. Kruger?"

"I've been working in a warehouse!"

Somehow, Esther sensed that the simple, rather blunt statement was all that the tall man intended to say. There was a resonance in him, and she felt there was some sort of mystery about him.

"And what have you been doing, Miss Winslow?" Kruger suddenly asked.

"Oh, taking a great many pictures—which is another reason why I came." She hesitated for a moment, then said, "I work for the *New York Journal*, and Mr. Hearst, the owner, thinks that it might be a good idea to photograph the lives of a family of newcomers to this country. There have been lots of pictures made, but my idea was to take *one* family and show what it's like to come to this country."

"Who wants to see pictures of people hungry and struggling for existence?" Kruger inquired almost harshly.

"Oh, I think many people might be interested—and it might

alert some people to the rather terrible conditions that exist. That's what I would hope, anyway."

It took some time, but finally Esther got her point across to Tony and Lucia. She finally said, "I would be very happy to have you help me with this project—and, of course, I would be glad to pay you for your time."

"You mean you pay us for taking our pictures?"

Esther smiled. "Yes, that's the way it seems to work. Not much, of course, but it might help a little."

At that moment a knock sounded at the door, and when Lucia opened it, Esther saw a dumpy middle-aged woman holding a child in her arms. The child must have been at least six years old, and she saw that his face was pale.

The woman spoke rapidly in Italian, and Tony turned to translate. "Mrs. Pappas, she says her son is very sick."

At once the woman came over to where Jan Kruger was standing, and a stream of sentences flowed from her lips, but Esther saw that the tall man understood none of them. She watched as he sat down and took the boy in his lap. He began feeling the boy all over, pushing gently on his chest, smiling at him at the same time. Once when the boy cried out, his mother hovered over him and passed her hand over his head, whispering to him some soft words of consolation.

"I need to look in his mouth," Kruger said. Lucia Scarlotta instantly interpreted, and the boy sniffled and opened his mouth. Kruger peered inside carefully, then turned the boy's head gently to one side. He found something there that interested him and took a handkerchief out. He dabbed at the ear and examined the handkerchief. Looking up, he said, "He has ear disease, and he has a temperature. He'll need to see a doctor at once."

When Mrs. Pappas heard this she began to speak, and Tony said, "She has no money."

"I've got a little," Kruger said. "He's got to see a doctor right away. He needs medicine."

"I think Dr. Burns would be glad to help," Esther spoke up. "You remember the doctor who examined you at the island?"

Tony's eyes brightened. "Very nice doctor—but we gotta no money."

"Dr. Burns wouldn't mind that, I'm sure. I'll go by the hospital and ask him to come. Better still, I'll bring him in my carriage. Is it urgent, do you think, Mr. Kruger?" She suddenly realized that they were all looking at Kruger as if he had all of the answers. There had been something expert and professional about the way he had handled the child, who now sat quietly on his lap.

"It should be very quick," he said. "The boy needs care right away before it gets any worse."

"Then, I'll go at once," Esther said, "and I'll be back with Dr. Burns as soon as I can."

She left the room, and two hours later Dr. David Burns was in the Scarlottas' apartment, with Esther standing back along the wall watching. Burns examined the boy carefully and looked up at Kruger. Esther had told him of the man's actions, and he said, "You're right about the ear infection. How did you know about things like that?"

Kruger merely shrugged his shoulders and did not answer.

Burns saw that he was not going to receive an answer to his question and said, "If someone will go with me, I'll get some medicine from the pharmacy down the street."

Dino jumped up. "I'll go with you, Doctor," he said.

"Fine." Burns closed his bag, stood up, and gave Kruger a curious look. "I'm glad you were here," he said. "A thing like this shouldn't be allowed to go untreated, should it?"

Kruger hesitated then shook his head. "No," he said quietly, "I suppose not."

Burns appeared ready to speak again, then seeing the adamant look on Jan Kruger's face said merely, "I'll order the medicine."

Esther said quickly, "I'll go with Dr. Burns."

"Thank-a you, miss." Tony came over and shook her hand warmly. "You're a good friend, and you can take-a your pictures."

Esther's face lit up and she smiled. "That's wonderful. What about if we begin tomorrow?"

"You talk to Lucia," Tony said.

"I'll do that. I'll see you tomorrow, Mr. Scarlotta."

After Esther and Dino followed Dr Burns out, the room exploded with talk, and Kruger stood, his face expressionless. He was thinking of the interest in Dr. Burns' face and knew somehow that the physician had guessed at his secret. *I don't suppose there's any great harm,* he thought finally. *We're a long way from South Africa. I doubt if they'd send the policemen all the way to America for one Dutchman!*

CHAPTER TEN

A STAR IS BORN

★ ★ ★ ★

Esther Winslow was enjoying a taste of fame. Her photographs of Ellis Island had made some impact when the Hearst papers had run a series on the problems of tenement dwellings and the squalid conditions of the slums. Her sensational pictures, made at the Keller murder trial, had brought her to the attention of others, so that now she was receiving a commission from other newspapers from time to time. None of them were interested in hiring a woman full time, but Esther was certain that this would all change someday.

Her big chance came when Theodore Roosevelt, recently elected President of the United States, came for a major political rally in New York City. He had been governor of the state at one time, and Mark Winslow had been on several boards appointed by Roosevelt. When Esther got the word that he was coming, she set her mind to getting some exclusive photographs and used her father shamelessly.

"Dad, you've *got* to get me in to see the President," she announced one morning early in July.

Mark lowered his newspaper and stared at her nonplused. "Why, he'll be so busy he won't have time for that. I understand he's only going to be here for the one day, then back to Washington."

Esther came over, took his paper from him, and sat down on the sofa close to him. Taking his hand she patted it and smiled up at him. "Now, Dad, you know that he's a politician. The Union Pacific is going to be asked to contribute to all sorts of future campaigns. He's going to be very nice to you—and as your only daughter, I think the *least* you can do is to get me an exclusive interview with him."

Amusement crinkled Mark Winslow's eyes. He leaned back and shook his head in mock shock. "I pity the poor fellow who marries you—he'll never have a moment's peace!"

Esther reached up and drew his head down. Kissing him soundly on the cheek, she said firmly, "Yes, but he'll have so much *fun!*"

Esther got her way, and somehow Mark Winslow finagled thirty minutes from the President's busy schedule. Esther was waiting with all her equipment when her time came. She was ushered into an office President Roosevelt was using for the day.

Roosevelt turned from the window and glanced at her with a trace of impatience. "Well, young lady," he said rather abruptly, for he had been making speeches constantly, "your father bullied me into this. Now, get on with your pictures."

Esther had her camera set up in seconds, but at the same time was charming the President. She spoke knowledgeably of political matters and was able to bring a gleam of humor to Roosevelt's small squinty eyes.

"Well, my dear Miss Winslow, I see you've been reading the newspapers—and now you're a photographer, too. What does your father think of your career? I'd think he'd want you to marry and give him some grandchildren."

"All in good time, Mr. President," Esther smiled. "Now, can you turn your head this way just a little? That's it—!"

The series of portraits turned out to be very good indeed—so good that the President himself had one of them enlarged and framed for his private study. Esther received a bonus for the series of prints. She determined to use part of the money to help the Scarlottas.

For several weeks she had been going to the Scarlotta tenement apartment between her assignments. She had gotten to know the family very well, and the cash that she paid for her photographic sessions there had been a godsend to the family. Early one afternoon, she went to their apartment building. She carried a smaller camera this time, not really needing more photographs for the moment, but it could serve as an excuse for passing along some money that she knew was badly needed. When the door opened, she was surprised to see Jan Kruger standing there.

He stepped back and smiled. "No work for me today. Come in, Miss Winslow."

Entering the room, Esther looked around and asked, "Where is everyone?" Only the two smaller Scarlottas, Emila and Michael, were there.

"Lucia is upstairs visiting with a friend of hers. The boys and Maria are out working."

"Well, I just stopped to take one or two shots, but I don't suppose I'll be able to get much with most of them gone." Somehow Esther felt intimidated in the presence of the tall man. This was unusual, for normally she was a young woman of great self-assurance and was rarely embarrassed. She was unable to analyze why she should feel that way, and finally murmured, "Well . . . I suppose I could take a picture of you."

"No, that wouldn't do your series any good," Jan replied, "but I have a suggestion."

"What's that?"

"Let me take a picture of you."

"Of me!" Esther opened her eyes with surprise. "Whatever for?"

"For the Scarlottas. They think so much of you. You've helped them a great deal. They'd like very much, I think, to have a nice picture of you."

"Well—"

"Of course, I'm no photographer, but if you set it up I can push a button."

Esther shrugged and said, "Well, I suppose it would be all right if you think they'd like it."

Jan smiled at her, his broad lips turning upward. "I'd like one myself," he said, "if you could spare an extra."

Esther was flustered, and to hide her feelings, she immediately began to set up her camera. She attached it to the tripod, composed the shot, using Jan sitting at the table, then said, "Now you come here, and I'll take your place. Look, then just push this button right here."

Jan moved behind the camera and stared at her. "Don't frown," he said. "You don't look natural then." He waited until she smiled, then snapped the picture. He made one more, then Esther rose.

"That's enough!"

"Let me fix you some coffee—some that just came off the boat," Jan said. "They broke a bag unloading it where Tony was working, and he brought home a big sack of loose beans—quite a windfall." He did not wait for an answer but moved over and put some beans into a coffee mill. He crushed them into fine grounds. When he was finished, he put a teakettle on to boil. While the water was getting hot he sat down and said, "I see where you made pictures of the President. There was a little story in the paper about the new woman photographer that's taking New York by storm."

Esther flushed. "Well, hardly that—but I have been doing well." They talked quietly for a while, then the two youngsters came in, beginning at once to demand attention. As Jan made the coffee, Esther entertained them by telling them stories. She had come prepared with a sack full of candy, and soon their mouths were stuffed and they grew quiet. She watched Kruger as he moved back to the table and thought how graceful he was for a big man.

He poured the coffee into a pair of mismatched mugs. "No cream—but here's some sugar."

"Oh, I always like it black," Esther said quickly. The coffee was excellent, and she smiled at him across the table. He was wearing a thin, white shirt, somewhat small for him, and his torso swelled the fabric. He was muscular and seemed to be very strong. Her eyes dropped again to his hands, which were roughened and callused now from the hard work at the warehouse where he worked.

As they were talking across the coffee cups, a knock sounded at the door. When Kruger answered it, a woman stood there, holding a small baby. "My baby, he's-a sick!"

"Bring him in, Mrs. Terrano—let's have a look."

Esther watched as Kruger removed the clothing from the baby

and examined him carefully. He encouraged the mother by saying, "Nothing serious. I'll make up something for his chest. He ought to be all right tomorrow."

Kruger moved over to a cabinet, took some elements out, and began mixing them. Esther could not see clearly what it was, but she was struck again by the certainty of his manner. After he handed a small bottle to Mrs. Terrano and patted her shoulder, she thanked him profusely and left the room. Coming back, he sat down and said, "Something about sick babies always gets to me. They're so helpless."

"You're very good around sick people, Jan. Have you worked in hospitals before?"

Kruger smiled at her. "Quite a bit," he said.

Something in his manner seemed to show his amusement. Esther suddenly had an intuition and said, "You're a doctor, aren't you, Jan?"

His eyes opened wide for a moment, then he glanced down at his hands as if reluctant to speak. He lifted his hazel eyes and said quietly, "I was once—but not anymore."

Esther was not greatly surprised. His manner at Ellis Island had been a tip-off, indicative of medical knowledge, and she had seen him help people each time she had visited. "How do you stop being a doctor?" she asked.

"You move to a foreign country where your credentials aren't valid."

"Oh, I see—but couldn't you qualify again in this country?"

"No, that would take a great deal of money and a great deal of time. I've got time, of course, but very little money."

Esther was puzzled, for he seemed resigned to the situation. Shaking her head doubtfully, she asked, "But you've been a professional man, Jan. How can you be contented being a laborer?"

Jan leaned forward, locked his long fingers together, and stared at them. For what seemed like a long time, he said nothing, and when he looked up there was an odd expression on his squarish face. He reached up and pushed his tawny hair back from his forehead, then said quietly, "I'm content to just be alive, Miss Winslow."

The way in which he said this startled Esther. "What does that mean?" she asked.

Jan hesitated, then told her about his service with the commandos. He ended by saying, "I was a noncombatant, but the English refused to believe me." He related how he had been sentenced to die and how God had spoken to him and delivered him from death.

He smiled again, this time more freely. There was a calmness about him that Esther found very attractive.

"So I really look on myself as a very fortunate man. They shot a great many of us during that time. It was only God's mercy and God's grace that kept me from being one of them."

Esther sat quietly, for his story had moved her strangely. Looking up, she said finally, "You've done so much, and I've done so little."

"We have to live the lives God gives us as best we can, Miss Winslow."

"Please call me Esther," she said impatiently. She had an appointment, and glancing at the watch pinned to her lapel she said, "I have to go, but I'd like to talk to you later and hear more about South Africa. I fear most of us Americans know very little about the issues." She stood to her feet, then remembering, reached into her reticule and pulled out some bills. "This is for the Scarlottas." She wanted to add "and for you," but dared not. "I'd like to help them more."

"You've helped them a great deal, Esther." Jan stood to his feet and took the money. He tucked it into his pocket and said, "You couldn't find better people. They were very kind to me. I think they really saved my life."

Esther had another thought. "You give medicine to some of the children in this building. Do you do that often?"

"When I can."

Esther took out some more bills and said, "At least let me help with that."

Jan hesitated only momentarily, then smiled and half bowed, saying, "You've got a kind heart, Esther Winslow."

His words caused a flush to redden Esther's cheeks. She turned to leave, but he suddenly extended his hand. When Esther took it, she felt the strength and vigor of the man in his clasp. He held it longer than usual, forcing her to look up.

"Thank you, for the children and for the Scarlottas," he said quietly. Then he released her hand and watched her as she left the room. As Kruger sat down and drank the coffee left in his cup, a thoughtful look came to his eyes. He had not met a woman of her class in America—but he was certain that most of them were not structured along the lines of Esther Winslow.

★ ★ ★ ★

Saturday was Priscilla's day off. She took the morning to wash her clothes, and in the afternoon she went to the theater where she was to meet Eddie, of course. They had grown very close over the past month. She had seen every performance of *Lilly Goes To Paris*, and their suppers after the performances had become a ritual. As she approached the theater, a troubling thought came to her. Eddie had continued to make advances to her that she felt were wrong, and she had surrendered herself to him more than she felt was wise. *I've got to be careful*, she said to herself as she entered the small foyer. Nodding at Charlie, who was cleaning the foyer, she passed through the doors and immediately heard the sound of angry voices.

The director, Robert Graves, was engaged in some sort of a shouting match with Florence Page, who played the second lead, right behind the star, Nellie Byron. Graves was a tall, lanky man, with a wild mop of gray hair. He was wearing a pair of gray trousers, a white shirt, and a string tie. His face was red with anger, and he was shouting. "You couldn't act your way out of a paper bag! And you've been late for every rehearsal—then half the time you're not sober when you step on the stage!"

Florence Page was a pretty young woman of twenty who considered herself much more of an actress than she really was. She had blond hair, dark brown eyes, and was somewhat overweight. Her singing voice was fair—a little better than her acting ability— but all that Graves had said about her was true.

"I don't have to stand for this!" the actress shrieked. She was so short she had to turn her head upward to look into the face of the director. "I can get a better part than this any day I want!"

"That's a lie!" Graves snapped. "This is the only job you could hold down. Nobody else will put up with you!"

Priscilla moved quietly down toward the stage, but no one

paid any attention to her. She saw that the other actors were standing back watching the scene in a rather bored fashion. Eddie looked up and caught her eye. He shrugged his shoulders and looked up at the ceiling as if to say, "Well, you know Florence." He had spoken of her often enough, and how she had contributed almost nothing to the play. Priscilla was aware that the girl was a very mediocre actress. She had often marveled at how a woman with so little talent could call herself a professional.

Florence Page had worked herself into a fit of indignation. Her face grew red, and she screamed out, "Well, we'll just *see* who's right about this—I quit!"

This caught Graves totally off guard. "You can't quit without giving us time to get a replacement!"

"Can't I? You just wait and see!" Florence walked off the stage, and Graves followed her, shouting that she couldn't just walk out—that he would ruin her acting career all over the city if she left without giving him time to replace her.

Eddie came down off the stage and put his arm around Priscilla. "Well, fight number ninety-two," he shrugged.

"This has happened before?"

"All the time," he grinned. "After they get through shouting we can get on with the rehearsal."

After what seemed like a long time, Graves came back, his face glum. He cursed loudly, then threw his hands up in the air. "She's done it! She walked out! That means no play tonight."

Sighs were heard from the cast, for no play meant no pay. Nellie Byron exclaimed, "The little tramp! She was no good, but at least we could get through the play with her. Now we'll have to wait until someone else breaks in."

A groan went up and Graves said gloomily, "I suppose I can find somebody over the weekend."

Eddie suddenly called out, "Robert, I've got a candidate for you."

Graves turned around to stare at him. "Who's that, Eddie?"

"Right here!"

Priscilla felt Eddie's arm tighten on her, and she was so shocked as he pulled her forward, she could not think.

"Priscilla knows every line and every song in the whole play, not just Florence's, but everybody else's. She can sing a dozen times better than that caterwauling Florence calls singing."

Robert Graves had thought of Priscilla as no more than Eddie's sweetheart. His eyes narrowed, and he asked instantly, "Have you ever acted before, Priscilla?"

"Why—just at amateur things," Priscilla managed to say.

"Well, I'm afraid—"

"Wait a minute! Give her a chance," Eddie broke in. "She can't act any worse than Florence, and she can sing a lot better."

Nellie Byron urged, "Let's give her a try. As Eddie says, she can't be any worse."

"All right, we'll give it a try."

"But I've never acted in a play—not like this," Priscilla gasped. It had all happened so fast she could not pull her thoughts together, but Eddie was insistent.

Finally she said, "All right, I'll try, but I don't think I can do it."

"Let's take it from act two," Graves said at once. "Just go through the paces."

Priscilla followed everyone backstage. She was trembling, and Eddie was standing beside her. "You can do it, sweetheart," he urged, his arm around her. "You've told me a hundred times how you always wanted to be an actress. So, now's your chance. . . !"

A cue came that took Eddie out on the stage. Priscilla stood there listening as the voices came to her. She knew them all by heart, but her throat was dry and her legs were trembling. Then she heard her cue and swallowed hard. Taking a deep breath, she stepped out onto the stage—and for one moment her heart failed her. They were all watching her, she saw, and she could imagine how much worse it would be if the theater were filled with people! Then she looked at Eddie, who winked at her rakishly, and his lips framed the words, "Come on, Priscilla—knock 'em dead!"

Priscilla said—or rather she gasped—her first line and moved to her spot on the stage. Somehow she managed to get through the scene until it came time for her to sing. The pianist hit the note, and when she opened her mouth and began to sing, she was shocked to discover how *easy* it was! She had a clear voice, rich and full, and it seemed to rise, filling the theater with sound. It was a love song, and she sang it to Eddie, who came and held her. Looking up at him, she found herself forgetting the stage, forgetting the other actresses, and singing the words to him.

And then—suddenly there was the sound of applause, and Priscilla was surrounded by the cast, all of them laughing and telling her she was great.

"Why, you sing like a canary!" Robert Graves exclaimed. "Why didn't you *tell* me you could sing like that?"

As the cast praised Priscilla, a warm glow came to her. She suddenly knew that this was what she had to do.

"Come along! We'll talk about terms. Can't pay much, you understand," Graves warned.

Eddie spoke up at once, saying, "I'm her agent. You can't get around me, Robert."

Graves slapped his forehead dramatically and groaned. "Just what I need—another blood-sucking agent! Well, let's run through the whole play—then we'll see what we can do."

They rehearsed the whole play, and everyone was amazed at how Priscilla knew every line and every song. When the rehearsal was over, she was warmly congratulated by the pianist, who grinned and said, "You'll have to be patient with me, Priscilla. I'm not really used to playing for people who can sing in tune!"

Eddie took her arm finally, and as they left, he said, "This calls for a celebration."

They went to a cafe, more ornate than usual, and were halfway through the meal when suddenly Priscilla put her spoon down, and her face turned pale. "Eddie," she said, "I can't be in the play."

Eddie Rich stared at her in shock. "What do you mean you can't be in the play? We've already agreed."

"But my work at the hospital—"

"But you're off every night, aren't you?"

"Yes, but I can't come to rehearsals."

"You don't need any rehearsals, sweetheart," he said, smiling.

Priscilla was filled with doubt. She was not certain that she could act every night in a play and carry on her demanding duties at the hospital. Finally, however, the temptation was too great, and she agreed to try it for a week. "At least," she said finally, "I can give Mr. Graves a chance to get somebody else."

Eddie Rich took her hand and kissed it. "You'll never get out of show business. Alcohol gets to some people—the theater gets to others. For you," he said and kissed her hand again, "the theater is in your blood. You'll never leave the stage, Priscilla. . . !"

CHAPTER ELEVEN

"SHE'S NOT FOR HIM!"

★ ★ ★ ★

A twelve-hour shift in a small, stuffy, windowless room and the heat of August had drained most of the energy from Maria Scarlotta. Her steps were slow and almost faltering as she made her way home through the dimly lit streets of the Lower East Side. Despite the lateness of the hour, Mulberry Street was still occupied by many peddlers who called out hopefully to her as she passed by their stations. The area she was walking through had come to be known as Little Italy, and one observer of the city described the area as a "sociable southern Italy, cramped and warped in the unfragrant and ugly tenements of New York."

It was common for ethnic groups to come together into settlements, for in these crowded, bustling neighborhoods, the inhabitants sought to reserve their old lifestyle from Europe. In these areas, the immigrants could speak their own languages, buy ethnic foods, exchange news of the homeland, and celebrate traditional holidays and holy days.

But though these neighborhoods provided warmth and familiarity, they also worked enormous damage on their dwellers. The districts were squalid, unhealthy, noisy, and overcrowded. The tenement buildings were six- or seven-story structures that occupied lots no more than twenty feet wide and a hundred feet deep. They were called "dumbbell" tenements—the term describing the shape of the floor plan. Narrow in the middle to allow for a central air shaft between buildings, each floor of the tenement had two apartments in the front, and two in the back. The New York Tenement House Law of 1901 mandated a toilet and running water for each unit, but many buildings had not caught up with this requirement, so tenement residents had to share two water closets located in the hallway. To make matters worse, many families took in boarders to help cover the rent. Not surprisingly, diseases—including tuberculosis, cholera, and typhus—were rampant.

A group of young loafers was congregated outside the doorway of a pool hall. Most of them wore black derbies and tight trousers, the style of the day. All over Little Italy they gathered in their groups, shooting pool, smoking cheap cigars, and seeking to find some excitement—oftentimes illegal in nature. Now they whistled and called out rude suggestions to Maria as she passed, and laughed to see her lift her nose in the air, ignoring them.

Reaching her own building, Maria turned inside and wearily climbed the dark flights of stairs. On reaching her floor, she took a deep breath, then moved toward the apartment. Opening the door, she stopped abruptly—for she saw Esther Winslow seated on one of the kitchen chairs, drinking coffee with her family.

"Maria, guess-a what!" Lucia Scarlotta exclaimed, her eyes beaming with pleasure. "Miss Winslow, she's a-gonna take us all to Coney Island tomorrow! That's-a your day off. We can all go and have a good time!"

Ordinarily Maria would have been glad enough to have made the holiday with the others, but she was acutely aware of Esther Winslow sitting next to Jan Kruger—and she did not miss the way he was watching Esther with a pleased expression. It leaped to her mind how that several times Jan had spoken of the rich young woman with warm approval. A rash streak of jealousy shot through Maria—not for the first time. Removing her hat, she hung it on a nail driven into the wall, then turned to say briefly, "I don't think I'd like to go."

Everyone in the room stared at her, for Maria was always anxious for a good time. Tony Scarlotta demanded, "What-a you mean, you don't wanna go? Miss Winslow, she's a-gonna pay for everything. You *gotta* go!"

Esther had not missed the look that had crossed Maria's face, and she understood the meaning of it. *She's jealous of Jan—which is foolish!* Speaking quickly she said, "Really, Maria, I especially want you to come. We'll need help with these young ones. They'll go wild on some of the rides there."

"Why, of course you'll go, Maria," Jan spoke up with surprise on his face. "It wouldn't be the same without you."

Maria turned quickly to Jan, and a faint color tinged her cheeks at his words. "Well—" She hesitated only for a moment, then nodded. "I suppose I should go."

"Of course you should," Esther said firmly. "Everyone needs to make a trip to Coney Island—and really it's all free."

"How do you mean *free*? Don't they charge for the things there?" Maria asked sharply.

"Well, they do—but I got some unexpected money, and I don't want to spend it on anything foolish." She laughed aloud and looked around the room. "I want to invest it wisely in having a good day with my friends, the Scarlottas."

Immediately Michael and Mario and Dino began shooting questions at her. "What have they got at that place?" Dino demanded.

"Everything! Rides, ferris wheels, horse races, you can go swimming—anything you like, and anything you like to eat, too. We'll all probably be sick." Esther smiled at their pleasure. Her eyes went to Jan, and she smiled. "Then you'll have to prescribe something for tummy ache."

"I'll probably have one myself," Jan smiled.

Esther rose, saying quickly, "I'll be here in the morning at eight o'clock. Everybody be ready—and don't worry about breakfast. We'll eat at a cafe before we go."

As soon as Esther left the room, a babble of talk arose, and Lucia said suddenly, throwing up her hands, "I forgot-a to cook supper!"

"The first time in twenty-six years that she don't cook-a my supper," Tony said in mock sadness. Then he moved over and put his arms around Lucia, who squealed loudly. He ignored her, saying, "We'll eat enough tomorrow to make up for missing a little bit tonight."

The rest of the evening was filled with excited talk about

Coney Island and what a great day they would have. Finally everyone went to bed except Jan, who was reading by a single candle placed on a table near the pad he slept on. He had not undressed, but had removed his shirt for coolness. The room was hot and uncomfortable, but he had learned to bear it stoically enough.

Maria, who shared one of the bedrooms with Emila and Michael, came out and went to sit beside the window, staring out at the city. She slowly turned her head and watched Kruger as he read. The yellow light caught the gleam of his tawny hair, and she admired his powerful arms and smoothly muscled shoulders. She arose from her seat, went over, and sat down beside him with a naturally graceful motion. "What are you reading tonight?"

Jan looked up from his book with a smile. "A book I found on the way home. Someone lost it, I guess." A smile tugged at his lips and he said, "It's called *The Wonderful Wizard of Oz*."

"What a funny title!"

"Well, it's a fairy tale."

Maria shook her long black hair free. She had loosed it from the ivory pin that held it, and now it fell down her back, glossy and black and rich. It made her look older, and her eyes looked very large by the light of the single candle that reflected her pupils. "I stopped reading fairy tales a long time ago."

"I don't think I ever will," Jan remarked quietly. He looked down at the book with silence for a while. Glancing up he added, "I think we need fairy tales in this world."

Maria was puzzled. She did not understand this tall, strong man that had fallen into her life. He said things that confused her sometimes, and she was well aware that he was out of her sphere in many ways. For example, she knew instinctively that he came from a better family than her own—better socially, at least. Now she said curiously, "What's the story about? I don't understand why you would want to read a child's book."

Kruger settled back against the wall and looked down at the book, speaking very quietly. He had a pleasant, deep baritone voice, and she always enjoyed hearing him speak.

"It's about a little girl who lives in the middle of the United States—a rather unhappy little girl in many ways. She gets caught up in a big cyclone."

"What's a cyclone?"

"A big storm with a funnel-shaped wind. Anyway, it took her into a strange and mysterious world, and she set out to find her way home with only her little dog, Toto, for a companion. On her way she hears about a wonderful wizard who can do anything, so she decides to find him. Then she meets three others who need something badly—a scarecrow, who doesn't have a brain, a tin man, who doesn't have a heart, and a lion, who is cowardly and needs courage. So they go together to find the wizard."

For some time Kruger spoke, telling the story of Dorothy and her adventures. Finally he ended by saying, "So they found the wizard, and even though he was a humbug, he tried to solve all their problems."

"How did he do that?"

"Why, he gave them what they needed. He gave the tin man a heart, the scarecrow a brain, and the cowardly lion some courage. Then he tried to send Dorothy home again. He failed at that, but Dorothy discovered she had the power to send herself home." He closed the book and grinned at Maria. The smile made him look much younger. He was a man of loose and rough and durable parts, like a machine designed for hard usage. His eyes were sharp and well-bedded in their sockets. His face held mixed elements of sadness in repose, and only when his face lighted did the humor that lay beneath the surface emerge. He looked at her closely and said, "You're tired and sleepy, Maria. It's going to be a big day tomorrow."

Maria, however, leaned forward, and the light of the flickering candle seemed to dance in her dark eyes. It gave her an intensely feminine look, and her lips and eyes were those of a woman rather than a young girl. She said quietly, "But things don't happen like that, Jan. People don't get what they want usually—and there's no place like Oz and no wizard."

"I think we need to have hope, Maria. It would be a pretty grim world if we didn't."

"That's-a no good," Maria said. She shook her head and bit her lower lip. "We have to think of things as they are, not like we'd like for them to be."

"I guess that's what fairy tales are for, to remind us that once in a great while we *do* meet the wizard—and sometimes he *does* give us what we desire. Only I think the wizard is just a symbol."

"A symbol? What's a symbol?"

"Why, it's one thing that stands for another. Like a ring can stand for love between a man and a woman. It's not really that love, but when you look at it you think of it."

"I see that; so what's the symbol in the Wizard of Oz story?"

"I suppose it would sound foolish and not theologically sound," Kruger grinned, "but in some sense I think Dorothy's search for the wizard is a little bit like our search for God."

"I don't understand that."

"Well . . . I think every one of us," Kruger said thoughtfully, "is deeply longing for something on the inside. I think every one of us is unhappy, and nothing can make us happy until we find God. If I understand what the Bible says, God has made us so that we're not complete until He has His place in us."

Maria listened intently as Kruger went on to speak about how people sought for God. This again puzzled her. She had gone to the cathedral all of her life back in Rome, but religion had never played much of a role in her life. She saw, however, that God was very real to him. Finally, though she did not understand it, she nodded. "Maybe I can read the book sometime."

"Take it with you," he said and handed it to her. "It's one of those books you can read when you are ten, and then come back when you're fifty and read it again, and get more out of it the second time." He smiled at her and said, "Good night, Maria." Then he lay down and closed his eyes.

Maria blew out the candle and groped her way into her bedroom, clasping the book. She lay awake for a long time thinking about Jan Kruger—how different he was from anyone she had ever known. Then she thought about the following day, and thought sleepily of Esther Winslow. *She may be rich and beautiful, but she's not for him!*

★ ★ ★ ★

Coney Island had once been a small middle-class seaside resort. The first hotel had opened in 1829, but Coney Island was hard to reach for most New Yorkers. The great era of the resort had begun in 1895 with the construction of large amusement parks. Captain Paul Boyton's Sea Lion Park opened in 1895, and the island became a refuge far removed from the risqué girlie shows and the lewdness of the concert saloons of the Tenderloin and Sixth Avenue. George Tilyou's Steeplechase Park opened in 1897. This was aimed at lower-class clientele, and people poured in. Coney Island became a refuge for those seeking relief from the boredom and the drab colorless work-a-day world of Manhattan.

With Jan Kruger towering over all of them, the Scarlottas arrived at Coney Island shortly after ten o'clock. Esther had come at eight and taken them all out for breakfast at a real cafe, then had hired a carriage to take them to the station. There they had exchanged the carriage for the railroad that went to the resort, and now as they piled out of the car, the younger members of the family were hard to control.

"I think we'd better tie a rope around all of them and yoke 'em to each other," Jan said and grinned at Esther.

Esther laughed. "I think that might be a good idea. Look, suppose we each make ourselves responsible for one." She reached out and grabbed Dino by the ear. "You, young man, stay close to me, you hear?"

"Ow!" Dino yelped. He tried to pull away, but she held him tighter. "Don't treat a fellow like that, Miss Winslow."

"All right, I'm sorry, Dino, but you'll have to help with the younger ones." She looked around and nodded. "If you ever got lost in here, I don't see how anyone could ever find you." This threat seemed to work its effect, for Emila, Michael, Mario, and Dino did not stray from the adults.

Esther enjoyed the trip more than she had expected. She had been to Coney Island when she was younger, and now it was a pleasure to take the Scarlottas by the amusement parks and watch them as they rode, shrieking wildly on the roller coaster. She, herself, had gotten into a car with Kruger sitting between her and Maria. Despite herself, she had screamed as the car had reached the tremendous speed at the bottom of the curves and had not noticed that Jan had put his arms around both her and Maria.

"Hang on!" he yelled. "I can't afford to lose you two!"

Maria was petrified by the apparent danger of the ride, but she was acutely conscious of Kruger's arm across her shoulder—and the same was true of Esther.

They rode the carousel, which was much more sedate, and even Lucia Scarlotta was cajoled until she mounted one of the brightly painted horses. When she got off, she said, "It's-a not dignified. What would my mama have thought of such a thing?"

"Your mama would have liked it, just-a like you did," Tony grinned. "Come on, let's go see the horses race."

They spent all day at Coney Island, and finally at four o'clock, despite protests from Dino and Mario, left for home. The smaller children were totally exhausted. Jan was carrying Michael, whose legs had given out, and Tony was carrying six-year-old Emila. They made their way back to the railroad, then got off and took the carriage back to the tenement. Twilight was falling as the carriage pulled up and stopped in front of the building. Esther laughed ruefully, saying, "I don't think I can get out. I'll never get back in again."

The younger children were too sleepy to thank her, but Tony's eyes glowed as he said, "Me and my family, we no forget this day, Miss Winslow!"

"Yes, it's been good," Lucia nodded. She reached over and patted Esther's hand and smiled. "You're an angel to our family!"

Tony grinned broadly and winked at Jan. "And now she's a-gonna give you another bambino to be an angel to!"

"Tony—shutta your mouth!" Lucia's face flamed, and she put her hands over her eyes. "How can you talk so in front of Miss Winslow!"

Esther leaped out of the carriage and hugged the older woman. "Why, I think that's wonderful, Lucia!" She was not usually so demonstrative with people outside her own family, but the weeks she'd spent with the Scarlottas had brought a warmth to her feelings for all of them. Now she laughed at Lucia, saying, "A brand-new American! What will you name him? Christopher Columbus?"

"No," Lucia said, lifting her eyes and fixing them on the young woman. "I already pick a name—is gonna be named *Esther*!"

Jan laughed aloud, pleased with the scene. "Better be a girl, Lucia. Hang a name like that on a boy and he'll spend his life fighting people!"

Esther was touched as she had not been in years. She patted Lucia's shoulder, saying, "That's a wonderful thing for you to do,

Lucia. I'm very flattered and happy—but if it's a boy, Jan's right."

"If it's a boy, he'll be *Jan*."

Jan looked startled, then smiled broadly. "A dark-headed boy with a Dutch name? Better stick with *Esther*."

The family went into the building, finally, but Kruger stood before Esther for a moment, still holding the limp form of Michael draped over his shoulder. He put his hand out, and Esther took it warmly as he said, "This was one of those days I'll never forget. I keep a little gallery of good things, like pictures, in my mind. When things get dark, I go through and look at the good things like today. I'll be looking at this one a long time, Esther."

"Why, what a nice way to put it!" Esther whispered. She noticed that Maria was standing close and quickly added, "I hope you had a good time, Maria."

"Yes, thank you very much." Maria's reply was formal, and she put her hand possessively on Kruger's arm, saying, "Good night, Miss Winslow."

Esther said easily, "I'm glad you had a good time. Good night, all of you. Move on, driver."

As the family made their way wearily up the stairs and began preparing for bed, Tony said, "That's-a fine lady, Miss Winslow, ain't she, Maria?"

"She's all right, I suppose."

"All-a right? She's better than that!" Tony nudged his daughter and grinned slyly. "I'm-a think she likes our Jan. Don't you see her hanging on to him on the roller coaster?"

Maria shook her head. "I didn't notice," she said coldly. "Don't be so foolish, Papa." She turned and went into her bedroom, shutting the door with more force than necessary.

Tony Scarlotta scratched his head. "What's-a matter with her?" he muttered. "The best time she ever had—and she acts like she got her toe caught in the door! I'm-a don't understand girls!"

CHAPTER TWELVE

PRISCILLA'S CHOICE

★ ★ ★ ★

"I understand that you have a matter to bring before us, Doctor Myers." Dr. Henry Cameron, general director of Baxter Hospital, looked around the table at the small group that had gathered to discuss the problems and plans of the hospital. The meeting had gone smoothly, but one look at Irving Myers convinced Cameron that that would no longer be true.

"I certainly do, Dr. Cameron!" Irving Myers was a small man with jet black hair and dark brown eyes. He had a pencil-slim mustache, and a Van Dyke beard, which gave him a Mephistophelian appearance. He responded tersely, his high tenor voice crisp, clear, and sharp. "I want to bring a charge against one of our nursing trainees."

Involuntarily Dr. David Burns tensed and exchanged glances with Nurse Agnes Smith, who sat across the battered walnut table from him. Neither of them spoke, but each knew exactly the problem that Dr. Myers was about to unfold. Myers had, as a matter of fact, spoken more than once to each of them on this matter, and now, noting the stern look on the small physician's face, both of them knew that trouble lay ahead.

"It concerns trainee Priscilla Winslow," Dr. Myers said. "I propose that she be dismissed from the hospital."

Dr. Cameron blinked his eyes with surprise. It was not common for nurses to be dismissed except on morals charges. "You're not suggesting that the woman you mention has committed a moral breach, are you, Dr. Myers?"

"I cannot say as to that," Irving Myers shrugged. "What I *can* testify to is that she is completely unsuited for nursing as a profession. She is consistently late for her duties, and when she does appear, she is inefficient and slovenly in her work. Some of the patients have even complained at how she responds to them."

Dr. Cameron thought carefully in the silence that followed, for he valued Dr. Myers highly. The small man was a perfectionist, but an excellent doctor and a tireless one. He was also willing to accept the relatively small salary that Baxter was able to offer. While Cameron felt that Myers created problems for himself by an unnecessary strictness in manner and in rules, he, nevertheless, spoke with a placating voice. "I'm sorry to hear this distressing news of one of our young women. I was not aware of it, Dr. Myers. Would you give us a few more details?"

Myers turned his head toward the two who sat slightly at a distance down the table. "I'm sure I do not have to convince Dr. Burns or Nurse Smith of the woman's total irresponsibility. I have spoken to them already on several occasions, complaining about Priscilla Winslow—and I am sure they, themselves, have noted her incompetence."

Cameron lifted his eyebrows in surprise. "Dr. Burns, what have you to say about this matter?"

David Burns was trapped between two forces. He was essentially a kind man, unwilling to hurt anyone—yet, he was an honest man too. He well knew that Dr. Myers spoke no more than the truth. He was also embarrassed, for he had promised Myers to speak with Priscilla Winslow and had half promised that he would see that her behavior changed. He knew that Priscilla had not changed, and now he said carefully, "I must confess that Dr. Myers has some grounds for his accusations."

"I make no accusations," Myers snapped. "I report the facts! Is the woman inefficient and slovenly with her work or not, Dr. Burns? That's a simple question, isn't it?"

Reluctantly Burns nodded. "I'm afraid she has not been up to our usual standards, Dr. Cameron."

"I should think not, and I have discovered exactly why."

Myers turned his eyes back to Cameron and leaned forward, placing his hands before him on the table. He pressed them against the surface until they grew pale, and his voice was cold as the polar ice. "I've just discovered that the young woman in question is leading a double life."

"A double life!" Cameron exclaimed. "What does that mean, Dr. Myers?"

"It means that every night as soon as she finishes her duties here, she rushes off to appear in a play. She's become an actress." The disgust in Myers' voice was unmistakable. He, himself, never attended the theater, sporting events, or any other social activity. His entire life was tied up with his work in the hospital and with his family, which consisted of a dainty wife and two very small daughters. "I found this impossible to believe when I first heard what I thought was a rumor," he continued, "but last Tuesday I investigated and discovered that the rumor was, indeed, based on truth. She's in a low play at Golden Nights Theater off Broadway. The name of the play is *Lilly Goes To Paris*." He turned suddenly and demanded, "Did you know of this, Dr. Burns?"

Once again David Burns was trapped. "Yes, I'm afraid I did."

"And you permitted it to go on? I'm surprised at you, Doctor!"

Defensively David answered, "I spoke to Miss Winslow about it. I pointed out that such a dividing of her loyalties was unwise. That it was causing her duties here to suffer and might jeopardize her training."

"That is not sufficient. She obviously has ignored your warning," Myers snapped. "Nurse Smith, you're also responsible for our nurse trainees. How do you account for your negligence in this matter?"

Agnes Smith was a fearless woman. She had led a difficult life and had learned to cope with hard situations. However, she had no ready answer for the enraged physician. Dropping her eyes in shame, she said in a subdued voice, "I'm sorry, Dr. Myers—and I must apologize to you, Dr. Cameron. I was aware of Miss Winslow's activity. I also spoke with her and urged her to devote herself full time to her work as a nurse." Nurse Smith shrugged her heavy shoulders and lifted her eyes, which contained more than a trace of resentment. "She ignored me, and I must say that she is not keeping the strict standards that I demand of all my nurses."

"Why have you been lenient with this woman? She should have been fired long ago," Myers stated flatly.

Feeling that some defense must be made, Dr. Burns said, "I appreciate your concern, Dr. Myers—and like Nurse Smith, I must confess I have failed the hospital in this matter." He saw a look of satisfaction cross Myers' eyes, and he continued slowly, "The fact of the matter is, I have been rather lenient with Miss Priscilla Winslow because of her cousin, Miss Ruth Winslow. You have found her a good nurse, have you not, Dr. Myers?"

"Why—yes, I have." Myers was surprised at the mention of her. "She is the finest trainee we have ever had in this hospital—a young woman to be highly commended." Then Myers shook his head sharply. "But I'm not bringing charges against Miss Ruth Winslow, only against Miss Priscilla Winslow. I fail to see the connection."

"Without going into particulars," Burns continued, "these two young women came from the West. They are cousins, and their families are very close. Miss Priscilla Winslow has a very fine family, Dr. Myers. Her father is the brother of Mr. Mark Winslow, who is the vice president of the Union Pacific Railroad, and he, of course, is the father of Miss Esther Winslow. You have seen some of her photographic work in the *Journal*, which has been helpful in bringing better conditions, I trust, to the immigrants who come to Ellis Island—and I know you're interested in that work."

As a matter of fact, Burns had touched on the one concern that consumed Irving Myers. Myers had immigrated to America himself and was vitally interested in helping the thousands of Jews who were streaming into Ellis Island. "I have been very impressed with Miss Esther Winslow's work," Myers said. He paused and finally shook his head. "I deeply regret that Miss Priscilla Winslow does not share the character of her cousins—but we are running a hospital here, Dr. Burns, not a clinic for wayward young women. I wish Miss Winslow well," he shrugged, "but I still insist that she be dismissed."

The talk went on for some time, but it was futile, Burns knew. Finally he heard Cameron make his decision. "I am sorry for the situation, of course, but the hospital's well-being is my first concern. We have a list of capable young women who will take their duties more seriously." He turned his eyes toward David, saying,

"Will you tell her, or would you prefer that I do it, Dr. Burns?"

"I think it might better come from me, sir."

"Very well. Handle it in your own way."

As they rose to leave, Dr. Myers said quickly, "I have no personal animosity toward Priscilla Winslow. You understand that, Dr. Burns?"

"Of course, Dr. Myers. These situations are always difficult."

When they were outside, walking down the hall together, Nurse Smith said quietly, "It was bound to come, Dr. Burns."

"I suppose you're right. There's no way to force people to do the right thing, is there?"

"It's going to hurt Ruth a great deal. She's very fond of Priscilla. I think," she said suddenly, "you ought to tell Ruth first so that she'll be prepared."

"You may be right aboot that, Agnes—but I'd rather take a whipping!"

*　*　*　*

Ruth sat quietly in the chair across from Dr. Burns. When he had asked her to come to his office, she was somewhat surprised. She had entered and noted that he was rather nervous, which was unusual for Dr. David Burns. He had talked for some time about small, unimportant matters, then finally had said, "I'm sorry to tell you, Ruth, but I've got to ask Priscilla to give up her post in the hospital."

Ruth had opened her lips to protest, but one look at the sad face of Burns convinced her of the uselessness of it. She looked down at her hands, squeezed them tightly together, and tried to think of some way to mitigate the circumstances.

"I know how badly you feel about this," Burns said. "I feel the same, and so does Nurse Smith. We all wanted to see your cousin behave differently and succeed, but I'm afraid there is pressure that goes beyond me and Nurse Smith."

"I know it's not your fault." Ruth looked up, and there was a sadness on her countenance. She was a woman of great compassion, and this was especially true concerning her cousin Priscilla. She felt doubly responsible and remembered that Priscilla's parents had laid it upon her as a special request to watch out for Priscilla. Now she had failed to do so, and a great heaviness settled on her.

Seeing Ruth's expression and knowing that she was deeply disturbed, Burns asked quietly, "What do you think she'll do now? Will she go back home again?"

"I can't think she'd do that. She hated it so much. I think she'll stay on the stage."

"Not a good decision for a young woman, I'm afraid," Dr. Burns said.

"No, but I think I know her well enough to say what she'll do." Ruth clasped her hands and looked at the doctor. Despite her agitation there was a steadiness in the young woman. "Have you told her yet?"

"No, and I wish I didn't have to."

"Would you rather I did it, Dr. Burns?"

Relief washed over the physician's face. "It might be better coming from you, Ruth."

At the use of her given name, Ruth felt a moment of comradeship with this young man. She admired him greatly and knew how hard he worked. He had to make many speeches that were painful to patients, and it pleased her that she could take this one unpleasant task off of his hands. "I'll do it. When will she be expected to leave?"

"She's relieved from duty now," Burns said, "but, of course, there's no rush about her leaving the living quarters until she's made other arrangements."

"I think she'll not want to stay."

"I suppose you're right." Burns shook his head and said dourly, "It wuid be nice if we could *make* people do the right thing."

A smile close to amusement came to Ruth's lips. It was the kind of statement she was accustomed to from David Burns. "You can't even do that with a child."

"Why, of course, you can make them be good." David Burns was surprised at her words. He returned her smile and said, "You're bigger than they are."

"No, you're not making them be good, you're making them *behave*. Inside they're still rebellious."

"I see what you mean," he said, his surprise breaking through.

Now that the moment of truth telling was over, he could relax a little bit. Thoughtfully he said, "My cousin once had a little dog—one of those yappy kind that loved to bite people on the ankle. That was back in Scotland, ye ken?" The memory brought a fondness to his blue eyes, and he shook his head at it. "My sister put a muzzle on the little creature—but that dog—he was still after people's ankles. Take the muzzle off, and he would've been right back at it again."

Ruth laughed aloud. She had a good laugh, vigorous for a woman, and her eyes crinkled up until they were almost hidden. "I think that's the sort of theology I could understand."

"It is, isn't it? The heart has to be changed or we'll go around biting people on the ankles—or destroying ourselves in some foolish way." For some time he sat there chatting with Ruth. Finally he realized that half an hour had gone by. With kindness in his voice he said, "You have a fine way of making difficult things seem pleasant, Ruth. It's a way I've noted in you since I've known ye."

His compliment confused Ruth Winslow, and as he watched her with approval, she said quickly, "We have to do the best we can."

A warm admiration for her steadiness rose in Burns. She was wearing the white uniform required of all nurse trainees, and her pleasant features and beautiful complexion made her seem very attractive at the moment. A thought came to him, *Why, she's almost as attractive as Gail Winslow!* The sudden thought shocked him, for the pain over the loss of Gail had never left him. Indeed, it had intensified for some time. Now, he had reached the state of numbness, having surrendered the chance of ever having the young woman. He was not basically a man who knew a great deal about women, but there was something in Ruth Winslow that drew him. Still, like a man who had a bruised thumb and protected it carefully from injury again, he blinked and said rather stiffly, "Weel now, I suppose we'd better get about our business. Thank you for your help, Nurse Winslow."

To Ruth his behavior was very obvious. She had noted that he would go warm and rather witty and with an openness of manner—then something would rise in him that would close this as firmly as a door shutting. The door was shut now as he called her

"Nurse Winslow" instead of Ruth.

"I'll tell her this afternoon, Dr. Burns."

★   ★   ★   ★

"I'm afraid I have bad news for you, Priscilla."

Looking up from where she sat on the edge of her bed, Priscilla instantly knew the content. "I've been asked to leave the hospital. I suppose that's it?"

"I'm afraid so, Priscilla. I'm so very sorry." Ruth saw that the news disturbed Priscilla greatly and went over to sit beside her. Putting her arm around her cousin, she said, "It isn't too late, even now. Dr. Burns will help, and Nurse Smith seems gruff, but she really has a kind heart. If we go to them and tell them that you want another chance, I'm sure they'll make a way."

Tears gathered in Priscilla's eyes, for the dismissal was rejection. Nevertheless, pride rose in her and a fierce determination to prove herself. "I won't do that," she said. "It wouldn't do any good, anyway."

"It would if you'd try, Priscilla. You can do anything you want to. I'll help you."

Priscilla dashed the tears from her eyes and stood to her feet. "That's just it, Ruth. I don't *want* to be a nurse. I want to be in the theater; can't you see that?"

Shaking her head, Ruth said sadly, "It's a bad decision for you, Priscilla. I know it's exciting and thrilling, but when you look at the theatrical profession you see a great deal—well, of—"

"I know you think all actors and actresses are immoral. Well, they're *not*!" Priscilla said defensively, lifting her chin. "I can name some doctors who aren't all they should be."

"That's no defense, and you know it, Priscilla. I'm not saying all the people in the theater are immoral, but it's a profession that offers great temptations, especially to a young woman."

Ruth talked as persuasively as she could for half an hour. She knew, however, that it was a losing battle and finally sighed. "What will you do? I hope you'll go back home and spend some time with your parents."

"I may do that—but not right now. They're depending on me to keep the play going." This was not exactly true, and Priscilla knew it. The role she played could have been played by someone else, but she could not face the thought of going back to the boredom of her life in Wyoming.

"Have you thought about what your parents will say?" Ruth asked quietly.

This was exactly what Priscilla did not want to think about. She shook her head stubbornly, saying, "They'll just have to understand. They have their lives, and I have mine." Then she turned to Ruth and said, "Oh, Ruth, try to understand. I can't stand the thought of going back—I wasn't made for that kind of life. I can stay in the theater and be a success. Please try to understand, Ruth!"

Ruth, however, could only see that Priscilla was making a bad and grievous error. Nothing she tried to say to convince her cousin to change her mind prevailed. Priscilla got up and soon left, saying, "I'll be back to get my things after I find a place to live."

★ ★ ★ ★

"Oh, I think it's the best thing that could've happened to you, sweetheart." Eddie Rich was fully aware that Priscilla was unhappy. She had just told him that she was leaving the hospital, and something about her wan expression warned him that he would have to be very careful. "I know it's a big change in your life, but you were born for the theater, Priscilla. You just wait and see. You're going to do better than a little play like this small-bit thing we're in—both of us are! Look, we'll go up together, you and me. It'll be exciting! Come along—let's go find you a nice room close to the theater. Then we'll go out and have dinner, and then we'll do the play."

Priscilla was somewhat encouraged when she found a very nice room only two blocks away from the theater. Eddie accompanied her back to the hospital, where she picked up her few belongings. She was relieved to see that Ruth was on duty, for she did not want to speak anymore of her decision. As she left the hospital, a pang of regret struck her. She thought of how disappointed her parents would be, but she firmly shoved that to the back of her mind. *I can explain it*, she thought. *They'll understand....*

Despite the sudden change, the next two weeks were the best two weeks that Priscilla Winslow had ever known. All of her life she had been searching for some sort of freedom, and freedom was what she had in abundance now. There was no one to tell her what time to get up, no one to tell her what to wear, no one to make her decisions for her. Her only obligation was to be at the theater for rehearsals and then back for the performance at seven o'clock—and this was still fun and exciting for her.

August was almost gone, and on the last day of that month, just before the performance, Eddie came rushing into the dressing room, his eyes bright with excitement. "Sweetheart," he said excitedly, "guess who's out front?".

"I have no idea. Who is it, Eddie?"

"Robert Glenn, no less!"

"Robert Glenn? Who's he?"

Eddie stared at her incredulously. "Why, I forget you don't know many people of the theater yet. He's one of the big producers on Broadway. I don't know what he's doing here, but they say he goes scouting third-rate plays like this one, looking for fresh new talent." Eddie reached out and took her into his arms. "And you, baby, are the talent he's looking for!"

"Oh, Eddie, really?"

Priscilla looked so bright and expectant that he kissed her at once. He held her for a long time, pressing her against him, saying, "Sweetheart, I love you. You're a sweet kid." Then he released her, saying, "If you ever sang in your life, do it tonight. It could be the big break we're looking for."

As Eddie left the room, Priscilla savored what he'd just said— "the big break *we're* looking for." Eddie had been pressing his suit with her, and although she had resisted his advances, she was captivated by him.

The play that night went better than it ever had. Perhaps it was the excitement that bubbled over in Priscilla Winslow. It seemed to catch the other members of the cast, who threw themselves into their parts with an unusual gusto. But it was Priscilla who dominated the stage that night. Deep within her own heart she knew it, and when the crowd demanded four curtain calls, she reveled in the thrill of such adulation.

She went to her dressing room and changed clothes, and her hands trembled as she waited for Eddie to come with the news of how the performance had taken Robert Glenn.

Eddie had gone at once, in his makeup, to meet Glenn, who stood talking to a small group. He waited impatiently until he caught Glenn's eye, and then said, "I'm Eddie Rich, Mr. Glenn. We're pleased to have you in our audience tonight."

Glenn was a short man, no more than five feet eight. There was, however, a power in his countenance. He had a shaggy bush of silvery hair and a set of keen gray eyes. Excusing himself from his companions, he said, "I was coming backstage. I'd like to talk to the young woman—I believe her name is Winslow?"

"Yes, my fiancée."

"Indeed?" Glenn gave Eddie a closer look and a smile. "I suppose you're her agent as well?"

"Well, I try to look after her as well as I can. She is a comer, isn't she, Mr. Glenn?"

They had reached the stage now, and as they stepped inside the wing, Glenn said, "I suppose I can talk to you as her business agent."

"Why, of course, Mr. Glenn." Eddie could hardly keep the excitement from his voice. "I knew it was only a matter of time before someone saw the star quality in her."

"Well, she's a long way from being a star," Glenn shrugged, "but she does have something promising. What I have is a play coming up that calls for a young woman with innocence who can sing. I'm doing it on a small budget," he warned.

"Oh, of course—but any play with you, Mr. Glenn, is a step upward in our profession. Would there be," he said, "a part for me as well?"

Glenn was an astute businessman. He recognized, at once, that he was being informed that Eddie Rich went with the territory. He smiled rather frostily and said, "We can find something for a man of your abilities, I'm sure. Not a starring role, of course—but you understand that."

Eddie Rich, as a matter of fact, did understand it. He knew that whatever magic transformed a human being into a star on the stage had not touched him. He would never be much more than he was right now. However, he was also a sharp critic of his profession. He was convinced that Priscilla could go to the very top, and his instincts led him directly to hitching his wagon to the star of the young woman. "Come along, Mr. Glenn. I must tell you that Priscilla is not your typical actress. She's new to the theater. She's fresh from the West, and that innocence and excitement you see in her is real."

They entered the dressing room, and Priscilla rose at once. She was still wearing her costume, a simple cranberry-colored dress with lace at the throat and at the cuffs. Her hair was done up in an old-fashioned way, and her eyes were enormous as she smiled rather tremulously at the great producer.

"This is Mr. Robert Glenn. Mr. Glenn may I present Miss Priscilla Winslow—my fiancée."

Glenn did not miss the startled look the young woman gave Eddie Rich. *That came as a surprise to her*, he thought sardonically, but that was none of his business. "I liked your performance a great deal. I'd like to see you in a play I'm doing. Would you come out and have dinner with me—you and your . . . fiancé."

The slight hesitation before the word caught Eddie's attention, but he said hurriedly, "Of course, we will. Won't we, Priscilla?"

"Oh yes . . . we will. If you'll just give me a moment to change. . . ."

★   ★   ★   ★

After the dinner with Robert Glenn, Eddie asked to accompany Priscilla back to her room to make more plans. For the first time she allowed him to come in. When they were inside, he took her in his arms, his eyes gleaming. "It's all set, sweetheart. We can't miss!" He kissed her then and held her tightly. He was pleased to feel her arms tighten around him, and knew that she was stirred tonight as she never had been. He drew her over to the sofa. He had bought a bottle of champagne and insisted that they celebrate their new adventure.

"You know I don't drink, Eddie."

"This won't hurt you a bit. Anyway, just one glass."

But one glass turned into two, two to three.

Priscilla's head, already swarming with plans, seemed to be spinning. She knew she should ask Eddie to leave. She was also aware that the wine had done something to her that she did not like. She was glad to hear him say, "It's all working out. We're going to be in the play together, and it'll be a hit. I promise you."

"Will it, Eddie?"

"Of course it will, and we'll be together." He put his arm around her, and for a long time sat there stroking her hair. His advances grew more bold, and when she protested he said, "But, sweetheart, we're going to be married. I love you."

"Do you really love me, Eddie? Honestly?"

"Why, of course, I love you! I've loved you from the first moment I saw you, Priscilla." He kissed her again, and she felt her resolve slipping away. As he kissed her she fought briefly a battle against what she knew was wrong, but he kept saying, "We're going to be married. Why, we're practically married already. I look on you as my wife!" Eddie's lips were warm and his arms were firm around her.

They were going to be married, and the future lay before them—and in that moment Priscilla surrendered herself as she never had to another man. . . .

PART THREE

ESTHER

★ ★ ★ ★

1903

CHAPTER THIRTEEN

SIMON IS UNHAPPY

★ ★ ★ ★

A frothy cloud of steam rose from the copper bathtub, frosting the windows into an opaque whiteness. Esther sank lower into the hot water, dreading to leave the warmth and comfort, for the room had no fireplace and was very cold. Outside, the winter wind of January whipped, nibbled, and clawed the casements like a beast trying to get in. Esther heard the low moaning sound and then abruptly forced herself to stand up. Almost wildly, she jumped out of the bathtub, shivering, making a trail of soapy water as she dashed across the room. Snatching up a thick, fluffy white towel she dried off quickly, her teeth chattering. Throwing on a heavy robe, she left the bathroom, dashed down the hall, then entered her bedroom, where a fire crackled cheerfully in the fireplace. Running over, she held her hands out, hugging her robe and letting the warmth of the fire soak in.

"I don't know," she muttered grimly, "why we can't have a fireplace in the bathroom—or have a bathroom in the bedroom." It was the kind of remark that Esther Winslow would make, for she had a practical, logical mind. Even as she marched across the room to her armoire, opened it, and began to pull out her clothing, her mind was busy with the problem. She loved bathing, and she loved cold weather—but not together.

Throwing her robe carelessly across the bed, she selected her undergarments, which consisted of a pair of white drawers with wide leg openings and a new garment for the upper body just coming into fashion. The French name for it was *soutien-gorge*, which she examined cautiously, then shrugged and slipped it over her head, thinking, *I'm glad we don't have to wear those awful corsets with metal stays. I always felt like I was dressed up in armor with those awful things!*

Esther felt fortunate to have escaped the styles of the Edwardian period which preceded her own. The clinging gowns, of that time, were worn over straight-fronted corsets that thrust the bosom forward and the posterior back, giving a fashionable—and rather ridiculous—"S" shape. Padding had been used above and below the waist, so that the waist appeared smaller. The corset had long metal stays in the front, fastening with hooks and eyes, while the stays were worn over a chemise that was tucked into drawers.

Quickly Esther slipped into her choice for the day, which was in the Gibson Girl style. Her outfit consisted of a blue-and-white striped bodice, high necked and pouched in front, and a skirt that came down to her ankles. She dressed quickly and efficiently, pulling on her stockings and a pair of brown leather boots with lacing at the side.

Moving to the mirror, she quickly arranged her hair, pinning it up in soft waves. She did not use the padding that many women used, for her hair was luxuriously thick. She fastened it in place with hair pins and an ivory comb, then applied just a slight amount of rice powder on her cheeks.

"There!" She grinned at herself. "You're beautiful enough, I suppose." Going back to the clothes press—a Regency mahogany with carved paneled doors—she picked a belted blue woolen coat that reached down to her half boots. Throwing it over her shoulders, she moved out of the room and descended the stairs. It was early morning, and the light coming through the windows that illuminated the stairways was as cold and hard as the inclement weather outside.

Moving down the halls, Esther heard the faint sound of music. Surprised, she turned and walked quickly toward her father's study. The door was open, and when she stepped inside, she saw him sitting on a chair listening to the new music box that he had purchased recently.

"What's that awful tune, Dad?" she asked, coming inside.

Mark Winslow looked up at her with a rash grin. His dark hair was ruffled, and he wore a soft gray shirt and a pair of charcoal trousers. He had the air of giving grace to whatever clothing he put on, and now he gestured cheerfully. "Why, I'm surprised at you, daughter! It's the latest thing. I don't know what I would have done without this new Edison phonograph."

In front of him on his desk was a square box with a large horn. Printed on the side was a small dog, his head cocked to one side, with one ear perked up as he listened intently. Underneath the logo the words *His Master's Voice* proclaimed the affair as one of Edison's new inventions. "Here, let me play it again," Mark said. He leaned forward and turned the crank several times, then threw the switch and sat back and listened.

Esther came forward, a smile twitching at her lips. Her father loved new inventions, and she knew that for a while this one would seize all of his attention. She had not heard the song before. Though the singer had such a tinny voice, her father informed her that the song was sweeping the country as a new ragtime favorite. The refrain was "Bill Bailey, won't you please come home?" It was some new music with a catchy syncopation.

"Doesn't that make you want to dance, Esther?"

"Not really. Do people really like that sort of thing?"

Mark shrugged his broad shoulders. "Some do, I suppose." They listened until it was over, then he put on another and said, "You'll probably like this better. I think it's the hit of the year. It's called 'In the Good Old Summertime.' "

Esther listened as the barbershop quartet sang the cheerful rendition of the song, then she sat down and the two listened to "Toyland" from Victor Herbert's musical *Babes In Toyland*. There was one sung by a soprano, "I'm Falling in Love With Someone," followed by "Ah! Sweet Mystery of Life."

Mark had a box full of the cylinders and obviously was set for the morning. "Sit down," he said, "we've got lots more, Esther."

"I don't have time to listen, Dad. I've got things to do. Do you think that Oldsmobile of yours will run today?"

Taken aback by her question, Mark glared at her. "Run! Why, of course it will run. You don't intend to drive it yourself, though?"

"I don't see why not. You do."

"But I'm a *man*. Men are supposed to do the driving."

Esther went across and plumped down on his lap. She grabbed a handful of his hair and pulled his head back. "That's what you think," she said pertly. "You just wait. Women are going to catch up with you men, and I'm going to be the one out in front leading the parade."

"Ow! You're pulling my hair!" Mark protested. Actually he liked it when Esther teased him this way. She had always been a demonstrative girl, at least with him, patting his cheeks, smoothing his hair, holding his hand.

Now, even though she was twenty-seven, he still enjoyed it. "Well, have it your own way," he shrugged. "When you hit a tree, don't come running for me!" She got up, and he turned to the newspaper on his desk. "You might be telling the truth about women. It seems like that's all that's in the newspaper these days. I see where Susan B. Anthony celebrated her birthday." He spoke of the Quaker abolitionist who had been leading a fight for the voting rights of women for nearly fifty years. He shook his head, saying, "The pioneers of the women's movement are getting on. Mrs. Stanton just last year was eighty-seven. I guess she's the one who really started the fight for women's rights." He spoke of Elizabeth Cady Stanton, for whom he had great admiration.

"Yes, those are both great ladies," Esther agreed. Her eyes gleamed and she said, "What do you think about Carrie Nation?"

"That woman's a menace!" Mark snapped. "There's an article in yesterday's paper. Where is it?" He rummaged through the papers on his desk and found it. "Look—last week in Topeka, Kansas, she made a march on a saloon. Threw her hatchet right through the door."

"Good for her!" Esther cried and clapped her hands together. "Let me see the article." She skimmed it quickly, saying, "Look, Dad, she marched right into that saloon and broke the bottles of whiskey and the beer kegs and the mirrors."

"Well, I'm against alcohol, but I'm not sure Miss Carrie has the right idea about how to fight it."

"Maybe not, but I admire people who have the courage to carry out what they believe in. You've always done that yourself, if I remember. If the tales Mother tells are true, you were quite a saloon buster-upper yourself in your younger days."

Mark shifted uncomfortably in his chair and ran his hand through his dark hair. Finally he mumbled, "Your mother ought not to be telling you those stories."

Esther came and threw her arms around him. "I've got to go," she said. Planting a kiss on his cheek, she whispered, "You are the handsomest thing I ever saw! No wonder Mama fell in love with you."

She turned and left the room, and Mark stared after her, shaking his head. "That's some girl I've got there," he muttered to himself, grinning ruefully. "The man who gets her is going to have to go some to keep up with her."

Leonard Bales, the handyman, who had been the chauffeur and jack-of-all-trades for Mark and Lola for years, looked up as Esther entered the garage. "Well now, Miss Esther. You need me to take you somewhere?"

"No, Leonard, I'm going to drive this infernal machine myself," Esther smiled.

"Why, you can't do that!" Bales replied, shocked by the audacity of her suggestion. "Just because you've had a few lessons doesn't mean you're ready to go off and drive it around. What would your father say if you went and ran it into a tree?"

"Just get this thing going, and I'll show you what I can do."

Ten minutes later, despite serious protests on the part of the shocked handyman, Esther put on a pair of large goggles and left the driveway and headed for New York. She was bundled up and wore a straw hat tied firmly down with a green ribbon under her chin. The wind cut against her face, but she was accustomed to the out-of-doors, having ridden her horse most every day, even during the cold weather, when she was home. She made the trip as the wind pushed the chugging machine from one side of the dirt road to the other. A sense of exultation filled her, and she laughed aloud, crying out as she might to her horse, "Come on, you ornery thing! Is this the fastest you can go?"

She had read only the day before that the members of the Automobile Club of America had been arrested in New Jersey for breaking the speed limit, which was eight miles an hour. Witnesses had sworn that the enthusiasts had reached speeds up to thirty miles an hour, and the Morristown Justice of the Peace had presented them with a lump fine of ten dollars. One of the cars had been an Oldsmobile, an exact double of the one she was driving.

When she reached the downtown section of New York, she slowed down to a sedate five miles an hour. Even then as she drove by, horses reared and pawed at the air, uttering shrill cries of fright. Some of those who drove the buggies and carriages cried out insulting remarks, but Esther simply waved her gloved hand at them and smiled benignly.

She parked at the front of the *New York Journal* and wondered briefly if she would ever get the car started again. Going inside, she spoke cheerfully to the young boy who had developed a tremendous crush on her, and made her way to the office of William Randolph Hearst.

"Hello, George," she greeted the secretary. "Is the boss in?"

George Sutter, a sour-faced man of fifty, grunted. "Yes, he's in. Sit down. You'll have to wait your turn."

Esther did not wait long and soon found herself speaking with the publisher. Hearst, as usual, was sitting behind his large desk cluttered with papers, books, charts, and all the other paraphernalia of his trade. His long face brightened as he said, "Well, I've been expecting you. The pictures on the Carrigan spread were fine, Esther. I've got them here somewhere." He dug through the mass of paper work, came up with an envelope, and soon the two were looking at a series of photographs that Esther had snapped of a society party that had degenerated into a brawl of sorts.

Hearst's eyes gleamed, and he laughed aloud. "They're suing us, of course—but we sold ten thousand extra papers with this story. A little bonus for you." He tossed the photographs down, and then cocked his head to one side. "What have you got on your mind now?" Without waiting for an answer he said, "I'd like for you to do a series on these animal dances."

Esther stared at him with bewilderment. "Animal dances? What do you mean by that?"

"You don't know about that? Why, it's the latest thing. Right out of the jungle, I call it. In the hot spots the young people are acting like bunnies hugging, horses trotting, chickens scratching, and kangaroos dipping." He laughed aloud, exposing long teeth, and his eyes glinted. "They call them the Bunny Hug, the Horse

Trot, the Camel Walk, the Buzzard Lope, the Chicken Scratch, and the Kangaroo Dip. You've never seen it?"

"No, and I don't think I want to."

"I took it in the other night. To Chicken Scratch you scuff your toes back toward the floor, to Buzzard Lope you dive with your arms extended like you were going down on a dead cow." With a humor that few people ever saw, Hearst went on to describe the dance crazes that had swept the country. "Some religious groups are pressuring towns to prevent all animal mimicry, and I don't know but what they'd be right this time. Well," he said, "never mind that. Let's get to work."

"Mr. Hearst, I want to push this thing about the slums. I think there's a good story in it, and with the pictures I can get, we can shake up the people who own those awful tenement houses."

Hearst leaned back, locked his fingers behind his head, and stared up at the ceiling. The room got silent for a while with only the muted echoes of voices from outside floating in. Finally he leaned forward and smacked the desk with his palm. "I think you may have something there. Get on it, Esther, and get lots of pictures of kids—suffering kids." He thought for a moment, then rubbed his cheeks with both hands in a habitual gesture. "If you could get some dying, that would be even better."

Over the weeks since Esther had been working for the *Journal*, she had rapidly lost most of her respect for William Randolph Hearst. The man would, she understood, go to any lengths and do *anything* to sell an extra newspaper. The sufferings of the Scarlottas would mean nothing at all to Hearst. He would simply use them to his advantage—as he used the Spanish-American War, and any other event that would sell papers. Standing to her feet, she said briefly, "Can I get Templeton to work with me on the text?"

"Yes, Templeton's good, but the pictures will make it go." Hearst nodded, his eyes alert and greedy. "Get lots of pictures. Make 'em look sad."

"I don't have to work at that," Esther replied rather shortly. "They're sad enough as it is." She turned and left the office, and as she made her way back to the Oldsmobile, she thought, *He doesn't care about anything in this world except making another dollar! I wonder why a man who has more dollars than he can spend wants to stack more of them somewhere in a cold vault?* It was more than she could understand. Thoughts flitted through her mind of how she would like to get her hands on Hearst's money and do something about the disease-ridden, filthy tenements on the Lower East Side of New York.

★ ★ ★ ★

When Simon Barfield pulled out of the circular driveway in front of Mark Winslow's home, he struck the horse pulling his buggy viciously across the hind quarters, then repeated the blow on the other matched bay. Both horses reared, squealed, then broke into a wild run. The carriage careened down the rutted dirt road, tossing Barfield roughly from one side to the other on the seat. He struck the horses again, taking a vicious pleasure in their cries. Somehow deep in him lay an innate cruelty that would surface from time to time. His outward manners were only a thin veneer of culture, but those who knew him best had seen this heartless side of him often enough to stay out of his way when he was stirred to anger. The horses, however, could not avoid Barfield, and within ten minutes, despite the cold, a white froth had appeared on them after a wild dead run.

Finally, Barfield allowed them to slow to a walk, and he managed to calm himself. Overhead the sky was slate gray, and he saw a red-tailed hawk plummet into a patch of stubble on a slight rise to his left. After a brief struggle, the hawk raised its head, with victorious eyes sweeping the terrain. Barfield's mouth turned upward with a smug smile of satisfaction. He saw a metaphor for his own life in the scene, for he, like the predator, took his prey swiftly, viciously, and without remorse. "Good job!" he said to the hawk that glared at him with an imperial stare, then lowered its head and began to tear at the warm carcass of the brown rabbit clutched in its talons.

Paying a visit was a rare thing for Simon Barfield. Usually, those he wanted to see were summoned to his office or to the lavish apartment he kept in New York. He had been unable, however, to find Esther for several days, and finally had left to drive to her home. When Mark Winslow had not been at the house either, Lola had informed him that Esther had gone to the city. "I think," she had said, "she's gone to see that family she's made pictures of—the Scarlottas."

Barfield had been courteous enough to Lola, but when the buggy was finally inside the environs of New York he felt a discontent. It drew his eyes together and down in a hard gaze, and finally when he reached the street where the Scarlottas lived, he pulled up to a hitching post. Leaping out of the buggy, he tied the team, ignoring their wild eyes as he jerked them around harshly. He had never been to the Scarlottas, but Esther had described the street, and he had no trouble finding the apartment. His nose wrinkled in disdain at the smell as he entered the door, and a poorly dressed woman coming down the stairs stopped and stared at him.

"Where do the Scarlottas live?" he demanded.

"Second floor, third door," the woman said, drawing back to allow the big man to pass. Her eyes followed him as he took the stairs, and she shrugged and continued on her way.

Simon knocked at the third door down the dimly lit hallway and waited impatiently until it opened.

"Yes, can I help you?"

"I'm looking for Miss Esther Winslow." Barfield stared at the man who did not look as though his name were Scarlotta. He was a big man with hazel eyes and a mop of tawny hair. His clothes were neat, but obviously those of a working man. "Is this where the Scarlottas live?" Barfield snapped.

"Yes, it is. Miss Winslow's down the hall. Shall I get her?"

"Just take me there," Barfield said.

Kruger looked back into the room and said quietly, "Emila, you and Michael stay here. I'll be right back."

"All right, Uncle Jan." The girl who spoke seemed no more than six or seven. She had enormous brown eyes and stared with curiosity at the visitor. "What's your name?" she asked.

"Don't ask people their names," Jan said, a smile touching his lips. "I'll be right back." Stepping outside he nodded. "It's this way. She's visiting a sick woman. Taking some pictures."

Barfield did not respond but followed the big blond man down the hall. The smell of cabbage, unwashed bodies, and other odors filled his nose. Trying his best to ignore them, he stopped before the door and waited until the other man had knocked. When it opened, Kruger said, "A visitor for you, Esther."

Esther had been sitting beside the bed of a young woman of no more than twenty. The woman had a flushed face, and her black hair was pasted to her forehead with sweat.

Kruger moved over and said, "I'll stay with Sophia."

The woman on the bed brightened up. "Dr. Jan," she said. She held up her hand, and the big man took it as he sat down beside her. Her eyes were bright with fever, and she held to his hand with both of hers. "You come-a see me."

Esther gathered her coat and stepped outside the door, staring at Simon Barfield with surprise. "I didn't expect to see you here, Simon. How did you find me?"

"I drove all the way out to your home." Barfield was irritated by the scene. "Can we go somewhere and talk?"

Esther looked around helplessly for a moment. "There's a little cafe down the street—not what you're used to—but we can get a table and perhaps something hot to drink. Come along."

The two made their way down the hall, descended the stairs, then exited upon the street. They made a strange contrast in their thick, expensive clothing, for those they passed were muffled with garments that had seen their best days. She led him to a small cafe and nodded to a table over at the back. "We can sit there," she said. Leading the way, she moved across the room and sat down. Barfield followed.

The proprietor came over at once—a very fat man, wearing a striped shirt with garters on his biceps. He had thick black hair pasted down, parted down the middle with two small curls on his forehead. "Ah, Miss Winslow," he said, beaming, "what can I get you?"

"Bring us some of that good minestrone soup, Luigi, and some coffee."

"Very good. Coming right up!"

As soon as the owner left, Esther leaned back and studied the man who sat across from her. She had learned to read him rather well, and she knew that he was irritated with her. "I'm sorry that you went all the way to the house. I wish you had gone by the paper first. I was there earlier."

"I can't keep up with you," Barfield said. He was still angry over his useless trip but covered it over smoothly. He could be charming enough when he chose, and now he smiled and cocked one eyebrow. "You're a busy young woman. Do you ever slow down, Esther?"

"There'll be plenty of time for that when I'm too old to do anything else."

"That won't be for a long time."

Esther touched her cheek, pressed the flesh in, then shook her head slightly. "It's sooner than we think. Forty years will be gone before you know it, Simon."

"Why, we can't think that far ahead." Barfield could not accustom himself to the shifts of this young woman's mind. Perhaps that was the fascination she held for him. Other women were more beautiful; many of them had been from wealthier families, but there was something about Esther Winslow that attracted Simon Barfield in a way that no other woman had. He sat there listening quietly as she spoke of the work she had been doing, letting himself relax.

Finally the soup and coffee came, and, after tasting it, Barfield lifted his heavy eyebrow with surprise. "Why, this is rather tasty," he said.

"You didn't expect it?"

"Well—not in a place like this." He tasted the soup again and said, "I could get this man a job at the Waldorf-Astoria."

"I don't think Luigi would like it," Esther smiled. "He worked for a big restaurant in Rome. He came to America so he could be his own boss." She looked around the small restaurant, plain without any adornments other than some pictures of Luigi's family on the wall and some silk flowers along the front window, and shook her head. "This is all Luigi wants, I think."

"A man should have more ambition than that."

Barfield's remark caught at Esther, and she sipped the coffee thoughtfully. "You have lots of that, Simon."

The remark seemed somehow critical, and Barfield lifted his eyes. "What's wrong with ambition?"

"MacBeth found it to be rather deadly," Esther remarked. She traced a scratch on the table in front of her with one forefinger, then said seriously, "Simon, I may need your help."

"Of course, what is it, dear? Anything."

"I've spent a lot of time in these tenement districts in the last few weeks," Esther said slowly. She gathered her thoughts, and a seriousness came to her eyes. "It's wrong for people to have to live as these people do."

"There'll always be poor people. Nothing you can do about that."

"Maybe not, but some of the things are so unnecessary." Esther gestured quickly, impetuously, with her hands sweeping across the front of the cafe toward the street. "These old buildings are rotten and falling down—and the owners never do any repairs. If a pipe bursts and goes bad, some of the tenants have to fix it half the time. Why, Jan had to clear the chimney out because the owner wouldn't do it."

"Who is this fellow, Jan?"

"You remember, if you read the story. He came from South Africa."

"The woman called him 'doctor.' What's his full name?"

"Jan Kruger. He was a doctor."

"Then, why isn't he doctoring here? He looks like a working man."

"He's not qualified. It's against the law. I've tried to get him to go back to school, but it's expensive. But he does all kinds of good things for the poor people in this district."

"But that's against the law, isn't it?"

"Not what he does. He never operates on anybody or anything like that," Esther said. "He's gotten to be good friends with Dr. David Burns at Baxter Hospital. Any sort of serious case, he gets Dr. Burns to take care of it."

"Doesn't he have a job?"

"He's had two since I've known him, but you just don't know how bad things are, Simon." Esther's brow furrowed and she shook her head. "I didn't know, myself. You have to live with these people, be around them before you know how bad it is. The men get up in the morning and go down to the docks, and they stand and wait, not knowing whether they'll get work or not. Sometimes they come home and haven't made a penny. And they live from hand to mouth." She went on describing some of the hardships of the people in the district, and finally she said passionately, "I'm going to do something about it, Simon."

Barfield blinked with astonishment. "What are you going to do?"

"I'm going to find out who owns these buildings, and I'm going to plaster their pictures all over the front page of the *Journal*.

They're responsible for what goes on. They gouge the Scarlottas for every penny they can get for that awful apartment, and then they don't do anything to keep it up. And if families miss one payment," she said bitterly, "they throw them out on the street."

Barfield stared at Esther for a moment, his eyes growing cold. "Esther, you're making a terrible mistake. You don't need to throw your life away down here."

"You're wrong about that," Esther said. "I was throwing my life away trying on new clothes and going from one boring party to another."

"You can't change the way things are."

"I can try," Esther said, and her mouth drew into a firm line.

She made an attractive picture as she sat there. She had a Latin look about her from her mother, and now the smoothness of her cheek and the curve of her full lips attracted Barfield, despite his dissatisfaction with her position. For some time he argued with her, but he had learned that Esther Winslow was not easily talked out of things once she had set her mind to them. Finally their discussion grew into a quarrel. He forced himself to say calmly, "We'll talk about this later. Are we going to the Rochesters' party tomorrow night?"

"Oh, I forgot all about it," Esther said, covering her mouth, her eyes flying open with surprise. "Simon, I'm sorry. I promised Jan I'd go to another neighborhood. He's going to help some of the people there. There's some sort of sickness going around. I wanted to get pictures of it for Mr. Hearst."

Simon Barfield made himself say graciously, "Well, I suppose it's important to you. It's, as you say, only a party."

Esther leaned forward and put her hand over his. "Thank you, Simon. I knew you would understand."

They left the cafe soon, and he walked her back to the apartment. Stopping at the door, he removed his hat. "I'll leave you here. When can I see you?"

"Wednesday," she said, "we'll have a night, just you and me." She reached out and patted his arm, then turned and went into the building.

Barfield did not say a word. Going back to the buggy, he stepped inside and drove to his office building. Going inside, he barked at once to the clerk, who looked up with a startled expression. "Get Hunt in here!" Stepping inside the inner office, he slammed the door and marched over to his desk. He opened a box of cigars, bit the end off one, then lit it. He watched the smoke rise slowly, and after a short knock the door opened. Myron Hunt was not an impressive sort of man—short, thin, his blond hair thinning, and a pair of innocuous green eyes were his chief characteristics. He wore a nondescript suit and could have faded into any crowd. "You want to see me, Mr. Barfield?"

"Yes, sit down." Barfield waited until Hunt sat down, then began to describe Jan Kruger. Then he said, "My fiancée wants to do a series of pictures on tenement owners on the Lower East Side. She's decided to expose them."

Hunt had an expressionless face, but a gleam of humor suddenly touched his faded blue eyes. "That comes pretty close to home, doesn't it, Mr. Barfield?"

"She doesn't know I own some of those tenements down there—and I don't intend for her to find out."

"I don't think she will," Hunt shrugged. "We've hidden most of your ownership in the Acme Corporation. We've covered your tracks pretty well, sir."

"Yes, I know. I'm not worried about that." Leaning back, Barfield puffed on his cigar and thought for a moment. "This man Kruger—put somebody on him, Hunt."

"All right. What do you want to do about him?"

"I don't know. Have somebody check on what he's doing. I think it's illegal. He's pretending to be a doctor, and there's probably a law against that. Talk to the lawyers and find out about it."

"Yes, sir. I'll do that."

"That's all. Get out."

When Hunt left the room, Barfield rose from his desk and went to stand by the window. Looking out, he studied the street below, but his mind drifted elsewhere. He was thinking of the warm way that Esther had spoken of Jan Kruger. It infuriated him. He looked with displeasure at the cigar, opened the window, and tossed it out.

"I'll have to know more about that fellow," he grunted, then turned and sat down at his desk and began to go through the stack of papers.

CHAPTER FOURTEEN

THE BIG CHANCE

★ ★ ★ ★

As Priscilla woke with a start, she realized that she had been having a nightmare. It was not one of those bad dreams filled with monsters, or the agonizing danger of falling off a high building— this kind of bad dream she seldom had. Lying in the bed under the covers, she opened her eyes—glad to come out of the land of the bad dream—and immediately heard the sound of whistling. Most of her life, Priscilla had slept alone—in her own room back in Wyoming—and then in her small room in New York, except for the brief time she shared a room with Ruth at Baxter. Until the days had become boring at the hospital, almost always Priscilla awoke cheerfully, ready for whatever the day might bring. Now, however, a grim depression seized on her as she realized that things had changed. For a time she closed her eyes and tried to escape back into the realm of sleep, but it would not come. She knew that it was because of the shame that tore at her heart.

"You gonna sleep all day, sweetheart?"

Pulling the covers close, Priscilla looked up to see Eddie, who was standing over her. He was half-dressed, wearing a pair of gray trousers and his shoes, but he had no shirt on as he looked down at her cheerfully. "It's ten o'clock. We've got to get down to rehearsal."

"All right, Eddie. I'm getting up." Priscilla turned her head away and threw the covers back. She was aware of Eddie's eyes on her as she slipped out of bed, and somehow this displeased her. She slipped into a robe and sat down before the mirror and began brushing her hair with quick, flurried strokes. She hesitated when she felt his hands on her shoulders. He had come to stand behind her, then bent over and put his arms around her, drawing her close. He kissed her cheek and whispered huskily, "Sweetheart, you're some kind of woman."

"Eddie, I've got to get ready!" Priscilla protested.

Eddie Rich laughed, kissed her again, hugging her in a possessive manner, then straightened up. "All right, I'll just have a quick shave."

As soon as the door to her room closed, and Eddie's footsteps sounded on the hall heading toward the bathroom, Priscilla stopped brushing her hair. Leaning forward on the dressing table, she stared into the small mirror, searching for signs of the shame and disillusionment that she felt must surely be visible. The only sign she saw, however, was the lines around her mouth, for her lips were drawn down into a frown. As she stared at the reflection that seemed like a different person, Priscilla asked her own heart, *I wonder if anyone can tell how I feel about what I've been doing?*

She sat there hoping, waiting for an answer that didn't come. Ever since Eddie had moved in, more or less, with her, she had kept away from Esther and Ruth. He did not stay all the time, for he had his own room; but whether he was there or not, her relationship with him was a keen knife that constantly seemed to be in her spirit. She managed to cover this up during those times when she was with others, but when she was alone there was no denying the shame that rose like a thickness in her throat and almost choked her at times.

As she slowly brushed her hair again, she tried to think back to how she had come to this. Somehow she felt sure she loved him, and that he loved her. She had fought off his advances at first, until finally she had given up when he had spoken of marriage. Since that time, however, although she had waited eagerly, Eddie had not said a word about getting married. She, herself, had mentioned it timidly once, and he had waved it away with an airy hand, saying something noncommittal—to the effect that when the time was right they would take care of that.

She sat there for some time, and was about to rise, when a knock at the door suddenly made her jump. Quickly she arose and went to the door. She had very few visitors and could not imagine who it was. Opening the door, she stood stock-still for a moment, for her cousin Ruth was standing there, a smile on her face.

"I'm sorry to come by so early, but I did want to see you, Priscilla," Ruth said. She was wearing a green wool coat and a dark fur cap over her red curls. She looked alert and her eyes beamed as she smiled. "I've missed you so much, so I thought I'd drop by, and we could make a date to have dinner some night."

Priscilla's mind went completely blank. She was totally aware of Eddie down the hall, and in a tone almost panicky she said, "Why . . . of course, Ruth. How about tomorrow? We could have lunch."

"Why, that would be fine." Ruth hesitated, expecting to be asked in. She saw that Priscilla was flustered. "Well," she said, "how about at Williams Restaurant? We've gotten some good meals there."

"Fine—that'll be fine, Ruth. I'll meet you there at noon." She would have said more, but suddenly to her horror she heard the door slam and then footsteps coming. "Well, I'll see you then," she said.

Ruth heard the footsteps also. She turned to see a man coming down the hall and recognized him at once. Her face paled, for he was wearing only a pair of trousers and the top part of long-handled underwear. He was carrying a shaving kit in his hand, and when he approached, she had no idea of what to say to him. Glancing back at Priscilla, she saw the girl's face had gone a deathly white. The truth of it all came to her then. Ignoring Eddie, whom she had met once when she had visited at the theater, she said hastily, "Well, I'll see you tomorrow, then. Goodbye, Priscilla."

Turning quickly, Ruth left the rooming house with a sickness in her throat. There was no doubt about the intimacy of the situation. She had feared for Priscilla, and now she knew the worst. Blindly she left the building and walked down the street, ignoring the cold wind that nipped at her nose and numbed her ears. "Poor

Priscilla!" she murmured sadly. "What will her parents think? It will almost kill them."

Back inside the room, Eddie knew at once that there was trouble. He picked up his shirt, put it on, and began buttoning it, wondering whether to say anything. Priscilla had not said a word but had gone to stand in the middle of the room, staring blankly at a picture that hung on one wall. Finally he came over and stood behind her. Putting his arms on her shoulders, he said, "Aw, look, babe, I'm sorry about this."

"Eddie, don't talk to me. I want to be alone."

Eddie recognized the terse quality of Priscilla's voice and hesitated. He had always been able to sweet-talk his way out of almost any situation with a woman, but this one was different. He knew that she was unhappy with their arrangement, that she was burdened with guilt. This was strange to him, for he had stopped having any guilty feelings over his escapades when he was eighteen years old. *Well, she's different*, he thought to himself. *She's led a sheltered life. I'll just have to be easy with her*. Removing his hands, he slipped into his coat and put on his hat. "I'll see you at rehearsal," he said. He hesitated one moment, then turned to look at her. She had not turned but stood as if frozen to the spot. "We'll talk about it, all right?" When she did not move or speak, he shrugged and left the room.

When the door closed, it seemed to break some sort of spell that held Priscilla. The sight of Ruth's face had told her all she needed to know. "She knows all about me," she said out loud. Moving over to the bed she sat down, folded her hands in her lap, and thought about her life. "I've made a bad mistake," she said once again aloud. The sound of her own voice seemed to echo in the small room, and she turned at once and buried her face in the tumbled bedclothes. Her shoulders began to shake, and soon she was sobbing her heart out, as she had not done since she was a very small child.

★ ★ ★ ★

Eddie Rich was not a sentimentalist. There was not really one romantic or idealistic attitude in his entire body. He had grown up in an orphanage and there learned the harsh facts of life—that a boy or a man has to take care of himself any way he can. Undersized and not particularly strong, he had been bullied by the larger boys in the orphanage, often carrying bruises on his light skin. All this had stopped one day when something had seemed to snap inside him. When Rafe Maddox had struck him in the face and taken away the small coin that Eddie had possessed, something took place in the boy's heart and mind and spirit. They had been in the barn, and when Rafe had assaulted him, Eddie bit back the tears. But when Rafe had laughed at him, something different happened that had never happened before. Like a red tide, anger began to boil somewhere deep inside. It had swelled through him until all restraint seemed to dissolve, and all he could see was Rafe's crude red laughing face. Without being conscious of it, he had reached down, picked up a two-by-four and raised it over his head. He had one quick glimpse of the horror in Rafe's face as the boy saw that he was not going to stop. The next sound he heard was the dead *clunk* as the two-by-four struck Rafe on the head. The boy dropped as if shot through the heart. Eddie had never forgotten staring down at him, the blood pouring from his head, matting the boy's hair and running over his ear.

And Eddie felt nothing at all except exultation. Reaching down, he picked up the coin and stuck it in his pocket. Then he drew up a bucket and sat, holding the bloody board in his hand. When Rafe had awakened and come to his senses, Eddie looked down at him with a cold, triumphant sneer on his face. Eddie had said, "You open your mouth about this, and the next time you won't wake up at all, Rafe."

From that moment on Eddie Rich had learned that a man has to take what he can get any way he can get it. He had experimented with crime on the Lower East Side of New York. At one time he had joined a gang and had somehow miraculously escaped being apprehended by the law. The same Rafe that he had learned his philosophy from was one of the gang. Eddie saw him caught and sent to prison when he was seventeen years old. He knew of the horrors of Sing Sing and determined that there were better ways to make a living than rotting away in a prison cell.

He had fallen into acting almost by accident. He did have a good singing voice and was a good dancer. One of his girlfriends had been an actress. She had gotten him a two-bit job in one of the plays, but he had worked hard at it, for he realized that fame and even fortune could lie at the end for those who were smart. He had learned his profession—but he had also learned that he would never be at the top, for he did not have that quality that makes a star.

Six days had passed since Eddie had been seen by Ruth, and since that time his life had been miserable. *Nothing* worked with Priscilla. She kept her distance and would say only, "I can't, Eddie—I just can't!" He had thought at first that this was merely a phase, but he knew that there was more to it than he had suspected. "She's got a religious streak," Rich muttered as he entered the theater for the evening's performance. "Her old man and her old lady must be Puritans. She's scared to death that they'll find out about us." A grim expression settled on his face as he passed into the lobby. To his surprise he had whatever affection lay in him focused on Priscilla Winslow. She was different from other women he had known. She didn't complain or badger him for gifts or favors. There was a sweetness and a goodness that even Eddie could treasure—though he had despoiled it. His mind was filled with ways he might regain her affection when he heard his name called.

"Eddie! Eddie Rich!"

Looking up, Rich saw the manager of the theater standing beside another man. Eddie took a quick breath, for the other man was Marvin Watts. He went over at once, wiping his face clean of the lines that were there, and smiled pleasantly. "Yes, Harry."

Harry Smith, the manager, said, "This is Mr. Marvin Watts, Eddie. I'm sure you know him."

"Everybody knows Mr. Watts," Eddie said. He took the hand the tall producer held out to him and shook it firmly. "I'm glad to know you, Mr. Watts."

Marvin Watts was a tall, thin man with a pair of keen green eyes and a shock of salt-and-pepper hair. He wore a tuxedo and held an overcoat on his arm. His lips were thin, and there was a calculating light in his eyes, but he said pleasantly enough, "I've come by to talk to you, Eddie. Do you have a minute?"

"For you? Always, Mr. Watts." Eddie's heart began to thump as he led the producer into a room, which the manager offered.

When they were inside, Watts laid his coat down and sat in

one of the chairs. "Sit down, Eddie. Let's talk."

Eddie sat down and tried to control the nervousness that came to him. Marvin Watts was the premiere producer on the Great White Way. Along with two or three other men, he was responsible for most of the big hits that made stars out of nobodies, and fortunes for the producers. Eddie's mouth was cotton dry, but he tried to preserve the illusion of coolness. "I've enjoyed all of your productions, Mr. Watts," he said casually. "You're between shows right now, I understand."

"You keep up with the theater, I see."

"Well, of course. It's my profession."

"You're right, Eddie," Watts said. He pulled a cigar from a silver case, offered one to Eddie, and then lit it for the actor. As the blue smoke curled upward, he said casually, "I've got a new property. I think it's going to be a winner. A musical."

Eddie could not control his anxiety. "Do you think I might have some chance at a part, Mr. Watts?"

"Well, Eddie, let's be honest. I'm really interested in Miss Winslow. I understand you're her manager."

A black depression swept through Eddie momentarily, but he did not let it show. "That's true. She's going up right away. Somebody's going to find her, and of course I'd like for it to be you, sir." He put away his own hopes then, for he knew that he would never have the talent necessary to qualify for one of Marvin Watts' shows. However, he was a man who knew how to survive, and he talked eagerly of Priscilla's talent.

Watts listened carefully, then said, "I'd like to sign her up. Why don't you drop by my office with her tomorrow, and we can talk terms. We might even sign a contract."

"Why, of course. You name the time, Mr. Watts." Eddie quickly settled on the time, and when Watts left, he suppressed a desire to leap up in the air and clap his hands for joy.

Then suddenly he stopped. He was painfully aware that his relationship with Priscilla was not exactly the best. He was not really her manager, although he knew that she relied on his judgment. His eyelids fell over his eyes, hooding them for a moment, and his lips drew into a tight line. *Gotta handle this carefully*, he thought. *It's my big chance, but without her I'll never be anything more than what I am now.*

He left the office and went to rehearsal. All during the time that they were on the stage, he said nothing at all to Priscilla. Finally, when it was over and the cast was leaving, he said quickly, "Priscilla, I've gotta talk to you." When she looked at him and shook her head, he said quickly, holding up his hands, "No funny stuff. I just want to talk. We can go anywhere you say." He put anxiety in his voice and said, "This is killing me. I can't stand it!"

Priscilla looked up with surprise. She had not seen him so disturbed before. Finally she shrugged and said almost in a whisper, "All right, Eddie, but . . . it's just talk, you understand?"

"Sure. Of course." Eddie quickly turned, took her arm, and led her outside. "Let's splurge," he said. "Let's go to the Astor House." He took her to lunch at the restaurant, and during the meal he said nothing personal. He talked about the play, about the theater, and finally when they were having coffee, he ran his hand over the snow-white tablecloth and touched one of the heavy silver knives that rested there. "This is fine, isn't it? Nothing like a great restaurant to make you feel good."

"Eddie, what do you want to talk about?" Priscilla's voice was weary, and there were circles under her eyes. She had not slept well for days, and now she had come to the point where she knew she had to say goodbye to Eddie Rich. It had been a difficult decision for her, and she knew she would have to live with the scars that he was responsible for on her soul. Now as she looked across at him she saw, with some surprise, that there was a different expression on his face. He looked somehow penitent, and he spoke quietly without the usual brash self-assurance. She wondered what he could add to what he had already said.

"Priscilla, I've been a fool. I never should have wronged you," Eddie said slowly. "I've had a bad life. You know a little bit about it. I never had a chance to learn good things like you did. . . ." He went on talking about his life, speaking soberly and looking down, not meeting her eyes. He was an actor, this Eddie Rich, and now he was playing the penitent lover. He played it to the hilt. Finally he looked up, and his heart leaped when he saw tears in her blue-green eyes. Reaching over, he took her hand and said as awkwardly as he could manage, "I'm . . . sorry for everything that's happened."

"That's . . . that's sweet of you, Eddie."

"I wish we could start all over again," he said quickly. He squeezed her hand and leaned forward. "And we can. Let's wipe out everything that's happened." He hesitated and knew that what he would say next would control his entire life. He whispered, "Let's get married, Priscilla. I love you more than any man ever loved any woman."

Priscilla had expected anything but this. She knew that he was a womanizer, but his story of his hard youth had touched her heart. *He can change*, she thought quickly, and all the affection she had felt for him came rushing back. "Do you mean it, Eddie?" she asked.

"Of course I mean it! I should have done it a long time ago. I just wasn't sure I could take care of you. A man wants to take care of his wife, and well—you know how it is in the acting business— feast or famine. I can't give you a lot of things, and you're going up in the world," he said honestly. He shook his head and said, "You'll be far above me in six months."

Of all the things he could've said, this appealed to Priscilla the most. She did not care about things like that, and now she dashed the tears from her eyes and said, "That doesn't matter. As long as you love me, that's all that matters."

"I do love you, and I always will. Will you marry me?"

Taking a deep breath, Priscilla nodded and said slowly, "Yes, I'll marry you, Eddie."

★　★　★　★

Peter Winslow was staring at the interior of the machine that he hoped would win a race for him. He had built it practically out of parts others had thrown away, and now the fledgling automobile looked not so much like a car as like a buggy made out of spare parts not related to one another. Peter had grease on his hands, and when he scratched his forehead he left a mark. He turned quickly and saw his father come striding across the lot toward the barn. "Hey, Dad," he said, "you want to give me a hand with this infernal machine?"

Dan Winslow stopped, looked at his tall son, and grinned suddenly. "I think I'll stick to horses, Peter."

Peter looked down at the automobile that he had worked on

so hard. "I sure wish I knew more about these things. Nobody around here knows any more than I do, and all any of us knows is one end of a cow from the other."

"Well, you can get a nice beef steak from a cow. You can't do that with that crazy contraption."

"Aw, come on, Dad. You can't ride a cow thirty miles an hour, either, can you?"

"You're not telling me that thing will do that? I've never even heard it run over two minutes!"

Peter grimaced and made a swipe at his forehead, leaving another mark. He stared down at his greasy hands and the scrapes that he had suffered putting the machine together and said, "Well, it'll go someday. This one or another one." He suddenly noticed the worried look on his father's face. "What's wrong, Dad?"

"We just got a letter from Priscilla." Dan Winslow hesitated and shook his head. "She's getting married."

Shock ran along Peter Winslow's nerves. He had known that Priscilla had gone into acting, and this had been a shock to all of them. "Who's she marrying?" he asked apprehensively. "Not one of those actors, I hope."

Dan Winslow's lips turned downward. "Yes, I'm afraid it is. It's bad news, son."

Peter laid the wrench down that he held in one hand and said, "Well, maybe he's all right. Not all actors are bad, are they?"

"I'm sure they're not, but this isn't the time for Priscilla to pick a husband, I'm afraid. She's too inexperienced in these things."

Peter knew his father pretty well. They were close, these two. Now his father's obvious grief touched Peter. "How's Mom taking it?"

"About like you'd expect," Dan said grimly. "She's dead set against it, of course."

"I don't suppose there's any way you can stop Priscilla."

"She's twenty-three years old, Peter. I'm surprised she hasn't married before this. She just didn't want to get stuck out on a ranch. Well, she won't be here now."

Dan turned abruptly and walked away without saying another word. By this, Peter knew exactly how disturbed his father was. He suddenly looked at the wrench in his hand and with a grunt threw it as far as he could heave it. It wheeled through the air, catching glints from the sun, and he watched as it struck, raising a small puff of dust. "Why did I do a fool thing like that?" Peter spoke aloud.

He marched over, knowing he had to have the wrench, and his mind worked on the thing that was before him. He had a logical sort of mind at times, especially in his fascination with machinery. The automobile was a fledgling invention, but the first time Peter Winslow had seen one, he knew he had to be involved. He knew nothing about them, but by pestering the local blacksmith, who was as much an authority on engines as anyone in that part of the state, he had put together the car that now sat in the middle of the lot. He moved around the automobile, looking at it critically, but his mind was on his sister, Priscilla. The two had been very close. Isolated as they were from town, they had played games together as children, and since he was only one year older than Priscilla, they had been close companions.

"She'll never run. You better get a horse." Peter turned around to see Jason Ballard, who stood there grinning at him. The tall cowboy always managed to look relaxed no matter what he was doing. His red hair caught the sun, and his blue eyes crinkled as he added, "I don't know why you fool with that thing."

"I don't know why you fool with bad horses. Gonna get yourself busted up one of these days, Jase."

"Never was a horse couldn't be rode."

"Well, that ain't so. I know two or three myself ain't never been rode," Peter remarked. He'd studied the tall cowboy with admiration. He knew of no man that was better with a horse or with a rope, nor one who knew more about the West than Jason Ballard. The two had become best friends, and now he thought suddenly, *Jase is sweet on sis. He's gonna take this hard.*

"What's the matter with you? You look like an accident going somewhere to happen," Jase said.

For one moment Peter Winslow hesitated, then said, "Bad news, Jase. It's about Priscilla." He saw the change in the man's face and knew that he had to give the bad news all at once. "She's gonna get married—to an actor there in New York."

Jason Ballard was indeed in love with Priscilla Winslow, and had been for several years. He had good control, however, and glanced toward the house. "Be tough on your folks," he said quietly. The pain that raced through him like a knife he did not allow to show. "I hate to hear it," he said.

The two sat down on a bench beside the barn and talked for a while. Both of them were stunned and disheartened by the news. Though Jason had not flinched outwardly at the news, Peter knew him well enough to know it hit his friend like a blow. Finally Peter said rebelliously, "Well, I'm going to do something about it."

Ballard looked at him with surprise. "*Do* something about it? What do you mean by that, Peter?"

"I mean I'm going to New York."

"You gonna shoot this actor fella?"

"Well, no I can't do that—but maybe I can talk some sense into Priscilla." A stubborn look crossed Peter Winslow's face. He stuck his jaw out and said, "I got a little money saved—enough for a round-trip ticket. She never would listen to anybody much, but she listened to me a lot. We're real close, Jase."

Jason Ballard sat there quietly, his long legs stuck out in front of him. He studied his worn boots, and then finally turned to look at his friend.

"I'm going with you," he said simply. He saw surprise light Peter's eyes as he said, "She never paid any attention to me either, but I reckon I'll never forgive myself if I miss the last chance to do something to stop this thing. She may not love me, but I love her."

It was the plainest declaration that Ballard had ever made. Peter had long known that the lanky cowboy was in love with Priscilla, and now he suddenly resisted an impulse to put his arm around his friend. Standing to his feet instead, he said, "Come on, there's a train out at four o'clock this afternoon. I plan to be on it." Jason rose and Peter grinned rashly. "Maybe we can do something. Let's go get the folks to praying on it, anyway."

CHAPTER FIFTEEN

A KISS IS NOT LOVE

★ ★ ★ ★

William Randolph Hearst had promised Esther that he would assign a good investigative reporter to work on the matter of exposing the slum landlords. As was not unusual, he neglected to come through on his promise. For over a week Esther waited impatiently, and finally when she spoke to her employer, he shook his head and snapped in a characteristic rebuke, "We have big things to do on this paper, Esther. My best men are all busy with other things. You'll just have to wait your turn." A thought struck him, and he lifted his eyebrows and smiled. There was a sharklike appearance to his long face, and his teeth looked almost carnivorous as he grinned. "Or you can do it yourself. You're a bright girl. In any case, you'll just have to wait until your time comes."

Esther had a number of assignments to work on, for her popularity had grown. She had developed techniques of getting pictures that others would not have been permitted to take. Undaunted by the rules, she roamed the city, appearing at any event or before any celebrity that caught her fancy. She did receive a shock when she was given a nickname by one of the local politicians.

Under indictment for embezzlement, the attorney general had been shielding himself against all newspaper people. Every reporter for every major paper in New York City had scrambled to get an exclusive interview—all had failed. He had isolated himself on his estate in Long Island, which resembled a medieval castle in many respects.

His name was Michael Dougherty, a second-generation Irishman who had fought his way up through the ranks of politics almost to the very top. He had been a likely candidate for governor of the state until the scandal had hit. Dougherty's usual tactics were to meet his opponents head on, but for some reason he had unexpectedly withdrawn, which had piqued Esther's curiosity. She had been having breakfast with her father one morning and had asked him his opinion of Michael Dougherty's business.

"It's hard to say, Esther," Mark shrugged. "I've always found Dougherty to be honest enough. He's always been one to come up front with any defense, though. He's a very aggressive man, and I can't understand what he's doing hiding out on that estate of his."

Esther started to answer, then suddenly cried out, "Ow!" Twisting, she grabbed Dickens, who had climbed the back of her chair and sunk his claws into her shoulder. "Will you get down and leave me alone!" she demanded. Picking him up, she shook him, holding him under his front legs. His lower body swayed, and he seemed to grin at her. Looking over at her father, she asked, "Dad, why do you suppose cats act like they do?"

Mark took a drink of orange juice and shook his head. "I don't know. I don't understand cats, and I don't think *anybody* does."

"I believe you're right." Esther stared into the huge, golden eyes of the tomcat and thought for a moment. "You know, if you feed a dog, give him lots of affection, and do everything for him, he probably thinks, *Say, this person must be a god!*" She suddenly put her nose against that of Dickens and muttered, "But with a cat, you feed him the best food, you love him, you care for him, and he thinks, *Wow, I must be a god!*"

Mark burst into laughter and nodded. "You need to take a stick to him. He's spoiled rotten."

Esther hugged the cat suddenly and kissed him on the head. "I know it, but I can't help it," she said, grinning ruefully.

"I hope you treat your husband as well as you treat that cat of yours."

"Not likely," Esther laughed. "Now get down, Dickens—go

away. Catch a mouse or something." Resuming the conversation, she said suddenly, "I'm going to see Dougherty."

"You'll have trouble doing that. He's barricaded himself inside that fortress of his. I understand there are even guards at the gates. Nobody goes in or out without Dougherty's say-so." He looked at his daughter and saw a familiar set expression on her face. A grin pulled the corners of his lips, and he shrugged. "I suppose that means you're going to do it?"

"I'm going to try, Dad. I smell a good story."

"I suppose it wouldn't do any good to try to convince you otherwise. Please be careful, Esther," Mark said slowly.

Esther stood up, walked over, kissed him, then smiled. "I promise, Dad. But somehow I'm going to get an interview with Dougherty. You see if I don't!"

For two days Esther thought of different plans to get in to see the politician but rejected all of them. She even took a drive out to Dougherty's estate, but she was careful not to be seen. As she waited, she watched as the guards turned several people away. Obviously Dougherty had no intention of allowing strangers, especially newspaper people, to come into his little kingdom. Somewhat discouraged, she almost gave up on the idea, but it still lurked in the back of her mind.

One Thursday morning she stopped by the Scarlottas. She had taken enough pictures of them, so she made no pretense of carrying her equipment inside. She found Tony at home, and he shrugged his shoulders, saying, "No work today. We got-a strike."

"What about Jan?"

"He's upstairs on the sixth floor with Mrs. Diviney. Some-a her kids are ill, they got-a something."

Esther visited for a while with Tony and Lucia, then made her way up to the top floor of the tenement. She found Jan examining some of the Divineys' smaller children and waited patiently as he looked them over. As he worked with them she thought, *He acts exactly like a doctor. There's always something about them. He knows exactly what he's doing. What a shame he can't practice medicine here.*

Finally, after Jan had examined the children, calmed the nerves of the mother, and promised to send some medicine back, they left the apartment.

"Were you telling her the truth? That the children are really all right?"

"I always tell the truth," Jan said smoothly, "except when it's necessary to do otherwise."

"You're a scoundrel, Jan Kruger," Esther laughed. She had learned that underneath the rather rough exterior of the man lurked an elfin sense of humor, and now she insisted, "Are they really sick?"

"Nothing serious, just as I told Mrs. Diviney." His eyes grew thoughtful and he shook his head. "I'm always very careful with children. They're so helpless, especially babies. They can't tell you anything that's wrong with them. You just have to examine them thoroughly and try to discover what the problem is."

"You're very good with them, Jan."

"Why . . . thank you, Esther. It wasn't my specialty." He thought back as they walked down the hall and said finally, "In the camps the most heartbreaking thing of all was seeing babies, some only a few months old, dying of starvation. A simple can of milk would have saved their lives."

"How awful!" Esther gasped.

He did not answer but shook his broad shoulders, trying to put the thoughts aside. "What are you doing here this morning?"

"Oh, I don't know. I'm just disgusted with myself."

"Disgusted about what?"

They had reached the doorway when she said, "Look, do you have to go inside? Do you have anything to do today?"

"No, I'm off too. I was working with Tony at the docks, but with the strike, nobody's got work. Why?"

"Come with me. I'm in a bad mood. I need someone to take it out on."

"That's the best offer I've had all day." Jan grinned. "Let me get my coat." He stepped inside, explained things to the Scarlottas, then emerged wearing a worn brown overcoat and a wool cap pulled down over his ears. "All ready. Dressed up, and ready for the ball," he said cheerfully.

The two of them left the building, and as they walked along, Jan looked up at the cold sky. "I'll be glad when summer comes," he said. "But spring in New York isn't much of a thrill, I guess."

"It is at Central Park—and out at our house, Jan." She looked around at the miserable, squalid street and shook her head. "I suppose some of these children have never seen flowers growing or run on green grass."

"I suppose not."

They walked around for some time, and suddenly Esther said, "Would you come home with me, Jan?"

He looked at her with surprise. "Home with you? What for?"

"I'd like for you to meet my parents and to see where I live." Suddenly it became very important that he go with her. She had no explanation for this sudden impulse, yet she was conscious of a need to talk, to be with somebody. She urged him by smiling up at him and saying, "I'll feed you and bring you back tonight."

"Well, I guess I can't refuse such a good offer. I'd like very much to meet your family."

"Good. Look, there's a cab stand. Let's go."

★ ★ ★ ★

"Dad, Mom, this is Jan Kruger." Esther turned to Jan, her eyes bright with pleasure. "Jan, these are my parents, Mark and Lola Winslow."

Jan bowed from the waist, in a foreign sort of military fashion. "I am delighted to meet you, sir—and you, Mrs. Winslow."

Lola quickly came over to him and extended her hand. She was somewhat surprised when he took it and kissed it. A deep blush came to her cheeks, and she said in a flustered fashion, "Esther has told us so much about you." Taking his arm, she continued, "Come into the parlor now and we'll have tea. I don't want to spoil your dinner, for we are going to have a fine one."

As Lola led the tall man away, Mark cocked one eyebrow and said, "What do you mean bringing a good-looking man into my home who fascinates my wife?"

"He is fine looking, isn't he, Dad?"

"Your mother thinks so," Mark smiled. "I never saw her take to anyone so quickly. Maybe I'd better start kissing her hand."

As they moved into the parlor, they saw that Lola had already begun questioning Jan. Esther took her seat beside her father on the sofa and listened. She had heard some of Jan's story, but it was different hearing him speak to her parents.

Mark Winslow was an astute man. He had to be to keep his position in the competitive world of railroads. Experience had taught him how to read a man, first as a cowboy on the open plains where he had to deal with the rougher sorts, then as a troubleshooter for the Union Pacific Railroad. Finally in the competitive world of big-time commerce, he had learned to assess quickly whether a man was real or not. His eyes caught Lola's, and she smiled at him, and he understood her meaning. He smiled back, then turned his attention to Kruger, saying finally, "You've had a pretty stiff jolt to your career, Dr. Kruger."

"You must not call me Dr. Kruger," Jan said instantly. "I am not qualified in this country."

Lola leaned forward, her dark eyes intent, and said, "But surely you intend to be?"

"I do not think I will ever be a doctor again. Not in this country." Jan had thought this over many times and had talked about it once with Tony. Now he said almost sadly, "I could be a doctor now in many countries. In Pakistan, for example, but I do not want to live there."

"Will you ever go back to South Africa?"

"I am not sure. There are . . . political difficulties."

"But you do like it here in America?" Lola inquired.

"He's gotten a very poor idea of it—look at his hands," Esther said. When Jan resisted, she moved over and picked up one of his hands, turning it over. "Look at the blisters! That's not good for a doctor."

"It's good for eating, though." Jan grinned, his white teeth flashing. "Please, this is too much talk about me. I would much prefer to hear about you, Mr. Winslow. Your daughter has told me much about you and your good wife and your struggles."

"Did you tell him I was a saloon girl dealing blackjack, and that they called me the Union Belle?"

Jan laughed. "Yes, she has told me that. I found it fascinating."

"So do I," Mark said. "It's exciting being married to a saloon girl."

"Not as exciting as being married to a gunfighter," Lola countered. "Now," she said, "let's stop all this foolishness. You'll have to stay overnight," she announced.

Jan opened his mouth to protest, but Lola overrode this. "We can't possibly hear all about you, and you can't know all about us unless you'll stay. We have plenty of room."

"Why, I have nothing pressing to do. Tomorrow I must return. There are some sick people who are depending on me—those who can't afford a doctor, you understand?"

"We'll get you back tomorrow," Mark said. "Come along. I've got a request."

"And what is that, Mr. Winslow?"

"I need someone to go hunting with me. Do you hunt?"

"Oh yes. I love to hunt, but I have no gun."

Mark nodded confidently. "Don't worry about that. I'm going to outfit you and arm you so that we could stop a herd of bull elephants if we run into any!"

"You're about the same size, you and Jan," Esther said. "Why don't you let him wear some of your hunting clothes?"

"Just what I had in mind. Come along, Jan. Let's stay on a first-name basis, all right?"

"That is most amiable, sir."

As the two men left, Lola looked at her daughter and said, "He's a fascinating man. I'm glad you brought him home."

Esther bit her lip and said, "I'm glad I did too. I know he needs friends. He's had a hard life. Some horrible things happened in the prison camp in South Africa. I want him to tell you about it tonight." Her eyes were bright and there was an excitement inside that stirred her. "I'll let Daddy have him this morning to go hunting, but this afternoon he's mine."

Lola watched her daughter carefully. She had not seen this kind of excitement in her in some time. For a while Esther's new profession had brought a certain sense of exuberance, but she had never seen her respond to a man so quickly and so positively.

"You like him?" she asked quietly.

Startled, Esther flushed. Reaching up, she tucked a lock of her black hair aside and said, "Yes, I like him."

★　★　★　★

Mark found Jan Kruger to be an excellent shot. The two of them brought back a bag full of quail, and he told Lola rather ruefully, "He shoots better than I do. I guess that's some of his army training. At least we'll have fresh game for supper tonight."

"What do you think of him, Mark? You had time to talk, didn't you?"

The two were standing in their bedroom where Mark was changing out of his hunting clothes. He had not shaved that morning and went to stand before a mirror. Quickly he worked up a lather with the brush, covered his face, then picked up a razor and tested it on his thumb. Stropping it several times on the leather strap attached to the side of the mahogany washstand, he carefully raked down one side of his cheek. Then wiping the foam off on a towel, he said thoughtfully, "I don't know as I've ever been with a more interesting fellow. He's foreign, of course, and that always has its fascination for us Americans—and he's not like I thought he'd be."

"What did you think he'd be?"

"Oh, I don't know. Just the pictures I've seen of the Boer War. The Boer farmers looked like stolid, dull fellows—honest and all that—but Jan's different. I guess being educated makes a difference, and being a doctor, of course."

Lola watched as Mark drew the razor down the other cheek and blinked against the pain of it. He had a heavy beard, and the razor made a rasping noise as it plowed through the whiskers. "I've never seen Esther so interested in a man."

Quickly Mark raised his eyes. "You don't think she really is, do you—interested in him?"

Lola moved about the room restlessly. "I don't know, Mark. I never felt good about her engagement to Simon. She doesn't seem to feel about him like—" She hesitated for a moment, and then came over and ran her hand across his hair. "Like I feel about you, for example."

Mark held his head still as he slid the razor down his throat. "Don't do that!" he growled. "You're distracting me, and I might cut my own throat when my hand trembles."

Lola laughed and waited for him to finish shaving. Then the two talked for some time as he dressed for supper. "I don't know. I guess I have my reservations about Simon like you do." When they were ready to go downstairs, Lola turned to him suddenly and put her arms around him. He held her with some surprise for the moment, burying his face in her dark hair, which had a clean, sweet smell. "I'm worried about Esther, Mark," Lola whispered. "She could make a terrible mistake, and I think she would if she married Simon."

"I know," he murmured, holding her tightly. He stroked her back and said, "I felt the same thing, but you know Esther. The surest way to drive her into a quick marriage would be to disparage Simon."

"She has to find it out for herself. She always was like that." Then she drew back and smiled. Pulling his head down, Lola kissed him lightly on the lips and said, "We'll pray about it."

"That always works," Mark agreed, then the two turned and walked out of the bedroom.

Dinner was a pleasant time. Kruger appeared wearing one of Mark's suits. It was an expensive Scottish tweed that Mark had outgrown, but it suited the tall South African well. He looked different, somehow, in the expensive, well-tailored garment. Mark laughed and said, "I've got a whole closet full of stuff I'm too fat for. You might as well take what you can wear with you, Jan."

Kruger fingered the sleeve and shook his head. "This is fine material. I'm lucky that you grew out of it, Mark."

The dinner was excellently served. Mark and Lola had persuaded a woman, named Aunt Jessie, to come from the old homeplace in Virginia. They both had learned to love Southern cooking, and Aunt Jessie was the best. She bustled in after the blessing with a huge platter in each hand. Both were full of crisp, tasty pheasants. "These here is guinea hens," Aunt Jessie announced as she set the platters on the table. She had already been introduced to the guest and had found him to be a perfect gentleman. She had her own standards, Aunt Jessie did, and now she explained the guinea hens. "Do you know what a guinea hen is, Mr. Kruger?"

"I don't believe I do."

"Well, they's little chickens, and they's hard to come by. But if you can get 'em like these, they are worth every bite. You have to be careful of them old guineas because you cook 'em all day and still can't bite into 'em. But these here is young'uns I raised my own self."

Kruger picked up a piece of the tender meat and tasted it. Lifting his eyes, he smiled at Aunt Jessie and said, "Wonderful! I never tasted better chicken in my whole life."

Aunt Jessie's face broke into a broad smile. "I wish I had me some possum. Now there ain't nothin' like roast possum, but not everybody appreciates that," she said, rolling her eyes at Lola.

Lola laughed and said, "No, they look like big rats to me, but I love your guinea hens."

"Well now, you save room for some of my sweet tater pie. I done fix it special for you, Mr. Mark," Aunt Jessie said.

The meal was different from most for Esther, especially those times when Simon had been with them. Simon was charming, when he chose to be, but he had little wit. Kruger amused them all by telling them tales of hunting in South Africa. He had traveled into other parts of Africa and hunted big game, including lion and elephant, and Mark found this fascinating.

"Daddy, you ought to go with him on a safari, and Mother and I'll go too!" Esther exclaimed. "Wouldn't that be fun?"

"It would not be fun if you got bit by a tsetse fly," Jan said.

"What's a tsetse fly?" Esther inquired.

"An insect that gives you sleeping sickness. Very bad. There are doctor flies, too. Once they bite you, the bite becomes infected, and it swells out into huge sores."

Lola laughed suddenly. "I think I'll rough it here, Jan. It sounds too strenuous for an old woman like me."

After the meal they went into the parlor, where Jan was entertained by tales of Esther's childhood and those of her brothers. He was very interested in the ministry work of Barney and Andrew. He listened carefully as Mark and Lola spoke of them with pride and Jan said, "You are right to be proud—to have sons to proclaim the gospel of Jesus. That is wonderful."

"Have you been a Christian a long time, Jan?" Mark inquired.

Jan hesitated, then shook his head. "Not very long. I would like to tell you how I found God." They listened intently as he told them how he had been captured by the English and condemned to die. When he was finished he looked down at his hands and said very seriously, "I do not know if I can ever be a doctor, but I would like to help the poor people. That is what God has told me to do. So far I have not found a way to do that—except in a small fashion in helping those who live in the tenements."

Lola was moved by Jan's story of his search for God. "You'll find the way, Jan. I'm sure you will."

Shortly after that the two older members of the party excused themselves, and Lola said, "Good night." As she turned to leave, she added, "We'll have an early breakfast. I wish you could stay longer."

After they had left, Jan turned to Esther. "Your father and mother are wonderful people. You're very fortunate."

"Yes, I think about that a lot, but what about your family?"

"My father died when I was only sixteen, and my mother only four years ago. I was an only child, so I really have no family."

Esther was moved for this man so far from his home with no family at all. Quietly she said, "God will give you a family."

Jan glanced up at her with surprise. "That sounds almost prophetic."

"Well, I'm no prophet or prophetess," Esther said, "but I just believe that good things will happen if we follow after God."

"I'm glad you believe that," Jan said. He dropped his head again and studied his hands. "Sometimes it is hard for me to think that, but I know that you are right. I hope you'll always feel like that."

They talked for some time, and slowly an idea began to form within Esther. She could not settle it at first, but finally it came clear, and she said tentatively, "Jan, I've been trying to think of a way to get in to see Michael Dougherty."

"Who is he?" Kruger listened as she explained, and finally shrugged his heavy shoulders. "I don't understand these things too well."

Esther said slowly, her brow wrinkling, "I've had an idea, but I don't think I can do it alone."

"This thing, this getting to see this man. It's important to you?"

"It would help me a great deal, I think. Every newspaper reporter and photographer in the city has tried to see Dougherty. If I could get in to see him and get some pictures, I think it would help my career a great deal."

Kruger smiled at her. There was an ease in his manner, and he said gently, "Any way that I can help you, I will, Esther. I've never told you, but your kindness to the Scarlottas has been an inspiration to me. I thank you for what you've done for them."

A rosy color touched Esther's cheeks, and she said quickly, "Oh, it's nothing really."

"Maybe not to you, but to them it's helped a great deal. Now, how may I help you?"

"Well," Esther said slowly, "it all became clear when you came in to dinner tonight wearing my father's suit." She laughed aloud and said, "It was like seeing another person. I was used to seeing you in your working clothes, and I guess clothes really do make a difference."

"I suppose so," Kruger smiled, "but what do my clothes have to do with your plan?"

Esther leaned forward, her brown eyes sparkled, and there was an excitement within her that moved Jan. She was a beautiful woman with a soft depth, a gentle spirit, and yet a vibrant quality about her. There was a provocative challenge in her beautiful eyes, and he knew that he could refuse her nothing.

"Americans are very impressed by royalty, Jan. Every time a prince or a princess comes to this country, society just goes wild for them. So when I saw you, I thought that if I could put you in the right clothes, and I put on the right clothes, we might pass for a prince and a princess. Foreign royalty."

"And you think Mr.—what's his name—Dougherty might be impressed by this?"

"I think he might. He worships power, almost," Esther said. "And to see a prince and a princess come to his door, I think he might let us in."

Jan laughed suddenly, his baritone voice filling the room. "I never thought of being a prince. I think it takes more than a suit of clothes."

"You don't have to pretend," Esther insisted. "You already have an English accent, and I'll do the best I can. Here's what I think we ought to do. It'll be fun," she said. Her lips curved upward in a smile, and she unconsciously took his arm as she began to reveal her plan to him. . . .

★ ★ ★ ★

"You say *who's* at the front door?"

Michael Dougherty stared at his right-hand man, a combination butler, bouncer, and general manager of the estate. He was a tall man names Patrick Spence with thick shoulders. Spence shrugged his burly shoulders and rolled his eyes upward. "So help me, Michael, I don't know what to think. The carriage that come up, I never saw the likes of it. Driven by four matched in hand bays, and then this fellow gets out dressed like he was going to the inauguration. I could see the woman accompanying him had diamonds dripping off her ears, and on her hand she flashed a rock that must have cost as much as this estate."

"Who are they?" Dougherty asked, interested in spite of himself. "What do they want?"

Spence stared at the small card that he held up to his eyes. "Sir Giles Montague and Lady Alexis Montague—they say they come from England."

Dougherty's eyes narrowed and he thought hard. "What do they want?"

"They wouldn't say, at least not to me, but they said they've come all the way from England, and they want to see you." Spence hesitated, then said, "I guess you better see them, Michael. They look like somebody real important."

Dougherty chewed on the cigar that he held firmly between his teeth, thinking hard. Finally he shrugged and said, "All right, bring them into the library, Pat."

Dougherty moved to the library, his mind working quickly. He couldn't imagine any reason why British royalty would come to see him—yet, he was always a man to take advantage of every opportunity. Whatever came into his sphere, he saw it in terms of power and votes. Now it occurred to him that in the next election it wouldn't hurt to have his pictures in the paper with a couple of swells from England. A smile touched his tough Irish lips, and when the couple entered he blinked, impressed in spite of himself.

The man was younger than he expected, no more than thirty. He had light yellow hair, hazel eyes, and a square face. He wore a square-cut dress coat evening suit with skirts that were narrow at the bottom, a single-breasted waistcoat that had a deep V-shaped front. The trousers were narrow with a braid running down each side from the waist. He was also wearing a small cambric bow tie and plain white silk gloves. He carried a black Homburg in his hand.

"My name is Giles Montague," he said in a clipped British accent. "I appreciate your taking time from your busy schedule to see us, Mr. Dougherty."

"I'm glad to meet you. Is it Sir Giles?"

"Yes, and may I present my wife, Lady Alexis."

She's a knockout, Dougherty thought. The woman who stood beside Sir Giles was wearing a gown with a cuirasse bodice, coming to a point in front. The dress itself was yellow and emerald green, the skirt train and flounce decorated with lace and velvet ruching. She was beautiful, indeed, and when she advanced and held out her hand, Michael Dougherty did something he never did in his life. He bowed over and kissed her hand, flushing at his own manners. "I'm glad to know you, Lady Montague."

"Mr. Dougherty, we are impostors."

Dougherty blinked with astonishment. Staring from one to the other, he asked, "What do you mean, impostors? Aren't you from England?"

"I am from South Africa," Jan said at once. "This is Miss Esther Winslow, who is from New York. She is the daughter of Mr. Mark Winslow, vice president of the Union Pacific."

Alarms went off in Dougherty's mind. His eyes narrowed, and suddenly the rules had been changed on him. "What do you want?" he demanded.

Esther had her mind made up. She looked directly in the Irishman's eyes and said, "Mr. Dougherty, I think you're making a mistake running from publicity. It makes you look like a coward. I studied your record, and the one thing you've always had is courage to face whatever comes."

"Wait a minute!" Dougherty snapped. "You're not with the newspapers, are you?"

"I'm a photographer for the *New York Journal*, and I've come to ask you to give us an interview and to let us take pictures of you."

Michael Dougherty stared at the pair in shocked amazement. He himself was audacious, but for the pair here who had tricked him, he first felt anger, then a growing admiration. Finally a smile tugged at his lips, and he chuckled deep in his chest. "Well now, lady, I've got to give it to you. You're the first one to get past my people at the gate."

"I can't apologize, Mr. Dougherty," Esther said. "I want something from you, but I'd like to think I could be of help to you too.

You need to hear what people like me on the outside are saying and thinking about you, and the best way to speak to that would be to say exactly what you want said to the public. I guarantee you Mr. Hearst will print with no additions to your speech."

Quickly Dougherty ran the proposition over in his mind, and suddenly he recognized that the woman was right! He had been running and hiding, which could hurt his political career. In one of his quick changes of mood, for which he was famous, he said, "Lady, you're something else! Where's your camera?"

"It's in the carriage. I'll get it."

"Let one of the guys do that. I'm telling you I'm going to give you the straight dope about Michael Dougherty."

★ ★ ★ ★

It had taken some time for Jan and Esther to return the clothes and the jewels that she had rented. The interview with Dougherty took over two hours, and both Esther and Jan had filled up pages with his words. Jan's writing was much better than hers, and he had an analytical way of speaking about the interview. After they had returned the carriage, and then rented another to take him home, they were riding along the streets that were now growing dark. "I'll stay in town tonight and take a room," she said. Then she turned to him in the carriage. The gas lights that they passed threw shadows onto his face, making his features look craggy and tough. "Wasn't it wonderful!" she exclaimed. "I've never been so excited in my life, and I'll develop the pictures tomorrow. You'll see Michael Dougherty on the front page of the *Journal*!"

"And the story, will you get credit for that?"

"I don't know. Mr. Hearst will have to decide, but we've done what nobody else could do. Oh, it was so much fun."

Unconsciously she caught herself staring at him in the carriage. It was a small carriage and they sat close together. She was aware of his hazel eyes fixed on her in a peculiar fashion, and finally she stopped and said, "Oh, dear. I've used you terribly, haven't I, Jan?"

"No, I enjoyed it. I thought for a while he might have us thrown in jail, but you could tell he appreciated you. I like the name that he gave you."

"Well, I don't know as I do."

The last thing that Michael Dougherty had said was, "You are one tough lady; as a matter of fact, you're an iron lady." He had chuckled and said, "I'm gonna tell the other newspapers now that I've decided to do some talking about you. Pretty soon all New York will know about the Iron Lady."

"That doesn't sound very nice—Iron Lady, indeed! I always think of the Iron Lady as the Statue of Liberty."

It had been a break from the boring, hard routine of his everyday life, and now as he sat close to Esther, Jan was very conscious of the self-possessed curve of her mouth. She had wide and clean-edged lips, and there was a richness in her that had always drawn him. Even in the semidarkness he saw her lovely features. He admired the roundness of her shoulders, the straight lines, tall and shapely in a way that struck any man. Her black hair lay rolled and heavy on her head, but her skin was fair. Even as she spoke, he was captivated by her. Suddenly she touched his hand in her excitement, and the touch was electrifying. The waft of fragrance came powerfully to him, and he looked at her in such a way that she ceased talking. There was a silence then, and in their closeness they were acutely aware of each other, of man and woman.

She had the power—this young woman who had come into his life—to stir him, to deepen his longings and awaken his need for companionship. A sudden impulse came to him then, and he reached forward slowly and turned her toward him. He gave her time to pull away, to protest, if she wished, but she did not. Her eyes suddenly seemed enormous in the darkness, and without hesitation he tenderly pulled her against his chest. She came to him with a woman's softness, and when his lips touched hers there was a sweetness in them that shook him to the core. The stirring force of something wonderful and timeless touched them both. In that moment Jan knew that Esther Winslow possessed all the richness of soul of a woman that could heal the empty places of his heart. He suddenly realized that the loneliness in him would never be satisfied with less.

As for Esther, she could sense that he was going to kiss her and had almost turned away, but there was a spirit within her that reached out to him. She was aware of the strength of his body as he held his arms around her, powerful enough to crush her if he so chose. There was a roughness to his embrace. His kiss was powerful—but not demanding in a way that she would have found distasteful—and somehow from deep within her heart rose a response. Unconsciously she reached up, put her hands behind his neck, pulling him even closer. The moment had swept her, and she was only aware of the pressure of his hands and his arms and his lips.

Finally, she moved away and whispered, "I shouldn't have let you do that, Jan."

"Perhaps not, but I meant it, Esther. You are a lovely woman."

"I'm . . . I'm engaged."

Jan said nothing for a while, and finally he said, "A kiss is not love."

"No, it isn't." Esther was deeply shaken and knew that it would be days before she would recover from the emotions that had swept through her. She felt somehow embarrassed that another man's kiss other than her fiancé's would so move her, and yet she could not deny that what she had felt had been honest—and pure. There had been nothing inappropriate or suggestive. He was a healthy man with a man's desires, and now she knew that her own yearnings were fully equal to his.

The carriage moved on, and the spellbound silence was broken by the clatter of the horses' hooves on the street. Finally, when they reached the tenement where Jan stayed with the Scarlottas, he got out and stood silently beside the coach. "Good night, Esther," he said.

"Good night, Jan—can I see you tomorrow? I have another idea."

Jan smiled at her. "I like your ideas. They take me places I never thought of seeing." He reached up and took her hand, which she extended to him. He kissed it, then squeezed it and said, "You are not an iron lady; you are a lady of flesh, and blood, and fire." Then he turned and walked away, his tall figure fading into the shadows of the building. He did not turn when the carriage started up. It was like entering another world as he came into the tenement, and he knew that he would never forget this day, not as long as he lived.

CHAPTER SIXTEEN

ESTHER GETS A SHOCK

★ ★ ★ ★

Jason Ballard and Peter Winslow never forgot the adventure of their journey by rail from Wyoming to New York City—the great coal-burning engine with its inverted funnel stack, brass bell, and brass kettlelike steam cone perched atop the black cylinder. The huge drivers connected to the steel rods churned with a massive power while the engineer, perched in a red square canopy at the rear of the engine, peered out, staring through goggles at the track ahead.

Winter was not the proper time to travel, for the cars were cold. If they had had the money to ride in one of the new Pullman cars, it might have been much more enjoyable, but both of the young men kept the little cash they had, and from time to time huddled around the coal-burning stove at one end of the car.

Halfway through their journey, the winter winds and snows descended in a fury upon the land. Snow fell so thick that all of the world outside of their car seemed to be a white void. Peter stared out once and said, "I can't see five feet away."

Jason put his nose against the cold window and peered out into the whiteness of the night. Drawing back, he shook his head and said, "I feel sorry for the cattle out in a blizzard like this. There'll be some of them that don't make it." As always, his mind turned toward cattle, for it was all he knew. He had sold everything he had to get the money for this trip, including his favorite roping horse, and now as the train plunged through the snow-drifts, he wondered if he had done the wise thing. He said little to Peter during those days, but a thoughtful expression remained habitually on his face as he sat hour after hour.

Once the conductor came in and said, "Got to ask you tough young fellows for help."

"What is it?" Jason called out.

"We got to clear the drifts ahead of the engine. We can't make it through unless we shovel some of that snow out of the way."

Jason and Peter arose at once and proved to be the sturdiest of the workers. Both of them were toughened by years of work on the open range, and the engineer nodded gratefully as he watched them make the snow fly. "If we had a bunch of fellows like you two cowboys, we'd make it fine."

Peter looked up and grinned, saying, "Now, a horse wouldn't get bogged down like this."

The conductor, an old cowboy himself from Montana, laughed and nodded. "You're right there. I'd like to be riding the range with you gents again, but I'm hooked to this here blasted train." He looked around and spat in the air and watched the spittle crackle. "Got to be thirty below." He shook his head. "We'll make it, but it won't be easy."

They cleared the snow and finally got underway again. The farther east they traveled, the milder the weather became. It was a grueling experience for the faint of heart—those who were not able to take advantage of George Pullman's special cars. The two cowboys did duck inside one, at the invitation of the conductor, to take a look, and marveled at the shiny lavatories and the fine food. The conductor winked and said, "You boys done good service gettin' that snow out of the way. Come and have a meal on the Union Pacific."

Jason and Peter followed him to the dining car, which was carpeted with gorgeous red, thick carpeting they seemed to sink into. The aisle was wide, and on each side tables lined the car. The seats were quilted red satin with gleaming walnut frames, and the tables were covered with snow-white tablecloths, on top of which gleamed silver and delicate crystal. Sitting down, the two waited while a black waiter, wearing a jet black suit with a white collar and a white apron, came and asked, "Yes, sir, what'll you gentlemen have?"

The conductor winked. "Bring them the best you've got, Sam. Guests of the UP."

"Yes, sir!"

The meal consisted of oysters, lobster, partridge, and steak, along with vegetables that had been obtained, somehow, even in the midst of a hard winter.

"I could get used to this," Peter grinned. "When I make my fortune racing cars I'm gonna have my own Pullman car. I read once that the big maybobs who own the railroads and the steel mines all have their private cars."

"Well, remember me when you come into all that fortune," Jason grinned. "I'll still be plugging along on a horse, I guess."

In spite of all the glamour and excitement, they both knew that railroading was a dangerous occupation. They had read of some of the spectacular wrecks, for the newspapers often had long articles about the gruesome details. They saw a good example of it before they left the freezing weather, when they watched a brakeman climb up the side of a swaying car. He had to set the brake by turning a steel wheel at the top at a whistle signal from the engineer. "That's all changing, though," the conductor said. "A new thing is air brakes. Fellow named Westinghouse invented them. We need 'em too. You don't see many brakees with all their fingers. They lose 'em when they try to manipulate the link-and-pin devices that couple the cars. Matter of fact, the cost of insurance is so high that the railroad brotherhoods had to form their own insurance companies to be sure they got took care of."

"Pretty rough job, I guess," Peter said. "One of my uncles works for the UP."

"Who's that?" the conductor asked casually.

"Mark Winslow. I'm Peter Winslow."

The conductor's eyes opened. "You mean the vice president?"

"I think that's his title."

"Well, you fellows should have wheedled your uncle out of Pullman car reservations. As a matter of fact," he said, "we ain't all full tonight. You fellows can sleep in the Pullman car unless somebody buys 'em up down the road."

This was a thrill for the two young men. They took advantage of the lavatories to wash and shave, and they thoroughly enjoyed the fine food in the dining car for the rest of the trip. They had clean linen each night, and both were amused at the sign that the porter posted, "Please take off your boots before retiring."

"I guess they got some rustic fellas ridin' in these cars," Jason murmured.

Peter winked and said, "We're just as rustic as anybody. I'll take off my spurs, anyhow. Come on, let's hit the sack."

★   ★   ★   ★

"Well, this is some place, but I got to admit it scares me a little bit." Jason and Peter had been walking down between the towering buildings of New York City. They'd gotten lost more than once, and both had stood aghast as they stared up at the magnificence of the Brooklyn Bridge. Neither of them could fathom how such an architectural marvel could be built. They had set out to find the theater where Priscilla was performing and had gotten completely lost. However, as they wandered about, they had a good chance to get a taste of what the big city was like. Both of them were impressed with the "EL"—the elevated railway system that traversed Manhattan. They actually got on the train once just to ride and look down on the city that lay beneath them. For part of the time, they walked through the streets that boasted the fine shops and were struck dumb by the exorbitant prices that were fixed on some of the items on the other side of the heavy plate glass.

"Would you look at that! That pair of shoes costs twenty dollars! Why, a man could buy a fair horse with that much money," Peter said in awe. Then he brightened up. "But when we make our pile we'll have a dozen pair of the best boots made. Come on, Jase, we're going to find that theater. I want to see Priscilla act in that play."

After asking around, they found someone who gave them directions to the theater. An hour or so later, after a lengthy walk, they finally stood in front of the theater where Priscilla acted. Jason looked at her picture and said, "That's her. Looks funny to see her picture up there along with those other actors and actresses." In his heart he was wishing it was not there. The city had cast a pall on him, for he realized that this was an alien world to him. It gave him little comfort to think that if one of the denizens of New York were placed in the middle of some of the savage country of Wyoming, they would be just as frightened of that world. Nevertheless, he set his jaw and said, "Well, let's buy the tickets and see what this show business stuff is like."

They had to wait until seven o'clock before the performance started. Finally, however, the curtain went up. Neither of them spoke a word, but Priscilla stepped out on stage and sang her first song. Both of them saw that this was not the Priscilla Winslow that they knew. They remembered a girl wearing gingham dresses, or linsey-woolsey skirts, or a girl riding a spirited bronc.

The woman up on the stage had poise and seemed much older. Priscilla had been tutored in the art of makeup, and now she seemed like a woman that they had never seen before.

"Something's happened to Priscilla," Peter said quietly.

"I reckon you're right," Jason said. He sat glumly through the play, impressed by the theatrics of it all, for he had never seen a play before. But he could not enjoy the music and could barely follow the plot. He was thinking, *I guess I never should have come here. She'll think I'm loco.*

After the play ended, and the cast came out for curtain calls, both men were standing and applauding. As the people began to make their way to the lobby of the theater, Peter said, "Come on, let's go find her."

"They'll probably throw us out," Jason murmured. "A couple of yahoos like us don't fit in here."

"You got to assert yourself, Jase," Peter nodded confidently. "Come on."

He led the way back, and suddenly they were blocked by a man who frowned at them and shook his head. "No visitors backstage."

Peter replied cheerfully, "It's all right, Mac, I'm Peter Winslow. Miss Priscilla Winslow is my sister. She wouldn't like it if you didn't let us back there."

"Oh, is that on the level? You're really Miss Winslow's brother?"

"Sure, don't you see the family resemblance?"

The stagehand grinned and waved them on. "Back there," he said, "you'll see her name on the door."

They found the door with Priscilla Winslow printed across it and Peter knocked. When somebody said, "Who is it?" he recognized Priscilla's voice and winked at Jason. "I'm from the Acme dress shop. Are you Priscilla Winslow?"

"Why, yes I am."

"Well, I've come to either collect for that dress or take it back with me. Now make up your mind. Pay up or give me the dress." Peter's voice was loud, and those actors and stagehands who were passing along stopped and stared at him with disgust.

The door opened and Priscilla appeared in a dressing gown, saying, "What are you talk—" Her eyes flew open and she cried out, "Peter! It's you!" She threw her arms around him and held him close, then when he released her she turned and stared at Jason, saying, "Jase!" She didn't hug him, but she put out her hand, which he took rather awkwardly. "I'm so glad to see you both," she said. "Why didn't you tell me you were coming?"

"We wanted to surprise you. Jase and me have come to see the big city. Gonna get rich and make our fortunes, but I had to see my sister in all her glory. You were great, sis."

"Come inside. No, wait out here, let me get dressed. I want to hear all about your trip. Wait right here now."

The two men waited as Priscilla commanded, and when she exited, she was dressed in an expensive outfit. "Come on, now. We're going out to get something to eat. Oh . . . oh, Eddie, come here. I want you to meet my brother and his friend."

Eddie Rich had exited to their right wearing a flashy outfit, cut in the latest New York fashion, and took the two men in with a swift glance. When he was introduced, he smiled and shook hands with both of them. "I'm glad to meet you. You just get in?"

"Just got off the train. Been looking the big city over."

"Here for a visit?" Eddie asked. "Well, you'll have to let me show you around. There's lots to see. How long are you here for?"

"We can talk about that later. Let's go get something to eat. I know these two are starved," Priscilla said.

As they left the theater to go to a restaurant, Peter laughed as he explained how they had eaten by courtesy of their uncle Mark. Jason, however, was not laughing. He stayed behind, walking in step with Eddie Rich, half listening to the smaller man who spoke cheerfully enough, but he knew in his heart that something drastic had changed. An earthquake had come that had wrecked everything he had pinned his hopes on, and he knew that his trip was a lost pilgrimage.

★　★　★　★

The next day was a busy one for the two men. Priscilla insisted on getting up early and showing them about the city. That night she had taken them to a dinner that was being held at one of the large hotels. "Mostly actors," she said, "but you'll enjoy it, I'm sure."

The dinner was sumptuous, and the two men met so many actors and actresses and producers that all the names began to sound alike.

Priscilla knew why Jason had come, but she said nothing. She was filled with the idea of getting married, and she tried her best to be kind to him. When she saw him sitting glumly at his table, she went to him and said, "Jason, I want you to meet somebody. I've been telling them about you."

"I don't think I'd like to meet anybody, Priscilla."

"You'll enjoy these men, and they are very interested in somebody like you." He rose and followed her to a table where three men were sitting, dressed in tuxedos. "I'd like for you to meet Mr. Jason Ballard." She mentioned the names of the three men, but the only one that Jason caught was Edwin Porter. "These gentlemen are into something new, Jason. You've heard of the Nickelodeons?"

Jason nodded cautiously. "I guess I have. I even seen one in Cheyenne."

"Well, that's just the beginning. These gentlemen are going to do a lot of picture making, even longer ones, and some of them are going to involve horses." She smiled at the three men, saying, "Nobody in America knows more about horses than this man right here."

The leader of the three men gave Jason an interested look. "Is that right? Well, we're looking for someone with experience. We've got lots of horses, and they seem to be getting out of control. Cowboys are a pretty rough lot. You look like you might be able to handle not only the horses, but those tough cowboys as well."

"Handle them? What do you mean?" Jason asked.

"Sit down," the second man said, "let's talk a little business."

"I'll leave you here, Jason. After you listen to what these gentlemen have to say, come and tell me about it." She turned and winked at the three men, saying, "Remember, he's the best there is."

The three men began to question Jason at once, and finally one of them said, "If you're going to be in New York for a while, we could use a man like you."

"I'm not sure," Jason said. "I don't know this place. Horses and cattle are about all I know."

Mr. Porter leaned forward. "There's more money to be made in making pictures than in punching cattle, I think, Ballard. Here's your chance to get in on the ground floor. The way I see it, there's going to be about a thousand cowboy films made. Somebody's got to be in charge of that. I think you might be a good candidate. Think about it and get back to us." He handed Jason a card, saying, "Just call that number, and we'll talk terms."

Later, after the dinner was over, Jason found one moment to be alone with Priscilla. Rich stuck close to them, but he finally left to go to his hotel, and now the two were walking slowly along the sidewalk. Jason waited until they reached her hotel, and she said, "I'd like to ask you to come up, but I can't."

Jason Ballard was not a man of many words. The street was almost deserted at this late hour. He stood there quietly, his honest, blunt features there for her to read. "I came to see you, Priscilla," he said simply.

Priscilla swallowed hard. "I know you did, Jase."

"I want you to marry me."

"I . . . I knew you'd ask me that, but I can't. I'm going to marry Eddie Rich."

Many things sprang to Ballard's lips, but as he studied her face his heart grew cold. *She's made up her mind*, he thought. *And nothing will change her*. He said finally, "I wish you happiness, Priscilla, but I'll have to say I'm afraid that you're not going to find it."

Priscilla never remembered how she answered Jason. He turned and left finally, and as he disappeared down the street, she felt she had lost something very precious. Tears came to her eyes, and she dashed them away. "I can't be like this," she said, reprimanding herself. "He's a good friend from back home, but I love Eddie."

★ ★ ★ ★

"Come in, Esther. Sit down there. I'd offer you a cigar, but I don't suppose you smoke, even though you are an iron lady."

Hearst liked to tease Esther for some reason. He showed this humor very rarely, for he was not really a man who was light-hearted. As she entered his office and sat down, he lit up his own cigar and said cheerfully, "So, things are going well for you. The Dougherty thing turned out better than anybody had ever expected."

"I appreciate the bonus, Mr. Hearst," Esther said.

The Dougherty story had hit the papers and sold so fast that the presses could not keep up with the demands. As it turned out, Dougherty had won his public image back by slashing attacks on those who accused him and had proven his case at the trial of public opinion. He also had complimented Esther, offering her another bonus. "You saved my bacon, Miss Winslow," he had said, giving her a glad Irish smile.

Esther had refused the bonus, but she had made a friend in the stubby, powerful Irishman. And now she sat smiling across the room at Hearst, who leaned back at his large desk and observed her critically. "The Iron Lady, is it?"

"I don't particularly care for that name."

"It doesn't matter much. You're stuck with it. You should hear some of the names they call *me*!" Hearst seemed to find some joy and perverse delight in the fact that he was vilified, almost daily, in many newspapers and magazines. "I don't much care what people say about me as long as they talk about me. It sells papers." He grinned, then took a long puff on his cigar, letting the smoke curl lazily upward.

"Well, I suppose I hope they'll get over it, but I'm glad you like the story, Mr. Hearst."

Hearst sat at his desk for a while, talking about the Dougherty story. He complimented her highly, and then finally his pale eyes grew serious and his mouth drew into a straight line. "I've got something for you."

"For me?"

"Yes, it's what you wanted about the slum landlords. I've found out some of the names of the owners."

Esther, at once, grew interested. She sat up straighter and leaned forward slightly. "How did you find out?"

"Wasn't too much of a job for some of our older hands. They know where the bodies are buried." The grisly metaphor seemed to please him, and he said, "It's going to raise quite a stink when we drag them out to the full light of day."

"They deserve it!" Esther said indignantly. "Are you going to do a special series on them?"

"I think we might, but you may not like it as much as you think."

Esther could not understand his words, which came slow and deliberate. "I've always wanted this. I was the one who brought it to your attention, Mr. Hearst."

"That's right, but people don't always really want what they ask for."

Esther could not imagine what the publisher was getting at. "That makes no sense to me. I've found a great wrong. I'd like to see it righted. Every decent person would if they had to live in those squalid conditions."

Hearst paused, and silence seemed to fill the room. Esther had discovered that he was a man of some mystery. Her observations told her his mind was deep and tenuous and took routes that few could follow. Finally he smiled, and once again Esther thought how much he looked like a shark when he *did* smile.

"Here's the list of some of the most prominent owners of the tenements on the Lower East Side. I think you might be interested in at least one of them."

Esther took the sheet of paper, held his eyes for a moment, then glanced down at it. She read the first three names—and when she read the fourth, she froze. *Simon Barfield*. The letters jumped out at her, growing larger, and she could not at first put together what seemed to be the truth. Looking up, she saw that Hearst was observing her carefully.

"That surprises you, I take it?"

"I don't believe it," Esther said vehemently. "Simon is not that kind of man."

Hearst leaned forward and locked his fingers together. "I knew you'd take it like that so I had my man run a double check. The property is not in Barfield's name, not directly that is, but he controls the corporation that owns a large number of these slums—including the one where your favorite family, the Scarlottas, live. I checked that out myself."

A ringing seemed to come to Esther's ears, and she felt a tingling. It was as if she had fallen into freezing water and her mind would not work as well as it should. She tried to think of something that Simon had said that would indicate that this monstrous thing was true. However, she could not, and finally she swallowed hard and said, "Are you *absolutely* sure, Mr. Hearst?"

"I knew you would question this—so here, I had the facts all printed out for you. They won't be hard for you to check. You can see who owns the company that owns the slums, and if you'll question Mr. Barfield, I'm sure he will eventually have to tell you that he is, in fact, the tenement house owner." Hearst leaned back and stared at the girl. It had been an experiment for him. He wanted to see what this pretty, wealthy young girl would do when confronted with a raw slice of life. He, himself, felt that life was the struggle of the survival of the fittest. He began to speak rather softly, and there was a sadness in his tone. "This world, my dear, is a terrible and brutal affair. The whole planet is made up of rascals and torment. There's a curse upon it, I daresay." He looked out the window, thought for a moment, then said, "We're nothing better than ticks scattered on the ground. Maybe we started clean, but now we are living in the filth made by ourselves. And we breed our own ignorance and vice." He turned and looked at her with emptiness in his eyes. "One day some big wind will blow all this out, and all the men and the foolish little pride that we have will be swept away. Maybe then," he said, "the world will be clean again, and maybe there will be a better breed than we are."

"I don't really believe that," Esther said. "The world has its scoundrels, men and women alike, but it has its heroes, too. Maybe somebody was robbing a bank this morning at ten o'clock." Her clear eyes observed him, and there was a passion in her voice that she could not hold back. "And at the same time there was a fireman giving his life trying to save a child from a fire. You forget that side of life, Mr. Hearst."

William Randolph Hearst listened as Esther continued speaking intensely, proclaiming the nobility that she witnessed every day in the world she photographed. It was as if he wished to believe her, but he had seen too much evil and injustice to convince him otherwise. When she had finished he said gently, "I wish I hadn't shown you this list."

Esther got to her feet, held the papers tightly, then said, "I'm glad you did." Her voice was quiet, and she asked, "May I keep these?"

"Of course."

Esther turned and left the room without another word. Hearst leaned back in his chair. He felt a sadness that was unusual for him, for he knew that he had tried to wreck something fine and good and pure. "Still," he murmured aloud, "I'm doing the girl a favor. She may be honest, but that fellow Barfield isn't. She's better off knowing it now before it's too late."

★　★　★　★

Simon Barfield looked up with something like shock in his eyes as Esther simply entered the door. She had walked past the clerk, who was now sputtering outside. She came to stand before him, and Barfield said, "That's all right. Shut the door, Williams." When the door was closed, Simon stood and came to her side. "What's wrong, Esther? You're disturbed."

Esther thrust him the papers without saying a word.

Barfield glanced at them and instantly alarms went off in his head. A dozen possibilities of explaining the situation came to him. None of them sounded good enough to put before the young woman who stared at him with accusation and sorrow etched on her face.

"Esther, these people have to have somewhere to live," Barfield said slowly. "Someday all those will have to be torn down and better places built, but someday is not good enough for those people. They have to have a place to live now. Those are the only places that exist. It's true I own them, and it's true I'm not proud of the condition they're in, otherwise I'd have put my name on them, but somebody has to provide housing for the immigrants that are swarming in here."

"Are you telling me you're doing it as a benevolent enterprise, Simon?" Irony was thick in the statement, and Esther was standing with her back stiff. "I thought better of you than that," she said, glaring at him.

"Now, wait a minute, Esther. You're not looking at this as clearly as you should."

"I'm looking at it the way any honest person would. You're charging those people three times what the filthy hovels are worth, and you never do one thing to improve their situation. In other words, you're growing rich off of their poverty. How can you take any pride in that?"

Simon at once began a spirited defense of his ownership, but Esther only stood and looked at him. Finally he grew angry and shouted, "It's easy enough for you to talk like this. You're only a woman. You've been raised with a silver spoon in your mouth. You never had to work for anything. If you were a man, you'd know that men do what they have to do."

"Are you telling me you *have* to do this, Simon?" Esther shook her head and realized that something had come to an end in her life. She studied Simon Barfield carefully, wondering how he could be two men. At times there was a good side to him. He could be charming and generous—she had seen an occasion or two of that—but now she saw him for what he really was—a vicious predator on helpless victims.

Slipping her ring off her finger, Esther held it out and dropped it onto the cluttered desk. "I can never marry a man who puts profit above character. I'm sorry for you, Simon. Please don't come calling again. It's over."

Simon Barfield was not accustomed to being dismissed, and he was so stunned, as a matter of fact, that Esther had turned and left the room before he could react. He picked up the ring and held it in his hand, looking down at its glitter, remembering the night he had given it to her, and she had seemed glad enough. He moved toward the door but stopped with his hand on the knob. *I can't go out there, calling after her, begging,* he thought, a fierce, bitter stream of anger running through his veins. He stood there wanting to shove his fist through the door, to run after her—to grab her and shake her, but he knew better than that. Slowly he mastered himself, turned back, sat down in the chair, and waited until the rage had subsided to a dull throb. He thought of what had happened. He thought of their courtship and knew that it was indeed over. She would never again have any respect for him, and despite himself, he felt a sense of shame. He thought of the clean honesty in her face and how she had not flinched as she stood before him. Somehow this made him even more bitter, and he said aloud, "She's not different from the rest of us, and she won't forget this. I'll see that she doesn't. . . !

CHAPTER SEVENTEEN

A MATTER OF LIFE OR DEATH

★ ★ ★ ★

"Well, Pete, you don't have to pull my arm off—I'm coming!"

Peter Winslow halted, gave a surprised look at his sister, and then grinned boyishly. "Sorry about that, but you just have to see this show." He pulled at her again, and Priscilla allowed herself to be towed along through the masses of people that were flooding into Madison Square Garden. They had entered the massive building with the rising towers that marked the showplace for exhibitions in New York City. Primarily it had become known for bicycle races and horse shows, and Peter had informed her that the really *important* show was taking place there—the National Automobile Show. He had approached her early that morning and practically forced her to accompany him.

"I've never *seen* so many people!" she said. "I wouldn't have thought there were that many people interested in these horseless carriages."

Peter shouldered his way through the crowd. His tall, strong figure gave him an advantage, and he was searching the area ahead as he answered, "Why, sis, you don't know what you're talking about. There's going to be over five hundred cars here, built by three hundred different automobile makers!"

Soon they found their way into the massive showroom, where Peter took her from one exhibition to the other, speaking so rapidly that Priscilla was amused at her brother's enthusiasm. She saw that this young brother of hers was completely enamored with this new invention that seemed to be sweeping America. They all looked, more or less, alike to her. Some looked like buggies without horses. Most of them were steered by a tiller that extended from the front.

"Look, you see this one? This is a Stanley Steamer made by two brothers, both with whiskers, identical twins. You just fill the boiler up, get steam going, and off you go. Why, as long as you had fuel and water, you could go forever!"

"That's wonderful, Pete," she said, trying to summon up her excitement and listen as he tried to explain all the new cars. She stared at him quizzically for a moment and said, "But I thought you liked horses."

"Why, horses are fun, all right, but you can't find a horse that can go as fast as this little hummer right here." He put his hand, almost reverently, on an automobile that was admired by throngs who crowded in closer. It looked a little less like a wagon and had two shiny brass lights over the front fenders, with two seats adorning the top. Peter said, "Look, it's got a steering wheel instead of a tiller. It makes it lots easier to drive, I bet."

"It's very nice. Who made this one?"

"A fellow called Henry Ford," Peter replied. He began spieling off information rapidly. "Ford made a Quadricle back in '96. It just had bicycle wheels and a buggy chassis and gas pipe hubs. It had two forward speeds, though, ten and twenty miles an hour, but no reverse."

"But what if you wanted to go backward?"

"I suppose you'd have to turn around in a circle, but that's no problem now. This Model A has a reverse in it." He went on speaking, and finally he stiffened and said, "Look, there's Mr. Ford now. I met him the other day. Come on, I'll introduce you to him."

Peter pushed his way through the crowds, dragging Priscilla behind toward the tall, thin-faced man who had entered the display arena. Without preamble Peter walked right up to the man and said, "Mr. Ford, I'm Peter Winslow. I met you yesterday."

"Why, yes, I remember." Ford's lips turned upward in a smile. "You still wild about automobiles after twenty-four hours, Peter?"

"Why, Mr. Ford, you might as well get used to me. I'm going to be around automobiles as long as I live. Oh, this is my sister, Miss Priscilla Winslow."

Ford's pale eyes lighted upon the young woman, and he nodded, saying agreeably, "I'm happy to make your acquaintance. This brother of yours is pestering me to give him a job. Can be rather dangerous driving these racing cars."

"But, Mr. Ford, it can't be any worse than topping an outlaw bronc," Peter protested. Ford was a handsome young man, and several had gathered around the famous Henry Ford to listen to the conversation. Peter paid no attention to them but presented his case more earnestly. "I'll do *anything*, Mr. Ford! Sweep the floor, mop up—just let me be around your factory and learn something about cars."

"And maybe drive that new racing car I designed?"

Peter grinned rashly. "That's what I've got in mind."

Henry Ford had incorporated his company called the Ford Motor Company that very year with only twenty-eight thousand dollars in capital. The first Model A Runabout with its solid L-head engine and twin opposing cylinders was taking the fledgling industry by storm. Ford was also interested in racing cars, however, and had done some racing himself.

"What do you think about that Oldsmobile down in Florida, Mr. Ford?" Peter spoke of an Oldsmobile racer called a "Pirate," which had broken the speed record, covering a mile in less than a minute and forty-two seconds.

Ford frowned and shook his head. "I think it'll be beaten many times over. Are you serious about working with automobiles?"

"Yes, I am, Mr. Ford. Just give me a chance, that's all I ask."

"Very well. Come to Detroit, if you can find your way there," he smiled frostily. "I'll see if you're any good—but no guarantees."

"That's great, Mr. Ford. I'll be there."

That was the high point of the automobile show for Peter. Filled with excitement at the unexpected prospect of actually working for Henry Ford, Peter babbled all the way back to the restaurant where they had lunch. "Can't wait to write the folks."

"They won't be happy to hear it," Priscilla observed. "Cass is gone. I'm gone, and now you're gone. They'll be lonely without us."

Peter's face fell, and he remained silent for one moment, toying with his food. "I suppose you're right, but I've got to do this thing. I've just got to, Pris!"

Priscilla leaned over and put her hand on her brother's hand. "I know, Pete, and maybe now you understand more about why I had to leave. I just couldn't face life there on the ranch forever."

Peter suddenly seized her hand and held it. His face grew serious and he said slowly, "I know you had to get away, but I'm worried about you, sis. You're jumping into this marriage too quick. You don't know enough about this man."

"I love him, I know that much."

"You're caught up in all the glamour of show business. He's a romantic sort of guy to you, but—"

"Pete, I don't want to talk about it." There was still a sense of shame in Priscilla over her affair with Eddie Rich. Somehow she felt now that if she didn't marry him, it would all have been cheap and tawdry. Marriage would make it what it was, a real love match. She had reproved herself and grieved over giving in to his demands, but now there was nothing to do but to go through with it. Besides, she really loved him. She told herself this constantly. Smiling at Peter, she said, "It'll be all right. You'll like Eddie when you get to know him."

Peter started to answer, and then a movement caught his eye. He turned his head quickly, saying, "Oh, there's Jase. I asked him to meet us here." When he turned back he saw that this disturbed Priscilla and said quickly, "It's all right, isn't it?"

"Oh . . . of course it is." Priscilla smiled and said, "Hello, Jase, you're still in time for lunch."

"No, I'll just have some coffee." Jason folded his lanky frame into one of the chairs. He always managed to look slightly uncomfortable in these highly civilized situations. He looked perfectly normal on a horse, but fancy cafes, restaurants, and theaters made him feel uneasy, and he longed to be back on the ranch.

"Let me tell you about my new job," Peter said. They listened while he explained eagerly about his encounter with Henry Ford. When he was finished, he said, "I'll get you a job there, too. We'll be together, Jase."

"No, no automobiles for me," Jason said almost languidly. He sat there quietly for a moment, then said, "I been doing pretty well with this job with Mr. Porter."

Edwin Porter, the producer who had hired Jason, was not famous as yet, and Peter was curious. "Tell us about it. What sort of work have you been doing for Mr. Porter?"

"Well, they're making what they call a moving picture. Something like the old Nickelodeons, but not exactly."

The Nickelodeon had been popular for several years, ever since its invention by Thomas Alva Edison. It consisted of a series of pictures being flipped in rapid motion, giving the illusion of movement. Its fame had spread across America like a prairie fire. Nickelodeon parlors spotted practically every town in America.

"What's the difference in a Nickelodeon and this here moving picture you're making, Jase?" Peter inquired.

"Well, of course, I don't know anything about it," Jason shrugged his shoulders, "but it seems to me that it's a story instead of just pictures."

"What kind of a story?" Priscilla inquired.

"It's just about a bunch of outlaws who hold up a train." He grinned and said, "Got a fella called George Barnes who's the star of the thing. He's never been on a horse in his life. I spent most of my time tying him on. That's my job, I guess. Taking care of the horses, and being sure if people fall off they get put back on."

"That sounds interesting, but it'll never take the place of a play on the stage."

"Mr. Porter says it will," Jason shrugged. "He's gonna make a whole bunch of what he calls Westerns. Stories about people out West, cowboys and Indians. Things like that."

"Are you going to stay with him, Jase?" Peter demanded.

"I guess I will—for a while, anyway."

Priscilla knew, in her heart, that Jason Ballard had no interest in such things, that he cared only for the life of a rancher. She knew, also, that he was staying in the hope that she would change her mind and refuse to marry Eddie Rich. She could say nothing, however, and she hated to hurt this tall man who had been such a devoted admirer for so long. Now as she thought about it, she realized how unfair she had been to him. She had led Jason on and given him cause to think that she cared more for him than she really did. She could think of no way to ease the pain she saw in his eyes. She was glad when the dinner was over and quickly excused herself to go to rehearsal.

The two men sat there and Jason said nothing. Noticing the silence of his friend, Peter said hopefully, "Maybe she'll change her mind. She's got sense, deep down, Jase. She's just blinded by all the glamour in this place."

"I don't think so," Jason said quietly. "She's got her head set on marrying this dandy, and you know how stubborn she is when she wants something."

★ ★ ★ ★

L. C. Baines looked more like a clerk in a dry goods store than a private investigator. This was a great asset to him, because he was able to fade into obscurity against almost any background. When he put on an expensive suit, he could pass for a minor stockbroker—but when he put on ragged work clothing, he could pass just as easily for a working man at the docks. He had chosen this latter dress to observe the movements of his quarry and had succeeded in attracting no attention whatsoever from the inhabitants of the tenement district.

"Keep your eye on this fellow Kruger," Simon Barfield had said. "I want him nailed."

"You want him roughed up, Mr. Barfield?" Baines had asked calmly. He was capable of providing this service, and had done so on other occasions, but he had been informed by Barfield that the thing must be legal. "What do I have to find him doing?" he had asked.

"It's against the law to practice medicine without a license. You've got to catch him doing something like that."

Baines had been doubtful. "Most people take care of ailments themselves—poor people especially. They won't put him in jail for putting a mustard plaster on somebody's chest."

"No, it'll have to be more than that, but I'm paying you good money to find out, so get at it!"

Baines had not been optimistic; however, for over two weeks he had shadowed Jan Kruger relentlessly. He had managed to keep himself out of sight, and Kruger, of course, had no reason to suspect that anyone was watching his movements. Baines had made several acquaintances on the street where the Scarlottas lived, passing himself off as a working man. He had learned at once the facts of the case, that Kruger had been a physician in South Africa, and that he was eagerly sought by the poor of this section when they had ailments they could not afford to take to a physician.

Thursday afternoon had come, and Baines was weary of his task. He was used to stakeouts and had the patience of Job when there was some hope of achieving his end, but there seemed to be no possibility of success in this case. "I'll have to give it up," he muttered to himself as he leaned against the outside of the building across from the Scarlottas' tenement. "Barfield's expecting results, and I can't manufacture something like that." He pulled out a pipe, loaded it, and began to smoke it. He finally muttered between puffs, "I'll give it two more days. If nothing comes up, that's it. . . ."

★   ★   ★   ★

Esther had made one of her periodic visits to the Scarlottas. After paying the cab driver, she climbed the stairs to the apartment. Jan answered the door, and taking one look at the strained look on his face, she asked instantly, "What's the matter? Is it Lucia?"

"Yes, it's almost time for the baby, and something bothers me about her condition—"

The door leading to the bedroom opened, and Maria came out, her face pale and stiff with fear. Ignoring Esther, she said, "Jan, she's not doing good!"

Esther said, "We need to get her to the hospital right away."

"I tried to tell her that," Jan nodded in agreement. He stood there thoughtfully, his brow furrowed, and shook his head. "She refuses to go. It's not just a matter of money; it's not the tradition of these people. They're really afraid of hospitals."

"But she knows Dr. Burns."

"Yes, and she likes him. Maria, come on. You've got to help me talk her into going right now!"

Esther tried to read a story to Emila and Michael, but she

found it difficult to keep her mind on what she was reading. She had grown very fond indeed of all the Scarlottas and did not like to think that anything bad would happen to Lucia. When she finished the story, the two children begged her to let them go down and play with the other children on the first floor. They had friends there, and finally when the door opened and they besieged Jan, he agreed at once. "Yes, go down there, both of you. Don't go outside, just play with Anna and Julio."

As soon as the children left, Esther rose, saying, "It's serious, isn't it?"

"Yes, it is." Jan gnawed on his lip, then shook his head. "I've got to check one more time. You can come if you want, but it's not something that most people like to be involved with."

"Having a baby?" Esther did not know whether to be insulted, but she was certainly surprised. "Why, every woman's interested in that."

Jan didn't argue with her but turned and walked back into Lucia's room. Esther followed him and was shocked at the haggard look on Lucia's face. Maria was standing beside her mother, holding her hand, her face stiff with anxiety. Esther spoke cheerfully, going over to take Lucia's hand. "Well, it won't be long now, but I want to get you into the hospital."

"No," Lucia moaned. "Not now. I want to have the baby here."

"I'm going to have to examine you one more time, Lucia," Jan said. He began to move the sheet that covered the enormous, swollen stomach and started his examination. Maria kept her eyes fixed on him, but Esther turned her face away. She held Lucia's hand, aware that Jan was using the stethoscope that she had purchased for him at a pawn shop. She spoke cheerfully to Lucia but saw the woman's eyes were rolling back and that her breath was coming in short gasps. Finally, after what seemed a long time, she heard Jan exclaim, "Lucia, your baby! He's dying!"

At first Esther thought she had misunderstood, but whirling, she saw that Kruger's face was still, and his brow was covered with sweat. "What's wrong?" she cried. Lucia's hands were squeezing her so tightly that they pained her, but she could not think of that.

"The baby's heartbeat has gone down," Jan said. "I can see the cord; it's right beside the baby's head. When that happens, the baby can't live." Jan was bent over, and an agony of indecision came across his face. "The only way the baby can survive is through the umbilical cord. When it becomes compressed, like it is now, the baby can't get adequate blood flow."

"You mean my baby's going to die!" Lucia cried. "No!" she screamed. "Save my baby, Jan."

"Jan—can't you do anything? Let's get her to the hospital!" Maria cried frantically.

"There's no time. There's no time at all. The baby will be dead in a few minutes if it isn't born soon."

"Do something! Please, Jan. Don't-a let my baby die!" Lucia sobbed.

"Isn't there anything at all, Jan?" Esther asked numbly. She had never faced a life-or-death situation such as this. The seriousness of it seemed to rob her of thought and will.

Jan Kruger's lips went tight. "We can . . . take the baby surgically."

Maria stared at him. "Take the baby—? What does that mean?"

"I can make an incision here and take the baby that way."

"Will that save the child?" Esther asked.

"Yes, but I'm not licensed here to do that."

Lucia was not concerned about qualifications or medical certificates. She was screaming now. "Doctor Jan, save my baby! Don't let him die!"

Jan Kruger stood there, his face twisted into a tortured expression. He knew that if he did not act soon, the baby would not survive if he did not perform the operation. He had done such operations many times and did not doubt that it was the medically correct thing to do. He also knew that he would be liable to the rigors of the law if he did perform the operation. Lucia was begging and pleading with him, and he looked over and saw Esther's face, which was set and pale, a pleading in her eyes.

Maria whispered, "Please—help us, Jan!"

"All right," he said abruptly. He snatched the bag that he had put together and said, "You'd better leave, Esther."

"No, I'm staying here. Maybe I can help."

"You'd be an accomplice if you do. Get out of here!"

But Esther's courage rose and she said firmly, "Go ahead, Jan. Do it! Quick, save the child."

Jan felt one brief moment of admiration for this young woman, then looked at Lucia and said quietly, "All right, Lucia, I'll try to save your baby. . . !"

★ ★ ★ ★

L. C. Baines became suddenly aware that something was happening in the tenement across the street when he saw two women standing outside, talking and gesturing excitedly with their hands. He was interested in anything in that building and moved quickly across the street to where he could hear the women's conversation.

"He's-a cut her wide open," one woman gasped. "Jan, he's-a cut Lucia. She's-a bleed bad."

Baines immediately said, "What's the matter? Do we need to get a doctor? I'll go get one."

The woman shook her head. "Lucia, she's going to die. Jan, he's cut her open with his knife."

At once Baines left, hollering, "I'll get a doctor." He did not, however, go to get a physician. Instead, he grabbed a policeman who was walking his beat. "There's a man that cut a woman," he said. "You've got to come and arrest him."

"What's that you say?" The Irish policeman stared at him with shock, then his mouth grew tense. "Let's go! Show me where it is."

When Baines brought the policeman back, he led the way at once to the second floor. "It's right in there," Baines said, pointing to the door of the Scarlottas' apartment. "Do your duty, Officer."

The policeman did not knock on the door but stepped inside. There was no one in the living area, but the door to a bedroom was open. Moving carefully, his eyes half-shut, knowing the possibility of danger, he held his billy club high and slipped over to the doorway. What he saw there caused him to halt—a bed, crimson with blood, and a man stitching a terrible wound in a woman's stomach. A dark-haired young woman was standing beside the man, helping him by applying cloths to the bleeding wound. "Stop right there!" he said.

At that moment a young girl, who was holding a newborn baby and washing him off, said, "Officer, you don't understand.

He had to take the baby." The officer stood for a moment, confused as he looked at the young girl with the baby and then back to the bed where the man was bent over the woman. "What do you mean *take* the baby? He's cut that woman! You're under arrest. What's your name?"

The tall man did not look up. He was stitching, making the stitches evenly, and his voice was calm as he said, "My name is Jan Kruger."

"Are you a doctor, then?"

"No, I'm not a doctor."

The officer shoved his hat back and removed it, and finally he turned it around in his hands. "I'll have to put you under arrest. You'll have a chance to defend yourself in court."

Esther, busy now helping Maria wash the new child off with a sponge, said nothing, but she knew that Jan Kruger now faced the greatest trial of his life—and she knew that she was in the fight with him.

CHAPTER EIGHTEEN

"GOD CAN STRAIGHTEN
IT ALL OUT"

★ ★ ★ ★

"You've got to do something, Dad. Jan's been arrested and thrown in jail."

Mark Winslow had been almost assaulted as his daughter had come storming into his office in downtown Manhattan. He had managed to quiet her down, and finally she told the story of Jan's arrest. Her face was pale, but her eyes flashed with anger. She ended by saying, "And so you see, we've got to get him out of jail."

"Let me get this straight. What was he charged with?"

"Well, at first they charged him with assault. When I showed them how ridiculous that was—that he had saved a baby's life—they seemed to get angry about it. It was like they didn't want to lose a suspect, Dad."

"Now, take it easy. They were just doing their jobs, I'm sure. What happened when you got to the station?"

"Well," Esther said, shaking her head in an angry gesture, "he told them what had happened, but they're so ignorant. They didn't understand why he had to take the baby. All they could see was that Lucia had been cut with a knife and that Jan held the knife."

"I imagine it was a pretty messy scene when the officer got there," Mark suggested.

"Well—of course it was. There's no way to do a thing like that neatly."

"So the officer saw a woman all covered with blood and a man with a knife. I don't imagine the poor officer had any medical training, so I can understand the confusion."

"Well, it was so foolish," Esther snapped, her eyes practically sparking with indignation. "They did a lot of talking and finally got a detective in there. Then he called somebody down at city hall and they charged Jan with practicing medicine without a license." Angrily she got up and took several quick paces, came over, and stood before her father, saying, "Dad, we've got to go get him out, right now!"

"All right, we'll just do that. Come along." Mark grabbed his hat and shrugged his coat onto his shoulders as the two left. When they were in the carriage, he gave the driver an address, then turned to say, "We're going to pick up some help on the way."

"What sort of help, a lawyer?"

"Yes, his name is Phineas Mott. He's a little bit strange, so don't be shocked at anything you see or hear."

"I don't care what he looks like. Is he a good lawyer?"

"The best I know," Mark said confidently. "I've tried everything I know to get him to work for the Union Pacific, but he's making too much money in private practice."

Ten minutes later they were in the outer office of Phineas Mott. An elderly lady stepped inside to ask if Mott would see them and was out again instantly. "Mr. Mott will see you. This way, please."

Esther followed her father inside the office, and once they had cleared the door, she stopped almost in shock, for there stood Abraham Lincoln!

The man who rose from his desk and came across the room in a shambling gait looked exactly like Abraham Lincoln. At least he looked like the pictures she had seen of Abraham Lincoln. Mott was over six four, lanky, lean, with a cavernous face, and a shock of black hair, salted with gray. His eyes were set deep in their sockets, and a large nose was centered between very high cheekbones. "How do you do, Mark?" he said amiably as he stretched out his hand.

"Hello, Phineas, this is my daughter, Esther. Esther, Mr. Phineas Mott."

Mott's hand seemed to be enormous, but he held Esther's very gently. A smile touched his lips, and his eyes opened slightly wider. "Well . . . the Iron Lady."

Esther flushed and shook her head. "That's a foolish name that was put on me, Mr. Mott."

"I think it fits you pretty well. It takes a lot of courage and determination for a young girl to throw herself into a world that's dominated by men. I enjoyed the spread you did on the slums. Very fine work, indeed!"

"Mr. Mott, I want to talk about a friend. He's in trouble, and we need help."

"Why, sure." Mott waved at two red plush chairs in front of his rosewood desk, then ambled over and unfolded his lanky body into the one behind the desk. He folded his hands into a steeple, leaned back, and said, "Let's have it."

Esther had collected her thoughts and soon found herself able to tell her story much more calmly. Mott missed none of the personal aspects of this. This Jan Kruger, whoever he was, was more than just a casual acquaintance of Miss Esther Winslow, the lawyer shrewdly deduced. He said not a word, but when Esther finished he said, "Well, it sounds like a strange case. He's charged with practicing medicine without a license. He doesn't have a license then, I take it?"

"No, not in this country—but he does in South Africa."

"Are you sure of that?"

"What do you mean, am I sure?"

"I mean, have you ever seen his medical credentials?"

"Why . . . no, I never asked."

"Do you know anyone who has seen them? Do you know anything about his life in that country?"

"I know that he's a doctor."

"How can you know that if you haven't seen his credentials?"

"Why, I've seen him treat sick people. He's wonderful with them, Mr. Mott."

Mott shook his head despairingly. "We have granny women and herb women back in the hills of Tennessee where I grew up who treat people too. They're able to help folks sometimes. They know some pretty good cures for minor things, but they're not doctors, and they can't operate."

Esther was nonplused for a moment, but then she lifted her chin, saying defiantly, "All you have to do is look at him. He has the air of knowing just exactly what he's doing."

"I'm afraid that won't impress a jury very much—or a judge."

Mark interrupted, saying quietly, "I think he'll be able to produce the proper papers, although it may take a little time. We need to get him out of jail, Phineas."

"That shouldn't be too hard. There'll be a bond."

"Oh, I'll take care of that," Mark assured him.

"Let me ask a few more questions, then we'll go."

Phineas Mott's "few more questions" turned out to be forty-five minutes of questioning Esther about everything she knew about Jan Kruger. He probed incessantly, not stopping for one moment, until finally Esther was exhausted.

"Well, I guess that'll do it. Let's go down and get the gentleman out."

Thirty minutes later they were standing inside the city jail in front of a blunt-faced sergeant. The man listened as Mott explained the purpose of their coming and said, "There's a thousand-dollar bond on him."

"I'll take care of that. Will a check do?" Mark asked, pulling a checkbook out of his inner pocket.

"You can get a bail bondsman to do that," Mott objected. "There's no sense paying all your hard-earned money, then."

"I'd rather do it this way," Mark said briefly. He scribbled on the slip of paper, handed it to the sergeant, who stared at it. "Will that do, Sergeant?"

"Yes, sir. I'll get the prisoner."

Five minutes later Jan Kruger came out of the interior of the building, shrugging into his coat. He needed a shave, and his eyes went at once to Esther, who said, "Are you all right, Jan?"

"Yes, I am fine."

"This is Mr. Mott, your lawyer," Mark said. "Mr. Mott, this is Jan Kruger."

The two men shook hands and Kruger said, "I didn't expect this. Thank you very much."

"Oh, don't mention it," Mark said. "You're going home with

us for a few days, until we get this thing straightened out."

"No, I really can't do that."

"Of course you can." Mark overrode Kruger's objection and said, "Will that be all right, Phineas?"

"Yes, I'll want to be having some long talks. Can you come by my office tomorrow?"

"Yes, I can do that," Jan Kruger said quietly.

"Fine. Mark, I want to talk to you a few moments. Maybe we can find a room here so you won't have to go back to my office."

They made the arrangements to use one of the rooms at the jail, and Mark said, "Take Jan down to the cafeteria off Thirty-second Street. I'll meet you there."

"All right, Dad."

As they left the jail, Esther said, "The cafeteria is down this way. I'll bet you're hungry."

"They fed us once, but I didn't have any appetite."

They strode along, and Esther said, "I hope you aren't too worried about all this."

"I'm afraid I am, a little bit."

Esther kept up a cheerful talk all the way to the cafeteria. Finally they got there, went in, and ordered sandwiches and coffee. "I have no money," Jan said, smiling grimly. "I hope you do."

"Oh yes. It doesn't matter."

"It does to me, but there's not much I can do about it."

Esther waited until the food came. As they ate, Kruger did not seem to have much appetite. He only nibbled at the sandwich. Finally he laid his head back against the padded surface of the divider and closed his eyes. He was silent for so long that Esther asked, "Are you all right, Jan?"

"Yes." He opened his eyes and gave her a wan smile. "The jail. It brought back some vivid memories of the prison camp."

"I'm sorry you had to go there."

"Well, it's all right, but I have bad memories of the camp, of people dying and being locked up. That's the worst thing of all. Dying is not so bad, but to be locked up, that's the worst."

He talked for a while and finally turned and saw that she was sitting with her back stiffly erect. Her hands were locked in front of her, white with strain as she clenched them together. A surprised look came to his eyes, and he reached over and held the two inside his own hands. "You shouldn't be so tense," he said.

"I can't help it. It's so . . . so wrong!"

"Many things in the world are wrong, but God is always right. Whatever happens is in God's hands."

"I wish I could think like that. I try to, but when things go wrong—like this, I just seem to get more and more angry."

"The wrath of man worketh not the righteousness of God," Jan quoted. "I know the feeling, though. I get angry sometimes when I see wrong and injustice, but we mustn't do that."

Esther was very conscious of his hands enfolding hers. They were big hands and strong. She enjoyed the power that was in them. It was a strange thing, for she was not a woman who had put great emphasis on the physical strength that a man had. She admired much more the other elements, such as character and courage. Jan had them all, and now as his hands held hers, warming them, she did not move for a long time but whispered quietly, "You mustn't worry, and you mustn't let me worry." She ducked her head and shook it, almost in despair. "They call me the Iron Lady, but I don't want to be like that. I want to be soft and gentle, like my mother."

"She was quite a lady in her younger years—somewhat like you, I imagine," Kruger smiled. The two sat there talking, and finally Kruger removed his hands self-consciously.

After a time Mark came in and said, "If you're ready, we'll go."

As they made the trip back to the house, they avoided talking about the case. Esther had decided that it would do no good to talk about it. When they got there Lola met them and went at once to Jan, putting her hands out. She squeezed his, saying, "It will be all right, Jan. Mark Called and told me everything. God is going to do something."

"It is good to hear you say that. When the skies are dark, we need to have those about us who are encouraging. You know," Jan said, looking at the three, "there's a verse I've always loved in the Bible. It says, two are better than one, and a threefold cord is not easily broken."

"I like that verse, too," Esther said almost shyly.

"Have you eaten?" Lola asked.

"Yes, but might we have some of that pie if you have any saved."

"Of course I have."

The three took off their coats and went to the dining room while Lola went to the kitchen. She came back in with slices of peach pie and thick mugs of steaming hot coffee. As they talked, the tension seemed to flow out of Jan Kruger. The only thing he said was, just before he went to bed, "I would not like to go to jail. I'd rather be deported than that, but whatever happens, I will always remember the Winslows." Thanking them again for what they had done, Jan excused himself and headed for his room.

A few minutes later, Mark stood and said, "Good night, Esther. I'll see you in the morning."

Esther remained and talked for a while with Lola. She felt the need for her mother's approval and the quiet confidence that she always found in her. Finally, they began to talk about Jan, and straightforwardly Lola said, "Do you love this man, Esther?"

"I think I love him," Esther said quietly, "but I'm all mixed up. I thought for a time I loved Simon, but I see now that I didn't. How can I know I'm right in what I'm feeling, Mother?"

"It's hard sometimes. We make mistakes . . . we get disappointments," Lola said, her eyes wise and her lips soft with compassion, "but we mustn't give up. We can't live in a cave and be hermits."

Esther reached out and her mother enfolded her in her arms. As Lola held her daughter, she said quietly, "It may be mixed up to you, but God can straighten it all out."

PART FOUR

RUTH

★ ★ ★ ★

1903

CHAPTER NINETEEN

DR. BURNS SPEAKS OUT

★ ★ ★ ★

Silver Moon had proved to be a most successful musical for Marvin Watts. This came as no surprise to anyone, least of all to the tall producer himself, for he had enjoyed an unbroken series of successful productions on the Great White Way. Watts had managed this without paying the astronomical salaries demanded by the stellar actors and actresses of the day. He had accomplished it by an astute sense of the theater—especially where personnel for his productions were concerned. He was considered a star maker, and hundreds of young hopefuls lived for the day when Marvin Watts would see them in a bit part and invite them to join one of his companies. As soon as his actors gained stature and started demanding larger fees, Watts usually let them go, having discovered another struggling young thespian.

Eddie Rich had not been able to integrate himself into Watts' good graces—at least not enough to obtain a part in *Silver Moon*. The play had packed houses every night for weeks, and already the rather small cosmos that made up the theater in New York was beginning to whisper the name of Priscilla Winslow. Being the protegee of Marvin Watts would have been enough to ensure that, but there was a charm and freshness in the young woman that attracted the rather jaded theatergoers of the big city. Somehow she gave the impression of enjoying her performances, as least as much as the audience itself. And though most singers were not great actresses, Priscilla threw herself into learning this art with all of her powers, and there was an almost pathetic effort to please that was obvious to those who came to see the play.

Eddie Rich saw Priscilla as his one chance to move in the upper heavens of the theater world, but he knew that this could not go on forever. As the play gained momentum, Rich became more and more aware that he was arriving at a crisis in his life.

Priscilla was happy—after a fashion. No young woman who loved the life of the theater as much as she did could be completely dissatisfied with all the attention that she was receiving. She was meeting legends, the living realities of those whose pictures had been pasted to the walls of her small room back in Wyoming. She was in awe of them, and, of course, the promise of even more success on the stage, as set before her by Marvin Watts and Eddie Rich, allured her to throw herself into her acting and singing even more. She never grew tired, and every night, when the curtain went up, became a new adventure for her. She would have performed matinees for nothing, for she was grasped by an intoxication that sometimes came to those who achieved success in the world of the theater.

But Priscilla, beneath the surface of all the outward excitement, was not content. She was a young woman who had been reared in a conservative world, though she, herself, had sometimes rebelled at the strictness of the rules. Nevertheless, she was sure that her parents and others had laid hold on a basic truth. She was never able to get out of her mind the knowledge that by surrendering herself to Eddie Rich she had deeply violated an inner consciousness, and she knew that something precious had passed away because of her surrender.

More than once Priscilla had decided to break with Eddie, and one Tuesday afternoon she was thinking on this as she sat in her apartment reading a letter from her mother. She always opened mail from her parents with a feeling of foreboding, for somehow she was certain they knew all about her arrangement with Eddie Rich—although they never rebuked her. Her conscience was quick and active, and as she opened this letter she scanned it quickly, then breathed a sigh of relief, thinking, *They don't know about Eddie and me, but they'll find out sometime, and I know what it will do to them.*

She had almost finished reading the letter when a knock sounded at the door. She rose, putting the letter aside, and went to the door. When she opened it, she saw Eddie standing there, a broad smile on his face.

"Hello, sweetheart," he said cheerfully. He stepped inside, kissed her lightly, then turned to her, an unusual light of expectancy in his eyes. "I've got to talk to you. Something you'll be glad to hear."

"What is it, Eddie?"

"I've been thinking about us," he said quickly. There was a coolness in her eyes that frightened him, and he hurriedly said, "I want us to get married right away!" He saw her expression change at once and knew that he had said exactly the right thing. "I would have insisted before now, Priscilla, but like I said, I don't have the money to support you, and I probably never will."

Relief surged through Priscilla, and she cried at once, "Oh, Eddie, money doesn't matter!" He put his arms around her and kissed her, and she held him closely. "We'll make it fine. You'll be a fine manager, and whatever play I'm in, we'll make them give you a part."

For the next ten minutes she talked rapidly, her eyes bright, the tension gone from her body, and finally she said, "I'll have to make all kinds of plans—to get a dress, find a church, and send out invitations."

Eddie hesitated, then said, "I wish we had time for all that, but really I don't want to wait. Let's just get married. What difference does a dress and a church and all that matter? It's two people in love, that's what counts. Isn't it, Priscilla?"

Priscilla halted, taken somewhat aback by the urgency of his words. "Well, I don't really know many people here—old friends that is. There're just Ruth and Esther, and of course my brother Peter will want to come." She did not mention Jason Ballard and was conscious of the omission. Jason had come by twice, but there was a constraint in Priscilla that she knew he must have felt. He stopped coming by, but she received a note from time to time.

Eddie Rich began to press his case. "Let's just get married and announce that we've done it. You can tell your friends and family about it afterward. Your folks couldn't come all the way out from Wyoming for the ceremony, could they?"

"No, they couldn't," Priscilla said reluctantly. She had always dreamed of having a wedding with her mother there, and her father walking down the aisle beside her to give her away, with her friends around. But now this seemed impossible. Slowly she nodded her head. "I suppose that will be all right, Eddie."

"Good! I'm a man who likes to get things done, especially with you, sweetheart. I'll whiz down to get all the paper work done and then find a minister. We'll get married right here, this afternoon," he said. "Then after that, since this is Saturday, we'll have Sunday and most of Monday for our honeymoon. That's not much, but it's all we can spare. With the way the play is going, we couldn't afford to miss the performances, could we?"

"I . . . I guess not."

"Swell!" Eddie kissed her and hugged her strongly. A big smile lit his features, and he was excited. "I'll be back as soon as I get things done. Why don't you go get yourself a new dress? But be back here by three o'clock."

"All right, Eddie. I'll be here."

After Eddie left, Priscilla walked slowly back across the room and stared out the window. She saw him leave the building, get into a cab, and drive off. Somehow she felt a sense of something closely akin to fear. "It's not like I thought it would be," she whispered, "but Eddie loves me, and that's all that counts."

Priscilla went out shortly after that and bought a dress and a pair of new shoes. She was home again by one and nervously paced the floor until three. At three-fifteen a knock came, and Eddie appeared at the door with a short, rotund man dressed in a plain black suit. "This is Reverend Horton, and this is the bride-to-be, Reverend, Miss Priscilla Winslow."

Reverend Horton had a pair of quick gray eyes and a ready professional smile. "I congratulate you, Miss Winslow," he said jovially. "Not only on your wedding, but I've seen your performance."

"You have?" Priscilla was somewhat surprised. "I didn't think the clergy approved of the theater."

"Some of the more strict ministers may not, but I think I may pride myself on a fine appreciation of the arts. Your play is very fine, wholesome, and can do no harm to anyone."

"Why, thank you, Reverend." Priscilla was pleased that the minister had seen her perform. "Have you known Eddie long?"

"Oh yes, we're old friends." Horton smiled, looking at Eddie and winking. "I've tried to do something with him, but he's a test of my ministerial powers."

"He's tried to keep me on the straight and narrow," Eddie grinned. "Now with you to help, maybe the pair of you can do something with me."

There was some light conversation, and then finally Eddie said, "Well, we're ready. I've got the license, and I've got the girl, so go ahead, Reverend Horton."

Priscilla never remembered much about the ceremony. It was brief, and it sounded official. Eddie was holding her hand tightly and slipped a gold ring on her finger at the proper time. When she heard the words, "I pronounce you man and wife," he took her in his arms and kissed her heartily, then turned and said, "I guess, Reverend, the knot's tied."

"Indeed it is!" Horton put his hand out, saying, "My congratulations, Mrs. Rich. Now, I wish you a long, happy, married life."

"Thank you, Reverend Horton." There was an awkward moment, and then Horton said quickly, "Well, I'll expect to be hearing from both of you. Goodbye now. Congratulations again. . . ."

After the door closed, Priscilla felt suddenly alien and lonely. It was, she supposed, the way most brides felt at this moment. She needed comfort and consolation and assurance, but Eddie suddenly approached her with his eyes gleaming. "Now," he whispered, "you're my wife."

★   ★   ★   ★

Maria Scarlotta had saved pennies and nickels for months, and now as she moved to the dress shop, she was facing an agonizing decision. She had been asked out to dinner and a concert with Jan. They were to join Dr. Burns and Ruth Winslow, and she wanted to look as attractive as possible.

The proprietor, exasperated at the young woman's uncertainty, shrugged his thin shoulders. "Vell, are you going to buy a dress or not? Other customers I've got already!"

Maria looked haughtily around the small, crowded shop and sniffed. "I don't see you being run over with customers," she snapped. "My money's as good as anybody's."

Finally, she settled on a dress that flattered her figure—a bright yellow creation with an abundance of ribbons at the bodice and cuffs. She insisted on trying it on in the small, grubby dressing room, and studied herself carefully in the mirror, which was of such poor quality that she could scarcely recognize herself. Then she glanced at the clock and said, "I'll take it."

"Good! Wear it in good health," the proprietor said, beaming from having made another sale. He waited until Maria had put her own clothing back on, then he wrapped the dress in brown paper and took the money from her.

Maria hurried home, anxious to prepare for the evening. Jan had taken her with him for walks, and twice to museums, which he seemed to like. She, herself, cared little for such things, but when he had mentioned casually three days ago that Dr. Burns had offered to take them out to a concert, she had, at once, begun planning the evening. When she reached home she found that Jan had not returned yet from his job. Quickly she heated water, bathed, and put on the new dress. She looked down at her shoes, which seemed shabby, but her savings had not stretched enough to buy new shoes. As best she could, Maria cleaned them and blacked them, then began working on her hair and makeup.

"Where you going, Maria?" Dino demanded. At sixteen he was short and stocky like his father and had become acclimated to the life on the streets quickly. He grinned, saying, "You got a date with somebody?"

"Jan is taking me to a concert," Maria said. She brushed her teeth with some of the new ribbon dental cream made by a company called Colgate, smiled at herself, and was pleased, for she had excellent teeth. And then she studied the rest of her face. She had a smooth complexion, and one of her girl friends had kept her supplied with Ivory soap, which was guaranteed to make even bad complexions beautiful. Her long, lustrous black hair had a willful curl in it, and she worked hard on it, staring at a picture of an actress that she kept pinned to the wall. When she had achieved the effect she wanted, she went at once to stand before her mother, saying, "Mama, how do I look?"

Lucia was nursing the new baby that they had named Antonio Jan. She smiled brightly, saying, "You look beautiful, and you smell good, too!"

"That's my new perfume. Do you really like it?"

"Yes, very nice. You look very good." She held the baby up, punched his cheeks, cooing, "Now, you see-a your big-a sister, how pretty she is?"

Maria leaned over and took the baby. They all called him Jan, which Tony pretended to dislike but actually rather approved of.

Just as Maria handed the baby back to Lucia, the door opened and Jan entered. He stopped short and smiled broadly. "Well, look at you!"

Maria flushed and said, "I got ready too early."

"No, I don't think so. I'll have to get cleaned up," Jan said. He looked at her with appreciation and said, "You ought to be going out with some young fellow. No sense wasting all that beauty on an old man like me."

"You're not old!" Maria said instantly. "You like my new dress?"

Actually, Jan thought it looked terrible. That particular shade of yellow made Maria's beautiful complexion look almost sallow, but he knew how desperately she needed approval. "Beautiful!" he said. He moved over and picked up the baby. "How's the big man today?"

"He's-a fine," Lucia said. She asked tentatively, "You hear anything about your case, Jan?"

"No. I have to wait for the hearing for that."

Maria suddenly felt a streak of fear. "What will they do to you if you lose?"

"Well, they could send me to jail—or they could deport me back to South Africa."

"No, they couldn't do that!" Maria cried suddenly. "It wouldn't be right."

"Well, let's hope they won't," Jan said. "Let me get cleaned up. Dr. Burns will be by pretty soon, I suppose."

★ ★ ★ ★

The knock on the door came at fifteen minutes after six, and

Maria darted to it and opened it at once. She greeted Dr. Burns cheerfully, and Ruth—and then she saw Esther Winslow and paused. "Oh, Miss Winslow," she said. She turned to Jan, who was slipping into his coat, and said, "They're here."

Jan did not catch the disappointment on her face and said, "Hello, Esther, I didn't know you were going with us."

Dr. Burns said, "Yes, she's the one who actually got the tickets for the concert. Well, the carriage is ready. Shall we go?"

As they made their way down the stairs, Esther said pleasantly, "I hope you like the music, Maria." When the girl merely nodded, Esther shot a glance at her face and saw that the girl was disappointed. *I shouldn't have come,* she thought. *I can see that Maria wanted Jan all to herself. I'll do the best I can to stay out of the way.*

Esther had guessed rightly. Some of the charm of the evening quickly faded, for Maria had hoped that she and Jan could enjoy the evening together.

Burns helped the young women into the cab, with Ruth in the front sitting by him, and the other three across on the opposite seats. "Weel, now," he smiled cheerfully, "I've looked forward to this evening a great deal. Rather hard to get tickets, wasn't it, Esther?"

"Yes, I had to pull a few strings. It'll probably be a full house," Esther said.

"Have you ever heard a symphony orchestra, Maria?" Jan asked, smiling at the young woman who sat on his right.

"No, I never have."

"Well, I've heard a few. I hear this is a good one."

Ruth leaned forward and smiled. "You look very pretty, Maria. Is that a new dress?"

Maria brightened at the woman's approval. "Yes, it is."

"You look lovely," Ruth said. She was an astute young woman and was aware, as was Esther, of the girl's hard life. Working in a sweatshop for a few pennies a day was difficult enough, and for a beautiful young woman like this, who had an urge for better things, Ruth thought how terrible it must be. *The poor girl must have had to save every penny for that dress!*

The conversation was cheerful enough, but everyone noticed how inhibited Maria seemed to be. They all made attempts to draw her out, but she answered in monosyllables, and Jan tried hard to make her feel a part of the group.

The concert, itself, Maria did not particularly enjoy. She was aware with one look that the dress she wore was not suitable, and she felt miserable. She could tell that Jan and Esther spoke with some knowledge of the music, and she felt ignorant and wished she had not come.

After the concert, Burns took them out to a restaurant, where they had a late supper. Maria ate very little and was glad when it was over and finally time to go.

When they arrived back at the Scarlottas' tenement building, Jan jumped out and helped Maria down. "It's been a wonderful evening," he said. "Thank you so much, Dr. Burns."

Burns nodded. "I'm glad you could both come. We'll have to do it again sometime. Good night, Maria."

"Good night, Doctor."

As the carriage moved on, Burns talked of the music until they reached the hotel where Esther was spending the night. They let her out, thanking her again for the tickets, then started back toward the hospital.

"I felt so sorry for Maria," Ruth said suddenly.

"Maria?" Burns said. He looked at her sharply. "What was wrong with her?"

"You didn't notice?"

"Why, I guess I don't think I did. What was wrong?"

"Oh, she was so out of place, and she's so much in love with Jan that it makes one almost cry to look at her."

Burns thought about this for a moment. "I'm not much for noticing things like that," he admitted finally. He listened to the sound of the horses as they made a sharp cadence on the street. He was aware of the perfume, very faint but provocative, that the young woman was wearing. Ruth had worn a pale green dress that fit her extremely well, and there was a certain air about her that pleased him. "You always seem to notice things like that," he said. "I'm just a plodding doctor, always looking for symptoms."

Ruth turned to him and smiled. "You always find them, too. You're a fine doctor, David," she said. She studied his sandy brown hair and added, "But you're not the most observant man in the world where romance is concerned."

Her words caught at Burns, and despite himself he frowned.

"No doubt you're right," he said dryly. "I have more to do than interest myself in romances. Ye wouldn't have me to start reading novels to learn about things like this, would you, Ruth?"

The music had worked a strange effect on Ruth Winslow. She loved music, and she had never heard such beautiful playing as she had this evening. It stirred her in a way that was surprising, somehow giving her the courage to say things she had never said before—at least not to Burns.

"I don't think you need to read novels to find out about love," she said.

"I don't think about things like that."

"You've never been in love?"

The abruptness of her question startled Dr. David Burns. He had grown very fond of Ruth Winslow. There were qualities in her that he had rarely seen, and he had found himself looking forward to occasions like this, where he could spend time with her. There was an honesty in her that he admired, and suddenly he said straightforwardly, "I . . . fancied a young woman."

"You mean Gail Winslow?"

"Why . . . how did you know about her?"

"People like to talk about things like that. Especially about doctors. You spent a great deal of time with her during the war, didn't you?"

"Yes." The word was sharp, almost like a rebuke, but David recognized that his tone was not gentle and said, "I'm sorry. I didn't mean to be short with you. It's just that, well . . . well, I guess you should know. I was in love with Gail."

"She's a very fine young woman. I've heard nothing but good about her. My cousin Aaron was fortunate getting someone like her."

David said slowly, "You and Gail are very much alike."

"Really?"

"Oh yes. I've often thought that."

"I take that as a compliment, David."

As the carriage rolled along, he was thinking about Gail. When Dr. Burns first came from Scotland to Baxter Hospital, he had been a busy man and had not been interested much in women. But young Gail Summers had caught his heart from the very first. He had never seen a woman who combined beauty and dedication to God in such a rare combination. Suddenly a thought came to him, and he spoke it aloud, "You're like her in many ways," he said. "For one thing"—he turned to her and smiled shyly—"you're as pretty as she is."

Ruth felt a warm surge of pleasure. The only other personal compliment he had paid her, aside from her professional duties, was when he told her he liked her red hair. Her cheeks glowed warmly and she whispered, "That's very nice of you to say so."

David felt he was getting into deep waters and said, "But that's not all. Gail has a love for God that I see also in you. And, of course, that is more important than physical beauty."

"Do you still think about her a great deal?"

For a moment David Burns was silent. He reviewed his life rapidly, then said with some surprise, "You know, now that ye mention it, not as much as I once did. Oh, I remember, of course, but I was hit pretty hard, to tell the truth. Went around almost in a state of depression after she turned me down and married your cousin."

"I can understand that. None of us likes to be rejected."

"Weel, I suppose that's true enough." He hesitated then said, "I think you are good medicine for me, Ruth. Now that I think on it, you've taken some of that sting away."

"Why, how could that be?"

"I dinna know," he confessed. He turned and looked at her. Her face was framed by the flickering of the lights as they passed, and he could not see the color of her eyes but knew they were as blue as cornflowers. There was a quietness in her expression that he admired. "You're the steadiest young woman I have ever known," he said. "I've watched you when things were bad for the cases at the hospital. You're never flustered."

"That's what *you* think!" Ruth laughed suddenly. "Sometimes I flutter like butterflies inside."

"Weel, you never show it, then." Without thinking he reached over and took her hand in both of his. "You've been good for me, Ruth. I can't tell you how much I admire and respect you."

Ruth Winslow sat there, her hand imprisoned in his. She had long known that there was more in her heart than just admiration for David Burns, but she knew also of his frustrated love for Gail Winslow. Now, in the closeness of the carriage, she suddenly felt hope rise in her heart. She said nothing, and in the silence, he leaned forward.

"You're very pretty," he said abruptly. "Would you mind—?"

"Would I mind what?" she said quickly.

"I was going to ask you," he said with embarrassment, "if you would mind if I kissed you."

Ruth's eyes opened wide and she smiled. "Most men don't ask," she said.

"I know, but I wouldn't want to offend you." He was studying her features and shook his head. "I'm sorry, I didn't mean to say such a thing."

"I think one kiss would be in order," Ruth said calmly. She saw his eyes fly open with surprise, and her lips curved upward. He leaned forward and kissed her briefly on the lips and then squeezed her hand.

"You're a bonnie lass!" he said huskily.

They arrived at the hospital, and as he helped her out of the carriage he said, "Good night. It's been a splendid night for me."

"It's been a splendid night for me, too, David."

She left him, then, and went to her room. When she was in bed, she thought of his request and smiled. *He's so proper—as if he were asking to pass the salt—but there is romance in him, I can see that.* She sighed deeply and smiled as she drifted off to sleep.

CHAPTER TWENTY

EPIDEMIC!

★ ★ ★ ★

Although Priscilla wanted to rent a larger apartment, Eddie argued against it. "This place is big enough for the two of us, babe," he said cheerfully. "After all, we hardly spend that much time here, anyway."

Making a home had always been a dream in the back of Priscilla's mind. She had grown up with this idea, as had most young girls of her generation. Subconsciously she had absorbed a vision of a woman who had a kingdom inside a house. Although she had always longed for a career of some kind, still her dream stayed with her, and the small clean room that she shared with Eddie did not satisfy her. She roamed the stores finding pictures, vases, and other small items to make the place more cheerful, but Eddie never seemed to notice. His whole life was tied up with the theater, and he was totally unaware of this desire on Priscilla's part.

Priscilla did her best, and her professional career seemed secure, yet there was a dissatisfaction in her that drove her one day to go by the hospital and invite Ruth out to lunch. "Come on, Ruth," she coaxed, "you can get off just for an hour, can't you?"

"I suppose so," Ruth smiled. She had seen Priscilla only once since her quick marriage and felt that she had not been faithful to the promise she had made to Priscilla's parents of looking out for her. Getting permission from Nurse Smith proved to be easy, and the two women left the hospital, got into a carriage, and finally arrived at a rather ornate restaurant. "This looks a little fancy, Priscilla," Ruth said as she got out and looked up at the imposing facade.

"I can afford it. Come on, let's go inside." The two women entered the restaurant and were approached by a tall, dark man, who proceeded to lead them to a table beside a large, open window. When they were seated, Priscilla studied the menu and ordered for herself, then urged Ruth, "Get whatever you want. How about lobster?"

"No thanks!" Ruth said instantly. "I always think I'm eating a big bug! I'll have a small steak."

The two women enjoyed a leisurely hour, with Priscilla doing most of the talking. Ruth noticed that there seemed to be an artificiality about her cousin's behavior. Priscilla talked almost non-stop about the play, about the actors and actresses she met, and the apartment that she was decorating—but Ruth noticed that she said almost nothing about Eddie.

"How is Eddie?" Ruth finally asked rather cautiously.

"Eddie? Oh, he's fine. He's managing me mostly now—although he's looking around for a part himself. He has real talent, Ruth. He just hasn't been discovered yet." Priscilla spoke somewhat too vehemently and seemed to catch herself and flush. Actually she was still trying to come to grips with the fact that she was the chief source of income for the two of them. This troubled her, for she had been brought up accustomed to a man bringing home the income, and somehow she felt vaguely guilty about the situation. There was nothing she could do about it, however, and she covered up by speaking glibly of projects that Eddie had on his mind.

Ruth listened quietly and made her own judgments. After a time she asked, "Are you happy, Priscilla?"

Suddenly an awkward silence seemed to fall, and Priscilla looked down at the tabletop. She fumbled with the silverware and arranged them into intricate patterns, as if hoping somehow to find there an answer to the simple question that Ruth had asked. It was a question she had asked herself many times and had not been able to answer satisfactorily. Finally she looked up and attempted a smile. It was a rather pathetic attempt, and she knew Ruth saw through her at once. "What is happiness, anyway, Ruth?" she asked quietly. "I was unhappy back on the ranch—or at least I thought I was. Now, I've got something that I've dreamed of all my life. I can't go back to the ranch again—so, I guess I'm as happy as most people are."

Dissatisfied by what she had heard, Ruth stirred in her seat and considered the young woman across from her. Priscilla was wearing an expensive dress with a pert hat tilted over one eye. She was healthy and successful in her profession—but something in her cousin's eyes troubled Ruth. *It would do no good to question her about it*, she thought and turned the conversation to other news.

Priscilla was relieved that Ruth had not continued asking about Eddie, and now she asked, "What about you, Ruth?" A thought came to her, and she smiled slightly. "Are you and Dr. Burns still romancing each other?"

"Priscilla, we're doing no such thing!" Ruth's cheeks flamed, and yet she didn't miss the delighted smile on Priscilla's face. Seeing the dancing eyes of the other woman, Ruth protested, "We're just professional associates. He's the doctor, and I'm the nurse."

"I don't think that always works, Ruth. There have been plenty of plays about the handsome doctor and the beautiful nurse falling in love and getting married."

"Those are just plays. They're not real life," Ruth scoffed.

"It happens, though. When a man and a woman are thrown together, why, they're bound to pay some attention to each other. What do you really think of him, Ruth?"

"I . . . I like him very much. He's a fine man. I don't know of a better doctor."

"Has he kissed you yet?"

Once again Ruth was speechless, and another flush of color tinged her cheeks. She had such a fair complexion that this happened to her often, and she hated herself for blushing. It was like a flag thrown up saying, "Look at me—you've caught me!" and she sat there wide-eyed.

Priscilla's eyes shone. "I see that he has, or you'd tell me so at once. Well, did you like it?"

"Priscilla, you . . . you ask the *awfullest* things!"

"I don't know what's awful about that. You've been kissed before. Not as many times as I have, I suppose. I was always more interested in romance than you were."

"Yes, you were."

There seemed to be some sort of rebuke in Ruth's short return, but Priscilla ignored it. Leaning over, she took Ruth's hand and squeezed it. "I wish you would fall in love with David. The two of you are so much alike."

Ruth was somewhat startled. "What do you mean we're alike?"

"I mean you're both serious and dedicated—and you're both religious, too. And he's not a bad-looking fellow."

Ruth shook her head. "He hasn't gotten over being in love with another woman."

"Oh? Are you talking about Gail?"

"Yes, she was training to be a nurse as well. He really cared for her. Of course, she's actually our cousin in a way, now that she's married Aaron."

The conversation turned away to Aaron and Lewis Winslow and their new brides, and Ruth was relieved. When they got up to leave, she asked, "Have you seen Jason Ballard?"

Now it was Priscilla's turn to be taken off guard. "Why—no, I haven't—yes, I have, I mean, but only once."

Seeing that Priscilla was completely rattled by the question, Ruth did not pursue it. She watched as Priscilla drew out some rather large bills to pay for the meal and a tip, then they went outside and hailed a carriage.

When Ruth had gotten out at the hospital and gone inside again, she thought about Jason Ballard. Ruth knew he was hopelessly in love with Priscilla. She guessed that he had followed her to New York, and now she thought, *I wonder what he'll do now that she's married! He really ought to go back home. It won't do him any good to stay around—he'll just be hurting himself.*

★　★　★　★

Eddie rushed in one day, saying, "You remember Edwin Porter?"

"Edwin Porter?"

"Sure you do, doll. He's the one that hired that big dumb cowboy friend of yours. What's his name. . . ?"

"Oh, you mean Jason Ballard."

"Yeah, that's him. Porter hired him to take care of his horses. Well, he's making some more of those motion pictures. I talked to him this morning." Eddie's eyes lit up, and he snapped his fingers with excitement, as he usually did. "He was looking for some young woman to be in one of them, but he can't find one that could ride. When I told him you could ride, he nearly jumped out of his shoes." Eddie stopped and stared at Priscilla. "Hey, you can ride, can't you? I never did ask, but I assumed everybody could ride out there in that hick state."

"I can ride all right," Priscilla said shortly, "but I don't want to be in one of those new moving pictures he's making."

"Wait a minute," Eddie protested, "you haven't heard it all yet. It pays good money, and you could stay in the play. Those things have to be shot in broad open daylight. It seems those cameras need lots of bright light. I've already agreed for you to go."

"You shouldn't have done that, Eddie."

"Well, I'm your manager, aren't I?" Anger had come into Eddie's voice, but he controlled it quickly. Coming over, he put his arms around her and said, "Aw, look, sweetheart, this is quick money." A thought came to him and he said, "We can get a bigger apartment like you've been wanting, and it won't take much time. A few days, that's all."

Actually Priscilla was intrigued by the idea and let herself be persuaded by Eddie. The next afternoon, he took her out to see what Porter called his studio. "Nothing but an old house," Eddie said, "but he's gutted it, and most of the scenes are done outside anyway."

"Are you going to stay here, Eddie?"

"No, you can take care of this. I've got some other deals to look into." He kissed her and left. She heard the roaring of the new Oldsmobile he had bought as it chugged down the road, then started toward the house. She stopped when she heard her name called and turned around.

"Hello, Priscilla."

"Why . . . hello, Jase. I wasn't really expecting to see you here."

"This is where I work." Jason was wearing a pair of worn

jeans, a checkered shirt, and a Stetson tilted back on his head. He looked tanned and healthy, but there was a question in his eyes. "Are you coming to be in the movie?"

"I've come to see about it. I don't know anything about movies, though."

"Come on, I'll take you to Mr. Porter. He's inside with the director."

The two walked on toward the house, and as they met, Porter remembered her at once. He introduced her to the cast that had gathered there and beamed. "We're glad to have a star like you in our picture, Miss Winslow.

The others seemed genuinely glad, and Priscilla smiled. "It'd be good to get on a horse again. I haven't ridden one since I left Wyoming."

"You'll have to see Jase about that. He spends most of his time seeing that these New York City dudes don't break their necks." A laugh went around the room, and Porter joined in. "You take care of this little lady, Jase."

"I sure will, Mr. Porter. We're old friends, you know."

Porter blinked in surprise. "I didn't know that."

"I worked for her father on his ranch back in Wyoming."

"Oh, well, that'll make it that much easier. You explain some of the riding scenes to her, will you, Jase? I want to get started as soon as I can."

Jason nodded and took Priscilla outside. "I'll just show you around," he said. "Actually there's not much to this thing—just a lot of riding and sometimes some shooting—just blanks, of course."

Priscilla felt very uncomfortable, but Jason had not said one word about her marriage. She was well aware of his feeling for her and had dreaded meeting him. However, whatever he felt he kept concealed. Instead he talked about horses, about pictures, and there was a calmness in him that made her feel much better.

The picture was made in three days. It was very short, actually, and on the last day of filming Jason told her, "They take these pictures, and then they glue them all up together somehow so that they tell a story. I don't know exactly how it works, but all I do is take care of the riding."

"Do you like it, Jase?" Priscilla inquired timidly. They were sitting under a shade tree in the front yard drinking iced tea. It was May, and the late spring sun was hot, so the iced tea was welcome. She was wearing a riding outfit, a divided skirt, and a vest with silver conchos for buttons, and she looked very lovely as she sat there. "It's not like being on a ranch."

"No, it's not. I miss the ranch," he said, shrugging his shoulders. "And I miss your folks a lot."

"So do I."

The brevity of her words and something in her tone caught at Ballard. In truth, her appearance had been a shock to him. When he had seen her show up on the set three days ago, it had taken all the strength he had to keep himself from running to her, but he knew that was over now. He had practically made up his mind to go back to the ranch, for he did not like New York. Porter had been telling him that he was moving his company to California, urging him to join them there. "It's open country," he had told Jason, "to get all the wide open spaces you want, and no freezing winters either."

Jason considered mentioning this to Priscilla, but thought, *Why should she care what I'm doing?* He said instead, "I got a letter from Peter. He's in Detroit now working for Henry Ford. He seems to be pretty happy out there."

"Yes, I heard from him. Have you heard from Mother or Dad?"

"Pretty regularly. Of course I write them often."

Guilt struck Priscilla, and she dropped her head. "I owe them two letters," she muttered. "I'll do that tonight."

There was a sudden awkwardness in the moment, and when Priscilla looked up she caught Jason's eyes on her. There was a longing in them, and for a moment she thought he meant to speak, but then he turned away and rose suddenly, saying, "I'd better get back to work."

Priscilla watched him as he strolled away purposefully, and she knew that he was fleeing from her presence. "He's still in love with me," she whispered softly. Her own thoughts remained on the tall man for a long time, and then she forcibly shoved them aside. She felt guilty for thinking about Jason but justified herself by saying firmly, "We've been friends forever, but I've got a husband now."

★ ★ ★ ★

Ruth was worried about Priscilla. She had written letters to her parents, making her letters as cheerful as possible, but when she and David talked about the couple she expressed her apprehensions. "I think she married too quickly," she said quietly. The two were moving down the street toward the tenement district, and, as usual, the dismal circumstances depressed Ruth.

Ruth had read the story in the *New York Journal* about the plight of the immigrants that had been illustrated with photographs by Esther. The article stated that there were already fifteen thousand tenements in the city. She knew that some of them housed as many as five hundred people at a time.

David began to speak of the deplorable conditions as they approached the building where the Scarlottas lived. "I've been worrying about this place. I read a study last night. It said that the death rate of the inhabitants here is the highest in the world."

"I can believe it," Ruth said. "It's just awful. The places are so foul and decrepit—especially these tenements crammed in behind others, trapped in an alleyway."

They made their way past rows of tenements, all of which were full of dirty children. The boys and girls were clustered on stoops, fire escapes, wash-hung courts, and trash-laden alleyways.

The streets were alive with men and women talking and shouting, bargaining in a dozen languages. It was an odorous open-air marketplace where one could buy bandanas and tin cups for two cents, peaches at a penny a quart, and damaged eggs for almost nothing. Children slipped by like eels as they passed by. Many of them were members of gangs that the slums had produced, and they thrived on petty thievery. While one or two would create a distraction, others would sneak up to a vendor and steal his produce and then slip into the crowds.

The two finally arrived at the building, and David Burns was at once thrown into his practice of seeing as many sick as he could on his time off. This was an unpaid duty, but he was recognized by most who called out to him. Some of them could barely speak English, and as Ruth stayed by his side as he saw child after child, and some adults who pressed themselves forward, she thought,

He's the kindest man I've ever known, but he's wearing himself out. He can't last like this.

They visited the Scarlottas', where David looked at the baby and said, "He's healthy as a horse, Lucia."

"He's-a gonna be a doctor like you and like Dr. Jan."

"That's fine," David grinned. "I hope he makes you very proud of him. Where is Jan, by the way?"

"Working at the docks."

"Is he still worried about being deported?"

"I think he is." Lucia's brow knitted together, and she said with a trace of fear, "You won't let them do that, will you, Dr. Burns?"

"If I have any say they won't. It'll all depend on how the hearing goes. He's got a good lawyer, though."

The two left the Scarlottas' apartment, and as they did, Ruth said, "You don't really think they'll deport Jan, do you? Or put him in jail?"

"It depends on the judge. It won't be a jury case. There are some pretty mean judges in this city. Anything can happen. If a judge has a bad night before he hears the case, he could hand down a stiff sentence just for meanness."

Ruth stared at him. "You don't mean that, do you? Things like that don't happen."

"Worse things than that happen, I'm afraid. Justice is hard to come by in this world." He saw that she was depressed and took her arm. "Don't worry, we are praying, and Esther's folks are praying. We'll get Jan out of this."

The two worked hard, and when they got to the last room, a dingy, dirty place with four small children, David was appalled. "Why didn't you call me before this, Mrs. Pappas?"

Mrs. Pappas merely dropped her head. She was worn down with work, and at least one of her children was always sick. "I don't know," she muttered. "Is he very bad?"

The baby, who was seemingly gasping for air, was a thin child, about one year old, undernourished, and with an unhealthy look about him. "It seems to be his throat, Dr. Burns," she said. "He keeps holding it."

Burns skillfully opened the child's mouth and looked inside and was silent for a long time.

"I want you to get the rest of your children out of here, Mrs. Pappas," he said firmly.

The woman stared at him. "Where am I going to put them? We got no place."

"They'll have to stay with the neighbors. I'm afraid they might all get sick if they stay with your baby."

At first Mrs. Pappas protested the doctor's suggestion, for she did not want to be separated from her children. But after some discussion, Dr. Burns finally impressed on her the danger, and the arrangements were made. He left some medicine with the woman and said, "I'll be back tomorrow. Be sure that you keep this child isolated."

"What's-a that mean?"

"Don't let anybody in here, and don't take him out."

They left the apartment, and Ruth saw that the physician's face was set in a stern frown. "What is it, David?" she asked, using his name unconsciously.

"I hope I'm wrong—but I think it's diphtheria."

The words sent a chill through Ruth. She knew how infectious the disease was—how it could strike quickly with a deadly force. She had been involved in one outbreak of the disease over on the other side of town, and it had been a frightening thing. "I hope you're wrong," she said.

"So do I," Burns agreed. "It'd give me no pleasure to be right about this thing."

★　★　★　★

Three days after the Pappas child had been diagnosed with diphtheria, it seemed that half the children on Mulberry Street were down with it. Ruth and Dr. Burns spent all their free time there, and other physicians were pressed into service. The disease spread so rapidly there was no keeping up with it, and one of the places it struck was in the Scarlotta household. Although there were three small children, not including Dino and Mario, strangely enough it was the oldest child of the family who was stricken.

Maria had come home from her work in the sweatshop feeling miserable, and by morning she was too sick to get out of bed. Jan had taken one look at her, and alarms had gone off in his head. He had not wanted to frighten her, but he knew Maria was aware of the epidemic.

"It's diphtheria, isn't it?"

"It could be," Jan said. He put his hand on her forehead and held it there for a moment, then said, "I think we better get Dr. Burns here to look at you."

Maria reached up and took his hand before he could move it. "Stay with me," she whispered.

Jan actually had a job, but there was a fear in the young woman's eyes that he could not deny. "I'll stay right here. Just let me go get Dr. Burns, then I won't leave you," he said.

Burns had come at once and examined Maria. The parents had lingered in the background, fear in their eyes, and when Burns turned to them and said, "We're going to have to isolate Maria," they knew the truth.

"We can't get all the children out of here," Jan said. "Have you got a place for her in the hospital?"

"No, don't take me to the hospital!" Maria cried out. There was an unreasoning fear of the hospital in most of the dwellers of the tenements for some reason, and nothing they could say changed her mind.

Finally, Dr. Burns said, "Well, if we can get a room, we can keep her isolated there."

"I'll find one, Dr. Burns," Jan said instantly.

"How are we going to pay for it?" Tony demanded. "We got a no money."

"Don't you worry about that, Tony," Burns assured him.

The problem was solved when Burns contacted Mark Winslow, who, at once, agreed to help with the expenses. Burns had taken the money and given it to Jan, who found a room in a building just down the street. It was small with only one window and one bed, but it at least provided isolation for the young woman.

As soon as Maria was moved, Jan began a constant vigil, staying and tending to Maria almost around the clock. Dr. Burns came by to check on her every day after his rounds. On the third day of Maria's illness, the two men stood outside talking in muted voices.

"I don't like it, Jan," Dr. Burns said. "She's not as well as she was yesterday. She's failing a bit more each day."

"I know," Jan said. "There's nothing to do in these cases. It's so frustrating."

Burns studied the tall young man's face, noting the shadows around his eyes and the marks of fatigue. "You're wearing yourself out, Jan," he said. "You'd better try to get some rest."

"I'm all right."

"You might catch this thing, too. It's worse for children, but you're not immune."

"God will have to take care of that."

Burns was tired himself, but the words of Jan Kruger cheered him. "I'm glad you're here," he said. "I'll come back tomorrow."

Kruger waited until the doctor turned and left, then went inside. Maria was sleeping fitfully, and he sat down beside her. Picking up his Bible he began to read. He had long hours now, just sitting and waiting, and he spent all that were not used on the care of the young woman reading the Bible and praying. He was fasting, too, although he had not mentioned this to anyone. A fear had grown in him that perhaps the girl would die. He had seen death in many forms, but if Maria died, it would strike him harder than others.

He struggled with God, praying, seeking for assurance—but none seemed to come. Hour after hour passed by, and he read until his eyes burned and the pages blurred before him. Then he simply closed his eyes and prayed, calling on God fervently. He reached a point where all the world outside seemed far away. The whole universe was inside this small room where this one young woman lay struggling against death.

And in this dark room, so bereft of any of the touches of grace or luxury, he found God closer than he had ever found Him. It was like his first days in the concentration camp when he had been driven to his knees by the abysmal conditions there. Hour after hour he would stay on his knees in the small room, unconscious of the passage of time. Prayer had become an ocean that he swam in, and although he did not hear what he wanted from God, he was conscious more than ever that God was in this dark, dingy room.

★ ★ ★ ★

Maria would awaken from time to time, and during that time, her eyes were fixed on him. They seemed enormous now, as her face had shrunk, and her lips were dry as paper. She would hold his hand and listen as he read to her from the Scriptures. She was almost past the point of speech, but she would ask, "Am I going to die, Jan?"

"I hope not, Maria."

"I don't want to die!"

"I suppose none of us do." Jan reached out and stroked her hair, which had lost some of its luster. Her skin was hot and dry, and she had taken so many drugs that she was not as clear-headed as she ordinarily was. "Would you be afraid to meet God?"

Maria thought for a time, then closed her eyes. "Yes," she whispered. "I would. Help me, Jan!"

"We are all going to die, Maria. Maybe today, maybe ten years from now," Jan said quietly. "But when we do, if we know Jesus Christ, it's just a slipping from this world into a much better one." He knew that Maria had been baptized into the Catholic church as an infant. He also knew that this had had practically no influence on her life. Now, he began to read Scripture to her. "As it is appointed unto man once to die, but after this the judgment," he read. "You see, Maria, we've gone wrong somewhere. We're sinners, every one of us, but God has made it possible to take us to himself. He is a holy God and He demands holiness, so that we must become holy."

"I'm . . . not holy," Maria whispered.

"No, I'm not either. Nor is any man or woman, but Jesus was. He was God come down to earth. He was born of a virgin, and He lived for some thirty-three years on this earth, and never once did He sin. That's why when He was put to death, His blood atones for our sins. He was the perfect lamb of God, and we must trust Him to make us holy in God's sight."

For long periods of time, Jan told Maria this story of Jesus. Over and over again he talked about the cross and how that through the blood of Jesus anyone could know God as Father.

The hour finally came when Maria looked up at him and whispered, "I want to know Jesus."

Jan's heart surged with joy, and he took her hands at once. "I'll pray, and you pray, too. Don't worry about being eloquent—just tell God that you have sinned against Him and that you want to come home. Tell Him that you believe in Jesus and are trusting Him."

It was really a simple thing. Jan prayed, and when he had finished, he looked down and saw Maria's face was damp with tears. "Did you call upon Him?" he asked gently.

"Yes, I did," she said, smiling weakly.

Jan did not ask her any more questions, but at that moment there was a peace in the girl that had not been there before. She was no better physically, but there was no longer the struggle in her mind and in her heart. He saw the serenity in her face, and more than once she would open her eyes and look up and smile at him and say, "I'm trusting in Jesus."

Physically, however, she grew rapidly worse. Finally, Jan had to send for her parents. When they came, they took one look at him and knew the worst. "I'm afraid she's not going to make it. God's chosen to take her home," he said quietly.

The parents huddled around the bed, and Maria opened her eyes finally, after a long time. She recognized them, and although she was almost gone, she whispered their names, "Mama—Papa, take care of the others."

She slipped away easily while the three of them stood around her bed. There was no struggle. She opened her eyes one time, looked at Jan, and whispered, "Thank you, Jan. . . ." Then she said goodbye to her parents. She closed her eyes, and her breath was so faint that they could barely discern when she ceased breathing at all.

When Jan saw that she had slipped away, he turned and went to stare out the window. Tears came to his eyes, and he felt a moment's bitterness. "God, why did you have to take her?" he said. But there was sudden knowledge that came to him, and he remembered many Scriptures that he had read about death and about the resurrection, and he turned back. Putting his arms around the two weeping parents he said, "She's better off with Jesus than she would ever be with us. We'll be with her one day. . . ."

CHAPTER TWENTY-ONE

THE LETTER

★　★　★　★

As the weeks passed and Jan's hearing loomed closer, Esther became aware that Kruger was brooding over the dim possibilities that lay ahead of him. She herself had been present at more than one session with Phineas Mott and had gained confidence in the tall, raw-boned attorney. He had said nothing to give them undue optimism, but there was a steadiness and a rocklike quality in Mott that gave her great encouragement. Nevertheless, this was not enough, it seemed, for Jan Kruger. Esther noticed that he had lost most of the excitement and enthusiasm that had been part of his character.

Searching for something to encourage him, she finally invited him to go on a shopping trip with her, and he reluctantly agreed. When she met him for the excursion, he was wearing one of her father's suits, and she exclaimed at once, "You look a lot better in that suit than Dad ever did!"

Her pert greeting brought a light to Kruger's eyes. He smiled and shook his head, saying, "I doubt that. Your father's a very impressive man. I don't know as I've ever met anyone like him."

Kruger's comment pleased Esther, and she took his arm, saying, "That's enough talk about you and Dad. I've got a lot of shopping to do, and you've got to help me with it."

"What's this about? Not another new dress, I hope."

"Well, that's a fine remark." Esther was glad that Jan seemed to be somewhat lighter in his mood. "I certainly do intend to buy a new dress, and you have to go with me into every dress shop. I'll have you know I've worn out strong men trotting around while I try on clothes."

She kept up the light conversation until they reached an enormous building with a gigantic dome on the top. "This is A. T. Stewart's. Have you ever been here?"

"No." Jan tilted his head back and stared upward at the huge building. "What do they sell in this place?"

"Anything you want, almost. Clothes, furs, furniture—come on, let's get started."

She led him not, however, to the ladies' wear, but to the toy department, which was the largest in the country. "I've decided to give the Scarlottas a party."

"You mean for Christmas? To give gifts?"

"No, I can't wait for Christmas. I want to get them something now. They have so little, and I've really grown fond of the young ones. You're going to have to help me shop for Tony and the boys."

Then began a shopping spree which Jan Kruger could not really comprehend. It was obvious that Esther intended to get gifts for the whole family, and so he started looking around for something that would please the boys. He found something very quickly but was not sure about it. He led Esther to the display and said, "Look, what about this?"

Esther looked up and saw the sign emblazoned in large letters, *It's a Daisy*. "Why, that's a gun," she said. "You can't give young boys guns!"

"It's not a real gun. Look," Kruger said, picking up one of the samples that lay in a rack before them. "It's an air gun. It doesn't shoot real bullets." He reached out and picked up a small round pellet and held it out in the palm of his hand. "This is what it shoots, and it couldn't kill anybody."

"It looks so real!" Esther exclaimed. "Are you sure it's just a toy?"

"Yes, I'm sure," Jan said. "They're very popular. I see ads for them all the time."

Jan was right, for an enterprising businessman named Clarence Hamilton had conceived a toy that few young boys could resist.

Whereas the other guns on the market were made of wood, he had invented a gun of metal that fired a tiny pellet. When he unveiled the idea to his company's directors, one eager manager exclaimed, "Clarence, it's a Daisy!" Thus the rifle had gotten its name.

For some time Jan and Esther stood there arguing about the gun, and reluctantly Jan finally agreed with Esther, who said, "I don't think this would be suitable for the boys. Those street gangs are getting worse, and you could put your eye out with one of these things."

"I suppose you're right. Maybe a baseball outfit would be better." He led her to another counter where they selected baseball bats, gloves, and caps for all three boys.

"Come along," Esther said, "I want to show you what I picked out for Emila. She led him to a section composed of nothing but dolls, and as they went she explained, "You know Edison who invented the phonograph? There's been a rumor that he's going to put one of his cylinder players inside a doll's chest. Just imagine," she exclaimed, "dolls that could say 'mama' and 'papa' in a real human voice!"

"That will never happen," Kruger said. "Think how large a doll you'd have to have. Those things are too big."

"I suppose you're right," Esther agreed, "but look at this." She held up a doll and said, "This is called, Suck-A-Thumb Baby."

"It's called *what*!"

"Suck-A-Thumb Baby. Look, she sucks on her little thumb." Esther was delighted with the doll but quickly moved along, saying, "Look, this is Tickle Toes. She's got rubber arms and legs. See? It feels just like human skin, and this one is Flossy Flirt. Look, Jan, she bats her eyelashes. Isn't that adorable?"

Jan stared at the lineup of dolls and shook his head. "I didn't know they made all these things."

"Yes, look, this is a cupie doll, and this one I like so much. It's called Raggedy Ann."

"What does it do, spit up?" Jan demanded.

"Oh no, Raggedy Ann doesn't really do anything, but isn't she poignant?"

"I like her better than some of the rest of the things."

The shopping for the children took some time, then they moved on to the clothing department, where they bought a new suit for Tony and a dress for Lucia.

They were walking toward another part of the store when Esther said, with some hesitation, "The only sad thing about this is that Maria is—" She stopped abruptly, seeing a break in Jan Kruger's face. "I'm sorry, Jan, I didn't mean to bring her up."

It had been almost a month since the funeral of Maria Scarlotta, and in all that time, Jan had not mentioned her—at least not to Esther. The two walked along silently, and Esther felt terrible. *I shouldn't have mentioned her to him,* she thought. *I've got to get his mind off of her now.* Seeing a small coffee shop she said, "Look, I'm tired. Let's sit down and rest our feet."

"All right," Jan said. Finding an empty table, they sat down and ordered coffee and sandwiches. As Jan was munching on one, he suddenly looked at her and shook his head. "I haven't been able to talk about Maria. Her death hit me very hard."

"You were very fond of her, weren't you?"

"She had her whole life before her. You can't imagine what a hard life she had in Italy; then when she came here, she had to work in a sweatshop that was not much better. I had hope for her, that she would marry, and have a good husband and children, and a good home. Now that will never happen."

There was such sadness in his face that Esther reached over and laid her hand on his arm. "I'm sorry," she said gently. "I've never really lost anyone to death. I can't imagine what it would be like."

Kruger lifted his eyes and managed a smile. He felt the pressure of her hand on his arm and was very much aware of it. "It comes to all of us," he said finally. "Who was it that said, 'Death has a thousand doors to let out life'? I don't remember—anyway, she went to be with the Lord Jesus." He went on then, quietly explaining how the young woman had accepted Christ into her heart shortly before she died.

"I'm so glad," Esther said. Her eyes were dimmed by tears, and she fumbled in her reticule for a handkerchief. When she did not find one, Jan held his own out and said, "Here, use this."

"Thank you, Jan." Esther dabbed at her eyes, then handed the handkerchief back. "I'm not usually so weepy, but she was such a fine girl."

They sat there for some time talking about Maria. Just when

they were ready to do some more shopping, a familiar voice suddenly came to them.

"Why, Esther."

They looked up to see Priscilla standing there carrying several packages.

Jan stood up at once and gave his rather military bow in the European fashion. He watched as the two women chatted, and then Priscilla turned to him.

"I've been thinking about you a lot. How are things going with your trial?"

"The hearing will not be for a time," Jan said. "I haven't congratulated you on your marriage."

Priscilla seemed to hesitate, then smiled graciously. "Thank you, Jan. I'm so glad I found you. It's Eddie's birthday day after tomorrow. I'm out trying to find him something, and I'm sort of lost. I never bought a birthday present for a husband before. You two will have to come along and help me."

Actually Esther was glad that Priscilla had come along at that time. She had talked to Ruth about the young woman, and Ruth had told her that there was an unhappiness that troubled their cousin. Now Esther saw signs of it, although through nothing that Priscilla said. There was a hyperactivity about her, as if she felt constrained to speak about her marriage . . . as if she had to convince herself that it was all right. She rose, and they found their way to the men's department where Jan supervised the purchase of a very fine shaving outfit.

"Eddie likes to read, but I don't read much myself. Let's go get him some books." Turning to Jan, she said, "You ought to know what a man would like."

When they got to the book department, Jan immediately displayed definite taste in books. The clerk tried to sell them a romance. One of them was a book that had been popular for some time, *Mrs. Wiggs of the Cabbage Patch*. Jan thumbed through it and shook his head. "This is a book for children," he said. "Not for grown-ups."

He also vetoed *Rebecca of Sunnybrook Farm*, and shocked the clerk by saying, "It's a book made up like a jelly donut, no form, just sugary sweetness."

Reaching out, he picked a book off the shelf and said, "Here's a book that a man should read."

"What is it, Jan?" Esther asked, curious about his taste.

"*The Call of the Wild* is the name of it."

"What's it about?" Priscilla inquired.

"It's about a dog that is stolen from the South in America and taken to the Yukon to serve as a sled dog."

"I don't think Eddie likes dogs, and he doesn't know much about the Yukon. My brother Cassidy would probably like it. He went prospecting there."

Jan smiled at her. "Just because there's a dog in a book doesn't mean it's a book about dogs."

"I don't understand that," Priscilla said with some confusion. "What is it about, then?"

"It's about how man has to struggle to make his way. I don't really agree with Jack London's philosophy. He says the strong always survive and the weak always die. That's not always true, but it's a rousing good adventure story."

He could not, however, convince her, and then he suggested *The Virginian*, which was the most popular fiction book for the year. She did buy that, and also at Esther's recommendation *The Hound of the Baskervilles*, a rousing detective story about Sherlock Holmes.

Finally, Priscilla had her arms full of packages and smiled. "Well, I think this is enough for one birthday."

"It looks like enough for half a dozen birthdays," Esther said. "Are you going to have a party?"

"No, just the two of us, I think." Priscilla realized her answer sounded suddenly cold and inhospitable. She said quickly, "But we've got to get together. Could we meet some time after the show and go out for dinner?"

"I'd like that, Priscilla. How about next week?" Esther asked.

"I think Tuesday would be fine," Priscilla said.

When Priscilla turned and left after making her goodbyes, Jan stared after her thoughtfully. "She's a very beautiful young woman, isn't she?"

"Yes, she is, and very successful at what she really wants to do. Few people are able to do that."

Jan, however, was not thinking so much of her success. "There's some sort of trouble in her eyes."

Surprised at his intuition, Esther looked at him silently for a moment. "You're very quick. I'd hate to think you were able to read me as easily as you do Priscilla."

Jan turned to her and smiled quietly. "There's nothing in your eyes that tells me you're in trouble. Just a pair of lovely brown eyes."

His compliment flustered Esther, and she said, "Come along, let's take these over to the Scarlottas. We'll stop and get a cake and some soda pop on the way."

★ ★ ★ ★

All the way home Priscilla thought about how pleased Eddie would be with her gifts for his birthday. When she reached the apartment, she took off her coat and began wrapping the gifts. This took some time, and she kept glancing at the clock, expecting Eddie to come in at any moment.

Finally, when they were all wrapped, she wondered where to hide them. She wanted the gifts to be a surprise, so she put the packages in a sack and placed it in the closet, then covered it up with other items. As she turned, her shoulder brushed against one of Eddie's coats, which was hanging on a hook on the inside door. It fell to the floor, and when she picked it up, a small envelope fell out of the inside pocket. Without meaning to, she read the address and saw that it was a woman's handwriting. She stood there uncertainly, for she knew that Eddie had been popular with women. He had not kept this from her, and she had learned to accept it. But she remembered he wore this coat just the day before for the first time since getting it back from the cleaners, so he had to have received the letter then.

Priscilla struggled with herself for a moment, then her lips drew into a fine line. She hung the coat up and pulled the letter from the envelope. It was a long letter—three pages—and by the time she had read the first page, she knew the truth. This woman had intimate knowledge of Eddie—this was obvious from the contents. She knew things about him that only a lover would know.

She glanced up at the top of the letter and saw that it was dated two days earlier. Then she sat down, her knees having gone unsteady. As she read the remainder of the letter, an emptiness came to her, for it was obvious that Eddie had been in contact with the woman since their marriage. The woman referred to an outing that she and Eddie had had at a hotel just outside Manhattan. The name at the bottom of the page was Irma Spencer, and she ended the letter with a plea for Eddie to meet her again. There was no mention of Eddie's marriage, and Priscilla sensed that she was not aware that Eddie was a married man.

Priscilla Rich had a temper, and by the time she had read the rest of the letter, it seemed to rise in her like a red tide. She felt betrayed, and for a long time she sat there struggling against the tears of frustration and humiliation that came to her. Finally, she calmed herself, and although her hands trembled as she replaced the letter in the envelope, she knew that nothing would ever be the same again. Then she thought, *Perhaps there's an explanation for this. I may be reading it all wrong. I'll have to give Eddie a chance to explain it.*

She paced the floor nervously, unable to sit, and thirty minutes later she heard the door open. She turned to meet Eddie.

"Hello, sweetheart. Sorry I'm late." Eddie came across the room, tossing his hat toward a chair, then stopped abruptly as he caught a good glimpse of Priscilla's face. "Why . . . what's wrong?"

Without a word, Priscilla handed him the letter. She watched his face carefully as his eyes focused on it and saw that he flinched visibly. "This fell out of your pocket while I was moving your coat," she said quietly.

Eddie Rich was a quick thinker, but for the moment he seemed to be totally unable to say a word. The evidence was right there in his hand, and he could not deny it. He held it while his mind raced, seeking desperately for some excuse. Finally he said hoarsely, "Look, Priscilla, I know this looks bad, and I should have told you about it."

"Yes, you should have," Priscilla said in a voice that was somehow even, but the river never ran colder than her tone. "Are you still seeing this woman?"

"No, I'm not. It was all over. She keeps writing me letters," Eddie said. "She won't take no for an answer. It was all over with Irma and me a long time ago."

Wanting desperately to believe him, Priscilla said, "I read the letter. It sounds like you went out with her just last week."

"That's nonsense," Eddie said. "Why would I go out with her when I have you? I tell you it's all over. Look, sit down. Let me tell you the whole thing."

Priscilla allowed herself to be persuaded to sit down on the sofa. Eddie took her hand, which was cold, and talked rapidly. He explained that the woman was one of those young girls who gets smitten with a crush. "It happens all the time to actors. It'll happen to you too, Priscilla. Doesn't make any difference whether you're married or not," Eddie said urgently. "When that happens, I'll just have to trust you, just like you'll have to trust me this time."

Priscilla desperately attempted to soften the feelings that were in her heart, and finally she said, "All right, Eddie. If you say that's the way it is, I'll believe you."

"Yes, that's the way it is," Eddie said with some relief. "Now, let's forget this crazy woman. It's time to get ready to go out and eat. We're meeting with some producers before the show. I think we might even get you a contract with Ziegfeld."

★ ★ ★ ★

Although Priscilla did not bring the matter up again to Eddie, she did one thing that she kept from him. The next day after discovering the letter, she sat down and wrote to Irma Spencer. The address was on the envelope. She informed the woman briefly that she was married to Eddie and that she would appreciate it if there would be no more letters. She tried to keep the letter as kind as possible, for she took Eddie's word that the girl was stage struck. She knew something about that, and when she mailed the letter, she hoped fervently that the young woman would not be hurt too greatly.

Life went on in a rather hectic fashion, for there were constant meetings with producers—important ones who wanted her to leave *Silver Moon* and star in other roles. She felt a debt, however, to Marvin Watts, and dealt with him faithfully. Watts was pleased with this rare display of loyalty, for he had often seen ingratitude in actors and actresses before when they got a little fame. "As soon as the run is over for *Silver Moon*," he said, "you'll be leaving me to go with someone else, and that's all right. You've been honest with me all the way."

It was actually two weeks after this conversation that a knock came on the door at eight o'clock in the morning.

"Who can that be?" Eddie complained, rubbing his eyes. They had been up until after two, and Eddie had been drinking most of the evening.

"I'll get it," Priscilla said. She climbed out of bed, pulled on a robe, and moved over to the door. Pulling the bolt back, she opened it cautiously and blinked at the bright morning sunlight. "What is it?" she asked the woman standing there.

"My name is Irma Spencer."

Shock ran through Priscilla, and for one moment she felt as if she might faint—something she had never done before in her life. Eddie scrambled out of bed and began pulling on his pants. Light streamed in through the side window, and one look at him told Priscilla the worst. She saw guilt wash across his face, and he gave her a despairing look.

"Priscilla—" he began, but then the woman began to speak.

"Eddie, I got this letter. It's from this woman who says she's your wife."

"I am his wife," Priscilla said dully. She saw then that the woman was older than she thought, at least in her late twenties. She was pretty after a fashion, but there was a hard look in her eyes as she entered the room and stood in the middle of the floor.

"You're *not* his wife," she said.

Priscilla lifted her head in astonishment. "What do you mean by that?"

"I mean he's got a wife in Troy." She turned and said, "You didn't tell her that, did you, Eddie?"

Eddie Rich could not act his way out of this one. He swallowed hard, and then said in despair, "Why did you have to show up, Irma?"

"Maybe I expected you to keep your word," Irma Spencer said quietly. There was a look of desperation in her face, and she added, "How many women do you have to have?"

"Wait a minute. What do you mean, he has a wife in Troy?" Priscilla demanded.

"I mean just that. That's the reason he never married me." The woman turned toward Eddie and shook her head. "At least I think he would have married me. I'm not sure about anything that Eddie says."

With her thoughts spinning wildly, Priscilla turned to face Eddie. "But we were married." Then something in Eddie's face caused a sudden thought to stab at her. "Eddie, who was that man? He wasn't a minister, was he?"

Eddie Rich shook his head wearily. He walked across the room and slumped down into his chair. "No, he was an actor friend of mine." He looked up at her, and despair clouded his eyes. "I couldn't lose you, Priscilla, and I couldn't marry you. I would've married you if I could've. I got married when I was eighteen years old, and she won't let me go. I support her, but we never see each other. I love you, but there's nothing I can do about it."

"That sounds familiar, Eddie," Irma said with disgust. "You told me the same thing, but at least you never went through the charade of a marriage." She stood there for a moment, then said, "I don't know why I came here. Maybe I thought I could get you back, but looking at you now, I don't think I want you. Goodbye, Eddie." She stopped for a moment, and then put her eyes on Priscilla. "I'm sorry for you. My advice is, get rid of him. He's no good."

The door closed softly, and a silence seemed to spread itself over the room. Eddie's face was stretched taut, and his eyes were wide as he stared at Priscilla. He got to his feet and seemed to stumble as he came toward her, his hands out. "Please, Priscilla!" he begged. "We can talk about this."

But even as Eddie spoke, Priscilla turned her back on him. "Please leave me alone, Eddie. Just get out. . . !" Somehow she managed to shut her mind down, although she was aware of his movements as he dressed. She was aware also that he was saying something to her about forgiveness, but it was too late for that.

Finally, the door slammed, and for a brief moment that seemed forever, Priscilla stood staring blankly at the walls. There was nothing in her now but a vast emptiness—and a grief that she knew would always be with her. She looked out the window and saw a cheerful couple walking by on the street, the woman holding to the man's hand and looking with delight into his eyes. She heard the pair laughing and talking, and then they moved on out of her range of vision. Slowly Priscilla turned, and going to the closet, she pulled a suitcase out and began to pack. . . .

CHAPTER TWENTY-TWO

"NEVER WAS A HOSS COULDN'T BE TAMED!"

★ ★ ★ ★

After working fourteen hours straight, almost without a decent meal, Dr. David Burns lowered himself slowly into a chair in the small cafeteria. He poured himself a cup of rank black coffee from the pot that had simmered on the gas stove throughout the night, and now sipped the bitter concoction. A copy of the *New York Journal* lay scattered on the table, and blinking his bloodshot eyes, he scanned the news wearily.

Paul Gauguin, the French painter, had died. Burns had attended an art show the previous October and had been stunned by the brilliant colors of the artist. He had not liked Gauguin's works much, preferring the more sedate style of the Victorian artists. Skipping across the page, Burns read that the first Model A Ford produced by Henry Ford's company in Detroit had made its appearance and was selling like hotcakes. He thought of Peter Winslow, who was working for Ford, and wondered if he was enjoying his new occupation. Automobiles seemed to be big news, for another story on the back pages described a race from Paris to Madrid, in which six people were killed, including Marseilles Renault, the French maker of automobiles. Across from that article was an account of contestants who had engaged in the first trans-continental auto race. Two exhausted men, Tom Fetch and M. C. Karrup, had steered their Model F Packard into Columbus Circle in New York City after a running time of fifty-one days.

Across from this article—which did not interest the doctor a great deal—was a notice that Calamity Jane had died. He had seen her once in Buffalo Bill Cody's Wild West Show. She had been dressed in buckskin and looked hard as a keg of nails. The article said she would be buried beside Wild Bill Hickok, her reputed and legendary lover.

He skipped over an article that spoke of the first World Series in baseball which would be played in Boston. He was not inter-ested in sports in the least. In fact, he was far more interested in the small article about Joseph Chamberlain's resignation from his cabinet post in England.

Abruptly the page blurred before his eyes, and he tossed the paper down, rubbing his eyes with the heels of his hands. The diphtheria epidemic had reached a peak a week earlier and now seemed to be ebbing out; nevertheless, there were still many ill, and the danger of it was never over with a disease like this. Al-ways, there was a chance of a flare-up and a new wave of sickness sweeping the tenements of the districts.

"I thought I might find you here."

Burns looked up and blinked through his burning eyes to see that Ruth had come into the small room used by the staff for breaks. Focusing his eyes with some difficulty, he saw that her face was drawn with strain, and when she sat down it was abruptly, as if she could not stay on her feet anymore. "I thought I told you to go to bed," he said rather crossly.

"I had a few more of the patients to see to."

"There'll always be a few more patients to see to." He felt ir-ritable, for fatigue had drained him of his usual good nature. "Mind what I tell you, Nurse Winslow. I can't have you getting sick."

"What about you, David? You've worked harder than anyone. Look at you—your hands are trembling."

Burns looked down at his hand holding the coffee cup and saw that, indeed, her words were accurate. Quickly he put the cup down and clasped his hands together. He hated physical weakness—at least in his own body—and snapped, "Never ye mind about me! I'm used to such things."

"I think you should go to bed and sleep the clock around. Dr. Simms is coming on, and he can take care of everything."

A wave of weariness swept over Burns and he nodded. "Aye, you're right, Ruth." He attempted a smile and shook his head doubtfully. "I think it's a good thing that this epidemic has played out—at least I pray it has. I don't think either of us would have lasted much longer."

Ruth sat there, her red hair glowing under the gas light. He had always loved red hair and wished that he had been one of those fortunate to have such. Now, as he sat there, he thought quietly, *She's a bonnie lass! I never saw anyone so dedicated in my whole life*. He realized, with surprise, that this even included Gail Winslow. It came as a shock to him. He had never thought to find two young women so dedicated, but so it had happened. And he had found himself drawn to both.

Ruth looked into his eyes and held his gaze for a moment. There was a warmth between the two of them that had grown slowly throughout the days of the epidemic. They had, of necessity, worked ceaselessly side by side, day after day, stopping only when they could stay awake no longer. Now as she held his glance, she was aware that he was a man who had what she most admired in a man—dedication, honor, and humility.

David Burns wished at that moment that he was more eloquent. He wanted to tell Ruth how much he admired her. It should have been a simple thing—but somehow in his boyhood he had been so stunted emotionally that it was difficult for him to make even simple remarks of this nature. Clearing his throat, he said haltingly, "Weel, now, Nurse Winslow, I've seen few women who were your equal." He hesitated slightly and saw that his compliment had startled her. Her cheeks were tinged with red suddenly, and she returned his smile. "After all this is over," he said, "we'll take a vacation. Maybe go around and hear some concerts. Maybe we'll find a bagpipe concert."

Ruth laughed suddenly. "There aren't many of those in New York, but I'd love to hear one."

"I wish you could go back to Scotland with me and see what it's like." There was a poignant tone in Burns' voice. He'd had a hard time in Scotland, but on occasion, in the midst of the hustle and bustle of the busy city, he missed the quiet hills and valleys of his native land. He spoke of them now, the heather-filled hills that rose and fell around his hometown, the lakes and rivers that he had learned to love as a boy. "I long to see them sometimes. There's some peace in that place."

"Will you ever go back there, David?"

"No, my place isn't there anymore." He hesitated, then said, "More and more, Ruth, I've been thinking that I'll be going to Africa."

Ruth's face lit up, and she exclaimed, "Why, David, that's what I've been thinking of! Ever since the first time we heard Andrew Winslow speak of the needs there, it's been like an echo in my heart. Africa—Africa—Africa!"

"Do you tell me that?" Burns said, a shock running through him. A sudden gush of pleasure took him, and he said, "I don't know how it is that God calls men there, and women, but somehow I feel like I'll be going someday. There's a pull in my heart for those poor people who need to hear the gospel of our Lord Jesus." He hesitated again, for these were feelings that were kept deep within his heart, and now he was happy to find someone he could share them with. "I'm glad, Ruth, that ye are feeling the same thing."

Ruth felt a sudden kinship with David Burns. She had known of his interest in foreign missions. He had spoken of it at times, and now that he had pinpointed Africa as a possibility, she felt very close to him. Although there was a weariness etched in her face after the long, hard days that she had endured, an eager light came to her eyes as she whispered, "It seems impossible."

"With God nothing is impossible," David said.

The two sat there talking, their voices quiet. From time to time David looked into Ruth's eyes, and as always, he was entranced by their cornflower blue color. They were like no eyes he had ever seen. He looked down at her hands and saw that they were not the smooth hands of a society woman, but were toughened by the hard work that she had faithfully done day after day. *She'd be a woman who would stand beside a man*, he thought suddenly. *Either here or in Africa*. Still he could not bring himself to say more. He did not recognize it, but Gail Winslow's rejection had scarred his heart deeper than he knew. In the back of his mind lurked a fear that he would never find a woman who would take him for who he was. Finally he stood up and said, "Weel, now—it's time you got to bed. I think the worst is over, and we'll not have as hard a time from now on."

As weary as she was, it was the most intimate conversation Ruth had ever had with David, and she longed to continue. Nevertheless, she rose slowly to her feet, knowing that she was exhausted, and felt that she could sleep forever. "Good night, David," she said, and as she turned and made her way to her room she thought of how his eyes had gleamed when he had spoken of Africa.

★　★　★　★

"Dr. Burns, I think you'd better come quick and have a look at Miss Winslow."

David had risen late the next day. Now, it was ten o'clock, and he was eating a late breakfast. The nurse who came in, Mary Wellsley, seemed agitated, and worry suddenly welled up inside the physician. "What's wrong, Miss Wellsley?"

"She's not well." A haunted look came into the woman's eyes, and she said, "It . . . it looks like it might be diphtheria."

Instantly David rose to his feet and left the cafeteria. He made his way, accompanied by Nurse Wellsley, to Ruth's room and stepped inside without knocking. He found Ruth still in bed, and immediately he saw the telltale symptoms that he had learned to recognize almost instantly.

It is diphtheria! he thought, and a fear seemed to break against him like a wave. It was only at that moment that he realized how much he had come to care for Ruth Winslow. As he went to her side, pulling up a chair, he sat down and put his hand on her forehead, which was hot with fever.

Her eyes fluttered half open, and she turned toward him, whispering painfully, "David—!"

"Don't try to talk, lass," he said, using the term unconsciously. With his free hand he held hers, took her pulse, and then slowly said, "We've got a bit of trouble here, but the guid Lord will see us through it."

Ruth was practically unconscious. She could hear his voice, but as she tried to focus on him, his face seemed to waver and fade. She began to cough and was aware that in a most unprofessional way he had lifted her from the bed and was holding her as one might hold a sick child.

★ ★ ★ ★

Esther and Priscilla had both come to the hospital as soon as Burns sent word of Ruth's illness. They were facing the physician now as he gave them an account of Ruth's condition. "I'm afraid it's very bad. Sometimes this hits adults harder than children."

"Like Maria," Esther whispered.

Burns looked at Esther and saw the fear in her eyes. "Yes, it goes very fast sometimes."

Priscilla stood silently, listening to the two as they spoke about the seriousness of Ruth's illness. She had never felt so helpless. Ever since she had left Eddie, she had walked around in a daze like a woman in a dream. Only when she was performing had she been able to escape the thoughts of what had happened to her. Each night as she stepped out on the stage, she had moved like a marionette, hiding behind the role that she played. But as soon as the play was over, and the curtain calls had been made, she would leave the theater at once. Now she whispered, "Dr. Burns, she's not going to die, is she?"

Burns bit his lip and shook his head slowly. "I pray not, but she's a very sick woman. We must all pray for her."

Priscilla dropped her eyes. Pangs of guilt stabbed her, for there had been no prayer in her life. A gnawing sense of shame had so filled her that she could not even think of turning to God. She turned and walked to the other side of the room and stood there until Esther and the doctor finished speaking. Burns left then, and Esther came over to say quietly, "It looks very serious. I think Dr. Burns is more worried than I've ever seen him."

"She . . . can't die!" Priscilla whispered, trying to choke back the fear that rose inside her. "She just *can't* die, Esther! That would be so unfair! I . . . I'm the one who ought to die, if anyone has to die."

"Why, Priscilla, what an awful thing to say!"

"It's true." Priscilla lifted her eyes, and despair was written over her features. Her lips trembled and she clasped her hands together to conceal her agitation. "You know it's true, Esther. You know what I've been—and Ruth has never done anything wrong."

Esther put her arm around the young woman. She had never seen such a bottomless pit of hopelessness in anyone's expression, and now she began to speak quietly. "You've made a bad mistake, Priscilla. We all make them."

"*You* don't!" Priscilla cried. "And Ruth has never done anything like . . . like what I've done."

"You don't know what I've done, and you don't know what Ruth has done. All of us have things in our lives we wouldn't want anybody, even our best friends, to know about. Things that we can only take to God."

"I couldn't go to God. Not after what I've done with Eddie."

"Priscilla, don't be foolish. You've been brought up better," Esther said gently. "You think God rejects those who come to Him confessing their sins? You know better."

"But I knew what I was doing, Esther." Priscilla tore away from Esther's grasp and went to look out the small window framed in the side of the room. Staring blindly out, she began to sob. "I knew exactly what I was doing. I knew that it was wrong— but I did it anyway. How can God forgive that?"

Esther felt almost helpless, but she knew she had to say something. Placing her hand on Priscilla's shoulder, she said, "You know God is love. We learned that when we were children—that Jesus loves us; but when you love someone you don't love them only when they are behaving. You love them when they are wrong—and even when they're hurting you. That's what true love is." She continued to speak for some time, offering what comfort she could.

Finally, Priscilla seemed to gain some encouragement and turned toward Esther. "I know you're right, but I can't seem to find God. All I can think of is how wrong I've been."

Esther spoke slowly and very carefully. "I think that's part of finding God," she said quietly. "I don't think it's a light thing to sin, and we shouldn't find it so. What you're going through now is what people call conviction, I think. The knowledge that we've done something very wrong makes us heartsick and we hurt, and there seems to be no peace for us. All of this brings us to the point where we can look to God and ask Him to forgive us."

"I'm so ashamed!" cried Priscilla as she starting sobbing again.

"I think that's good. If you weren't ashamed, *that* would be terrible. Now, because you realize that you were wrong, God is waiting to take you back. He's like the father of that prodigal son, Priscilla. You must turn to Him, and I think you should do it right now."

A startled look swept Priscilla's tear-streaked face. "Now? You mean—right here?"

"I mean right now, this moment," Esther said determinedly. "I think we ought to pray. I think you should confess what you did—to God—not to me, and then you ought to ask Him to forgive you. And then you accept His forgiveness—no matter what you feel like."

It was a novel concept to Priscilla, and she stood there thinking hard for a moment. Esther continued to talk, and finally it seemed that she could stand no more. "Pray for me, Esther!" she cried, reaching out to her.

Taking Priscilla's hand, Esther began to pray. She prayed with more fervency and assurance than she had ever prayed in her life, for somehow God had given her a burden for her cousin. It was unusual for her, for she had not done this sort of thing a great deal. Now, however, as she prayed there came a sudden sense of knowledge to her—that God would do exactly what she was asking for. She prayed for Priscilla to be forgiven, for her to be cleansed from the very guilt of sin, and finally that she would find great peace with God.

Priscilla sobbed during most of the time Esther was praying—but then somehow she became calmer, and in her own heart she began to call upon God. It was not an eloquent prayer, but an earnest, agonizing cry from her heart. As she prayed—to her shock and amazement—the shame and the humiliation began to fade away. She stood there for a time feeling Esther's hand clasping hers, and then she finally opened her eyes and gasped, "Esther . . . I feel so . . . *clean*."

Esther sent a silent prayer of thanks heavenward, for she knew God had answered her prayer. The two women wept and rejoiced together, and then prayed for Ruth at length. When Priscilla left the hospital, she walked the streets of New York for over an hour, marveling over the sense of relief that had come to her. The calm peace she now treasured in her heart meant more to her than all the fame and attention she had ever received on the stage. It was the first time in her life that she had ever thrown herself on God's mercy and forgiveness and felt the presence of God as He entered her heart.

★ ★ ★ ★

A knock at the door startled Priscilla. She had been sitting quietly in her new apartment, staring out the window. A pair of sparrows had been building a nest in a crevice of the building next door to hers, and she had been observing their progress for several days. She was amazed at how busy they were, bringing straw and string and nesting materials into what would be their little home. There was something about the scene that pleased her, and she had become so engrossed that the knock had caught her off guard.

Going to the door, she opened it, then stood for a moment shocked into silence, and finally smiled. "Jase . . ." She hesitated only for a second, then said, "Come in."

Jason Ballard swept off his Stetson, and as he stepped in, he studied her face carefully. At once he smiled and said, "I guess I'd make a pretty good private detective. I found you, didn't I?"

"You must've talked to Mr. Watts. He's the only one who knows my new address."

"That's right. He wasn't going to tell me at first, but I made such a pest out of myself, I guess he'd have done anything to get rid of me." Jason stood there, his tall body adorned in a fashionable gray suit; but no one could have mistaken him for an easterner, for the West was stamped all over him. One only had to look at his tanned face, and the creases caused by facing the sun day after day, to know that this was a man used to the rugged outdoors.

"I had to find you, Priscilla," he said. "I'm sorry . . . I know you don't want to see me, but—"

"Please come in, Jase, and sit down. Tell me what you've been doing."

Relieved at her ready welcome, Jason sat down on one of the two chairs in the sitting room. It seemed to be rather frail and he sat down gingerly, as if afraid it might collapse under his weight. "Well," he said, twirling his hat around nervously. "I've been pretty busy working for Mr. Porter. He's making another Western film." He went on to tell how the production company seemed to be set on making a great many films. Then he said, "Mr. Porter's decided to move the whole outfit to California. Better weather, he says, for making pictures out there."

"Will you go with him, Jason?"

Ballard hesitated, then said quietly, "I guess that depends on you."

Instantly Priscilla knew his meaning. Her face grew still, and she could not speak for a moment. "You heard about"—she had difficulty saying the word—"about Eddie and me."

"I guess everybody has heard about it." A streak of harshness came into Ballard's face, and he clenched his fist. "I know what I'd like to do to that bird!"

"No, don't do anything, Jase! Please, promise me you won't." Priscilla knew that Jason Ballard was capable of violence, and looking at him now, she was afraid of what he could do to Eddie if he let his anger control him.

Jason Ballard was a plain, simple, straightforward sort of man. Now he said plainly what he had come to say. "I love you, Priscilla. No way I can stop, and I don't want to."

Priscilla started to say something, but she could not speak. She sat there, sensing the strength that seemed to flow out of Jason. There was a simplicity about this man that she had always admired.

He fumbled with the Stetson that he was holding in his hands and said quietly, "I know you don't love me. Maybe you never will, and you can't help that. We can't make ourselves love folks, I reckon."

Suddenly a great sense of longing for the kind of strength that Jason Ballard possessed came to Priscilla Winslow. All her life she had yearned for what she now had—the theater, the big city, fancy clothes. But as she sat looking at the tall man who slouched in the chair, she thought, *He's happier than I am!* Aloud she said, "It's too soon to even think about such things. I don't know—if I'll ever get over what has happened." She smiled tremulously then and said, "But God has forgiven me; I know that much."

Jason studied her face and said with a glad tone, "I'm pleased to hear that. You know what I think you should do?"

"What, Jase?"

"I think, as soon as you can, you ought to go to your folks."

"Why, that's exactly what I plan to do. How did you know that?"

"I think a lot of your folks," Jason said simply. "They've been worried about you something fierce. I think it would help you a lot if you just go tell them what you've told me. Let them see that you've passed through this thing. It hasn't made you bitter, Priscilla, and I'm glad to see that. I wanted to hurt that man when I heard what he had done, but I can see by the look on your face that you're not filled up with hatred as some women would be. I'm glad of that."

Priscilla sat there quietly, listening as Jason talked. Finally, she knew that he was right. "The play ends in two weeks. I'll go home as soon as it's over."

Jason's long face lit up. "You're making the right decision. Could you stand some company?"

Priscilla knew that he was asking for more than a train ride to Wyoming. She thought suddenly, *I must not hurt this man anymore! He's been put through too much already on my account.* Aloud she said, "Jase, I'd be glad to have you, but—"

"I know," he said, "you don't want to give me any encouragement, but I found out a few things, even though I'm just a dumb bronc breaker." He grinned at her rather crookedly, and humor twinkled in his eyes. "Never was a hoss couldn't be tamed!"

Priscilla laughed aloud. "You have a fine way of complimenting a young woman, to compare her to a horse!"

Suddenly Jason reached out and pulled Priscilla to her feet. He did not embrace her but held her arms tightly, saying, "We've got different ideas, but this city life in New York—I don't think it's good for you."

Priscilla knew instantly that he was right. She would always have bad memories of New York City. "I think you're right, Jase," she said, "but I can't go back and live in Wyoming on the ranch."

"No, I don't think you could, but I'll tell you what you *could* do. Come to California. Mr. Porter's been after me all the time to get you to come with him and make movies out there." Again he did not press her, but he released her arms and stood there before her, his face filled with a love that he could not put into words. "I think it's going to be a whole new career—this thing they call motion pictures. Mr. Porter says they're going to be making a lot of Westerns. There'll always be a job for me, and a pretty good one, but it wouldn't mean anything much if you weren't there, Priscilla."

Tears suddenly flooded Priscilla's eyes. The faithfulness of Jason Ballard seemed to her exactly what she needed after the faithlessness of Eddie Rich. She tried to blink the tears back, and finally dashed them away. "I can't say right now, Jase, but—it sounds awfully good to me."

Jason leaned toward her, then held himself back. It was too soon, he knew, but somehow there was a sudden sense of excitement in him as he said simply, "Good, we'll shake the dust of this place off our feet. When we get out in California—well, there'll be things to say then."

Priscilla reached out, took his hand, and laid it against her cheek. It was hard and strong, and yet somehow it gave her pleasure.

"Yes, Jason, we'll have things to say then."

CHAPTER TWENTY-THREE

A DAY IN COURT

★ ★ ★ ★

The ethics of William Randolph Hearst, the publisher of the *New York Journal*, may not have been the highest—but no one ever questioned his innate sense of what would sell newspapers. The name "yellow journalism" came into the language to describe the polemic newspaper wars that existed between Hearst and his great competitor Joseph Pulitzer. Between the two of them, they managed to drag the name of journalism from a high professional level to a subterranean depth. Neither publisher ever showed any remorse over what they did to newspapers, and it was Hearst who eventually won the battle.

Esther Winslow had never been ignorant of the low caliber of much of the newspaper she worked for. It had been an open door for her from the beginning to get her career off the ground, and she often made a wry face upon looking at the front page of the *Journal*. Once she remarked to her father, "It seems that Mr. Hearst, for all his high and mighty ways, enjoys nothing more than wading through scandals that stir up quite a stench. He seems not at all affected by them." Nevertheless, Esther understood that the attention of the public could be reached through the brazen, spectacular headlines, and the garish, often slightly risqué photographs than it could through an essay issued by a dusty scholar in some ivory tower at Harvard. Having a hard, practical side as a foil to her streak of romanticism, Esther accepted this fact as a way of life that Americans had to live with.

The story that she had inspired concerning the abysmal living conditions in the tenements on the Lower East Side of New York had been a matter of pride for her. Cheerfully she accepted the Hearst policy that exaggeration was the way to sell newspapers. It was, however, impossible to exaggerate the horrible conditions that existed in that part of the great city. She had not had to pose subjects in the process of looking miserable, for misery was a miasma that hung like a dismal cloud over this whole section of New York. More often than not she had been tempted to put a certain photograph aside, saying to herself, "No, this is too horrible for people to look at." But nothing was too horrible for the Hearst papers. It seemed the worse the condition the more the publisher gloated over it. Hearst seemed to take a perverse pleasure in looking at the underside of a rather horrifying world.

On the heels of the story about the tenements had come great success for Esther in the feature story she did on the diphtheria epidemic. She had been sickened by the numerous deaths that swept through the tenements. There were days when she could barely force herself to go back and face the grim totals that seemed to rise geometrically. She realized that always before, when she read about an epidemic, there was a certain remoteness for her. It was entirely one thing to read about a hundred thousand Chinese dying in an outbreak in a far-off city on the other side of the world, but quite another to see a small baby choking to death in his mother's arms. Never had she learned to accept such tragedy, philosophically or clinically, and the heartrending deaths she had witnessed firsthand during the entire epidemic had done much to change her outlook on life.

Jan Kruger had traced this development in the young woman's character, and one afternoon as they were moving along through the district, carrying Esther's equipment, he remarked, "You've changed in the last few days, Esther."

Startled, she looked at him with a query in her expression. "Changed how, Jan?"

"You've been touched by all this—deep in your heart." Jan was wearing a pair of dark blue trousers, a white shirt open at the throat, and a light brown cloth cap on his head. He had lost weight throughout the days of the epidemic, for he had willingly been at Dr. Burns' beck and call to help.

When the epidemic had first broken out, Burns had approached Jan, saying, "You're working for me now as an aide. You can't be arrested for that, and we need all the help we can get!"

Esther thought quickly about what Jan had said as they moved down the street. Her eyes searched the throngs of people that crowded and jostled one another. "I suppose that's true," she admitted finally. "I don't see how anyone can go through a thing like this and not be touched by it."

"Some people do," Jan said calmly. "I saw it happen in the camp back in South Africa. People who lived on the next farm by a group of settlers who had been slaughtered didn't seem moved by it—at least not for long." He sidestepped a pair of men who were carrying a long length of pipe on their shoulders. Quickly he reached out and touched Esther's shoulder, edging her over closer to the building. "Careful there. It looks like they'd run over you and not even notice." When the men passed, Jan took his place on the outside of the sidewalk and said thoughtfully, "It's like when we almost have a bad accident but escape. For a while we move very carefully, but then the sense of danger passes away and we don't think about it anymore."

"I don't think it's the same thing, although that's true enough. I don't think I'll ever forget this. It's burned into my memory, Jan! I wake up at night sometimes," Esther said, shaking her head slightly, as if a sense of helplessness had taken her. She tried to put what she felt into words.

As she talked, Jan studied her profile—so clean and almost classic in the bright sunlight. She was wearing her usual outfit, a rather strict black outfit composed of a skirt that brushed the top of her ankle-length shoes which laced up the side, a long-sleeved jacket, and the only touch or ornament about her was a silk white blouse with a frill at her throat. She had a hat perched on her head that made her appear rather youthful as it rode her black curls. She seemed suddenly very beautiful to Jan as they walked along, even in the plainness of the black outfit. Again he said, "When I first met you, you were a rather formidable young woman. I was somewhat afraid of you."

Quickly Esther turned and looked at him, astonishment washing over her face. The sunlight coming down from between the two rows of buildings touched his face, and she was aware that never had she met strength so chiseled in a man's features. His face was square, strong, and his broad lips expressed a strength that reflected the inner discipline that was so much a part of his character. His eyes were half-shut, and slight lines marked the edges of them—a reminder of the days under the hot sun that made the African veld. Several curls of tawny hair escaped from under the cap, and his hair was long on the back of his neck. There was a grace about him that she had never seen in any other man, an athletic ease that expressed itself with every move he made. "I don't see why you were afraid of me," Esther said finally, somewhat disturbed by his remark.

"Well, you'll have to remember, Esther. I was on the run—a fugitive, and there you were, a rich young woman, very self-possessed. As a matter of fact," he said, "the thought came to me when I first saw you that I could strike a match on you, you were that hard." Instantly he reached over and took her arm, saying, "But that was the first time I saw you. And as I say, you've changed quite a bit since then."

Esther was not completely happy with his analysis, although she recognized the accuracy of it. They turned the corner, and as they approached the newspaper office, she said, "I suppose I was pretty self-sufficient. I've always had my own way. Daddy's spoiled me hopelessly."

"Yes, he has," Jan said, a slight grin turning the corners of his lips upward, and humor shading his eyes. "But"—he shrugged and sobered, almost at once—"you're different now. There's a softness in you. A gentleness, I guess I should say. I think it becomes you very well. You needed a little compassion, and I think this epidemic has given it to you."

By the time they reached the newspaper office, Esther had absorbed what he had had to say. She stopped before they entered, and they had one moment's privacy, for at that particular instant no one was entering or leaving the building. "Some of it has been your doing, Jan," she said, looking up at him. "I've learned from you how unselfish someone can be."

There was a warmth in her voice and a vulnerability in her that was very attractive to him. She stood with her lips slightly parted, and her eyes opened wide as she looked into the eyes of the tall man. Then, as if she had said too much, she turned abruptly and entered the newspaper office.

They went upstairs to where the feature editor was working on the story that was to come out the next day. His name was Mike Delaney, a cheerful, husky Irishman, with a red face and small twinkling blue eyes. "Well, now, darling," he said jovially as Esther approached, "you'll be wantin' to see the layout. I've got it right here."

Eagerly Esther bent over the table where the paper was laid out and cried with delight, "Look, Jan! Here's the picture we made of the baby next door to the Scarlottas. Isn't he darling?"

"He's healthy—that's the important thing."

"Oh yes, he is, but he's such a *cute* baby."

"I think all babies are cute, like all puppies."

"Oh, Jan, what a thing to say!"

"Well, have you ever seen a puppy that *wasn't* cute? I never did—but the baby is a fine young fellow, all right." He stopped suddenly when he saw his own picture, standing and holding a small child in his arms. "I didn't know you took this," he said haltingly.

Esther had been delighted with the picture. Jan had been so taken with tending the baby, that he had not known that she had snapped the picture. She had caught his face, half-turned toward the camera, as he looked down at the child, and somehow the miracle of photography had captured the look of strength and compassion that sometimes leaps out from a photograph. "It's a wonderful picture," she said, and hastily added, "I don't mean my part. I mean it has caught the whole story of the epidemic, and those of you who have been working so hard to do something about it."

"You're right there," Mike said quickly. He rolled his cigar around his lips and ran his hand over his reddish hair. "It's a great picture, and the story tells all about you, Jan."

"I'm not sure I need to be in the paper."

Esther, however, was far more practical at that moment than was Jan Kruger. "Your hearing is coming up day after tomorrow. We timed this so it would come out just before that. Whoever the judge is, he probably reads the *Journal*, and he's going to have a hard time being tough on a man who has sacrificed so much to help stop this epidemic." Esther nodded firmly, and there was an aggressive line to her body as she spoke.

Noting this, Jan smiled slightly. "I wouldn't be surprised if you didn't take a copy of this to court and make the judge read it!"

"I would if I thought it would help, but he'll read it. Everybody reads the *Journal*," Esther said. "I haven't read all the text. Come on, let's go sit over here and take a look at it."

She pulled Jan after her, and the two read through the paste-up version of the story. Everything had been said about the epidemic, one would think, so the story had focused on the life of Jan Kruger. It described his adventures in South Africa, including his capture, and it dwelt at great length on his selfless work in the prison camps. It even made a romantic thing, indeed, of his escape to Europe. Finally, it described his coming to America with the Scarlottas. Somehow the story of Maria's death had gotten into print here, and Esther knew this had been Mike's doing. She started to rebuke him for it but said nothing as they continued reading the paper. It ended with a laudatory account of Kruger's attempts to help with the unfortunate dwellers in the tenements, with a closing statement about the need for getting the man qualified to practice as a doctor. "America needs a man like this" was the last sentence.

Looking up with a wry expression on his lips, Jan said, "I didn't know I was such a hero."

"Well, you are," Mike said, slapping Jan on the shoulder with a meaty hand. "You might as well get used to it. Why, this will sell ten thousand extra papers tomorrow. You'll be signing autographs—watch what I tell ya, me boy."

Jan looked at Esther silently for a moment and shook his head. "I am not a hero," he said. "I'm just a poor Dutch doctor trying to do what I can."

Disregarding Mike's steady gaze, Esther reached over and took Jan's hand. She held it in both of hers for one moment and squeezed it, saying, "You *are* a hero—and we'll prove it to that judge at the hearing. You wait and see!"

★ ★ ★ ★

Judge Asa Harding was displeased to find his courtroom packed. He was the least spectacular of judges on his circuit, and he disliked any sort of flamboyant behavior in the cases that he tried. He was a stickler for the law and was widely known as a hard judge.

When the judge entered and looked around with some displeasure, Phineas Mott whispered to Jan, who was standing by him, "He's a tough nut, but an honest one."

"He looks like he could bite a nail in two."

"He probably could, Jan, but in a way I'm glad we got him. That story in the paper yesterday won't hurt our case any."

Judge Harding took his seat, and as the bailiff commanded the people to sit down, Harding looked over the crowded courtroom. He was a man of sixty years with a thick head of snow white hair and a pair of frosty blue eyes. His lips were drawn tightly together, and very few saw him smile when he was carrying out his duties as a judge.

Harding had been a judge for many years, and early on he had learned to pick out the key players in the legal dramas that played out before him. His glance went at once to the young woman dressed in black with a perky hat on her head. *The Iron Lady*, he thought almost sourly. *I thought she'd be here.* Suspiciously, he peered to see if she had a camera concealed and was almost disappointed to find that she did not. He disapproved of women with careers, thinking them better off at home rearing their children and taking care of their husbands. Nevertheless, he had been forced to admit that the pictures this young woman made were stark, dramatic, and extremely telling.

Shifting his eyes, Judge Harding saw the tall form of Mark Winslow, the father of Esther Winslow, an acquaintance of his. He and Mark Winslow had been on several political committees together, although they had had no social communication whatsoever. Nevertheless, his eyes met the steady countenance of the vice president of the Union Pacific Railroad, and he thought, *That girl has got some of her father in her. She'll be a challenge to some man somewhere along the line.*

Then his eyes went at once to the accused, and with some curiosity he studied the tall form of Jan Kruger. He met Kruger's eyes and looked sharply for any faltering, but the hazel eyes that met him did not waver for even one second. *Well, he looks tough enough, but he's broken the law, and we'll see how it comes out.*

The charges against Jan were read out by the bailiff, which were very simple—practicing medicine without a license. The prosecutor in this case was Arlo Quinlan—a short, trim young man of thirty with high political ambitions. He and the judge had met before in the courtroom, and while Harding had some admiration for Quinlan's skills in the law, he had some apprehensions about the shortcuts that the attorney took at times. Harding listened as the prosecutor related the incident of the accused's arrest, his eyes going at times to study the lawyer, Phineas Mott. Mott looked almost lackadaisical as he sat in his chair, and, as everyone else did, the judge marked his resemblance to a young Abraham Lincoln. *He better be a Lincoln in this courtroom if he's going to get his man off*, Harding thought wryly.

Quinlan concluded his case by saying, "I hardly see, Your Honor, why this case is even being tried, except as a matter of form. The accused performed a caesarean upon Mrs. Lucia Scarlotta. Mr. Kruger makes no attempt to deny this, and there are enough eyewitnesses to convict any man. I, therefore, propose that you make an instant judgment and find Jan Kruger guilty as charged."

"I will hear the case for the defense first, if you don't mind, Mr. Quinlan," Asa Harding said dryly. Despite himself, he sat a little straighter than was usual, for the case interested him. He had read the newspaper account of Kruger's life in South Africa and had a certain amount of sympathy for the man. And now as Phineas Mott seemed to unfold himself in sections until he came to his full height of six feet five, he awaited to see what rabbit the magician might pull out of a hat, for that is what it would take to get a dismissal of the charges.

"Your Honor," Mott said in a pleasant high baritone, "we would not deny anything that the prosecutor has said."

A little hum ran over the courtroom, for some had been expecting that Mott would attempt to cloud the issue, to confute the testimony of the policeman—who was, after all, not a physician. The judge, himself, was so surprised that his frosty blue eyes opened slightly, and he listened more intently as Mott ambled across the courtroom, seemingly at odds as to what to do next.

Finally, he came back to stand before the judge and said, "Let me just put this before you in very simple terms, Your Honor. We have no defense as far as the *act* is concerned."

"But you pleaded not guilty," Harding said, his tone sharp. "Whatever can you mean by this, Mr. Mott?"

"I mean that there are acts that go beyond the law. This may sound strange," Mott shrugged his bony shoulders, "especially for a lawyer to say to a judge—and especially to such a judge as yourself."

"Never mind the flattery; just get on with your defense—if you have one."

"Why, I indeed have a defense, Your Honor," Mott nodded, "but first I would like to lay before the court a summary of Mr. Kruger's past life."

Instantly Arlo Quinlan was on his feet. "Objection, Your Honor. His past life has no relevance whatsoever to what he's done."

"I beg to disagree with my worthy opponent," Mott said, arching his thick black eyebrows. "It has *everything* to do with the case. As a matter of fact, I might say that Mr. Kruger's character *is* the case."

Harding ordinarily was a stickler for the law. In this case, however, he hesitated slightly. He said after a moment's pause, "Objection overruled, we will hear what you have to say—but mind you, Mr. Mott, make it pertinent."

"I hope to do exactly that, Your Honor." Mott then launched into a narration tracing Jan Kruger's life. He knew the story well, having elicited it, point by point, from Jan on more than one occasion. He touched on the main events, such as had been underscored in the newspaper story, and the audience throughout the crowded room listened almost breathlessly.

"So you see, Your Honor, we are not dealing here with a criminal."

"He broke the law; that makes him a criminal," Quinlan raised his voice and would have said more, but the judge interrupted.

"You know better than to interrupt, Mr. Quinlan. I will ask you to put your protest into a formal mode."

"Then, I object!"

"Objection overruled!" It gave Harding some distinct twinge

of pleasure to see the feisty young lawyer flush and sit down, showing as much displeasure as he dared. Harding turned his gaze back on Mott. "I have not allowed the objection, but that's the truth—we must stick to the law."

"Yes, Your Honor, I would like to put some character witnesses on the stand. . . ."

For the next hour a steady stream of people took the stand. Most of them were from the lower classes, parents of children that Jan had helped in the tenements. All of them made very good witnesses, for they spoke in glowing terms of how Jan Kruger had helped them, buying medicine often out of his own meager wages to help their children.

"I call Mrs. Lucia Scarlotta to the stand," Mr. Mott said.

Lucia was wearing a new dress. She was still heavy and bore her baby in her arms.

"Can't someone take care of your child?" Judge Harding inquired querulously.

"He's-a fussy, Judge, I'm-a sorry."

"Very well," Harding mumbled, "get on with it."

After Lucia took the witness stand and settled herself, with the baby on her lap, Mott said, "Would you please describe what happened in your room on the date in question."

Lucia Scarlotta began to pour her heart out. She began to weep halfway through and held up the baby, saying, "He-a save-a my baby's life. You see he's alive. We call him Jan, because Dr. Kruger, he-a save him."

"You must not call the prisoner, 'doctor,' " Judge Harding said instantly, but inwardly he was saying, *What a witness! How am I going to go against a thing like this?*

Finally Lucia left the stand, begging the judge all the way back to her seat to have mercy on Jan Kruger.

Mott was a shrewd master of timing in trials, and he saw, at once, that the time had come. "I call Jan Kruger to the stand."

Kruger rose and made his way forward. He was sworn in and sat down half facing the judge. Mott said, "Do you understand the charges, and how serious they are?"

"Yes, I've always understood that."

"You understand," Mott persisted, "that you cannot practice medicine in this country without a license."

"I have always understood that very well," Jan replied calmly.

"Then will you tell the court why you violated the law."

"I violated the law because a child's life was at stake. If there had been any way to avoid surgery, I would have done it."

"Are you certain that the child would have died?"

"Yes, in my judgment, there was no hope at all." Jan went on to describe the medical aspects of the case, and when he was finished, he looked at the judge and said calmly, "I realize that there must be laws to protect people against those who are not qualified. I knew this at that moment, but I could not turn my back on the oath I took to preserve life."

A murmur of admiration rose from the crowd, and Mott knew that the moment had come. "Your Honor, I can go no further than this, nor can my client. Yes, Mr. Kruger did violate the law, but if he had not violated the law, we would have had a tragedy—a terrible loss for this family." He paused and looked at Lucia, who was rocking the baby in her arms. Then he turned back toward the judge and said, "I move, Your Honor, that the charges against my client be dismissed."

Silence fell on the courtroom, and never in his experience at the bar had Judge Asa Harding felt such pressure. True enough, no one was speaking, but every eye was fixed on him. For one moment he felt a perverse notion to stand against this pressure, but he, himself, had been moved by what had taken place in his courtroom. He turned now to face Jan and said, "Will you stand to your feet, Mr. Kruger?"

When Kruger was standing before him, Mott by his side, Judge Harding said, "By your own admission you have broken the law, Mr. Kruger." A sigh went over the courtroom, and Harding thought he heard at least more than one sob, for it seemed that this was the beginning of a sentence. However, he nodded and said briefly, "In this case, I feel that you were justified, and I therefore dismiss these charges against you. You are a free man, Mr. Kruger."

Pandemonium broke out in the courtroom, and Harding recognized the impossibility of doing anything with these shouting people. *After all*, he said to himself, and allowed a smile to touch his lips, *they are excitable Italians. I suppose I can put up with it this once.*

But the next moment he saw that at least one of those who was shouting was not an Italian. Esther Winslow had reached up to give her father a quick hug of victory, and then had run across the room. The judge noted with interest that the newly freed accused was waiting for her. He held out his arms, and she flew into them, hugging him and pressing her face against his chest. *Well now, that's interesting,* Harding thought. He glanced at Mark Winslow and their eyes met, and Winslow gave him a broad wink.

Suddenly, a light caused the judge to blink, and he saw that a photographer had managed somehow to bring his camera into the courtroom. He had snapped a picture of Kruger holding Esther in his arms and yelled out with triumph, "It'll be in the *Journal* tomorrow!" Then he turned and ran out before the judge could call for the bailiff to stop him.

Kruger turned, and holding tight to Esther's hand, he approached the bench. "I'd like to shake your hand, Judge," he said.

Harding reached out, took the strong hand, and this time he smiled more broadly. "You must get yourself qualified, Mr. Kruger."

"He will, Your Honor," Esther said. "I promise you he will!"

Judge Asa Harding leaned back and looked at the two. "Well, if the Iron Lady says so," he remarked ironically, "I suppose it will be done."

CHAPTER TWENTY-FOUR

WINSLOW WOMEN – AND THEIR MEN

★ ★ ★ ★

Although President Teddy Roosevelt spent most of his waking hours working furiously to negotiate a canal through the Isthmus of Panama, he did take time to come to New York to speak. After all, there was an election coming up in the next year, and Roosevelt, master politician that he was, weighed this carefully when he agreed to come. With a sense of drama found in few United States Presidents, Roosevelt chose to speak in the shadow of the Statue of Liberty. An enormous crowd had gathered, and somehow the idea of the fiery president speaking under the very shadow of what was rapidly becoming the symbol of liberty to the world caught the imagination.

In the forefront of the crowd a small group had firmly entrenched their positions. The Scarlottas, with their faces turned up, listened as President Roosevelt made a soaring, eloquent speech, presenting America as the land for the outcast. He ended his speech by saying, "We're all immigrants in this country—except for the Indians."

A roar went up from the crowd at this dynamic proclamation, and Roosevelt bared his large teeth and, raising both hands, shook his fists in a gesture of exultation.

After the speech, a dinner was held by the three cousins—Ruth, Priscilla, and Esther Winslow—and their families. Esther had made reservations for everyone in an expensive restaurant, and Mark Winslow, the host, grinned at Lola during the meal, saying, "I wish Dad could have been here to see this. He would've been proud of the Winslow women, I think."

Lola looked down the table to where Priscilla was sitting next to Jason Ballard. "What do you think will become of that pair?" she asked Mark.

Rubbing his chin thoughtfully, a sly look touched Mark Winslow's eyes. "Well, I think that young fellow reminds me of another young cowboy I knew." He reached over and took Lola's hand and held it. Squeezing it, he added, "This young cowboy saw a beautiful young girl—the prettiest he ever saw, and nothing would do, but he had to have her."

Lola flushed at his words, for he still had the power to move her. She held his hand and nodded, "I think you may have something there, but they may have a harder time than we did."

Down the table Priscilla was listening as Jason spoke of their trip. He was excited, and somehow this touched her. She knew that he was deeply in love with her, and although she respected him, and found in him an honesty and a rock-hard streak of integrity that she admired, she was not ready yet to return his affection. However, when he paused, she did say quietly, "It's been good for me to have you around, Jase. I need someone to keep my feet on the ground."

Jason turned quickly and searched her face. Then he said quietly, "I'll always be there for you, Priscilla, no matter what happens."

At that moment a voice cut through the hubbub of talk, and everyone turned to see Dr. David Burns standing and tapping on the table with his knuckles.

"Let's have a moment's quiet," Burns said. There was a pleased expression on his face, and when he had everyone's attention, he said, "We've all been edified by the President's speech—a good man he is—but I have more important news for you than any presidential speeches." Laughter went up, and Burns held his hand up with a warning gesture. "Let's have no levity now. I have an important announcement to make." When the room fell silent, and he had everyone's attention, he said, "I wish to announce the engagement of Dr. David Burns to—" He turned to Ruth, who had now recovered from her illness, and smiled at her, resting his hand on her shoulder and said, "Miss Ruth Winslow."

Applause broke out, and Faith and Tom Winslow, who had come all the way to New York to meet their future son-in-law, came to the couple at once. There was a fury of embracing, and when things calmed down, David said, "One more announcement." His face grew serious then, and he said quietly, "I wish to announce that Ruth and I have given our lives completely to God, and He has directed us in a marvelous way. We will be leaving soon after we are married to go to Africa as missionaries. We'll be joining Barney Winslow and his family on the field there, and we ask for your prayers."

Mark and Lola grew misty-eyed over this, and Mark said huskily, "The Winslows are going to make an impact on that dark continent, it seems."

Esther went at once and embraced both Ruth and Dr. Burns. Jan Kruger was by her side, and their congratulations were warm.

Jan went back to his seat, and then looked up as Mark Winslow began speaking. As Kruger realized that Mark was speaking about him, his face grew warm, and he shot a quick glance at Esther.

She returned his look fully and smiled with satisfaction. "You can't run," she said. "I won't let you." She took his hand under the table and held it firmly.

Mark said, "We have been very proud of our daughter—the Iron Lady as some call her—and the work that she has done. And of nothing have we been more proud than the way she has been able to be of service to Jan Kruger, our honored guest here tonight. I have an announcement to make, and I have not shared this with Jan, for I'm getting to be old and set in my ways." Mark looked at Kruger, who was staring at him almost in a state of shock.

"My wife and I wish to announce that we are sponsoring an internship for Jan Kruger at City Hospital. I've been informed that in a period of two years the requirements will all be met, then it will be—Dr. Jan Kruger."

Jan sat there as people applauded and laughed. He felt Esther squeezing his hand, and finally he rose to his feet. The room grew quiet and Jan swallowed hard, for there was a thickness in his throat. "I have never met such kindness," he said simply. "I did not know there was a family such as the Winslows in this world, but I know now that this country is producing men and women who will be the envy of the world. It is hard for a man like me to receive such generosity. I was brought up to give," he hesitated slightly, then nodded, "but God has given me the grace to say thank you, Mr. and Mrs. Winslow. I receive this gift with deep gratitude, and I will never forget as long as I live what you have done for me. . . !"

★ ★ ★ ★

"I didn't know that a party could tire one out so much," Esther said. She was walking along the garden path beside the house with Jan at her side. They had come back from the party at the restaurant, and now it was after ten o'clock. Her parents had already gone to bed, proclaiming themselves to be exhausted, and Mark had told Jan that they'd talk about the details of his internship tomorrow.

"I know what you mean," Jan said. He looked up at the silvery moon, which shed its beams over the grounds, highlighting the graceful contours of the house. "I feel like I've worked for a week. That's what excitement does for you." He turned to her suddenly and took her hands. "I can't say what your father's offer means to me, and I know that you were behind it, Esther."

"No, I was not," Esther denied quickly. "It was all his idea—his and mother's." She was very much aware of his hands on hers and was almost serene in her composure.

Her face was lighted by the moonbeams and seemed to grow prettier as he watched her. Laughter and a love of life seemed to lie impatiently behind her eyes and her lips, waiting for release. There was a fire in this girl that made her lovely and brought out rich and headlong qualities of a spirit otherwise hidden behind the cool reserve of her lips.

Jan could smell her perfume, a faint scent that seemed to affect him deeply. There was a femininity about her that he had always found enticing, and now in the quietness of the night, he felt that he had never seen anything so lovely.

"I can't say anything about what's to come," he murmured, "but I can say that I love you, Esther."

Esther remained absolutely still. There was a simplicity in this man that she had learned to admire, and she knew now that of all the things that she wanted to hear, what she had just heard was what pleased her most. Without thought, she reached up, laid her hands on the sides of his neck, and pulled him down. "I love you too, Jan," she said softly.

No other woman stirred him as this one, and as Jan's lips fell on hers, he knew that her completeness was all that he would ever desire in a woman. She was rich in a way that a woman should be rich, and there was a depth in her that he had not found elsewhere in his entire life. Now as her soft lips yielded under his, he held her protectively. Finally, he lifted his head and whispered, "I have nothing, no money. It will be a long time before I'm qualified as a doctor."

Esther said, "I don't care. I love you, and that's all that matters."

His arms tightened around her, and he held her for a time, savoring the clean strength of her body and the softness of her touch. Finally, he smiled and said quietly, "You're no Iron Lady, Esther. You're gentle and sweet and everything a man could ever want. I wish I had a ring to give you."

"I don't need a ring," Esther said. Laughter bubbled up in her, and she hugged him closely, leaning her head against his chest for a moment. This was what she had longed for, and now that she had found it, a singing seemed to fill her. She lifted her face and whispered, "We have each other, Jan!"